AFTER
THE
MONSOON

Robert Karjel was a lieutenant colonel in the Swedish Air Force for twenty-five years. His job as a helicopter pilot took him all over the world, from peacekeeping missions in Afghanistan to pirate hunting in Somalia, and he is the only Swedish pilot who has trained with the US Marine Corps and flown its attack helicopters. He is the author of *My Name is N*, his first novel to be published in English, and is one of the most sought-after motivational speakers in Sweden. He lives with his family outside of Stockholm.

🐦 @RobertKarjel
www.robert-karjel.com

Also by Robert Karjel

My Name is N

AFTER THE MONSOON

ROBERT KARJEL

Translated from the Swedish by
NANCY PICK & ROBERT KARJEL

HarperCollins*Publishers*

HarperCollins*Publishers* Ltd
1 London Bridge Street,
London SE1 9GF

www.harpercollins.co.uk

Published by HarperCollins*Publishers* 2018
1

Originally published as *Efter monsunen* in Sweden in 2016 by Partners in Stories

A catalogue record for this book is available from the British Library

ISBN: 978-0-00-758608-0 (PB b-format)

This novel is entirely a work of fiction.
The names, characters and incidents portrayed in it are
the work of the author's imagination. Any resemblance to
actual persons, living or dead, events or localities is
entirely coincidental.

Printed and bound in the UK by CPI Group (UK) Ltd, Croydon CR0 4YY

MIX
Paper from
responsible sources
FSC™ C007454

This book is produced from independently certified FSC™ paper
to ensure responsible forest management.

For more information visit: www.harpercollins.co.uk/green

For Josefin and Elvira

AFTER
THE
MONSOON

1

Mortal fear. Not anger, not surprise. Fear. He jerked so violently that he knocked the machine gun out of the sailboat's cockpit, before he could get ahold of it again.

The sea was glassy, without so much as a ripple. The sails on the *MaryAnn II* hung limp. The boat sat motionless, the nearest land five thousand meters below. A nameless position in the middle of the Indian Ocean.

He picked up the gun and stood in a crouch, holding it to his chest. The safety still engaged. He hesitated. A feeble, half conscious hope: what if they saw that he was armed, the way he saw that they were? But it was useless. They kept closing in.

The fast motorboats—skiffs—had come out of nowhere. They were speeding toward him at the stern. Someone shouted from there, he couldn't make out the words. He turned toward the hatch, where his family was still unaware, below deck, spending the day out of the heat. He was just about to warn them, when he heard even louder shouts from the skiffs, and his protective instincts took over. They had to be kept down there. Not a chance in hell he'd let them set foot on deck. He cocked his rifle and glanced at the spare magazine lying on the cockpit floor. The only thing he knew was bottomless dread.

The first shot was his, fired straight up into the sky. More a hopeless plea than a warning. A few seconds later, the pirates answered with a volley that hit like whips around the stern, the bullets raising white jets in the water, tall and slender as spears. The last shot tore a trail through the wooden deck, splinters flying.

In that moment, his world was reduced to the men maneuvering their boats and his own gun sights, which at first he found impossible to control. He fired shot after shot, driven by his instinct to keep them away, unable to focus, much less correct his aim. They moved in fast, so close that he could now see their faces. He saw how the recoil threw them backward when they fired. Yet he was completely oblivious to the white trails their shots made in the water around him, or to the dull thuds in the canvas behind. In the battle frenzy, they all shot wildly, and despite the short distance, no one had hit his mark.

But then one boat made a slight change of course, so that he could see not just the bow but also down along the side, and he fixed his eyes on the man steering the outboard motor. A clear target—one that might actually stop them. After a few long seconds, he paused and aimed.

The shot hit the man's shoulder, the bullet's power at short range shattering the bone as it burst inside his body, nearly severing his arm. It hung by skin and tendons, while his torso was thrown sideways. In the shock of the moment, a very brief moment, the man sat there, expressionless. The throttle also got thrown to one side, and the boat made a violent turn. The second shot was luckier, hitting the man in the middle of his chest. Just a tremor before he collapsed, dead.

Sailing around the world. A family that dreamed of going to the Great Barrier Reef and back. But this wasn't just an adventure, it was a new beginning in a life that would otherwise have fallen to pieces. They'd passed through Gibraltar in February and spent a few months in the Mediterranean. It wasn't hard to find destinations: the Riviera, Sicily, the Messina Strait, and then the whole odyssey of the Greek islands. Outside Rhodes, for the first time they saw dolphins playing by the bow. Near the Balearic Islands there'd been a few days of sun and Jenny had gotten some color, and with her tan came the bright lines around her eyes, the ones she hadn't had since she sailed as a professional. Her hair was thick and wavy; she'd worn it down past her shoulders as long as anyone could remember. She was the type that, if she felt pressured or uncomfortable, quickly turned defiant, and in school, she often got blamed for starting fights. But here on the boat she felt at home; she felt strong now. For the first time in ages, she liked how her husband looked at her. Carl-Adam, who could win over almost anyone. He was not yet forty, and the first thing people always said about him was that he made you laugh. Yet beyond his joking, there was something larger-than-life about him, and not just because he was a big man. The years of overwork, red-eye flights, five-course meals, and sauternes had gone straight to his waistline. He'd stopped playing golf several years ago, and tennis was out of the question. But he still needed the competition, so instead he'd pushed to become ever more well-informed, quick with the numbers, convincing in arguments. With his brusque smile, he was the one who closed the deals. It became a kind of relentlessness, his trademark, getting things his way in the end, driven to always be the best. Yet out here, he accepted that he'd never come close to Jenny's level as a sailor. He'd started to lose weight, and he no longer made a nasty comment if she smoked a cigarette in the evening breeze. In Porto Salvo, they'd even left the children on board overnight and gone to a small hotel near the harbor.

"They have the cell phone if they need us," Carl-Adam said, when she hesitated for a moment. They hadn't felt this kind of fire in a long time, and they didn't just make love at night but were also surprised by their desire for each other at dawn. Not sleepy caresses, but instead a force that took ahold of them. This wasn't dutiful lovemaking, it was pure sex for the first time in years. Back on the boat, Alexandra asked about the bite mark on Carl-Adam's neck.

They'd talked about it before, but not until they left Crete heading south did Jenny begin to worry. The Suez Canal and the Red Sea lay ahead—no dangers there—but then came the Gulf of Aden. They'd read about it. The pirates. Checklists in the sailing magazines, websites listing the latest attacks. Experts saying: keep away from the obvious trouble spots and stay in close communication with navy ships. Still. Reading about it from far away was one thing; sailing straight into it, another. Carl-Adam dealt with it in his own way. As usual, he preferred action, not just vague advice and relying on others. Alexandria was their last port stop in a big city. They tied up for a few days in the empty cruise-ship harbor not far from the center. A little sightseeing for the whole family, a trip to the pyramids of Giza, and Carl-Adam made his own little excursions in the city.

He returned to the boat one evening carrying something slender wrapped in burlap. He glanced at the port guards through the windows before cutting the strings and taking it out. A Kalashnikov, with two magazines and four hundred cartridges. "Arab Spring," he snorted with contempt. "They're losing their grip. Would you believe it, this cost me only two hundred dollars. Two hundred."

The object lying on the dining-room table didn't convey the slightest sense of security. Dented wood and dirty metal. With a flimsy bayonet attached below the barrel, and reeking of gun grease. It had to be hidden going through the Suez. Carl-Adam didn't want trouble from the inspectors sent aboard by the canal company to take bribes, or to give them any excuses. But in the Red Sea, he took it out. Carl-Adam emptied a magazine into a plastic jug he towed behind the boat.

Afterward, he rubbed his shoulder with his thumb. "If they come too close, they'll eat it." Sebastian, the boy, played with the empty shells, while his big sister, Alexandra, was quieter than usual that evening.

They passed through Bab el Mandeb, at the southernmost point of the Red Sea, and continued into the Gulf of Aden. The fishing was good here, and Yemeni fishermen steered their skiffs in small fast-moving clusters. The same open boats that the pirates sat in, from those photos online. The same thin, dark figures. Although the fishermen often waved as they passed, Jenny grew uneasy. The Somali coast lay no more than a few days' sail away.

Moving on, they passed by Djibouti, where convoys of ships seeking protection from Somali lawlessness were organized. The convoys required a speed of twelve knots, but that was impossible for the *MaryAnn*, as she would have to rely solely on her engine to keep her place in line. Carl-Adam and Jenny took down the sails and joined a convoy for slow-moving vessels. A collection of the lame and crippled. Freighters and tankers, real tubs, flying the flags of East Africa, Pakistan, and North Korea. Twenty merchant ships— and the *MaryAnn*. Radar showed them in a formation of two lines, with a few Japanese and Chinese naval ships making a weak show of power on either side. On the common radio frequency, there was constant chatter. Strange languages and obscenities in broken English. "Fuck you, Pakistani monkey." One night they heard strange moaning and wet sounds on the frequency. Finally they figured out that the night watchman on some ship thought he'd cheer up the convoy by playing the soundtrack to a porn movie. For hours it continued, you could turn down the volume but had to leave it on. Because all of a sudden, things would change into terrified shouts and uncomfortable silences. "They are shooting, shooting . . ." "Where, where . . . ?" It always sounded confusing. "Who is calling?" Chaos. "Pirates, pirates . . . !"

They knew the navy ships didn't scare off the pirates. Ships were getting hijacked even within the convoys. Jenny and Carl-Adam tried, but they couldn't both stay up all night. They had to take shifts, sleeping badly in between. It wasn't for this that they'd left home, Jenny thought at some point, but said nothing. Old patterns repeated themselves; they shared shifts up on deck, but she still cooked all the meals below. The children were listless, often seeming downright spoiled, and Jenny got angry when they complained about helping with chores or started fights. Often, it felt crowded on board.

In the Gulf of Aden also came the heat. With the sails down and the engine running, there was almost no shade on deck. Only the black finger of the mast, moving through the hours like the shadow of a huge sundial. The air was thick and hot with every breath, and the children stayed below. Jenny and Carl-Adam took four-hour shifts under the canvas roof of the cockpit. On the digital nautical chart, the northern Somali coast passed by too slowly. Their eyes fixed on what lay ahead: a timber freighter burning coal, its dense smoke rising in a black plume. A couple of ship silhouettes to starboard, and now and then a navy ship speeding past them, making sweeps that seemed mostly random.

"Jenny! Jenny!" It was always Carl-Adam who sounded the alarm. Sometimes he was already carrying the Kalashnikov when she came up on deck, sometimes he nodded with only a "There!" while he followed through the binoculars. A lone freighter in the distance, or a group of fishermen that navy ships had already checked out and reported on over the radio. He didn't have Jenny's ear for languages and still had a hard time deciphering what was said over the airwaves. Yet whenever he shouted, her heart would pound. The kids exchanged frightened glances whenever their mother raced up on deck. The seconds it took to understand what was happening, their temples aching before the danger could be dismissed.

They passed the Horn of Africa, and the convoy broke up where the Indian Ocean opened out. The *MaryAnn* returned to good form and set sail again. They continued east—following the advice of *Yachting World*—to get beyond the pirates' range. Nearly to the Arabian Gulf, before turning south to head down through the middle of the Indian Ocean. They were on their way to Mombasa to refill both diesel fuel (the tank nearly empty after the Gulf of Aden) and their food supplies. Even better, they'd spend a week at a hotel and live at the beach. Jenny looked forward to taking walks, to the smell and feel of leaves, and to sitting at tables already set, with someone else cooking the food.

But somewhere out there, the wind died. Mornings, the sea was often glassy, despite their being in mid-ocean. They moved slowly, while the heavy gray storm clouds passed by, always missing them.

Jenny longed to get drenched and cool off. At best, the clouds brought a few minutes of teasing, a few barely cool gusts of wind, without the sun's burning flame being obscured for even a second in the sapphire blue sky.

They didn't see a single ship for more than a week. Only a gray military helicopter heading straight on its course, far away. A brief crackle on the radio, and the sound of the distant rotor fading out. Then gone. Jenny was the one who saw it, hearing the crackle. Everything so still that she saw no reason to mention it to Carl-Adam.

Jenny was down in the children's cabin, distractedly helping Alexandra with her math homework, when she heard her husband's clattering on deck. She listened. A shout in the distance. It wasn't Carl-Adam's voice. And then a shot, followed by silence.

And suddenly, all hell broke loose. A bullet tore through the deck, whistling just above their heads. Jenny shouted at the children to lie down on the floor and ran as she'd never run before, like an arrow, to get her head up into the cockpit. She saw Carl-Adam standing at the rail, holding the Kalashnikov in front of him. And there beyond him, a fast little skiff. Full speed in a wide arc around them, not even a hundred meters away. Dark figures, flapping T-shirts. Weapons in hand, a couple of them raised in some kind of gesture. Threat, victory? Her thoughts stuttered as she tried to understand—not here, nobody would come here, there was nothing here. A shout again, a strange voice from somewhere behind her, at the bow, her view blocked by the cabin roof in front of her. All her impressions converged in a split second, while she was still on her way up to the deck.

The instant she took the final leap, there was a series of quick shots. She flinched, and in the same instant the vicious bullets hit the water at the stern. Carl-Adam followed the skiff with fear in his eyes, raising and lowering his arms a few times.

Jenny sensed something at the bow. She turned around, and now with a clear view, she saw a second skiff. "Carl-Adam," she cried. They were close, heading straight at the *MaryAnn*. "Turn around!" He didn't react, was overwhelmed, unreachable. Only watching the one boat he could see. "There are two!" Not even ten meters left, before the other one would reach the bow.

New shots came from the boat farther out, throwing up spray at the stern, where Carl-Adam stood. Jenny's gaze wandered from the bow to her husband. He raised his arms at last and fired a few shots. He must have hit something, she didn't know what, but the boat veered away sharply, out of control.

She shouted: "Bow! The bow!" And watched the man who sat at the front of the skiff, the one her husband couldn't see, stand up and take aim. Straight at her, it seemed. She crouched behind the cabin roof in fear. A shot.

Carl-Adam twitched as if he'd been punched. His weapon was tossed aside, and he fell to his knees. Blood. Something thudded into the *MaryAnn*. Jenny ran to the stern, grabbed Carl-Adam with both hands, got a confused look in response.

"I shot," he said. "I shot one."

Blood covered her hands. Behind her, she heard steps running. In the bow, they'd already come on board. She tried to say something to Carl-Adam, and he said something back that she didn't understand. There was something wrong with his leg. The man who came on first was tall and gangly, with bloodshot eyes. Barefoot. Without a word, he pulled back his gun and rammed it into Carl-Adam's back. Jenny lost her grip on him when he collapsed. Two other men pushed past. They disappeared with their machine guns leading, down below deck. She thought about the children and was overwhelmed by the feeling that something had come to an end.

2

The helicopter pilot on the HMS *Sveaborg* shoved the magazine into his pistol, pushed the pistol into his shoulder holster, and pulled on his flight helmet. All the other shit, he was already wearing. It was time to take off, again.

He'd lost count of how many times he had taken off from the ship. Had lost count of most things now. No longer kept track of how long they'd been out on their mission off the Somali coast, or even when they'd return home again. *Mission*, the word alone—whose salvation were they seeking here? His flight suit had salt stripes from old sweat, like the rings on a tree. He hadn't washed it as often as he should. There were so many shoulds. He shaved at most once a week, something so unlike him that at least he noticed. There was also the creeping feeling that maybe he'd stopped caring about real things. That idea bothered him more than his stubble when he looked in the mirror. In his emails home, he didn't think there was anything to say, nothing to talk about in a stream of identical days. His wife sent pictures of the house, of the flower beds and bushes turning green again in spring, and of the kids' sports practices. They struck him as familiar and so terribly distant at the same time. He sent no more than a smiley face or a thumbs-up in reply. The last time they'd escorted a ship into Mogadishu, he'd stood on deck and watched the shelling around the port while he ate a packet of biscuits. Were there two bloated corpses floating past him as he took out the last one, or was it three?

Now he sat strapped into the cockpit and waited for final preparations to be completed on the helicopter deck. He leaned forward and squinted up through the glass canopy at the aft mast. A peregrine falcon was sitting there, despite the noise from the engines and the spinning rotor. For a week, he'd seen it following the ship, mostly perched there, watching, or gliding on the winds around the ship. Now it had prey in its beak, Christ knows where it'd been caught, because it was not a fish.

A fresh splash of seawater hit the rotor, spotting the glass. The ship rocked in the rough seas of the southwest monsoon. Newly arrived, it had brought strong winds over the past few days. The pilot tried to get comfortable, but he couldn't, not with his bulky vest bursting with all the survival equipment someone else had decided he needed. The worst, comfort-wise, was the bulletproof vest beneath his flight suit, with its heavy protective plates front and rear. It weighed almost twenty kilos. But he wanted that vest, even though it would drown him if he crashed into the sea. Stray bullets were what scared him the most, beyond the fear of being taken hostage by any of the insane militias based in the Horn of Africa. The flight crews no longer joked about why they'd save one last bullet in their gun.

The ship lurched again, and the helicopter's shock absorbers reluctantly responded. The copilot rattled off the final checklist items, and the gunner in the rear, after swearing about something, announced: "Cabin check complete." Outside, the flight deck crew stumbled off, carrying the lashings they'd removed from the helicopter. Already, big flowers of sweat darkened the pale blue fabric of their jumpsuits. Even in the strong wind, it was impossible to defend against the heat.

They had an extra passenger in the helicopter. An hour before takeoff, the ship's first officer had told the pilot: "You know, we'll have Lieutenant Slunga aboard, the head of MovCon."

MovCon, the logistics unit, normally kept to their unloading duties in Djibouti. The HMS *Sveaborg* had made a brief stopover in Salalah a few days before, when the ship's air-conditioning had broken, and they'd quickly arranged a delivery of spare parts to the nearest port. It was Slunga himself who'd organized it, then stayed on board when they cast off again. "MovCon performs miracles, but they work their asses off, especially Slunga," said the commander. "He'd probably appreciate a ride." One of the few rewards the brass on board could give their men was a trip in a helo, if the pilot in command didn't object.

"Of course we'll take him."

Before takeoff, the pilot helped Slunga put on his gear, a slimmed-down version of what the others wore, and they'd introduced themselves. The lieutenant, with his white-blond hair, projected something both friendly and preoccupied. He chatted about his family, especially his son whom he clearly missed a lot, and never stopped asking questions. But as soon as Slunga's attention wasn't required, his thoughts drifted away, and he seemed startled when the conversation started up again. He grabbed a cup of coffee before takeoff but took only a sip.

Now Slunga was in the aft of the cabin with the gunner. Amid all the commotion around him, he seemed finally to have forgotten what was bugging him, and he sat down looking expectant as the engines roared.

A gust ruffled the falcon's feathers up on the mast, while on the helicopter deck, the pilot tried to get a feel for the motion of the ship, looking for the sweet spot in the erratic rhythm. The deck light turned from red to green, and he got his chance as the aft heaved upward. The helicopter lifted off through the gusty winds in one long sweep over the starboard side.

They flew under radio silence at low altitude toward the coast. After the tension of takeoff, they got a half hour of peace. The sea always seemed calmer and bluer from the air than when you stood on deck. The short period of calm invited conversation, sometimes even confidences.

"So . . . ," asked the pilot, "how's it going?"

The gunner knew exactly what he was talking about. "I was in her cabin yesterday, but she said that now that we're on duty, everything's off. But the next time we're in port, she wants to go out."

"And you want to go in," laughed the copilot. The gunner said nothing.

"Are you serious about her?" asked Slunga, the extra passenger.

"Yes, he is," replied the pilot for the young gunner.

"Do something special, then, don't just take her out for a few beers."

"It's hard," replied the gunner, sounding blue. "You know, you only get one day ashore."

"Not beer and a disco ball," continued Slunga, "not with the life you live out here. Give her peace every minute of those twenty-four hours. Take her away from it all, to the beach, where it's only her and you, with no one from the ship around."

"That's a sweet dream, but how can I make it happen from here?"

"Not you. I'll do it, and I know just the place. If you say she's worth it."

"Are you serious?"

"Doesn't MovCon have anything better to do than arrange love nests?" the copilot tried to joke.

"What could be more important?" said Slunga. There wasn't a trace of irony.

They flew in silence for a minute, before the pilot broke it. "The first officer says you're working hard these days."

"Did he mention me specifically?" replied Slunga.

"Why?"

"No, nothing. We have enough to do, sure, we work around the clock. But I have all the people I need. I've even managed to hire a crew of locals on the base in Djibouti. It's just that you're on the ship out here, while I'm ashore with my little gang. Strong personalities, and lots of distractions near the base and in town."

"Discipline problems?"

"Sometimes."

"You've got to keep them on a short leash."

"I try to."

For the last few days, the Swedish patrol vessel HMS *Sveaborg* had been skulking outside a known pirates' nest not far from Bosaso.

As they reached the beach, the helicopter climbed to a few hundred feet, and then the cabin door opened wide and the machine gun emerged, ready in case of trouble. With their powerful cameras, the crew started taking videos and stills. The beach was more than a kilometer wide, but what interested them stood by the water's edge: a half-dozen open boats, their hulls resting wearily on their sides, right on the sand where the tides came up, along with some improvised shelters built from rubble, and the fuel storage, with oil barrels covered by orange tarps.

"Not many awake," said one of the pilots, about the stillness below.

"Sleeping off their khat highs." With the cabin door wide open, they had to half-shout to make themselves heard over the wind and the rotor's roar.

"There, at two o'clock," yelled the copilot. The gunner turned the high-magnification camera sitting in a gimbal under the fuselage, the movement making the TV screen flicker. Then it stopped and came into focus.

"Weren't there some oil drums here before?"

"Nothing left but marks in the sand."

The camera moved again. "And I can't find that pile of RPG grenades we saw yesterday."

"High tide was just after sunset."

"Seems a few snuck out at night."

On the second lap around the camp, the radio crackled. They couldn't hear a thing but figured it was the ship. Distance was a problem, and the pilot had to corkscrew up to a higher altitude before they got a voice.

"Snowman from Mother, do you read us?" It was the combat control officer on the *Sveaborg*.

"Not even a half hour out. Always something," said the copilot in a tired voice, as he pressed the transmit button. "Snowman here."

The *Sveaborg* had received a distress call from a merchant ship. The helicopter was given a position, and the pilot turned around and picked up speed toward the sea. While the copilot went over the adjustments on the radar screen, the gunner pulled in his machine gun and closed the cabin door. Instantly, the wind noise died down in the helmet headphones.

Soon afterward, an agitated voice came on the radio, heard through constant interruptions in the transmission. It was the skipper of the MV *Sevastopol*, a Russian freighter. If there was anything you learned in the Gulf of Aden, it was how to understand all the world's accents in English, shouted over Channel 16. "Calm down, calm down . . . Please, say again . . . Who is shooting?"

But they got the gist. "Shit!" swore the gunner, who felt tricked by the pirates sneaking out at night. It took a while to get more out of the skipper than "Two boats, two boats" and "Please hurry up!" The pirates were shelling the bridge with bursts from their automatic weapons, and it seemed the ship had also taken some grenade hits. The men in skiffs had tried more than once to hook ladders onto the sides, and one of the freighter's crew members was badly hurt. But so far, no pirates had gotten on board, and the captain was maneuvering his ship as well as he could to keep them off. "Please hurry up!"

The MV *Sevastopol* had grown into a fat cigar-shaped blip on the radar screen, matching its swelling dot on the horizon, and now had a clear wake.

Only in the last few hundred meters did the helicopter slow down. The same routine as before: door open, machine gun out. Although they weren't taken by surprise, the men in the motorboats hesitated for a moment. The pirates had been so close, the prey almost in hand, just one more minute and . . . Even if you looked right into their faces, you'd never see disappointment. The skipper kept yelling over the radio, and on another channel, the *Sveaborg* kept asking what was happening, but the helicopter crew couldn't care less about that. They had a single focus: the men in the boats, and what they did with their hands. The only one actually aiming with a weapon was their own gunner. The MV *Sevastopol* had stopped zigzagging and held a steady course, with one pirate boat just a few meters from her side, and a man still holding on to the long, hooked boarding ladder. The other boat was farther out. Five men in each—bare feet, skinny arms,

T-shirts and shorts. A few moments to decide who was strong and who was weak. "Shoot! Shoot the monkeys!" shouted the *Sevastopol*'s captain.

As if on cue, the two pirate boats revved to full throttle, spraying arcs behind their outboard engines. The Russian freighter remained on course, a tired old dinosaur, while both skiffs disappeared, leaving white streaks.

The pilot had already caught up. He could see how the men below shook as their boats hit the waves, even though their speed was child's play for the helicopter. He felt a shameful wave of satisfaction, for in that instant, it was all just a game. An interlude between the pirates' firing on defenseless people and the consequences that would bring. Now they were trying to escape, but escape was impossible.

"Give them a few rounds, see what happens."

The gunner, who already had them in his sights, pulled the trigger. Twenty meters in front of the first boat, the water leapt up in white columns. The skiffs didn't slow down. But the second boat, which had been following the first, made a wide arc and took off on its own. One helicopter, two boats; they'd certainly lose half their catch. The pilot continued straight ahead, a hundred feet up, just behind the remaining boat. The copilot updated the *Sveaborg* over the radio about what was happening. They needed no further orders or permission to pursue. It was obvious what they were facing, and what the people in the boats had done— piracy, no small thing; someone had been seriously wounded on a merchant ship. They were to be stopped at any cost.

"Fire again."

The second volley hit just in front of the bow, so that water from the impact splashed into the boat. Some of the men ducked, as if the splashes were shrapnel. A chink in their armor, revealing that they were afraid. "We'll give them a chance." The pilot had dropped closer, less than a hundred meters between them now. Here the helicopter was at its most vulnerable, given that the pirates had more firepower: four or five Kalashnikovs and at least one rocket-propelled grenade.

But these wouldn't be an option now. The language of power was spoken through shiny technology, thundering rotors, and targeted firepower. Had anyone so much as reached for a weapon on the floor, the gunner would have instantly opened fire on the boat, without even an order from the commander on board. It would have been self-defense, clear and simple. And the men in the boat knew it. They might have been too high on khat or too afraid, but mostly they held their fire because of the balance of power. They had to accept their futility first.

One last chance, the pilot had said. The third volley sprayed from bow to stern next to the rail of the skiff. Impossible to shoot any closer without hurting someone, and none of the pirates wanted to risk a challenge. They just wanted to survive, and maybe get back home again. The boat stopped abruptly, and all five raised their hands. The helicopter pulled away and began circling. There was an intense burst of radio traffic, and they calculated their fuel reserves.

"How much time?" asked the pilot.

"Keep us at just below sixty knots, and we might have enough for an hour." The HMS *Sveaborg* had been traveling at top speed for a while. Down below, the pirates had lowered their hands and sat bobbing in the boat, while the gunner kept them centered in the viewfinder of his TV camera. "Now they're dumping the ladder," he said. That was also part of the game. The Somalis were trying to get rid of evidence: they lowered the ladder into the sea while the gunner filmed.

"And there go the guns."

Five nameless men in an empty boat somewhere in the Gulf of Aden.

The helicopter circled. They'd done this before. But then the radio crackled—an unexpected surprise.

"Snowman, Snowman, this is Russian Federation warship *Admiral Chabanenko*."

"Shit," swore the copilot. The Russians had a handful of warships in the region that didn't belong to any task force. Instead, they ran their own show. Well-armed and aggressive, their approach to Africans with flip-flops and Kalashnikovs was: gloves off. The Russian destroyer *Admiral Chabanenko* was moving in like an arrow. And the fact that she could be heard over the VHF radio meant she couldn't be very far off.

"Snowman, confirm you have the Somali pirates under your control." The Russian combat controllers had a distinct accent, and their tone was never polite.

"Answer them," said the pilot.

"You know what they'll demand?"

"Answer them."

The copilot replied to the *Chabanenko*, telling them where things stood. Then he radioed the *Sveaborg*: "Following the traffic?"

"We follow."

"What's happening?" asked Slunga, who'd been sitting silently in the cabin.

"We'll explain later," said the pilot.

"Just make sure to get a video of that damn boat down there," the copilot reminded the gunner.

"Confirming your position," said the Russians.

"They already see us on their radar," the pilot explained to Slunga, and then added, resigned: "They're taking over."

"Mother, what are our orders?" radioed the copilot to the HMS *Sveaborg*.

"Wait," said the Swedish combat controller.

It was obvious. The Russians had contacted their own military headquarters through other channels. Made their demands. Asserted their rights. Somewhere a Swedish admiral was sitting down with a lawyer, reading the fat paragraphs of rules and conventions: a Russian merchant ship attacked in international waters, a sailor seriously injured. Rights and wrongs—and politics. And keeping his hands clean. Chasing pirates was less about battle operations than about mastering these paragraphs.

The helicopter circled while the five men in the boat sat dazed and unsuspecting. A destroyer was on its way, doing at least forty knots. Somewhere in the Russian hull, weapons were being loaded and grenades readied.

"Snowman from Mother," the Swedish ship radioed, "hand over the suspects."

The copilot was silent for a second, letting it sink in before he answered. "Mother, we are handing over five men to the Russians. You are fully aware of this?"

"Drop it," snapped the pilot, over the intercom. But the copilot had scored his point and wouldn't do any more grumbling. The admiral had decided that he couldn't put up a fight. Who knew what he really wanted? Certainly he realized what was happening. But Legad, the military lawyer, had pointed to some lines in the rule book and showed the admiral that, even though he was cornered, he could come out with his hands clean.

"Hand over the object and document your actions," repeated the combat control on the HMS *Sveaborg*.

"You bet your ass we will," muttered the copilot, and called out, "Confirmed." Then he asked the gunner: "You noted the time of the order, right?"

"Of course."

Then the Russian destroyer arrived, first a blip on the radar, then a dark gray shape through the haze. A warship on the open seas—for the Russians in the twenty-first century, everything was still about flexing their muscles: huge spinning antennas and guns in every direction. A death star.

Now it was their show.

"Snowman, stand by, boarding team on the way," said a voice that no human being would want judging his fate. Two rubber boats shot out from the destroyer carrying the boarding team: black boats, with men dressed entirely in black. On the helicopter's TV, the men in the pirate boat looked vaguely anxious—they'd probably seen the destroyer and the rubber boats coming. They raised their arms again, straight up like exclamation points, all five.

"You still filming?" asked the copilot.

"Yes," replied the gunner.

"Turn it off now and put away the camera," commanded the pilot. Hands clean.

The rubber boats had barely another two hundred meters to go. The pilot turned, leaving the pirate boat and the whole scene behind them, while the copilot announced: "*Admiral Chabanenko*, we are handing over pirate suspects to you."

"Affirmative," answered the voice of doom. "Good hunting."

The pilot looked at his wristwatch. "Note that when we left them at zero seven fifty-three, all five were still alive."

The silence in the machine was palpable. The logistics officer must have been feeling some kind of internal moral struggle. They'd gone without a word for more than ten minutes when Slunga finally asked: "What will happen to . . . ?"

"You don't want to know," replied the pilot.

And then, silence again.

They'd seen nothing. Hands clean.

3

Jenny never said it, could never stand to think it, but the *MaryAnn II* had been hijacked. Seven pirates on board, their two skiffs towed behind. They waved their guns around impatiently, everywhere, always a finger on the trigger. The first hour, they'd been full of victory and rage. Searching and looting, dragging Jenny along to open lockers, cabinets, and bulkheads. Mostly, they seemed to be looking for food, or racing to find valuables to stuff in their pockets. They'd wolf down a chocolate bar, clear out a bathroom cabinet, nab a little knife with nail scissors, and push on to the next cabin. The slightest misunderstanding was seen as defiance, and then the muzzle was up against Jenny's face again. Worst was the crushing feeling of powerlessness, every time they grabbed or shouted at the children.

In one of the skiffs lay a dead man—the one Carl-Adam had shot. Carl-Adam himself had been shot in the hand, and there was a long gash in his thigh. But all in all he'd been fortunate, given the number of shots they'd fired. His luck had only held out so far, however, and now it was over. He'd armed himself, killed one of their own, and now he was the pirates' defeated enemy. They forced him into one end of the cockpit. He was guarded the whole time, by the unlucky bastard who got back at his prisoner for missing out on all the looting. Random bursts of kicking, rifle-butting, and yelling. Carl-Adam tried to defend himself, barely noticing his wounds, but soon the cockpit was covered in long streaks of blood where he'd braced himself, crawled, and slipped as he was being beaten. His corner looked like a pen where some animal was slowly being slaughtered.

The whole time, the *MaryAnn*'s autopilot kept the boat on the same steady heading it was on before the pirate skiffs appeared.

Jenny managed to keep the children with her while she was being dragged around the ship. Only one thing mattered as long as she had them with her: preventing them from seeing what was happening to their father out on deck. When the first numbing terror subsided, her head spun with one recurring thought: it's all on me! The thought didn't exactly make her stronger, but it did make her more wary.

One face among the pirates, with his narrow almond-shaped eyes and henna-dyed beard, etched itself early in her consciousness. He ransacked the cabinets and ate like the others, but carried his rifle on his back, not in front, and the other pirates were careful never to get in his way. Seeing the way he observed his surroundings, Jenny always made sure to stand between him and Alexandra whenever he looked at her. Despite the looting, he kept the others from stealing the radio and the navigation equipment on the chart table.

When the thieves had gotten what they wanted and given in to the drowsiness of victory, their leader went up on deck. His rust-red beard shone intensely in the sun. It took Jenny a while to realize that the man was kicking Carl-Adam like the others, but he wanted something specific. "Here!" he shouted, waiting a few seconds for the prisoner's reaction, and then starting in again. "Here!" Then Jenny got a glimpse of the man's handheld GPS and understood.

It would take several days before the pirates grasped that Jenny was the skipper of the *MaryAnn*. But this time, when Redbeard kicked, she managed to go up on deck and get his attention. With a final kick to his side, bringing Carl-Adam down once again, the pirate leader turned around.

"Here!" he repeated, reaching out his arm with the GPS right in front of her. The display showed a point on the Somali coast, just south of Harardhere.

Jenny set the course with the autopilot. They veered to starboard, a gentle turn in the breeze. A new course to the west, toward a place everyone had been told to avoid. Redbeard watched her quietly during the entire maneuver, then checked the course on his own GPS. After that, she was allowed to take care of Carl-Adam.

The shot had gone straight through his hand. She picked out bone chips, then washed the wound and bandaged it. At least one bone in there was shattered. The gash in his thigh was inches long and deep; she did what she could with a first-aid kit. She had a hard time getting a hold around Carl-Adam's heavy thigh, and the wound started to bleed badly again, while her arms got shaky before she finally managed to squeeze so hard that it stopped. Her hands were shiny with her husband's blood, so much of it on herself and her clothes that she could smell the iron. Carl-Adam was panting from exhaustion, and at times his gaze went blank. She started to take off his stained shirt but stopped when she saw all the big bruises forming and the lump rising on his back from the first blow with the rifle butt. How much more, for how long?

"They'll miss us" was the first thing he said, when she was nearly done. Carl-Adam was leaning back, and she put an arm around his head in an attempt to comfort him and get close. She thought he meant the kids, that he was already thinking of himself and her as dead.

"I'm all right," she said, and tried to smile. Not a second passed without her thinking about Alexandra and Sebastian, left alone in their cabin below deck.

But Carl-Adam had seen a glimmer of hope, knowing that they'd turned west toward the Somali coast. "The link," he explained, his voice a whisper. "Everyone will see."

On their blog, which they kept so friends and family could follow their trip, their location was automatically updated every ten nautical miles with a small red dot on a map. They probably wouldn't be able to write another word, but their dotted trail now went counter to all their previous posts about where they were heading. "They'll sound the alarm." Even in his weakened state, this was Carl-Adam's way of relating to what had happened, maintaining his distance, shunning the blood and vulnerability with his hope that someone would see the conflicting data. Jenny didn't know what to think. He was busy finding a logical solution, while she was doing everything to keep them alive. Below deck, the children were still alone, with at least five pirates.

"Of course," she said, kissing Carl-Adam's forehead. "Someone will get worried, and they'll find us."

The days went by. A sixty-two-foot sailboat towing two skiffs close behind. Westward went the dotted trail on both the *Mary-Ann*'s GPS and the family's sailing blog. The corpse, left exposed in one of the skiffs, had begun to swell. There were only a few meters between the boats, and from the quarterdeck they could clearly see his face, the teeth shining white in an unnatural grin. Starting from the mangled shoulder, the flesh was turning a bad color and slowly cracking. Whenever they went up on deck, it was impossible not to look, and the weak wind blew the stench at them.

Below deck, Jenny tried to restore order, unwilling to give in. She kept picking up, even though the floor was soon covered with trash again. Wads of paper and food packaging lay everywhere. She gave up on the toilets, which reeked ever more strongly of urine. But for her own sake and for the dignity of the children, she tried to keep their regular routines. She got up at the same time every morning, tried to cook at least one meal a day in an orderly way, kept busy, supervised Alexandra's schoolwork. Her efforts were often blocked, as sometimes activities would be forbidden, or stuff would disappear, or someone would take away their food, but still—she'd try again. Jenny's patience was all that kept the creeping resignation at bay, creating a sense of safety and keeping them from giving up: they are there, and we are here. Before the pirates, on board she'd always worn shorts and gone barefoot, but now she covered her legs and wore shoes. And as a mother she was forced to choose: the children or Carl-Adam? So their shared cabin had become his infirmary, and she slept with Alexandra and Sebastian. She didn't leave them alone for a moment, unless absolutely necessary. On board, she and the children moved as a pack. For an hour or so every evening, she tried to make sure all four were together, although her injured husband mostly slept.

The second time the pirates went after Carl-Adam was when they wanted to go faster; the weak wind was making Redbeard impatient. They shook Carl-Adam and landed a couple of decent punches before Jenny understood and started up the engine. She didn't try to explain that the tank would soon be empty. They ran out of diesel two days later, and then there was more shouting and a few kicks before they were powered only by the wind again. Carl-Adam recovered somewhat, but he had trouble putting weight on his injured leg, and his hand was an ominous red. He mostly just sipped water and lay on his bunk, and Jenny washed and dressed his wounds every day. They'd run out of bandages, so ripped sheets had to do. When she asked him to move his fingers, only his thumb twitched.

It wasn't long before Alexandra made an innocent mistake. One afternoon, on her own initiative, she sat down at the computer on the chart table, to send an essay in for school. Despite all the chaos on board, she still wanted to do well in her last semester of junior high. Jenny couldn't stop her, and Redbeard saw and understood what a satellite link could lead to. He yelled, Alexandra glared, a loud slap was heard, and she cursed in defiance before Jenny stepped between them, and then he furiously snatched all the cables out of the computer. The link was broken; there was no more dotted trail. Later that evening, when she and the children were below with Carl-Adam, he asked about the commotion. Alexandra shrugged, and Jenny said Redbeard had gotten upset when she'd opened some cans. She held his hand in bed, and in his eyes, saw that he didn't completely believe her.

"Someone will notice?" he said.

"Of course," she replied. "Someone will miss us."

Her lie in front of the children, her own sense of hopelessness while needing to keep up an appearance of strength. It was the loneliest moment she had ever known on the boat.

Redbeard was called Darwiish by the other pirates, and after the incident at the chart table, Alexandra kept a close eye on him. She'd slip past Jenny and say: "We have to watch out, Redbeard is drunk." The liquor bottles on board had disappeared from the cabinet on day one. No one saw when he drank, but after nightfall, they sometimes saw his awkward movements and moist lips. From time to time, he'd fire shots into the night, but mostly he kept to the cockpit at the stern, or the middle of the cabin below deck, sitting up straight and thin, and watching everything and everyone through narrow eyes.

The slowness, the heat, and the weak wind that kept them at a crawl took their toll. Fights broke out among the pirates, and there were new outbreaks of looting to relieve the boredom. When Darwiish roared at or hit one of his own, it was impossible to say if he was settling a dispute or simply acting on impulse. Once, he forced one of the younger pirates, not much more than a boy, to sit at the bow for the whole afternoon without shelter from the sun. Only when he fainted did someone go up on the deck and pull him away.

Finally, the situation with the bloated corpse became unbearable. Three pirates stepped into the skiff with handkerchiefs tied over their noses and mouths, and they rolled the body over the side. They'd wrapped a chain they'd found on board around his feet as a sinker, but the dead man was so bloated with gas that he floated anyway, with one arm strangely sticking up above the surface. He looked like someone in distress who'd been frozen in his plea for help, as he slowly drifted away, disappearing into the mist.

Only once was Darwiish caught in a moment of indecision. When a military helicopter crossed the horizon, the pirates came to a standstill on deck, all eyes focused on the same point in the sky. A burst of static on the radio. Darwiish looked at the speaker as if it were a weapon aiming at him. Suddenly there was a chance. The emergency flares, Jenny thought. They were right there in a box next to the cockpit, still intact, she knew it for a fact. She could do it. She had time; they were two steps away. Just tear off the tape and pull.

Poof—a red light rising into the sky. What a sight, what defiance. It would have cost them, maybe a life. But still.

Then she thought of the children, especially Sebastian. She hesitated. The sound of the helicopter died away.

She should have fired that flare. It was the first thing she thought of two days later when she saw land before the bow of the *MaryAnn*.

4

Annoyingly, he felt himself breathing hard, although he hadn't moved a muscle. His adrenaline hadn't yet kicked in, not like for the others. But he could feel the fatigue behind his eyes. As usual, he hadn't slept.

Ernst Grip stood outside an apartment door in the Stockholm district of Husby, eyeing the second hand on his watch. In front of him stood a handful of SWAT guys, way overequipped as usual. They'd even brought a battering ram, though they called it something else. At the briefing beforehand, someone had suggested they could just pick the lock—but no, they wanted shock and awe. They'd use "the big master key," as they called it. No one even laughed when it was said, just a few quick and knowing nods, then the matter was settled. Shock and awe.

Two men, one on either side, took hold of the bars. Arms out, they clenched their gloved hands into fists, like overtrained athletes winding up to throw something extremely heavy as far as possible. In Grip's row, lined up behind the strike force, stood the two others from Säpo, the security police. They were the ones in charge, the ones who'd received the order, who wielded the power. The atmosphere was both serious and amped up, as if they were facing something decisive, something at once important and extremely dangerous. And Grip didn't like it. From where he stood, there were too many murky agendas. Of course, there was fear, but also a kind of unchecked enthusiasm before they'd even begun. What was it they were actually about to do? He looked at his second hand—fifty-five. Just seconds to go.

Ernst Grip had only a vague idea about the men standing around him. Within Säpo, he worked in the bodyguard detachment. Official visit to Dubai one day; the next, standing by the queen as she cut a blue-and-yellow ribbon for a hospital in Skövde. Working for the royals had no cred among the bodyguards, who saw it as a place for newbies needing to prove themselves or old guys who'd lost their touch. The ones who were for real got to accompany the foreign minister to some refugee camp on the Syrian border, despite all threat analyses flashing red. There were a few among Grip's colleagues who thought he'd been shunted aside, but those who'd been there longer and had heard the rumors guessed at the real reason behind Grip's job. He had a reputation for being good with his fists, among those who'd seen him. Maybe that was why he'd gotten called in so fast for this apartment raid. At least, that was what he hoped. Nothing more than that.

Now it was late Sunday afternoon, and already Grip had taken the royal couple to a fund-raiser at Stockholm Concert Hall. He'd driven them back to Drottningholm Palace, then returned to Säpo headquarters in Solna to drop off his equipment, planning to head home.

Everything at headquarters was dead, except in a room full of people where the phones and printers were going crazy. Grip hadn't paid attention, only walked by. But then while he sat alone in the echoing locker room, a face that had nothing to do with bodyguards looked in: "Come on, we need you too." So Grip had stood up.

The operations room was in chaos, with more information coming in than the staff could handle. The people around Grip were barely familiar to him, by either face or name. The instructions were unclear. "You know, on a Sunday you can't fucking reach anyone, and we need at least one more to tag along."

They passed him some papers with signatures. "The boss has given you clearance." There were dozens of bosses in the building, but Grip didn't ask questions. He saw it as a simple matter: they were shorthanded and needed extra muscle. Besides, a Sunday afternoon alone in his apartment wasn't something he looked forward to. "Can't just rely on SWAT for this." Someone winked at him. A forced entry apparently, but then what? People were so stressed that they were dropping things. Someone spoke nonstop in English on an encrypted phone, mostly obedient strings of: "Yes, yes," and "Please say again." Body armor and firearms began to appear on a large table. An apartment blueprint was taped to one wall.

And then SWAT sauntered in.

Already dressed for action, they sat down, while the security police officers quickly took their equipment from the table and improvised a briefing. Stress and loose ends, sure, that's what they had to deal with at times, Grip had seen it before. But it was during the briefing that Grip felt his first wave of uneasiness. The thing with the lock, for one. Not so much the battering ram itself, as the sense that they were going in full force. A piece of the larger world would play itself out in an immigrant neighborhood of Stockholm on a Sunday. They were facing a suspected terrorist cell linked to ISIS, and they had to strike now.

Obviously, they were acting on foreign intelligence, though no one said that out loud. The jargon always sounded a certain way, whenever Washington and Paris were involved. There was talk of weapons caches and suicide bombers. Sweden had long been dismissed as a backwater that didn't take matters seriously enough. A safe haven for the naive. No one could remember the name of the guy who blew himself up a few years before near Queen Street, and there'd been some change in attitudes afterward, but still. They'd never gotten wind of something big, always been relegated to the B team. Then suddenly, this active cell. Apparently, there were people in that apartment right now. Hands in jam jars: money, weapons, bombs. It was like a perfect hand in poker. You could take the whole pot. "Now, you little fuckers!" There was no limit to ambition, and that was precisely what gave Grip the sense that something was wrong.

Two seconds to go. Grip pressed the button on the little voice recorder in the pocket of his bulletproof vest.

The battering ram was swung back, on the second, like a freight train picking up speed toward a pile of boards . . . "Now, you fuckers!"

The entire door collapsed in a shower of splinters. And then they went at it.

Two dark men were in the first room—at the briefing, someone had said Somalis—and a third ran back through the apartment as the wave of police and weapons swept in. When one of the overtaken men raised his arm, probably just for protection, the blow that followed knocked him flat on his back. The officers yelled, nonstop, and one drove his knee into the back of the other man who was already down on his stomach. Grip looked for weapons or suspicious devices with electrical wires. As he moved past, he noticed a table with a few stacks of foreign bills. He hadn't lost speed, hadn't stopped for a second. He and two of the SWAT officers rushed ahead to find the third man. A bedroom door slammed shut in front of them, but it was ripped right off its hinges by two flying shoulders. The Somali, if that's what he was, had been pushing from behind and was thrown back into the room. The two SWAT guys dressed in black were on him in an instant. Grip saw a trail of blood spatter on the carpet. It was impossible to determine if the man on the floor was just whimpering in pain or still resisting.

"I got this," Grip said, moving in quickly between them. He'd already holstered his pistol; the other two struggled to hold the man while they fumbled with their equipment. Grip approached, taking control. He was bigger than the two police officers, despite wearing only body armor, while they were dressed for two weeks of rioting.

"You check the bathroom."

No one would be in there, he was certain of it. He trusted his instincts. He thought it was enough now, with all the punches, knees, and shouting. There were only three, and their hands were under control. No one would be able to press a detonator. The SWAT men left to check. The man beneath Grip had a bad nosebleed, dark blood running over dark skin, and stared at him wide-eyed and confused. Grip hadn't even brought along handcuffs, but that wouldn't be a problem. He pulled the skinny young man to his feet with a single move, the man's arms hanging like fragile pendulums.

The two SWAT officers came out of the bathroom, the first giving a quick shake of his head, and then they hurried out with heavy steps. There was another bedroom somewhere. Grip heard loud voices and commotion behind him—they were ransacking every inch of the place. Just a few more seconds, before the others would also realize that they'd gotten all of the men. Then it all would wind down. Grip held the African with one hand wrapped in the front of his loose shirt. Blood was dripping on his fist—at least he'd brought gloves. With his other hand, Grip reached for a hand towel slung over a chair and gave it to the young man for his nosebleed. He took the towel but left it dangling from his hand.

Grip was alone in the room at the back of the apartment. Still all that noise and struggle behind him. What the hell were they doing? Everything in the operation had gone as it should, and now they were done. A feeling of vulnerability came over him. He looked around, both ways, but no one else was there. The man in his hold gasped and trembled. A creeping sense of unease. Something was going on. Grip scanned the face of the man standing in front of him but got back only a blank stare. No, the world could not be read so easily. Matchstick arms and frightened eyes revealed nothing about the people they were facing: petty criminals or hardened terrorists. But wasn't it enough now? What the hell were they doing? Just a few more seconds, then it would all wind down.

5

The HMS *Sveaborg* had docked a few hours before in Djibouti, home base during her mission in Africa. The sun had passed its peak, but still no one moved, not if they could help it. The ship's dock guards suffered in their desert hats, kept to short shifts, and drank huge quantities of water. When sailors hauled garbage bags from a cargo door and threw them into an empty dumpster, it instantly began to stink in the heat.

A white Toyota Land Cruiser drove onto the loading dock, which was the size of two football fields, with huge cranes on rails guarding either end. The car, with Swedish military plates, pulled right up to the dock guards' table. A lone sergeant stepped out, wearing the same desert uniform as the watch officer on the dock, but a more pleasant expression. As if he'd sat in an air-conditioned office all day and knew that within half a minute, he'd be inside again. Or possibly because, even though he was Swedish, he'd spent much of his adult life in this climate and knew how much everyone else suffered.

"Hi," he said, nodding to the watch officer, who raised his head just enough to see under the brim. The sergeant walked around the car and opened the tailgate. "Jönsson, make sure you come ashore for real this time. There's plenty to do here in town. Whatever you want." He took out two metal suitcases covered with baggage tags, slung a small cooler bag across his back, and slammed the door. "Damn it, all you have to do is ask, while you're out on the boat, you've always got MovCon here. We know all the places." He stopped in front of the desk, slightly raising up both bags. "Just some spare parts, arrived by plane this morning while you were out at sea."

The watch officer nodded and the sergeant went up the gangway.

The helicopter stood on the flight deck, as pampered and fragile as a patient in intensive care. A tarp draped over the rotor blades gave some shade to the men working below, naked from the waist up. The fuselage panels were stripped off, exposing the engine and the gearbox, while a few pairs of arms reached inside.

The sergeant nodded as he came up to the last ladder on deck, but he said nothing until he was under the shade of the tarp. "Where is . . . ?"

"I'm here." An older technician looked out from behind a door into the cockpit. "And both of them made it." He smiled and took the bags, moving much more cautiously than the courier handing them over.

When the sergeant pulled out the cooler bag, the technician said: "Thanks, but don't get me mixed up in that. Take it to the guys over there." He nodded toward a few others who were working on the machine.

Two of them met him by the tail rotor.

"Six cold ones," said the sergeant, smiling wide like someone with an answer to everything, "and you can knock them back as soon as she's fixed and ready to go. And a whole bottle of Talisker. It was Talisker that you wanted, right?"

"Yeah," replied one of the technicians. He looked at the cooler bag, his body shining with sweat. "Salminen's totally sick of this ship. He can't stand being on board anymore, and he needs cheering up."

"Beer's on me, but for the whiskey, it'll be nine hundred."

"Nine hundred!" said the other one under his breath, clearly annoyed.

"Hello? This is Djibouti." Very discreetly, he took a look around the deck beyond the helicopter. If the wrong officer saw them, he'd be in trouble.

He got a shrug in reply from the pissed-off technician. The other said: "We'll drink it on shore, promise."

"Doesn't bother me, either way," said the sergeant.

"The cash?"

"We can settle up another time. Or else, you can take me on a helo joyride. My boss just got one."

The technicians laughed for a moment. Everyone knew it would never happen.

The sergeant drove back out in his white Toyota. It took a while to get out of the port, a landscape of containers and miscellaneous cargo waiting to be sent somewhere else. There were long rows of little Chinese trucks, hundreds of them, of a type never seen inside Djibouti, and huge stockpiles of pipes. By this time of day, the few longshoremen around lay sleeping in the shade next to their water bottles.

At the gate, a uniformed guard was stationed at the entrance and exit, and anyone leaving had to show proper identification. The sergeant pressed his ID card against the side window without turning his head. In the photo, he was clean-shaven and had an intensity in his eyes that seemed to question what the photographer would actually do with his picture. The guard had to settle for seeing him in profile—with cap, sunglasses, and beard. Neither man bothered to care, and without a moment's hesitation, he was waved through.

The road out, one of the few that was paved, led through the city's low-rise downtown. Despite the miserable state of the roads, there were many roundabouts, a legacy of the French, the last outsiders to hold official power. The sergeant drove through one with a few tired dolphins made of concrete in the center and passed by a small amusement park that never seemed to be open. The neighborhood was a mixture of filthy vacant lots, small workshops, and walled houses. Everywhere, wild dogs limped and stared. He turned down a busier street, with shop advertisements painted on the facades, and a big poster mounted on a pole, with the president's broad smile and a message of progress. Here people were out, and along both sides of the street stood small stalls, every ten meters, with burlap roofs shielding them from the sun. The same damp burlap covered the goods on all the tables. The vendors were women, and all they sold was khat. The leaves had to be kept fresh to stay potent. It was long after one o'clock, when the women were allowed to set up their stalls, and nearby shopkeepers waiting for customers had been standing for a while, chewing in their doorways. An entire nation was getting its daily buzz.

The sergeant picked up speed where the buildings thinned out and the asphalt turned to gravel. He passed a few warning signs that marked a military training area, drove a few kilometers without seeing a soul, and then stopped at a gravel yard.

Even here, they were expecting him. "Damn it, Hansson, we've been waiting for almost half an hour," said Slunga, his lieutenant, when he got out of the car.

"Had to make deliveries to the helicopter," he said effortlessly.

"And that was all you left on the *Sveaborg*?"

"What else?"

Slunga looked incredulously at Hansson. Behind the lieutenant sat two white Land Cruisers and a small bus. There were half a dozen Swedes wearing his same desert uniform, and an equal number of civilian Djiboutians. Beyond the gravel yard were a few low shrubs, otherwise only stone and dust. The others had gotten out, some just standing there, others joking around, some of the soldiers pointing and showing their equipment to the Djiboutians.

"Yes, but what now?" said the sergeant, swinging his AK-5 onto his shoulder.

Mr. Nazir, the Djiboutian foreman, looked concerned. He spoke to Slunga in English but looked at Hansson. "I really do not think we should. Maybe tomorrow."

Slunga hesitated. "Let's do this the way we said," said Hansson, and he started walking. And the whole group set off in a muddle of English, Swedish, and Somali. Several of the younger Djiboutians talked loudly and spat khat juice around themselves, already much too interested in the weapons they got to carry.

"Are we really?" asked one of the soldiers in disbelief, keeping a tight hold on his own gun. "But we'd set conditions, and Nazir promised that . . ."

Slunga heard him and turned to the foreman: "Mr. Nazir, you promised us. Why?"

The man made a slow gesture with his hands, a prayer for understanding in the face of defeat. Apparently, he'd promised that none of the men would arrive high, and at least he wasn't chewing himself, but most of the others unabashedly kept a ball in one cheek, and their teeth shone green with the juice. "Please," he said, "tomorrow instead, but before lunch, like we agreed." It was not only the Djiboutians who had failed to keep their word. Slunga said nothing but hurried to get away from the foreman.

"Damn them," muttered one of the soldiers. One Djiboutian posed with an assault rifle, while another took pictures with his cell phone. "Great, great," shouted one of the Swedes to them. "You see what fucking nonsense this is," said another to a third, under his breath, in Swedish. The camaraderie was playacting that existed only in English.

One of the Swedes stopped walking.

"Come on, what the hell's wrong?" someone asked.

"No fucking cell phones. I will not be in the fucking picture if we're doing stuff like this. Tell them!"

One of the Africans lay on his back in the dust with sunglasses on his forehead, pretending to surrender, while another straddled him holding a gun without its magazine and saying "ta-ta-ta" while making his whole body jerk. Mr. Nazir tried to stop them and was clearly humiliated by their refusal to obey. Walking at the head of the whole entourage was a man humping his surroundings with an AK-5 held against his crotch like a huge cock, while his friend shouted encouragement from behind and took pictures.

A corporal tried to restore order, but finally Hansson had to yell at the top of his lungs to get through to them, so that at least the cell phones disappeared.

Soon they arrived at the actual shooting range. Hidden behind a hill, it was desolate and flat, with only a few dirt berms built up at the end.

"We'll be in deep shit for this."

"It's okay. Not a single fucking person around."

"Damn hot, no?" asked a soldier in English, trying to take the edge off what had been set in motion.

The Swede got a shrug for an answer and a questioning look from khat-shiny eyes. "Bullets, you have the bullets?"

6

With Ernst Grip still clutching his shirt, the young man began to return to his senses. He said nothing, had barely come around, but at least he'd wiped his nose, and he stared down at all the blood on the towel. Then he cleared his throat low, as if to regain his dignity, and looked up at Grip. It was as if he'd said he was ready to proceed, to wait patiently, to do whatever was expected of him. Beneath the arch of his eyebrows, his eyes revealed an underlying sadness.

"Secure!" someone shouted from farther back in the apartment, and just as Grip was about to pull the youth out toward the living room, the other two security police officers came rushing into the bedroom. They were dragging the suspected terrorists along with them, both with their hands cuffed behind their back. One looked scared and stumbled along, while the other looked tall and defiant with every step.

He glared at Grip and the one who was dragging him. Impressive, thought Grip for a second, that the man could resist such a show of force. But that didn't explain the look in his eyes. At the same time, the young man he was holding grew anxious, lurched and mumbled something, as if the other's expression was a call to arms. Grip shook him and he grew still.

Grip wondered what they were planning to do to the two men in the bedroom. "What'd you find out there?" he asked.

"We need to get more," said one of the security police officers, without looking at him. All the SWAT guys were somewhere else. At first, Grip didn't realize what was happening. Something unspoken had been agreed on, and the three detained men understood more than he did himself. He had a deep sense of foreboding when one of them whimpered. Out of reflex, he tightened his hold on the young man's shirtfront. When one of his coworkers yanked open the bathroom door, the terrified prisoner threw himself down on the bed, trying to stay away from the open door. He lay on his back and kicked, before he was captured again. He pleaded. They were going to get him in there, some kind of shit was about to go down, but the Säpo guy who held him couldn't drag him by himself, so the other officer had to let go of the defiant one and grab the man's legs. And in that instant, the man wound up and threw a powerful kick.

Ernst Grip saw in a split second what was happening, the step back and the kick that would have hit his coworker from the side. But its force, just as it was about to land, rebounded right back as it met Grip's own kick. Not a clean hit, but the impact went straight to the gut. Sensing something, the police officer turned around. Behind him, the man lay curled on the floor, groaning, his arms cramping from the handcuffs when he tried to pull them to his stomach.

"Never mind," said Grip. "What are you . . . ?"

"Just hold down those two."

The man who'd tried a futile escape over the bed was pulled into the bathroom by the security police officers. The last thing Grip saw before the door slammed shut was that they'd turned on the bathtub taps. Soon, from the other side, came terrified screams.

Now Grip was alone with one man who was bleeding, and the other, who was doubled over in a bedroom. Trapped. They knew that Grip would be loyal. None of the SWAT team was in sight; they must have been told to stay out and look for evidence. That way there were no witnesses, at least, no one who wasn't 100 percent loyal. That was that. All this unspent energy, when the final confrontation never happened. They probably hadn't found anything useful out there, maybe some cash and a few unused cell phones. But then again, they had these men, three terrorists traced to ISIS, that's the thing. Tips, notifications, hundreds of cell numbers, intercepted calls, transactions traced and lost—the Americans, or the French, or whoever they were, they knew. They'd pointed their finger, and now the Swedes would seize their chance. They had to. They couldn't leave empty-handed, not again.

And Ernst Grip, that bodyguard who kept to himself, the one no one cared about, but who was a hell of a fighter, would keep watch outside. He was the type who couldn't afford to say anything if you needed to turn up the heat. Two security police coworkers with far more influence than he in the corridors of power, and totally single-minded, had seen their chance. Grip had anticipated only the kick, not the other thing that was coming. Not until the bathroom door had closed.

The man with the nosebleed moved restlessly at the end of Grip's fist, while the man on the floor looked up. He was still panting, and there was something broken in his eyes. The whole world knew what anonymous security officers, handcuffed men, and full bathtubs added up to. Behind the closed door, they heard the water still running, and their friend's senseless shrieks.

"Wipe yourself off" was all Grip could say, picking up the towel again. The bloody young man didn't take it, didn't see it, but kept his hands gently cupped around Grip's tense fist and looked at him with that sadness in his face. He said something strange, it sounded like a plea. Grip didn't look at him, or anywhere. All attention was on the closed door, and the turmoil behind it. Screams, voices, unintelligible words, splashes, and several thuds heard through the wall.

The adrenaline was pumping and Grip's entire being protested. An unholy agreement—they were counting on his muscles and his loyalty to shut out the world. It was within him that the moral line would be drawn, not in the bathroom, but he couldn't possibly let himself get involved like the other two in there. Not with this, not the splashing and the screaming.

"Stop it," he screamed and kicked the bathroom door. "Now!"

It took a few seconds before there was silence. Grip registered the bleeding youth's pleas and yet again felt his hands on his own hand.

All had gone quiet on the other side of the bathroom door. The man on the bedroom floor swayed and shook his head, and it seemed that he was crying. The young man in his grasp swallowed and repeated something; it sounded like a name. Grip looked at him, tried but didn't understand. "What are you saying?"

Again the sound of running water from the bathroom.

The bleeding man still held on to Grip's hands, trying to pull him closer, then whispered again what he'd said and continued in broken Swedish: "He man you want."

His eyes were terrified; he thought he was next.

"He is man you want."

Grip raised his foot. "That's fucking enough," he shouted, and kicked so hard that his shoe broke through the door, and the lock gave way.

7

When the first shot rang out, people cheered. It hit the dusty ground of the shooting range, and a little cloud rose up like an exclamation point before falling again. Without a breath of wind, the smell of gunpowder clung to the shooter. In the harsh sunlight, the only shadows were made by the men waiting to shoot and by the row of cardboard figures against the berm. And so only human-shaped shadows darkened the ground—the targets were shaped like soldiers on a rampage.

One of the Swedish soldiers had tried to give an introduction to rifle shooting, but it became a dull recitation of weapon parts, firing procedures, and which orders meant what. A necessary ritual. Some of the Djiboutians tried to follow along—this was useful information about weapons, after all—but the lesson was ruined by the others, who couldn't stop fooling around. Even the interested ones lost track, and the Swede sped up to get it over with. He fired a shot for show, afterward explaining how to unload and how to secure the safety on a semiautomatic machine gun. After looking into the barrel and dropping the bolt back with a click, he turned the selector to lock and repeated in English: "Very important, do not forget."

The Djiboutians were anxious, once the mandatory introduction was over. When some of the Swedes disapproved, they'd split up into several small groups. Not much was said. A few pushed cartridges into empty magazines, one stood and drank water with a hard gaze, turning away from it all.

"Okay, one of us for every weapon," said the sergeant, Hansson, raising his voice to make something happen.

"Do we start now?"

"Yes, now we start!" Hansson pushed hard into the back of the soldier who asked, forcing him to get moving.

This got a few others going, and soon all the weapons had been picked up, and the soldiers began instructing the Djiboutians, the *click-clacks* sounding as the bolts slid back and forth. The magazines were pushed in with a final slap, at the end. Most of the fooling around was over. Proper shooting positions were tried out, with the rifle butt pressed fully against the shoulder. A helping hand went to the man's other shoulder, and one to his hip, making his chest turn and lean forward. The back leg was extended to provide support behind, creating stability to absorb the recoil again and again.

"No one fires until I say," shouted the sergeant who'd given the lesson. Lieutenant Slunga went up to Mr. Nazir and cajoled the foreman to participate, to get a feel for the weapon, fire a few shots. Wouldn't it be harmless to try it, have a little fun? Mr. Nazir nodded and smiled, but he retained his island of self-respect and didn't budge. Slunga clucked, but Mr. Nazir pretended not to notice.

"Damn it, keep after that one!" someone shouted when a muzzle was pointing every which way.

"Please, only point forward."

A shot rang out and everyone jumped. The shooter laughed.

"Goddammit!"

"What did I say?!"

Glances were exchanged among the Swedes, both among those who were worried and those feeling they maintained a sliver of control. Hansson stretched and grinned with a glance toward Slunga. He thought for a moment and then said: "Let them shoot it off."

And so the shooting began. First with a furious volley that whipped across the shooting range, and the shell casings flew among the shooters. Those not holding a gun clapped their hands over their ears. A thin haze spread around them, carrying the acrid and almost arousing smell of burnt gunpowder, airborne dust, and a hint of something metallic.

The intensity dropped a notch, to a persistent *ta-ta-ta* of firing. Some wanted to learn something, others just to shoot. Although they stood at only thirty meters, many shots landed in the dirt in front of the targets.

"Did I hit?"

"Not even close."

Then things grew calmer. The most enthusiastic had emptied their magazines, pressing their triggers in disbelief a few extra times before lowering their weapons. The sergeant who'd volunteered to lead the shooting was trying to say something, but he was constantly interrupted by those who had bullets left. A few still flinched with every shot they fired.

There was silence for a while. In some of the paper soldiers, light shone through the holes of the hits.

"Should we check the targets?" asked one soldier.

"Of course," said Hansson.

"There isn't a single hole in the one mine shot at," said another soldier. "Can you believe it?"

"I bet your barrel is warped," the man next to him joked. He got no answer.

"Well then," said the sergeant, "all weapons down, while we check the targets."

Most went to see how they'd done, though a few lacked the energy to walk the thirty meters.

In the next round, the pace was slower. Most of the Djiboutians were still anxious, but the khat and the heat had their effect. There was a kind of low-key disorder: scattered shots and then suddenly one shooter managed to switch to automatic fire and get off a good round. One Swede winced and covered his head; others just looked at their watches.

They could have stopped right there.

But the sergeant was feeling ambitious. "We'll mark again, and then a final round. Don't we have a little ammunition left?" He got no response. Mr. Nazir looked at Slunga, silently asking to end things. But now it was Slunga who pretended not to see.

"Well then," said Hansson. "One more time."

"All weapons down," the sergeant reminded them.

Half the men went up to the cardboard figures. One of the Africans smiled broadly and pointed to his sweet spot. All his shots were clustered in the chest of the paper soldier. He shouted to the others in Somali. "Rambo-man," someone said back.

"It's always like this," said a Swede. "They can, if they want to."

"Sure, one by one," replied someone.

"Put the tape on."

"I don't want to do this, I want a beer."

"Tape!"

They spread out to put black patches over the holes.

A bang.

Everyone at the shooting range jumped, looking around in fear, even those who'd stayed lazily in the back with their weapons. It took several seconds before they realized that a shot had been fired.

"No!"

One man's shadow missing in the afternoon sun.

Lieutenant Per-Erik Slunga lay flat and motionless on his stomach. The dry sand soaked up the blood that streamed from his head.

8

Ernst Grip suffered from insomnia. He never got to bed before midnight. He'd sworn to himself that he'd turn in at a reasonable hour, but then when it came time to get ready, a bad feeling would come over him, or else he'd just sit there. Right there, until the clock said past two in the morning, the hours sifting away like sand. Simply gone. So it was, night after night. Up for work the next morning, no more than four or five hours of sleep in the bank. At the end of the week, he wasn't all there. Everything felt fuzzy. He ate badly and often had headaches. The world was just something that went on outside the thick glass that surrounded him. And so it had been, for almost a year.

Or more accurately, since June 5 of the past year. It was at about eleven in the evening when Benjamin Hayden had died. Around eleven—it was always hard to decide which was the last breath, when there was barely any breathing at all. To Grip, Benjamin had only ever been Ben. It was just them in the room. For more than two days, the vigil had gone on. Hour after hour, Grip had struggled with his conflicting emotions, from his powerful desire to keep Ben with him, to the hope that he would finally let go. Hours of silent tears, comforting words—both for the dying and for himself—along with small confessions and the desire for forgiveness for any wrongs that still gnawed at him.

From Ben, in return, came nothing more than barely perceptible breathing. He'd gotten dehydrated and thin as a thousand-year-old mummy over the past few months. Watching his decline and hearing his sighs had been painful for Grip. Those last weeks, when he

49

barely stuck out from the sheets, had been disturbing. It was more than just the idea of a corpse, it was the tangible presence of death. He saw his own impotence in Ben's withered figure. There was not the slightest thing he could do to reverse the direction. Death would triumph and told him so. Powerlessness was a condition Ernst Grip despised, as much in himself as in others. Being a victim. And here, there were two. When he thought about it, he told himself that he wanted to remember the way Ben had been before, and that this was his understandable excuse for looking in the other direction the next time the body was exposed. But even though he was ashamed, he turned away.

For there were still traces of life in Ben: in the heat of his hand, in the squinting, brief glances that occasionally rose out of the fog of death. As long as he was able to look up, he saw Grip. He stared Ernst Grip straight in the eye. Seven years they'd been together, seven years to a greater or lesser extent defined by his illness. Ben belonged to the group of gay men who'd held on long enough for the dramatic arrival of antiretroviral drugs in 1996. But by the time help finally arrived, the disease had already made deep inroads. The virus wasn't defeated, though Ben's decline was less steep. In the last year, he'd been in and out of hospitals, at first just a few days at a time, and then, toward the end, he couldn't stay in the apartment in Chelsea more than an occasional long weekend. They went from the joy of a life together to a split in their roles. One who was dying, the other who looked on— and who had to deal with everything that life involved.

Grip yo-yoed between Stockholm and New York. Torn between the desire to take care of and to be with, and the need to work all the overtime he could get in order to pay the bills of his dying lover in Manhattan. For despite it all, Ben wanted to have health care, good doctors always nearby. He'd endured it for so many years, survived so many of his friends, not always out of love of life as much as his all-consuming fear of death. It was fear that had kept Ben alive. But the stream of hospital bills was also an excuse.

Grip's trips to Stockholm weren't just about duty and money; they became a way for him to breathe. Not just to be there for someone else, watching and standing by, but to be himself. Himself. To work, to take something on, to do some good. To hear people laugh at a clumsy joke, to get angry with someone without having to hold back. The flow of impressions during the workday kept other thoughts from rising up. There was the vaguely pleasant satisfaction of dealing with the car in the Säpo garage and with equipment in the office, and realizing that he didn't have to devote every single moment to Ben when he got to work in the morning. But finally, Ben was too weak, and Grip couldn't work more or borrow more than he already had.

Then there was a hospice for Ben, with a good reputation but grim single rooms. Run by volunteers, the care they offered was essentially a last few days under morphine. Once they moved in, Ben and Grip realized that these four bare walls would be their last room together. Sometimes Ben yelled out, full of anxiety and accusations. Those who worked there called it the release of a dying person's unresolved thoughts. Grip knew better.

A couple of times at the end, they'd still managed to talk about the good times, agreeing on which were their best memories. Trips to Cape Cod, the house with the fireplace they'd sometimes borrowed by the sea. The café at the Whitney Museum, where they'd sat down and decided to try each other out. These were the bright spots, because when the morphine erased the pain, it also destroyed the ability to hold on to thoughts and talk. The awareness in those squinting eyes became increasingly rare. Just a few quiet words. When did everything fall silent? The breathing slowed. One evening in June, shortly after eleven o'clock, Grip let go of the cold hand.

He sat with the body for a couple of hours and then went home and curled up for the rest of the night. Never in his life had he felt so alone. The worst was knowing it would continue. The feeling of not really knowing what he'd left behind or what would come next.

Grip had never even met Ben's family. Lawyers, mostly, with a friendly manner and a penchant for living lies. There was a barrier that Ben himself had created. He'd managed to be out everywhere, except to them. Twice a year he went home to Houston to play the returning son, a little sickly, admittedly, but above all straight. In that world there was no Grip—and what they suspected, he could only guess. Given that even the most casual acquaintances knew that Ben was a gay man who ran a gallery, it was as simple as that. He'd forbidden Grip to contact the family before his death. When he died, his elderly mother came up immediately, and his father a few days later. In their eyes, apparently he'd come to New York to clean. "Thanks for your help" and a handshake, that was all they had to say to Grip. He was less surprised by their attitude than by their efficiency. A family of lawyers, with hired henchmen to slash straight through the administrative details. Not even a week after Grip had let go of his lover's hand, the Flatiron gallery was boarded up.

At a tense meeting in the apartment, Grip was permitted to go around and take what was unmistakably his—not much besides clothing. As soon as he picked up or looked at any of the things that represented shared memories, his parents glared. Even when he lifted up an unremarkable piece of driftwood from New London, the mother stretched her neck vigilantly. Despite his mounting anger, Grip restrained himself. But when he was about to leave, and the father held out his hand for the keys, Grip pointedly held the bundle a few seconds too long above his open palm before he released them. A lawyer was also present, which Grip saw as some kind of passing acknowledgment.

Grip returned that same night. Of course there'd been a spare key. He brought a suitcase with him, and after a half hour going through their possessions, the worst of his anger from earlier in the day had subsided. The twisted driftwood branch lay in his overstuffed bag. When he was done, he moved some furniture around in the apartment, pulled out a couple of drawers, and yanked up the carpet as if someone had kicked it. And then he left, leaving the front door of the apartment unlocked.

After a few blocks, he threw the spare key into a storm drain. Not so much to hide his tracks, as to make sure he wouldn't be tempted to return for more.

9

It wasn't until after lunch on Monday that the syrupy feeling started to go away. He hadn't slept much the night before. Once again, it was past two when he got into bed.

Ernst Grip was supposed to be with the crown princess that afternoon, but someone had fixed his schedule so he could go to the debriefing after the Husby raid. The meeting was a mere formality, with not a single SWAT guy there, because no matter how you spun it, the operation had failed. Sure, there was still a little game with the evening papers: the prosecutor who approved the action and a security police chief made it sound like something major. But they had failed. Three Somalis with Swedish residence permits, a little over a hundred thousand kronor in cash, and a box of mobile phones with SIM cards. In short, a complete bust. No suicide vests, no weapons, no USB sticks with grandiose plans. Something had gone wrong, or gone cold, and now no one at Säpo headquarters wanted to speak English over the encrypted phone.

No one said a word about a bathroom.

He sat through the half-hour debriefing while a chief who hadn't been on the scene explained to the others what they'd done. A boiled-down version, summarized in a few bullet points on a single PowerPoint slide. Nods, agreement. They'd done what they could—wasn't that true?—based on the intelligence they had—wasn't that true! When the review was over, and a paper had been circulated approving compensation for new front and bathroom doors, the two security police officers who'd actually been there went up to Grip.

"They really didn't talk?" asked one, while the other sized Grip up. A question repeated from the day before.

When the bathroom door had caved in from Grip's kick, and he'd stared at them with rage and contempt, both police officers had worn guilty looks. Later, they told him they'd simply been trying to instill fear. The Somali had been lying on the floor, exhausted and soaked to the bone.

"So, did he spill his guts?" Grip had asked defiantly, a little later, when it was just the three of them. Obviously, there'd been no confession, only violent splashing, and a man weeping and praying for his life in Somali. But his coworkers figured it was the men in the bedroom who'd give up the important stuff. The two under Grip's control. They were the ones who'd be scared into talking. The ones who didn't yet know but who imagined what was coming. Grip had told the officers that they hadn't said a word, that they were speechless with fear. Now they repeated the question a day later, beyond the chief's ears: "They really didn't talk?"

"Not a sound," Grip lied again, and then left.

The small voice recorder that Grip brought to Husby in a pocket of his bulletproof vest was his own idea. He often took it along; you never knew when you'd need to back up your own version afterward. What had been said, and what hadn't. He'd listened to the recording afterward, to the chaos and the shouting, but it was really only the last part that interested him, when the young man with the nosebleed said something in Somali.

From that, he'd sensed a bigger picture. On Monday morning, even before the debriefing and the questions, he'd gone looking for a translator. He found the academic who did work for the security police, originally from Yemen, fluent in both Arabic and Somali. In his office, Grip had played the last few minutes, keeping the recorder in his hand. Sure, Grip could have started further back, but he was anxious to keep an outsider from getting the larger context. If he'd played the recording from beginning to end, the actions would have been obvious—and given the prayers and screams, it could have started people talking. And if some damn lawyer got involved, Grip had no out. He was just as entangled as the two police officers if someone started flipping through the statute book.

"Yuhuudi," the translator said, repeating what was on the recording.

"Yup, I have ears too," said Grip, with unnecessary annoyance. He was feeling uneasy and wanted to get this over with. Here he was, facing an educated immigrant—one who certainly wouldn't brag to his friends about whom he was working for—about an operation in which Swedes, his own coworkers, completely lost control.

"Yuhuudi—the Jew," said the translator.

Grip looked puzzled. "The Jew?"

"That's a Somali speaking on the tape, right?"

"Yes."

"The Somali is saying that you need to find the Jew." The translator was quiet for a few seconds and then said thoughtfully: "He seems scared to death."

"I believe he was. Thanks."

"What is . . . ?"

"The larger context? Today's *Expressen* and *Aftonbladet* are probably out by now." Grip was already heading from the room. "But, please, let's just forget about this."

The Jew. Something was going on with those Somalis, Grip didn't doubt it for a moment. But this wasn't about blowing up the Parliament or destroying subway stations. Naturally, that "Jew" was somebody, but it was only too easy to imagine what would happen if he reported the detail. His coworkers from the day before, and probably a couple of directors above them, needed vindication after their wholesale failure in the apartment in Husby. They'd put their heads together, dreaming of revenge, and Grip would bet a month's salary that they'd find another opportunity to use the battering ram.

That's how it was when you were hunting terrorists. You'd get the smallest scrap of evidence—and then you'd go ballistic. There would be more shattered doors in immigrant neighborhoods, more screams, more kicks in the gut, and more people with bloody noses. And maybe they'd finally find something real, or maybe they'd only find a few more boxes of mobile phones and SIM cards, which is to say—nothing. Sure, Grip could live with that. But at worst, when everything had gone wrong and they needed someone to blame, the stink could blow back in his face. With the right mix of insider tips, angry Muslim representatives, and prosecutors smelling blood, he himself could be held accountable in a courtroom, because he hadn't intervened before the splashing and screaming in the bathroom began. A goddamn little Nuremberg trial, you taking the stand to say you'd followed an illegal order. He'd end up as the face of the Waterboarding Association in Sweden. And the others would leave him holding the bag. They'd waste no time in closing ranks, shutting out the one who came along as an extra, the one no one really knew but that they'd heard stories about. They'd dig up all the old shit.

Why did they think he'd bear the cross for his coworkers? Just for a good cause?

Already on Sunday night, he'd told them that no one had said anything in the bedroom. Now he knew more, but it wasn't worth the risk. And besides, who in ISIS, Al-Qaeda, or any of their supporting ranks and Koran-obsessed affiliates would be crazy enough to be called the Jew? No one. So Grip dropped the whole thing, erased the recording, lied again after the debriefing in the afternoon, shrugged his shoulders, and went on. No more bathrooms, that had crossed a line. At least, not with Ernst Grip as both witness and hostage.

Grip was back in his usual hallway, trying once again to go home for the day, when an assistant yelled as he passed by.

"Yes?"

"Someone named Thor is looking for you. He said it was important."

"Thor?"

"I'm sorry, but that's all I wrote down. He seemed to think you'd know." The assistant was new.

"Could it have been Didricksen, Thor Didricksen?"

"Sounds right."

Grip had never heard anyone refer to Didricksen as just Thor. Didricksen belonged to the top ranks of the security police, but, lacking clear responsibilities, he had the title *At large*. That is, he'd take on what none of the other directors wanted on their desk, the unpleasant emergencies. Usually matters from outside, and usually things that people with careers and political ambitions feared would make a stink. For items requiring special care, it was good to have someone experienced with the dirty side of things. It was said that he participated in very few regular management meetings. He acted through other channels, something of a detested court dwarf, who sat and whispered, glaring by the prince's side.

Besides, "old" Thor Didricksen's age was hard to gauge. He'd seemed to be on the verge of retiring for at least a decade. It was assumed that he was waiting for a scandal of the right magnitude, and then Didricksen would take himself and all his dirty laundry with him. Only for all these years, he'd somehow managed to keep himself and those he protected out of trouble.

Most people even avoided calling him Didricksen. When he called to find someone in the various departments, the person who picked up would say something about "the man upstairs" or "the dog on six," with a gesture of resignation, and then you knew who you needed to see. Immediately. Also, Didricksen always made the messengers imply that people should know what the meeting was about, when in fact they hadn't the slightest idea. The contradiction lay in the fact that in Didricksen's world, very few knew much of anything. During the short periods that people worked directly for him, he was called simply the Boss.

In the circle of ambitious middle-aged types at Säpo, the ones always looking to move up a notch, they often spoke in low tones about violations and breaches that bore Didricksen's stamp. Mostly, it was about jealousy. The Boss had no regular staff, but from time to time, he took what he needed. You couldn't go to him; he did the choosing. Too many considered themselves next in the pipeline, or, in any case, thought they'd done it—gotten "on the list." Grip and Didricksen went way back. Perhaps that was what made people uncomfortable, when they found themselves alone with Grip at the coffee machine.

"Should I call to say you're coming?" asked the assistant.

"Don't bother, I think he's expecting me," said Grip, and walked toward the stairs.

The dog on six. Something about his hanging cheeks. The floor of his office was covered by an oriental carpet from Afghanistan. "From before the war," he'd point out, "even before the Russians." A souvenir from a trip in the seventies. The carpet—deep red with black geometric designs—made visitors move cautiously and made the room strangely quiet.

"Did you read the paper today?" asked Didricksen, when Grip closed the door behind him.

Grip hesitated for a second. "You mean the apartment in Husby?"

"No, no, I don't care about that. And not the tabloids, but this morning's *Svenska Dagbladet*."

At best, Grip skimmed the *Dagens Nyheter* online for breakfast. What could Didricksen be interested in, beyond the result of yesterday's soccer derby at the Tele2 Arena, or the fan brawl in the subway afterward?

"About the soldier who got killed," Grip began. "Can't say I read the whole article." In fact, he hadn't read anything at all, but only briefly glanced at the morning news on TV. Grip felt the Afghan carpet sag beneath him. "Did the Taliban blow someone up again?"

"A soldier, yes," replied Didricksen, "but you're on the wrong continent. It was at a shooting range in Djibouti."

"Aha." Didricksen hadn't offered Grip a seat. With anyone else, he'd just sit down in the first chair he saw, but their clear division was one of few hierarchies he conformed to.

"Just to be sure, I got out a map." Beside Didricksen lay an open atlas, and he spun it so that Grip could see.

Africa.

Didricksen pointed at the map, his finger indicating the little thumbnail of land sandwiched between Eritrea and Somalia, inside the Gulf of Aden.

With the mention of Somalia, Grip felt a vague sense of anxiety overtake him again. The apartment, the bathroom. "Yesterday—I was in the apartment of the Somalis."

"Drop it, nothing to do with this. There's a fleet chasing pirates down there, and one of our men is dead."

Grip struggled to shift gears. "A Swedish soldier?"

"Yes. A Per-Erik Slunga, hometown of Gothenburg," Didricksen read from a page, "lieutenant, in fact," he said, as he looked up and leaned back. "You see, we had a little discussion . . ."

And only now did Grip start to get it

". . . about how this kind of thing can be tricky."

Grip assumed that "we" having the discussion meant the chief of security police, the commissioner of the National Police, and those involved from the government side.

Someone was worried, that's always the way things worked, and that's why Grip found himself standing here. But he still had no clear idea what was involved. "And now a Swede is going to be stoned to death, by Sharia law?" A feeble attempt at a joke.

But Didricksen smiled. "No, no. The military has agreements when they're on foreign turf, country by country. Swedish law applies to Swedish soldiers, no matter what trouble they cause, fortunately. But that also means any investigation falls under Swedish jurisdiction."

Grip nodded. And let go of the apartment in Husby.

"So it appears, in theory," continued Didricksen. "In practice, things might get more or less complicated."

Grip understood a little more.

Didricksen returned to the atlas. His gaze lingered there, before he said, without looking at Grip: "Swedish soldiers are national heroes." Raising his eyes, he continued, "And our politicians sent them there to do good. If our soldiers make a mess, someone treacherous could start asking what they were doing there in the first place. At the same time"—Didricksen stopped himself in mid-thought—"At the same time, we need to find out what happened. A man is dead, after all."

Right.

Didricksen continued. "Not just any police officer feels comfortable in this situation." The old dog played with a pen. "But during our discussion, I said I had an idea about how to tackle this. And a suggestion for whom to send."

"Down to the desert uniforms?"

"Exactly."

"So how much do we know?" asked Grip.

"Nothing, beyond that a Swedish officer got shot in the head at a shooting range."

"An accident?"

"The reports from down there are muddled, and the context of that shooting seems . . . somewhat unclear. But yes, maybe just a shooting accident. Still, you know, people worry about matters like this. The Foreign Ministry, the supreme commander, the minister of defense . . ."

Obviously. That's why Didricksen was involved, and why Grip stood swaying on the Afghan rug. The truth was one thing; what to do with it, another.

"And you're the right man for the job, for the simple reason that you need to get away, don't you?" Didricksen didn't wait for a reply. "Get away, go where it's quiet, have your own world, your own investigation for a while, that doesn't sound so bad, does it?" There was something close and confidential in his eyes. "It's time for you to rediscover yourself, Ernst. After what, I'd guess almost a year. What was his name?"

They'd never discussed anything personal, but of course Didricksen knew. He, if anyone.

"His name was Ben," Grip said.

"A man must mourn properly, there's no way around it. Otherwise you can get lost in missing a person, the way so many do. And some-times a little privacy helps you find a way out."

"Maybe," said Grip. He stood silent for a few seconds and added: "And when has the Boss decided I'm leaving?"

"Tomorrow—via Paris."

"Djibouti?" Grip said, without hiding his skepticism.

"Yes."

"An invented country?"

"From what I understand."

"Like Monaco?"

"Not exactly."

10

Djibouti. Little more than a stretch of stony desert and oppressive heat. A colonial leftover, a shard of a country, and a city by the same name. A backwater with only one thing to offer the world: its location. At the crossroads of ship traffic to and from the Suez Canal, the pirate-infested Gulf of Aden, the turmoil of the Arab world, the tentacles of Al-Qaeda and ISIS, the civil wars of Sudan and Ethiopia to the west, and the total anarchy of Somali in the east—there lay Djibouti. An oasis of apparent order, for anyone willing to pay. South of the international airport, the Americans had thousands of troops stationed, in their ever-expanding and only permanent base on the African continent. North of the airport, the French kept their installations, while also housing half a brigade of Foreign Legion soldiers in another part of the city. A flurry of other uniforms came and went.

Grip stepped out of the air-conditioned Air France plane straight into an oven. Africa. It had been a while. The air actually shimmered in the heat. Already, as he turned toward passport control and customs, the sweat was dripping down his back. Grip carried a stack of papers he'd been handed before he left and hadn't really examined, but after a few stern glances, his passport got stamped with a visa. None of the officials asked questions, not to a single person in the line. Everyone who came to Djibouti obviously had a job to do. The posters advertising desert ruins and camel caravans were merely for show. Grip didn't see anyone among the passengers who looked like a tourist. You arrived in Djibouti either as crew cut military, or with a briefcase and laptop for business.

A dozen aggressive taxi drivers swarmed in the arrival hall, but they stopped when they saw that Grip had someone waiting. His eyes met the gaze of a tall, ruddy man with a cautious smile. Grip had no idea who'd be meeting him, but he'd spotted the small blue-and-yellow flag on the desert uniform.

"*Hej?*" the man said in Swedish, more a question than greeting.

"Yes, I'm the one," Grip replied, and kept walking.

The man, who introduced himself as Captain Tommy Mickels, wore the black armband of the military police on one bicep, marked with a big MP. "I have the car right out here," he said, pointing through the glass doors.

They loaded Grip's bags into the white jeep and got in. Once the engine was running, it took a few more minutes for the air conditioner to cool things down. Grip sensed Mickels's hesitation.

"So, where will it be?" Grip asked.

"The commander is expecting you."

"The commander?"

"The captain of the *Sveaborg*. He's the top brass, in charge of all the Swedes on this mission."

"And he knows I'm here?"

Mickels smiled without looking at him. "Everyone knows you're here."

People within the ranks always worried whenever an outsider stepped in. Grip hadn't expected anything different, but he was in no rush to make a courtesy call. Shaking hands with a nervous boss, that kind of nonsense could wait. First, he wanted to know what had actually happened, and wasn't that why the MP was hesitating? The car still hadn't moved a meter.

"The captain will be around, I'm sure, so why don't you start by . . ."

". . . bringing you up to speed . . ." Mickels nodded. They pulled out.

Turning off, they headed to Mickels's office, not more than ten minutes away. As they drove, he explained that when the *Sveaborg* was out at sea, the Swedes who did shore jobs stayed inside the French base.

The entrance was tightly guarded: speed bumps, barbed wire, lots of weapons.

"Al-Shabaab and Al-Qaeda," Mickels said, not needing to explain more.

Behind the walls and fences, they drove slowly along the base's neat grid of streets. A whole self-contained community: office buildings, little dusty parks, bunkhouses, a bar with plastic chairs and umbrellas, and rows of hangars.

"Here." White, windowless containers with sprawling antennas formed a little lunar base on the gravel, their air conditioners clattering in the heat. On a pole hung a limp Swedish flag.

They stepped into the cool of a small meeting room. Mickels closed the door to the hallway, shutting out the sound of office work.

"Water?" he asked, opening a refrigerator. Along the walls stood plastic crates of bottled water, stacked as tall as a man. Grip caught the bottle that was thrown to him. Mickels pointed to a chair, and Grip sat down. He tried to quench his thirst while he listened.

The MP was well prepared, starting right in with a PowerPoint and sketches on a big flip chart. It had been just forty-eight hours since the shot was fired. And with cool sincerity, Mickels concluded that the situation was totally fucked up. Grip soon realized that Mickels probably wasn't the ship captain's favorite. He was a little too thorough and outspoken to be liked by a manager. Grip let the information wash over him, not bothering to take notes. The way everything flickers at the moment of takeoff.

Six Swedes had been out on the firing range. They belonged to a MovCon unit. Their job was to keep a steady flow of equipment and supplies arriving from around the world, so that the war against the pirates could roll along without interruption: ammunition, fuel, bottled water, Band-Aids, DVDs, and sunscreen. Mostly, they handled air transports to and from Djibouti, the loading and unloading, sorting and checking off. They were led by Lieutenant Per-Erik Slunga, who now lay with rigor mortis and a hole through his head.

For help, MovCon relied on a handful of local Djiboutian staffers. They were the ones who'd been at the shooting range. No—of course no one else had any inkling that the group had planned an outing to a shooting range, far beyond where they could be seen or heard. The escapade had apparently been Per-Erik's own idea, an attempt to do some bonding and team building. Socializing over a thousand 5.56 cartridges. There wasn't a rule book on the planet covering that kind of insanity.

It was all the lieutenant's idea, the dead man's idea, his five subordinates said afterward. Good, that was something concrete to hold on to, Grip thought. Forty-eight hours since it happened, forty-seven hours for them to talk among themselves.

Mickels had prepared personnel files for Grip. Six folders, each showing the solemn face of a person in uniform, inside a plastic cover.

"What's the group doing now?" Grip asked.

"Same job, same place, only now with their sergeant as boss. The planes keep coming and going, you know. They still need to be loaded and unloaded for the war against the pirates. Nothing stops."

Grip looked at the sketch on the flip chart showing who stood where when the shot hit: a circle for a Swede, a black dot for a Djiboutian. Some were shown up by the targets on the embankment, others thirty meters in back. A dotted line was drawn from two circles that stood close together on the shooting range, a black one and a white one, leading to Per-Erik Slunga's position.

"Everyone in the group agrees, that's where the shot came from."

"Uh-huh," said Grip.

As if to underscore his fairness, Mickels said, "I've spoken to each one individually, and also in groups."

"The Swedes?"

"Yes, exactly."

"And the locals? The Djiboutians?"

"Difficult, only once through an interpreter."

Grip nodded, then asked, "So whose finger was on the trigger?"

Mickels pointed to the black circle where the line began. "It was Abdoul Ghermat's."

"And he was standing next to?"

"Milan Radovanović, who witnessed it."

"What does Abdoul say himself?"

"He denies it."

"And the other locals?"

"You have to understand . . . I don't have a police force here, it's only me. I heard them only once in a group, right after it happened, with the interpreter. Couldn't get a coherent story out of them, it was all just a mess."

"Were they high?"

Mickels hesitated. "Everyone, except maybe Mr. Nazir, the foreman, was high on khat. They were high when it happened, high every day before and every day after. But I didn't mention the khat in my report." Grip just looked quietly at him, waiting for what would come next. "The captain wanted it that way." Grip kept silent. "We don't talk about the local workers being high on the job. It's impossible to apply Swedish rules. They are, after all, employed by us."

"So the captain has already read and approved your report?"

"He wanted it that way."

"You mean, so everything would be neatly sewn up before I arrived?"

Mickels didn't answer but was clearly embarrassed.

"Per-Erik Slunga's body has barely cooled down," Grip went on, and then he added, "Did the captain change much in your report?"

"He cut a few small things." The ruddy military police officer's cheeks flamed with indignation.

Grip kept pushing. "Like the khat?"

"Yes, like the khat."

"Anything else?"

Mickels's gaze said that was as far as he'd go. "The report is accurate as written."

"Certainly," Grip said curtly. And he made a sad mental note: he'd already lost his chance at an unfiltered first impression. Mickels had been too talkative from the start. Grip swore at himself, blaming the heat and thirst; he'd stepped off the plane and wasn't on his game. And Mickels had quickly drawn a convincing mental image: Swedish soldiers, Djiboutians, a shooting range, weapons, khat, and a deadly dotted line on a flip chart. It would be hard to erase that picture and see something different. An almost endless desert, a few men, and a shot. It was so beautiful in its simplicity that it almost seemed staged. What had been going on, and what had taken place beyond the frame? He was being strung along, and even worse, the report was already finished.

Grip didn't distrust Mickels but realized that he was, after all, being loyal to his boss. There'd be no free lunch for Grip—he was dealing with someone who only allowed himself to see a narrow slice of reality. Grip would have to get past that.

"And this Abdoul . . . ?" Grip continued.

"Abdoul Ghermat, what about him?"

"Where is he now?"

"The Djiboutians took him. The police, that is. He's being held at the main station here in town."

"Arrested?"

"Something like that."

"Suspected of murder?"

"Not by me."

Grip was annoyed. "Come on, this isn't exactly a trivial incident. Why?"

"The Djiboutian authorities want to stay on our good side. Once we'd reached a clear conclusion, the captain of the ship called up the local police chief. He was informed about the incident and who took part. And then I assume the local chief wanted to look decisive, and he arrested Ghermat."

"Once you'd reached a clear conclusion, you said. So what actually happened?"

Mickels looked blankly at Grip. "It's obvious."

"Is it?"

"A stray bullet. Fucking arrogant Swedish soldiers and Negroes high on khat. That bastard fumbled, he'd probably never held a weapon before. And so the shot went off."

"The cocky lieutenant's own idea?"

"Yes, to his eternal regret. And here we sit in this shit. But one more thing . . ." Mickels was fired up, and he kept pointing his finger at Grip as he searched for the words. "We haven't pressed formal charges against Ghermat. An accidental discharge, under the circumstances," he said, shrugging. "Why the Djiboutians are detaining him is their call."

"Accidental discharge, you said?"

"Yeah, if you ask me. But now that you're here, you can decide the rest. You have the personnel files, and at the bottom you'll find my report: who said what, where they stood, all that. I collected the weapons that were there too. They're here with me, in a locker."

For Mickels, it really was cut-and-dried. The incident had taken place two days ago, and he'd already drawn his conclusions.

"Might as well take a look at the weapons too," Grip said, trying to look methodical. They went into a room next door. Mickels entered the code into a large cabinet and swung open the heavy door.

There they were, lined up in a rack: six identical assault rifles.

"It was this one," Mickels said, pointing.

To Grip, that didn't mean a damn thing. Only that he was being fed too many simple truths.

11

"See you later."

"Sure," Grip replied, opening the door to Mickels's jeep at the gangway of the HMS *Sveaborg*.

The dock was nearly a kilometer long, but the *Sveaborg* was the only ship there. Huge container cranes loomed, unmoving and seemingly abandoned, on either side of her. Whether their red-brown color was rust or the original paint was difficult to say. In the late afternoon, the sun shifted from white to yellow, and the only human in sight was the watch officer.

An hour before, when they'd left the French base in Mickels's car, Grip had said on a whim, "Can't we go to the shooting range first?"

It turned out that all Mickels had to do was make a call from his cell, since the shooting range was officially part of the US base. Fifteen minutes later, Grip stepped onto the dusty gravel. Just as he'd expected, the place was completely surrounded by desert, with the city barely visible as a gray zone to the southeast, and, in the other direction, the silhouettes of distant mountains in the haze. The place felt alien, a no-man's-land. After a few steps, the black of his shoes disappeared under the fine dust. He kicked an empty shell. There were hundreds near where he stood. How many bullets were buried in that embankment—and which one was *the one*?

In front of the mound, he saw the big rusty stain in the sand, shapeless and darkly ominous. When Grip pressed the toe of his shoe into the middle of it, the bloody sand cracked like crusty snow. Tens of thousands of bullets and shell casings, six identical assault rifles in a locker. Here was a job to keep the forensics technicians busy for a decade. A troubling thought. This shooting range in the desert, this blank space that gave up nothing. Only silence. If he were looking for the right questions to ask, he wouldn't find them here. Grip did a dutiful lap, but then flattened the stain with his shoe and nodded to Mickels that they could get back in the car.

The empty dock looked as battered and unchanging as the desert. And just as with the bloodstain, Grip saw the *Sveaborg* as an island of uncertainty. Not an intruder exactly, but out of place.

"You'll find the duty officer on the third deck," said the watch officer, once Grip had presented his ID. He walked up the gangway and into the shade below the helicopter deck.

"Welcome aboard!" said a man in a navy T-shirt and shorts. He wasn't wearing the khakis of the watch officer on the dock: everything past the gangway was Africa and desert, but everything on board was pure Sweden. The man led the way. It cooled off as soon as they reached the ship's interior, passing the whirling fans and the clatter of activity in that endless maze of gray corridors and steep ladders. Even if Grip wouldn't admit it, the layout was confusing. He could never have found his way back out if he'd had to. They moved inward and upward. Gradually the detailing became more polished and a little quieter, and then they came to a door made of varnished wood. The man knocked, and when a voice replied within, he said only, "Please," and disappeared.

The door opened. Grip left the noisy jumble behind and saw in front of him: power expressed in mahogany and fine rugs. Also, it was two against one. The captain's cabin resembled the boardroom of a shipping company, down to the pair of ship portraits on the walls. The captain himself sat in a corner sofa, with his arms confidently outstretched. The first officer stood to the side, and slightly in front. A well-rehearsed chamber play, Grip thought, taking a few more steps forward.

"Welcome aboard," the first officer added. He was the third person wearing a Swedish uniform who'd said that to Grip in the past few hours, only now, he didn't buy it. The captain nodded quickly; he was the meaty type who gave the impression of being very busy. Always making people feel he'd rather be doing something else. The first officer was dark and more chiseled, with a penetrating gaze.

"Right, you're the one from the police," he said.

"Security police," Grip corrected him. That little addition was rarely a disadvantage, when it came to balance of power.

"Yes, this is tragic," continued the first officer. "We're still . . . shaken." He seemed to mean it.

The captain drummed impatiently on the leather sofa. "Tragic, but completely out of bounds."

The first officer followed his lead. "We didn't know anything beforehand about the excursion to the shooting range." The captain's career had to be protected, no blotches on his record. "You've got everything there, in our report about the incident." The first officer nodded toward a printout on the coffee table, which was otherwise bare.

"Thanks, I already received a copy from Mickels."

The captain stopped himself, just as he was sliding the report over.

Mickels would catch hell for that, Grip thought, for upstaging his boss with an outsider.

"By the way, where are you holding Slunga's remains?"

The captain looked vacantly at Grip, who'd directed the question his way.

"Where's the body?" Still that same look, and Grip realized that he didn't know. The captain only waited, hoping to be rescued.

"We're keeping it on board," said the first officer. "In the cold room. We have a couple of mortuary compartments, just in case."

"How convenient. Autopsy?"

"We're a combat unit, not a forensics clinic. He's down there, in the same condition as when he came in."

"Excellent, then at least there's one thing that's been left untouched."

"Excuse me, what are you driving at?"

"Just that everything seems to keep rolling along, even though a person has just been shot to death."

"Yes, it probably looks that way," replied the first officer, "but that's because we have other problems to deal with. It's real here. Every extra hour in port is an hour lost at sea. Out there, ships are getting hijacked and people are being shot all the time."

"And a dead Swede . . ."

"An accident at a shooting range in Djibouti is tragic, but the world doesn't stop for it. So what do you want us to do differently?"

Well, what the hell *did* he want? They couldn't have isolated all the Swedes in the MovCon unit, he realized that. Was it the report that annoyed him, slapped together and approved so quickly? No, it wasn't that either. Or not that alone, but the way it all added up: the atmosphere of arrogance. Expecting that he'd made the journey simply to sign off on their version. He had no other theory than the one they were feeding him, but it all seemed so simple, the slightest question met by a perfectly reasonable answer. What did he want? He didn't want to feel stupid, but he did now, because he had nothing else to go on.

Before Grip answered, the captain, who seemed uncomfortable with the tone, cut in. "Everyone under my command has received an explicit order from me to cooperate with your police investigation. Your inquiry, that is."

"And you think you need to give an order," Grip said, "for that to happen, I mean?" Now he was being rude, and he knew it.

Silence.

"When do you head back out to sea?" Grip asked instead.

"Two days from now." It was the first officer, stepping in once again. He held Grip in his gaze. "MovCon will be busy transporting matériel to the ship until then, but of course you can question anyone, anytime. I think Mickels has given you background on who they are and how they work."

"He has."

"And what about the Djiboutians?"

"Only that the local police have arrested the man accused of firing the shot."

"What goes on there is completely beyond our control," said the captain.

"And where can I find the rest of the Africans?" Grip asked.

"I spoke with Sergeant Hansson, who took over the unit after Slunga," said the first officer. "Apparently, most of the locals quit after this incident, and I'm afraid they'll be difficult to track down."

"It is what it is. But the Swedes are all back at work?"

"Of course."

"Well then, I'll want to question them tomorrow, the whole gang at once."

"Question them? You mean you already have suspicions?"

"Journalists interview, and police question, that's all."

The first officer shrugged.

"We . . ." The captain sounded conciliatory. "We're thinking of holding a small dinner tomorrow, here on board, and we'd like you to come. At seven, that was the idea."

"Dinner, thank you. And I guess MovCon is busy during the day, so I'll meet with them at five. That should leave them enough time to do what they need to."

"Think jacket."

Grip didn't understand.

"For dinner tomorrow. If that works."

Grip, who hadn't changed since he landed, stood there without a tie, looking rumpled. What was this about, he wondered, some sort of game, giving him a dress code?

"Jacket, of course," Grip replied with a nod. "And my questioning?"

"I'll take it up with Mickels," replied the first officer.

Then there was silence again.

"For me, there's just one detail left before I call it a day," Grip said. "Where am I staying?"

"Hm," said the first officer, taking a moment to remember. "The Sheraton was completely booked, so it must be the Kempinski. A

75

night there costs a bloody fortune, but that's what's available, from what I understand."

"The Kempinski?"

"The best Djibouti has to offer."

Grip had done his homework. The Kempinski. Not just the best in Djibouti, but possibly the best anywhere in Africa. Did they want to smoke him out, get him to stay as short a time as possible, fearing what some police chief would say about his travel expenses?

"That will be perfect." The navy men were apparently accustomed to a different kind of boss.

"Until seven o'clock, tomorrow, then," said the captain. Time to go.

"The quartermaster will drive you to your hotel," said the first officer, glancing at the clock. "He's out running an errand in town. It shouldn't be long. You can wait for him in the officers' mess."

Grip hadn't taken more than one step toward the door before the first officer noticed his hesitation. He had no idea how to get out. The maze had won.

"I'll call someone on watch to show you the way."

12

Grip had managed to get to bed before midnight but soon woke up again, freezing. Several times, he wrestled with the hotel's air-conditioning controls, increasingly annoyed. Finally, as the clock by his bed turned to four, he gave up and took a sleeping pill. Most of the morning disappeared in its haze. The rest of the day, he kept to himself. Read the report and the personnel files, pondered, planned, called Mickels and then a few others. Made sure both suits that had been lying in his suitcase got pressed. Easily arranged, at the Kempinski.

The hotel stood alone on a peninsula north of downtown. Its palm groves and lush gardens were enclosed by sand-colored walls, which cut straight lines through the barren landscape. On the inside was abundance, for a select few; on the outside, patches of stubby grass and plastic bottles spinning in the sea breeze. But there was no barbed wire, and no shards of glass poking up, not like on the walls in the wealthy residential neighborhoods. Someone had been thoughtful. The impression was meant to be inviting; people were meant to see an oasis. And for those who knew exactly which credit card to flash, it truly was a place out of *One Thousand and One Nights*.

Opinions differed as to whether it was a sheikh or the Chinese who owned this twenty-first-century take on a fairy-tale palace. Did it matter? What mattered was that the Swiss hoteliers pulling the strings behind the scenes knew exactly whom to hire. The local middle-class daughters worked the reception desk, smiling shyly and adorably, having wasted years studying languages at foreign universities so they could serve Germans wanting to park closer to the main door and Chinese wanting massage appointments at the spa. The Filipino maids managed to do the impossible, keeping every horizontal surface free from dust without being visible themselves, and making sure not to miss all the nooks and arabesques. This was fabulous Islamic architecture, the Alhambra reimagined: geometric patterns covered the tiles and lanterns, while the colonnades and ornately carved wooden panels created a kind of labyrinth. It was rare to have an unobstructed view, and generally many things were not to be fully seen but only imagined at the Kempinski.

There was a French pâtisserie, and in the evenings, the Egyptian singers in the Lebanese dance bands, who smiled down from the posters, did their best imitations of Umm Kulthum at one of the hotel bars. Everyone was supposed to feel at home, yet at the same time get a whiff of something foreign, even exotic. Like the fact that the outdoor pool was chilled. This was one of the first things the hotel told its guests, so they'd understand that the hotel had thought of everything.

That afternoon, Grip slowly swam laps, cutting through the fog that lingered from the previous night. The pool was lined in deep blue mosaics, and its chilled water felt pleasant in the shimmering heat. He showered in his room and put on his freshly pressed linen suit. The tie seemed like overkill, but he had that dinner to go to. Earlier in the day, he'd arranged for a rental car, and at lunch, Mickels had stopped by with entry cards for both the port and the French base. Now, he could move around.

Grip left the car in the shade of some containers on the dock and walked the last hundred meters to the warship's gangway. He'd said he wanted to meet the MovCon unit at five o'clock; now it was quarter past. They were soldiers, so they were sitting where they'd been told to, looking at the clock.

The group was waiting in a small mess hall for the ship's crew. It looked like the common room of a dorm, with its shelves of battered

DVDs, game consoles, and computer games. Five pairs of soldiers' eyes told him he was late. Grip wanted them to start off feeling they had an advantage.

"Hi," he said. He took a chair and sat down, as they'd already formed a U around him. Grip pushed autopilot, letting his mouth babble on about his assignment and his investigative mandate. He spewed nonsense while he looked them in the eyes, the whole circle, again and again. All between twenty and thirty. Sleeves carefully rolled up on their uniforms, with just the right amount of wear. They all dressed in khakis, definitely not navy blue. Grip knew their personnel files by now, and every single one had a background in the army. His own linen suit was out of place. His mouth ran on, something about combatant status and international accords, a few heads nodding in agreement, as if they followed the nonsense point by point. Four men and one woman. A pair of tattooed forearms, a mustache, two with beards—probably a look the veterans brought home from Afghanistan. Three met his gaze, one looked around at the walls, the last stared down at the floor in front of him.

". . . therefore, I'll be around for a few days asking some questions." Nobody reacted, not the slightest movement. "So, when did you get the idea of heading off to the shooting range?" Grip looked at the person sitting directly in front of him.

"The lieutenant told us."

"Lieutenant Slunga?"

"Yes, the day before, around lunchtime last Saturday," one of the beards answered. It was Fritzell, the biggest of the bunch, who no doubt lifted dumbbells when he had an extra hour or two.

"And what time did you go?"

"At three." This was Fredrik Hansson, the sergeant who'd had to take over command. "I booked the shooting range and went to pick up ammunition. Did anyone have objections?" Hansson answered his own question. Laid-back style, expensive watch. "Most of us probably did."

"Most, probably?"

"Well, I was against it," said Hansson, "and I told Slunga the minute he came up with the damn idea."

"But he insisted?"

"Yes." Hansson shrugged.

Grip let it go. "So the point was to do a little bonding between you and the locals." Grip smiled. "You needed that?"

Silence.

Hansson looked at Jondelius, the other beard, who leaned forward and replied, "I think the Djiboutians had been pushing him, saying they wanted to shoot."

"And Slunga caved in to the pressure, just like that?"

"Yes."

"And the Djiboutians, what did they do, the day after the shooting?"

"The next day, only two showed up—Mr. Nazir, the foreman, and his nephew," answered Philippa Ekman, the only woman in the room, speaking up without a look from Hansson. "Where the others went, who knows?"

"And that means more work for you, delivering supplies to the *Sveaborg* before she casts off again?"

"It's okay. Mr. Nazir hired six new people today."

"I see."

Philippa Ekman nodded. The mood among those in the room remained total self-confidence. It was in their body language, and in that "bring-it-on" look in their eyes.

"Just for my own information," Grip continued, "many of you have worked together before? On missions?"

"Yes, of course," someone answered. Another nodded, and the one gazing at the floor raised his head.

"Where, for instance?"

"The Balkans, I guess everybody started off there," replied Jondelius, the second beard. "I met Philippa for the first time in Kosovo."

"What about you?" Grip said, turning his gaze to Radovanović, who'd looked up from the floor.

"Me . . . ?" He shifted in his seat. "Well, before this, twice in Afghanistan."

Milan Radovanović's personnel file said his parents were Bosnian Serbs who'd come to Sweden when he was five.

"Afghanistan, of course," said Jondelius. That got them started, pointing at each other, talking about who served together when, names flying with locations and units: Mazar-e Sharif, Sheberghan, OMLT, FS-17, Marmal. All of them had served there, one of the beards doing the most tours, it seemed. Someone laughed: "We've done everything: drivers, grunts, vehicle mechanics—you name it."

"And now you do MovCon." Grip got a thumbs-up from one member of this traveling circus. Fritzell, the muscular one, smiled broadly behind his beard.

"You like to dig into things?" Grip asked, looking at him.

"I like to dig into things," he replied, with the indulgent gaze of a bouncer looking at a drunk trying to get past him.

Philippa Ekman snorted at the comment. She wore her long blond hair up and sat with her legs wide apart like the others.

"And in Africa?" Grip continued.

"This is a first for me," said Jondelius. Radovanović nodded.

"Me and Hansson were in Chad together," said Ekman.

"Yeah, I've done my fair share around here," continued Fredrik Hansson, the new leader. "Chad, Sudan, a few other little missions."

"Always MovCon?"

"Something like that. My thing is logistics."

Grip nodded. "And now you're here. There aren't many of you, and I hear there's a lot to do. How do you divide the work?"

"What do you mean?"

"You know, mornings, evenings, nights, how do you arrange your shifts?"

"We work as needed."

"Around the clock?"

"Not always, but it happens."

"And the Djiboutians?"

"During the day. But really, they only get things done in the morning."

"Why?"

There was silence.

"I said, why?" Grip saw Hansson look at Fritzell, so instead he went to Radovanović. "Why, Radovanović?"

The soldier fiddled and twisted his index finger nervously.

"Too hot in the afternoon sun?"

The staff sergeant struggled for words.

"The real reason," Grip went on, "is because at lunchtime, the khat stalls open in town. After one o'clock, nearly everyone is chewing, and by two, they're no longer useful . . . right?"

"Something like that," said Hansson, to break the deadlock.

"Then I understand better. And another thing I was wondering, since you've been out on so many missions. How often have you taken the locals to a firing fest at a shooting range? And I don't mean when you were training some ex-Talibans to be police officers in Afghanistan. I mean people who have jobs on the base that have nothing to do with weapons. Do you have a single example? Chad, Liberia, Kosovo?"

Silence again.

"Anything?"

"It was the lieutenant . . ."

"I know, Slunga told you to. And not just that you were going to shoot with them, but that you'd do it in the afternoon, when the entire gang was high. You've said it yourselves, right?" Grip leaned forward, looking at Hansson, Fritzell, and Ekman. "The idea was so goddamn stupid that the lieutenant couldn't have done it alone. No way in hell it was five against one, and he won just because he was a lieutenant. Never, not with this crew. You need to work on your story, it's too polished."

This hit home. But Grip had more. "Was he a good shot, by the way?" He'd turned to Radovanović, who looked down at the floor again. "Hello? How well did he shoot?"

"Huh, who?" asked Radovanović, looking up.

"Abdoul Ghermat, was he a good shot?"

"When?"

"C'mon, you stood next to each other on the shooting range. I've seen the sketches. It was you who instructed him—was he a good shot?"

"I don't know, the idea was just that they'd give it a try. We taped over the targets as they went." Radovanović tore a little sliver off his cuticle.

"But did he hit the target at least?"

"I guess so."

"You guess? It was only three days ago. Did he hit the cardboard soldiers or not?"

"Yes, he did."

"And then he shot Slunga?"

Radovanović didn't know what to say.

"Let it go," said Fredrik Hansson at last. "I was standing in the back as well, when the others walked up to the targets. The shot, when it happened, fuck, it wasn't something you were expecting. Whether he aimed before or not . . ." Hansson shrugged. "In any case, it was Abdoul Ghermat who fired the shot."

Radovanović nodded. Saved by Hansson.

"Ghermat," mumbled Grip. He glanced at the clock and stood up. "I'm sure you also took a lot of photos with your phones. That goes along with doing something so goddamn stupid." No one denied it. "Exactly. And I want to see pictures, enough pictures so I can see the faces of everyone there. Email them to me. I want them by ten tonight." Still no one said anything, and Grip tossed some business cards on a table, nodded, and left.

The next time Grip stopped, he was out on deck. Alone in the late dusk, he looked out over the water and the lights on the other side of the harbor. Behind him, the ship's funnel whirred, towering behind him.

Already he'd found the weak link.

The whole MovCon unit stayed at the Sheraton, with the other Swedes and foreigners who didn't serve aboard the ships. They'd go back to their rooms now, on the same hallway. They'd have a few beers, trying to come up with a new strategy, because the pig wouldn't just go away. What photos had they taken last Sunday, and which would they send? Some would be for, and some against. They didn't agree, only pretended to, and pretty clumsily when Grip was in the room. Grip knew an inbred group when he saw one. Those smug little smiles, from spending way too much time together and playing entirely by their own rules. They were a world apart.

Grip would be surprised if there weren't something in his in-box before ten. They understood that much. It remained to be seen how useful the images would be. The really interesting part would come at ten thirty, when Grip figured he'd still be at the dinner aboard the ship, with the captain.

He picked up the phone and covered his other ear to mask the noise from the chimney. Waited for someone to answer.

When Grip met Mickels at the Kempinski earlier that day, Mickels had given him the business card of a French colonel. He'd explained that Colonel Frères was responsible for the security of all European military personnel stationed in Djibouti, and he knew that Grip was there. Apparently, he wanted Grip to contact him.

Grip had called the Frenchman as soon as Mickels left. The colonel, who was well-informed and totally self-assured, brought up the difficulty of doing this kind of investigation alone. He suggested using a couple of his own military police. Not for the long term, but if there was some specific errand . . . Grip had gotten a phone number. "Just give my name, they'll know it."

So Grip had started making arrangements. The concierge at the Kempinski recommended a small but well-run hotel on the outskirts of town. There, he booked two rooms. Then he called the French military police. A phone call, a name dropped. "Ah, Colonel Frères, no problem. When do you want them? . . . Well, two men plus two would be good enough . . . No, no, we won't tell anyone about it." Mickels and all other Swedes would be kept out of this.

All set.

Now the French were waiting for his signal. Two men in uniform would go into the Sheraton and knock on the door; two plainclothes-men would take over and stay a few days at the hotel that Grip had booked.

The ringtone stopped. Grip pressed his hand harder against his ear to shut out the noise from the ship.

"*Oui?*"

"Yes, it's me— the Swede. Milan Radovanović is the one."

"Milan . . ." repeated the voice. He'd already given them all the names and photos. A brief pause on the line. Perhaps the French military police officer was writing something down. "Still half past ten?"

"Exactly."

"Good, then."

Grip hung up.

13

They'd set up a small bar in one corner of the captain's spacious cabin. The ice rattled as a junior officer wielded a cocktail shaker. Daiquiris and martinis were it. The officers wore all-white uniforms, and even their shoes were white. Only their ties broke the rule—black stripes beneath their jackets. There were a few civilians too, visiting from the Swedish embassy in Addis Ababa, apparently the nearest Swedish legation in the Horn of Africa.

The first officer ran interference as usual, overseeing political correctness between the sliced goat cheese hors d'oeuvres. He explained to the diplomats, and eventually to Grip, that liquor was rarely served on board—never at sea, only in port and on special occasions like tonight. So that they'd feel privileged. He rambled on about the keys to the liquor cabinet, some sort of complex system. The professional drinkers from the foreign office nodded politely, reminding Grip of the many times he'd observed the king getting lectured at a corporate event on some piece of trivia. The captain himself didn't contribute much to the buzz, not until dinnertime, when he invited his guests to take their seats in such a loud voice that everyone winced.

The captain's table was set for ten: pressed linen tablecloths without the slightest ripple, heavy sterling-silver cutlery, and crystal. It was as if the captain had been waiting offstage, and now he came out, turned and gestured. Handwritten place cards—with the only woman at the table, one of the diplomats, of course seated on his right. He began his monologue as soon as they sat down, while the guests' eyes wandered around the room, pausing at the framed foreign flag or the broken tip of an oar mounted on a plaque. There were many stories to tell, and the cabin provided props for well-rehearsed snippets and harmless anecdotes.

A male chef came in to present the menu, describing at length what had been sautéed and reduced in the dishes that awaited. Otherwise, the waitstaff was entirely female, made up of a couple of nurses and some of the kitchen's off-duty personnel, wearing white uniforms that were simpler but just as sharp as those worn by the officers they served.

It was a nostalgic kind of theater, one that hadn't changed in decades.

Everyone already knew which appetizers would be served, since this was the week before Midsummer: cheese, butter, and herring. For the sake of argument, they debated which schnapps would go best. On a tray stood a few fogged-up bottles—Skåne, Östergötland, OP—"Take this one . . . no, not on your life . . . sure . . . fill it up." The dock outside the porthole had disappeared in the darkness. They sang a Swedish drinking song, and most took sips, except for the chief engineer, who knocked his back in a single gulp. After another song and a couple pieces of herring, most of the glasses were empty. People gazed at the icy bottles, but despite the captain's asking, the first officer's glare made them think twice, and no one took him up on the offer.

Grip was seated at the corner, with the woman from Addis to his left, but she was completely monopolized by the captain. Grip saw little besides the hair at the back of her neck. Across from him sat the grizzled ship's surgeon, who ran the small hospital on board. Here, the conversation was better. A headstrong type, he'd just retired from general surgery at Sahlgrenska Hospital in Gothenburg, when he heard that the military was struggling to find doctors willing to go out on missions. His peers preferred sterile operating rooms, MRIs, and triple-digit hourly fees on call—not dealing with soldiers' gunshot wounds and heatstroke, and in between, being quartered in a cabin so run-down you wouldn't offer it to a drunken dance band on a Baltic ferry. He laughed at his own words. Still, the navy had its charms, and after a life of working all the time, he was scared by the thought of doing nothing. At sixty-six, he'd gone out to a shooting range for the first time since he'd done his military service at eighteen, brushed up on his military ranks, and a few weeks later boarded the HMS *Sveaborg*. He sometimes cupped one hand behind his ear and sang a bit too loud.

Somewhere in the middle of the filet mignon, when the conversation around the table had split into a few groups, Grip asked him about Per-Erik Slunga. About the body. Yes, the doctor had seen it and put it in the ship's morgue himself.

"Autopsy?" Grip asked

"No, no, that's a job for pathologists, and we don't have one on board. We're here to sew people up and keep them alive. If everything goes south, the cause of death is usually pretty clear. That poor bastard Slunga was shot, as you're probably aware."

"Yes, of course, but beyond that."

"In the head."

Grip spun his index finger, in a gesture of wanting to know more.

"You know, pathologists, they're peculiar people," the doctor said, sipping his wine, "and they do a particular type of science. An autopsy, if it's going to happen, will have to be done in Sweden."

"Takes too long."

"What are you looking for?"

"Whatever you can figure out. I don't know, maybe the angle of the bullet."

"There was just one shot, right?"

"If you say so."

The captain raised his voice to get everyone's attention. "As I mentioned, I received confirmation today that in little more than a month, the foreign minister will make an official visit." He got a couple of satisfied nods in reply, and the male embassy official started talking about plans for the event, something about a motorcade, and soon the other guests at the table fell back into their little conversations.

"Shot angles, bruises, and whether he was under the influence when shot, that much I can handle," said the doctor, who'd swallowed the bait during the break in conversation. "I can run some tests here, through the French hospital in the city."

"When?"

The doctor didn't hear Grip. "But no fine points. I can't tell you the caliber of the bullet, or what he's had for lunch. I don't want to slice him up too much."

"When can you start?" repeated Grip.

The doctor had stopped debating with himself. "Tomorrow. I can start in the morning."

The women in white began to clear away the empty plates.

"And when exactly will you have the results?" It was the first officer, looking across the table at Grip.

"Sorry?"

"I mean, in terms of the foreign minister's arrival."

Grip understood exactly. The first officer couldn't possibly have overheard his conversation with the doctor, but Grip was the bull in the china shop. Not even filet mignon and schnapps from Östgöta could disguise the disturbing fact that there was a dead man on board. The first officer needed to clean up the mess before his boss's proud moment, when the big man was coming to visit, something no doubt planned months before. Long before Slunga's group decided to have some fun on a shooting range, on the outskirts of Djibouti. Surely the bloodstain in the sand would be gone by then?

Closure.

Signed and sealed.

Perfectly reasonable.

The first officer smiled. But his self-assured gaze left little room for alternatives.

Grip looked at the clock. Half past nine. An hour to go. While MovCon argued about which pictures to send, the French military police were putting on their boots. "I can't imagine there will be a problem," he replied. "The formalities will certainly be over before the minister arrives."

Cognac was served. The chief engineer's eyes grew hazy. The first officer told the diplomats about hunting pirates, how it all worked, who did what. The attacks they'd thwarted, and the times they got away. How the ransom money was paid in cash, delivered by parachute from small planes leased from Kenya. Eventually, the woman from the embassy got up and smoothed out a few wrinkles in her skirt as she thanked the hosts. Then the whole contingent left, heading down to the car waiting dockside.

Ten thirty. Grip could make his exit, just as the other events were gearing up, but he'd rather wait it out in the captain's cabin than sit at the bar of the Kempinski. Once again, it would be impossible to fall asleep.

At the Sheraton, two military police officers knocked at Milan Radovanović's door. Friendly enough, but one on either side as they accompanied him out. Into the waiting car with two plainclothes MPs, disappearing into the night. Everyone would see it, and the rest was just a matter of waiting.

In the captain's cabin, the officers were in a good mood. Some sat at the table, while others sprawled on the couch with their jackets unbuttoned. Grip's pocket buzzed. A text. He didn't even pick up the phone—he knew it was the French, saying the deed was done. If something had gone wrong, they would have called.

Despite their bloodshot eyes, among the naval officers there was more laughter than stifled yawns. Then came a knock, and a head appeared. As usual, the first officer went to meet the messenger. A glance at Grip, a few words with the captain.

Grip stood up. Both the captain and the first officer were coming toward him, but Grip beat them to it. "What's the protocol for having a car drive up to the dock?"

"We . . ." For a moment, the captain fumbled for words. "They say that one of the soldiers in MovCon has been arrested. By the French."

"The French military police, but that doesn't mean that he's been arrested. They've only taken him in for questioning, on my instructions. The car, what was it . . . ?"

"Radovanović." The captain read aloud from the note he'd been handed, pronouncing the name as if it were the first time he'd ever seen it. "What are you trying to say," he asked Grip, "that my own people have been lying to me?"

"I don't know yet."

"Drop the false humility," the first officer said. "What is your intent?"

"You've done your investigation, now I'm doing mine. Thanks for tonight."

Grip had all eyes on his back as he walked out.

"That little bastard" was the last thing he heard behind him.

Grip didn't bother to wait on the dock. Instead, he walked to the port's guarded entrance and took a taxi from there to the Kempinski.

14

As the *MaryAnn* approached land, she anchored a few hundred meters out, on the outskirts of a village. Darwiish let Jenny go about her tasks, making sure everything on board was properly lashed, stowed, and shut tight. Half the pirates went ahead to shore in one of the skiffs they'd been towing. Jenny worked slowly, feeling that with every rope she coiled, she was digging another shovelful of her own grave. Alexandra stood by quietly and watched, while Sebastian stayed below deck with his injured father. But then when a few curious people appeared on the beach, Darwiish got annoyed and impatient. They barely had time to gather up their belongings, once the boat was secured. It went badly; they had to grab things at random, no more than what could fit in a few plastic bags and a canvas tote. Then, herded into the second skiff, they sped toward land.

Carl-Adam staggered ashore with only Alexandra to help him. It seemed that the pirates wouldn't touch him, much less help, and Jenny had her hands full just carrying their plastic bags and keeping Sebastian calm. They were split up into two cars with four-wheel drive. The last thing Jenny saw, before the scarf was tied over her eyes, was Alexandra clutching the sleeve of her blindfolded father, while a pirate took out another twisted scarf for her too.

It was a bumpy ride. Sebastian trembled with fear and gripped Jenny's arm and leg the whole way. She comforted him, trying to hide her own despair. Lacking any sense of time or distance, she simply prayed to God, really prayed to God, that Alexandra and Carl-Adam in the other car would at least be taken to the same place.

Something to be thankful for. Both cars stopped in front of two stone houses at the top of a gravelly hill, the sea barely visible at the horizon. It must have been a settlement once, even a fairly well-built one, but now it was a hideout. A haunt chosen for its isolated location and its perfect vantage point. Jenny realized this the instant they took off her blindfold: even if you managed to escape, there was nowhere to go, and the tracks in the sand would betray you, no matter how much of a lead you started with. The vast 360-degree view and the sandy expanses made you more powerless than barbed wire and walls ever could. Even the guards realized that the family's situation was impossible. At sea aboard a hijacked yacht, the world was capricious, and they held tight to their Kalashnikovs to assure themselves and everyone around them that they were in control. Here at the two houses on the sand, at times they didn't even bother to carry their weapons, knowing their power was absolute.

Even though the family was allowed to go outside, they preferred to stay indoors. Inside those four walls, they had a world that was predictable, keeping them from thinking too much about their situation and simply giving up. They had a room with two camp beds, a mattress on the floor, and two plastic chairs. That was it. There was a wooden door leading to an outer room, but it had to be kept open, and one or two guards were always posted there. In the second house, the men slept and ate, a force of usually five, sometimes six. They worked a week at a time, then a new gang came and they changed over. Most of the ones who hijacked the boat were here, along with a few new faces.

The biggest problem was water. Every day they were given a bucket. The first morning it had felt generous enough, but soon they understood. Four people, washing and drinking, and also trying to keep Carl-Adam's wounds clean. Their only container—that bucket. If they washed in it, the rest became undrinkable; if they poured water over their hands after every trip to the toilet pit outside, they soon ran out. They were given enough to eat: a pile of flatbread every night, with rice and lentil stew—but only that one bucket of water.

And Jenny understood. Maybe this was why the people who first settled here had abandoned the place. There was no well. Only the water brought by car every afternoon. You could see the dot far out on its path along a distant ridge, as it turned and climbed the hills in their direction. Sometimes the guards changed; otherwise there was just food, water, and khat. The same procedure every time: one of the guards carried the new bucket to them, his cheek already bulging with green leaves. Jenny tried to explain, more indignant every day. Gesturing, yelling, right up in their faces. Whichever one it was, he'd shrug his shoulders or shove her out of the way, then take the old bucket away. It was important that they'd drunk the last drops before that happened.

From the outer room, Alexandra managed to get ahold of an empty bottle that the guards had left behind. With that, they could pour and measure. Their days were taken up with water rituals. Carl-Adam needed the most—the wound on his hip had started to heal, but the one in his hand looked bad, and although he didn't have a fever, he was exhausted. Sebastian was the only one they had to force to drink. Jenny always accompanied the children to the toilet pit, partly to avoid the risk of them ending up alone with the guards and partly to make sure their urine hadn't gotten too dark. She adapted her own ration accordingly. As the water in her own allotment fell, thirst began to eat its way into her emotions, magnifying her sense of powerlessness. When her sticky mouth screamed for more in the room's dry heat, she blamed herself for what she'd done to the children. In her dark and twisted thoughts, Carl-Adam was completely innocent, because she was the one who'd pushed them to break free of their conventional lives and escape. The dream of the sea. A few days later, her ration level in the bottle dropped by yet a few more sips. She held back for her children but still felt the same shame and guilt. What kind of mother takes her children on a sailboat trip in the Indian Ocean?

They didn't see Darwiish at first, but one day he showed up in their room. His beard was freshly dyed red, his eyes shining from khat.

He looked at them as if they'd been taking liberties, like uninvited guests. Carl-Adam was asleep on one cot and hadn't woken up. But he did, with a loud kick to one of the bed legs. Then Darwiish turned his beard toward Sebastian, who was slouched on the mattress in the corner. He made a motion with his head that the boy didn't understand. A command, but Sebastian just sat there. Then he lifted up the mattress, dumping Sebastian onto the floor, and looked angrily underneath it, as if searching for something that had been hidden. Then he went out.

The second time, they saw through their little hole of a window that two cars had arrived in the evening. Two guards entered their room, forced Carl-Adam out of bed, and took him away. No one stopped Jenny when she followed.

Outside, a crowd of men: the familiar guards, Darwiish and a few others he'd brought with him. It got loud as soon as Carl-Adam emerged from the shadows of the house. One of the guards yanked on his shirt, as if he were showing off a thief. The matter seemed to involve an elderly man who'd come to see Carl-Adam. The man didn't say much, but after looking him over, he turned to the red-bearded pirate with a short quick phrase and an extended finger, indicating that nothing more needed to be said. There was something both resigned and unforgiving about him. Darwiish nodded, as if he'd given in. Jenny sensed that the man walking back toward the cars was the father of the pirate that her husband had killed.

The third time, Jenny was looking from the inner room toward the outer one. There, the two chairs the guards normally used had been placed on either side of a small table. As if for a game of chess. Darwiish on one side, her husband on the other. Carl-Adam held his aching hand in his lap while Darwiish repeated, "How much?" Carl-Adam didn't understand. The guard who was standing next to him jammed his rifle muzzle into his back.

"How much?" Darwiish held up a printout. A photo from the Internet, of Carl-Adam smiling in a suit and tie. The others around him just as clean-shaven and smiling as he. It was a picture from his time at Scandinavian Capital. All the lions were there, some sitting, others standing, and underneath appeared their name, age, and the titles that were part of that scene: Junior Partner, Founder, Chief Financial Officer . . .

"How much?"

Carl-Adam shrugged his shoulders uncertainly.

"Ask for more water," Jenny yelled from inside.

Darwiish threw a cigarette lighter on the table and waved his hand toward the guard, who wasn't visible from where Jenny sat. A couple of steps, and then the door closed with a bang.

The pirates, and not least Darwiish, had figured it out. Of course they reeked of money, the sailboat spoke for itself, and now they had Googled Carl-Adam.

The *MaryAnn II*, sixty-two feet long and forty tons' displacement. She represented the kind of money that only a very successful forty-something could get his hands on. An elegant hull with teak decks that reeked of venture capitalist a mile away, when she slipped into Sandhamn or Smögen in the summertime. But just as much, a sailor's dream in a gale in the North Sea. Carl-Adam had gotten looks of both approval and envy when friends who knew boats came on board the first time. In fact, Jenny was the one who'd made the decisions. Decided to buy a sailboat, and decided on the *MaryAnn*. "That one or no one," she'd said. A matter of course. And how could Carl-Adam have argued? They'd bought it from a German, and then she was the one who got her ready. After all, it had been her dream, more than anyone's. Roller sails, electric winches, satellite link. Her escape.

Yes, they'd cast off from posh Sandhamn, that had been Carl-Adam's idea. Not hers. But she'd gone along with it. A final celebration, a send-off from the old world. One last time, she'd be nothing more than the wife of Carl-Adam Bergenskjöld. A weekend at the Sailor's Hotel in Sandhamn and on the wide planks of the docks below. A three-day party, with Carl-Adam footing the bill: chartered boat from town, hotel, dinner, bar—everything. All his friends were there, which is to say, basically Carl-Adam's colleagues with their wives and families. As if for a damn costume party, they'd shown up in Vineyard Vines polo shirts and Sperry shoes, like a bunch of New England preppies. A couple of them had actually raced in the Round Gotland. But those were in the minority, and the others were mere posers, there by virtue of being as rich as trolls. They'd even gotten ahold of a cannon, some sort of miniature version of one on the ship *Vasa*.

Finally, the late Sunday-morning brunch was over, and more than a few were red-eyed with hangovers from the night before. Time to go. The cannon was loaded and aimed, and the glasses of pink champagne raised by everyone on land.

"Keep in touch." "We love you." "Chin chin!"

The whole Bergenskjöld family was on the boat, held by a single rope. Carl-Adam stood quietly with a pained expression. Second thoughts? The entire Scandinavian Capital office was gathered there, and now he was no longer one of them. Everything associated with that place, his rise, all the good harvests. Dividends, bonuses, rhythms. Life. Confident Carl-Adam—King Carl, on the way up—that was his thing. A social über-machine, graced by God, never down for long, always with the killer line and the twinkle in his eye that made the obnoxious investors and cutthroat comptrollers start laughing again. Not a single accountant raised objections in his presence. But now—quiet. Jenny saw it, the umbilical cord stretched taut. All the faces on land. She stepped up and kissed him. He stood at the helm; she was still the wife. The conventions were powerful, she knew that part, had lived with it. He seemed unmoved. Her only thought—steer out and away. He was at the helm, and all she had to do was let go of the rope.

"Wait, wait," said someone on land. There was commotion and smoke around the cannon, amid the Henri Lloyd jackets and Dockside shoes.

"*Kabooom!*" Everyone jumped. Then they laughed. She let go of the rope, and smiled, still her smug Djursholm smile. Ten seconds after the cannon was fired, most on the land were already glued to their phones. Jenny Bergenskjöld had liberated herself from that hateful life.

And Carl-Adam didn't even turn around.

Starting out, Jenny Bergenskjöld was Jenny Stensson, a wind-surfer girl from the west coast. Even a professional for a few years. She cruised between races and photo shoots, with her sun-bleached hair and peeling lips. Although she was sponsored by board and sail companies, she made only enough for a roof over her head, living on noodles and chicken. In the end, it got boring, and she began crewing on luxury yachts, mostly in the Caribbean and the Mediterranean, usually on large sailboats. This paid better, but it also meant Internet millionaires who expected some adventure between the sheets in addition to the salary they paid. It was good training for all sorts of balancing acts, and smiles. She turned twenty-six. And suddenly her friends back home had finished grad school, begun careers, wore engagement rings, and no longer came alone when they visited her in the sun. They were less and less interested in her stories. It hit Jenny hard. She didn't want to get stuck speaking sailors' English for the rest of her life; she didn't want another twenty years of celebrating Christmas wearing sunscreen. She began to look anxiously toward home. For the first time, she longed for the north.

When she went to a party in London that fall, she broke loose. Sigmund Freud would have had a lot to say about random behavior versus unconscious desire. Her life had always moved in distinct phases. Now she found herself at a party in a circle of attractive acquaintances. It was time to move on: to spin the wheel and bet everything on red. She could read the force fields in a room—the power—in an instant. It took her only a few minutes to scan twenty, thirty, sixty new people at such a feast. From among the suits, the bling, the men, the dresses, and the hand gestures, she could see who was real and who was only playacting. Picking out the alpha females, and the males, was easy enough. She was introduced to many but felt the burning energy in only a few. Jenny needed only a few words to know exactly what she was dealing with, after all the years of men trying to impress her, and her trying to impress them back. She'd always been the one who broke things off, when, after a few nights together, the energy fizzled. In that vast apartment in London, it soon became clear which was the one. They bumped and slid apart a few times in the crowd, before they naturally found themselves standing together, and then other interested people, and even their friends, sensed nothing but their complete exclusion of the outside world. The evening ended at the Four Seasons at Hamilton Place in a room that cost 428 pounds a night.

She wore a sweater of the thinnest imaginable cotton under her jacket. When everything else was off, and he lifted it up, she said: "No—touch!" And then his hands were all over her softness, the silky fabric enhancing every sensation as it ran under and between his fingers. Before his attentive gaze, she felt playful, and her undisguised pleasure aroused him. He drew his face along the length of her, capturing the essence of her, inhaling her through the thin fabric, as if he were smelling the scent of a woman's body for the first time. They were already on the floor, and she clasped her legs around him, so the caresses could continue, the intensity mounting with him inside her.

For her, desire made her turn inward, and she made love almost unconsciously, with her eyes closed. With him on top, she felt the full weight of him, not fat, not then, but overwhelming in his embrace. He didn't try to hold her tight or force himself on her in any way, yet that was the effect, by virtue of his sheer physical presence, his strong thrusts, and his firm grip. He had an almost childlike unawareness of his own power, and she liked that. She could tease him, give herself up to him, and still get what she needed. She held back, as they braced against each other, and he thrust even harder. Just before he came, she opened her eyes and looked straight at him.

They saw each other in the days after, but she thought she'd pushed things too far and sensed that he held back when she tried to see if she was more than the thinnest of sweaters on a fit body. Soon enough, she'd be heading back to the Caribbean, where a new mahogany deck awaited. But, and this was crucial, he'd become persistent and kept in touch during the weeks that followed. It was as if insight came with distance, and most of all, he didn't want to lose her. He wanted to meet again, but once she was free, she gave evasive answers and lame excuses. He wanted to spend a long weekend with her in Scotland. When she hesitated, he emailed her plane tickets and a picture of some friend's family estate. Who could say no to that? It drew her in. There had been something between them, and it had stung when she'd left him in London the last time, not least the feeling that she was just a sailor girl and he, after all, something else. She traveled with only a carry-on bag, so typical of her, and the weekend was everything one could hope for. Beautiful views and some kind of hunt she didn't understand, dinners amid silly pranks of men who'd spent too many years at boys' schools, and what they'd both really come for—three nights in the same bed. There was his slight awkwardness, but also those unhesitant games with his tongue, the savoring of every smell, and the tasting of each other's saltiness, and there was the falling asleep and waking up and falling asleep again. And hanging over it all, an unmistakable sense of sadness.

On the last day, they went for a walk in awkward silence. "And now?" she finally said, turning to him. He cleared his throat. She didn't know it then, but he too needed to take the next step.

Carl-Adam Bergenskjöld was doing his time in the financial coal mine: paying his dues, putting in the late nights, flaunting his ambitions for a few years at the flashy banks in London. He was far from the noodle-eating-windsurfer-in-a-studio-apartment, more Östra Real prep school, MBA at Handels, and summerhouse on the water in Smådalarö. He was walking the narrow path his father laid out for him. Not without resistance, but it was indulgently swept aside by his wealthy family. Of course he had other plans, the kind that always began with: "You know, actually . . . ," spoken eye to eye late at night, after a few drinks. Dreams of long trips, and of writing a book. But that was just steam released by the valve from time to time. A thousand passionate ideas and longing in his eyes when he was drunk, and a one-way track forward when he was sober. He made his dad proud, did well—London—built his own stock portfolio, and his own accounts started to fill up. And he learned some other tricks too, how it wasn't hard to get a pair of tanned shoulders to join him at Nobu. He shopped around.

But when he walked along that gravel path in a park in Scotland, what he'd felt after the first night at the Four Seasons in London burned even more intensely. Now what? Soon she would slip out of his hands a second time. He had enough self-awareness to realize that the woman he needed didn't belong to the usual crowd. He'd joked about it a lot since then—at parties, with the others—that he'd found himself a commoner. But that didn't hurt Jenny in the least. "You might as well move in, then" was all he'd said on that walkway, after a few seconds of silence.

And that was all he needed to say. Never a word about being a gold digger, although her own demons rose up sometimes to remind her. She was a sort of trophy wife, that was true, and she'd brought along nothing besides her carry-on bag. But so what? It meant no more living hand to mouth, the end of the noodles and guys running their hands between her legs while she made the beds in their cabins. On his side, he admired her independence and wished the same for himself. To choose her was a rebellion against his father, not on the outside as much as on the inside. It gave him the satisfaction of having obtained something different, and she put him at peace. And soon enough the magical change—family. Alexandra was born first, and then the friend who'd hooked up with an engineer from Ericsson in Kista had a reason to come visit again.

Although it continued for a few years, London was just a phase. That, they already knew. Real life would begin when they moved back to Stockholm. Then Scandinavian Capital came into their lives. Direct recruitment. Private equity, hedge funds, no limits. Quick moves. First the apartment on Karlavägen, but soon Carl-Adam became King Carl—and with the annual bonuses a year later, it was time to start building his very own temple. He came home one evening with paperwork for something she'd only heard mentioned in passing, already signed.

"But . . . ?"

"You have to understand, you only get one chance." A turn-of-the-century villa, of course. Djursholm, obviously. Huge rooms, almost like halls. It needed work. Not that the house was in bad condition, but the people who'd lived there before were old money. Creaking wooden floors, ancient stucco. King Oscar II might have felt at home there, but now it would be different. The dark wood paneling would be torn out and the French tapestries taken down. There was no limit to how many rooms would eventually be furnished, once the swarm of Polish carpenters was done ripping out the old. It became a full-time job: the catalogs of gas stoves, a Pompeii of marble and travertine samples, coordinating shipments, firing the incompetent plumber and finding his replacement. Jenny had probably imagined that they'd make these decisions together. She had the painfully naive idea that all of Carl-Adam's overtime and late nights would be done after the years in London.

"We need to decide on . . ."

"Can it wait until tomorrow? Oh, and by the way, tomorrow I'll be . . ."

In London, Carl-Adam wasn't really a player, but now at Scandinavian Capital, he was somebody. And somehow, there was always a final negotiation he alone was responsible for. Always some acquisition or divestment that needed a final push. Decisions hung in the balance, a little nudge needed over dinner to convince some investors, or a trip to close the deal. He came home after midnight when she was already asleep, with the last whiskey hanging in the air around him; when it was Zurich, London, or Frankfurt, that meant at least one night away, and always the last flight home. No planning, everything on short notice. But what had she expected?

And for Carl-Adam himself? King Carl, he shut down as soon as he stepped out of the taxi in front of his house. Slow steps in the gravel. He'd stopped doing his "You know, actually . . . ," as if trying to confide. He merely gave Jenny mumbled versions of no longer being able to distinguish between what he wanted and what he ought to do. But what did it matter to her? It was all empty air. At the next dinner party, he sat back and rambled on with a colleague about *grand cru* wines and some damned car, as if that really were his greatest wish, while Jenny stood in the kitchen, cleaning up, talking with some wife about the usual drivel.

Guilt spread like a weed, into every niche.

When they'd first met, Jenny had worn a silver bracelet set with a few gemstones, a beautiful piece that cost considerably more than what she could afford. It was a gift from a skipper who hadn't expected anything in return. For Jenny, the bracelet was the only thing she'd saved from those years. It was a fond memento that Carl-Adam had mistaken for an interest in jewelry. He thought he'd figured out her one weakness. And so he'd gotten in the habit—when he disappeared without warning, or when the last flight home had been pushed to "tomorrow" too many times—of standing there, when the front door finally closed behind him, with a small oblong package and that expression of knowing exactly what she wanted. Chopard, Tiffany, Cartier. How could she object? She wore a smile that she too had rehearsed. There was a whole bathroom cabinet full of necklaces and bracelets in boxes. She had to remind herself to wear them.

Jenny became obsessed with the thought that she couldn't feel gratitude. Truly obsessed. She tried therapy, and the therapist obsessed instead over the word *meaningfulness*. She quit, and started working out without anyone else around. No gym, no personal trainer. She ran in the dark, after Alexandra had fallen asleep for the night, and that worked better, as a painkiller. At any rate, she could deal with the status quo.

Until Sebastian was born.

15

Milan Radovanović hadn't slept well that night, mostly going back and forth to the toilet, then tossing and turning in bed. That's what the French had said, when Grip called the next morning. One of the MPs watched Radovanović while the other slept in the room next door. Taking a couple of shifts, they'd gotten through the night. At the small hotel Grip had booked for them, they brought breakfast up to the room, but Radovanović had only sipped at his orange juice. It could very well go on like this for a while. Radovanović spoke no French, and the military police only broken English. Nothing valuable would be said, no steam let out; the atmosphere would simply grow heavier with guilt and uncertainty.

Grip had checked his in-box, and sure enough, Fredrik Hansson had emailed photos from the shooting range. He'd sent them at just before ten o'clock the night before, with a short note saying he'd chosen pics that showed everyone. Grip scrolled through them, and although they'd obviously been carefully selected, still the screwing around came through—in the poses and khat-glazed eyes. One image said it all, a group shot, probably taken with the self-timer, since all the players were there. You could see the Swedish desert uniforms mixed in with the Djiboutians, and the weapons, and all the faces. They were close together, some on their knees. One tried to look serious, another couldn't hide his skepticism. In this cauldron of simmering feelings, the only Swede smiling was Fredrik Hansson himself. His superior, Per-Erik Slunga, who twenty minutes later would leave this earthly life, gazed absently at something far out in the sand.

Grip's cell buzzed; it had been going off the whole morning. The first officer and Mickels were both trying to get ahold of him. Grip didn't answer. He'd let temperatures rise. It was easy to imagine: officers asking each other why Radovanović had been taken in, and everyone in MovCon wondering what their colleague would spill. There'd be gut reactions and accusations and what-the-hell-do-we-do's and why won't that fucking Grip answer his phone.

Grip had his own to-do list. After a breakfast of eggs Benedict and fresh fruit at the Kempinski, he drove his rental car to the city jail. "Could I ask a few questions?" After showing his ID, he got a shrug in reply and a guard to accompany him. If the jail in Djibouti looked exactly the way he had imagined a jail in the Horn of Africa, at least Abdoul Ghermat got his own cell. Maybe that was what they did with suspected murderers.

Ghermat was lying on his bunk, but he rose slowly as the cell door opened and Grip was shown in. Other than the bunk and a floor drain, there was nothing. Their eyes didn't meet, but the Djiboutian sat up, with his elbows on his knees and his hands clasped around his neck, as if for protection. Grip said a few words to introduce himself.

Silence. Yet Grip felt sure the man understood. Abdoul Ghermat was wearing his own clothes, which were covered with fresh stains. They looked like blood.

"Can you tell me what happened on the shooting range?"

The same silence as before. The guard who'd accompanied him had also entered the cell. Abdoul moved his leg slightly, with a pained expression.

Grip turned to the guard. "Could you wait outside?" He pointed to his identity card, as if it showed obvious authority. The guard left, and they heard a wooden chair scraping on the concrete floor in the hallway.

"The shooting range?" repeated Grip.

The man moved his leg again. "I did not shoot anyone," he said.

Grip searched in vain for a feeling, an impression, something to grab onto. Who was the man he faced? What was his background, and how could he get him to talk? Would he need to get rough? In the echo of the long narrow space, he got no answers.

"Can you tell me what happened? Where were you standing?"

"I did not shoot anyone." Looking straight ahead, in quiet defiance. One eyebrow swollen, the opposite corner of his mouth skewed. What damage was hidden by his clothing, Grip couldn't know.

"You say that," Grip replied. "But a group of Swedes say that is exactly what you did—you shot someone. And an officer, at that."

The man took a few deep breaths, keeping his hands on his neck. "I did not even have a gun. It was my turn to shoot, I was waiting for my turn. I had no gun." Then Abdoul turned around to face Grip with a look that said the rest. That what he said didn't matter, and that he and the whole world knew it. Then he turned his eyes back to the wall, moving in his slow, tense way.

"The Swedes say," he repeated. "I have a daughter, and the Swedes say."

Grip saw how he touched his bracelet. A moment of clinging to something real, in a cell where nothing was respected. Was it his daughter who'd braided the thin leather strap they hadn't yet taken from him?

Djibouti lived off the Europeans and Americans, who paid large sums to keep their soldiers, warplanes, and ships there. A thumbnail of apparent calm on the world map. Everyone there feared extremists and, most of all, the jihadists with their gaze fixed on the kingdom of heaven. The few Djiboutians who built fantasy palaces for dollars and euros gritted their teeth, seeing the crap that every country surrounding them had to deal with—and worried that their own people would start blowing things up, and then start killing foreign soldiers. So when a Swedish lieutenant fell dead on a shooting range, it was like an amen in church. The incident would lead to feet being beaten with cudgels, and then to car batteries attached to the nipples of the man they all accused. At best, maybe they'd come out with some names, but, more likely, they'd simply sow fear and unbridled hatred.

At least Abdoul Ghermat remained alive. For now.

Grip didn't even say good-bye when he left the cell. Here he had absolutely nothing to gain. Maybe Ghermat would receive a few extra blows to the kidneys in the next round, simply from his having been there.

His legs almost gave out, as Grip walked the last few steps to his rental car. Abdoul Ghermat's gaze had struck a nerve. Grip suddenly felt he'd tossed too many balls in the air over the past twenty-four hours. Was this really the best approach, making everyone his enemy? Was this what a real homicide detective would do? Grip was something else. He made knots magically disappear; he wasn't the guy who untied them.

Grip drove absentmindedly from the outskirts of town toward the roundabouts in the center, with the bad sculptures of dolphins and the garish national monument made of crumbling concrete. He couldn't shake the feeling that he was responsible for the prisoner, that he'd done something wrong. An ugly clock had begun ticking. How long before they'd beat him to death? One thought rose above his churning emotions and his mounting self-loathing: play the game anyway. Impossible to back down, now that the die had been cast. If Grip had no easy way to save Abdoul Ghermat's life, he was still in the lead, and the others would have to chase him. His cell phone rang and rang, while Milan Radovanović licked his lips nervously. The circles cracked. The clock ticked. He had to stay ahead.

Grip exited between roundabouts and stopped in a dusty parking lot. He searched for Didricksen's number in the contacts on his cell. Got his voice mail, as expected, but Grip left a message anyway. "Hey, it's me—in Djibouti. Things heating up here, I need an extra. Send von Hoffsten or Skantz for backup. See ya."

Von Hoffsten and Skantz: people he knew well from his bodyguard days, the ones he knew had also investigated murders.

The HMS *Sveaborg* would remain in port barely another twenty-four hours. Then it was time for another two-week stint hunting pirates.

Grip found the surgeon he'd met over dinner down in the ship's sick bay, with its green walls. The grizzled doc was arguing with a nurse standing next to an open medicine cabinet when Grip came down the hall. They seemed to be talking past each other about something. She was indulgent; he was annoyed. No more than that, before he said, "The police . . . yes," and brightened up, as if this was just the excuse he'd been hoping for. His stubby bangs, the eyes that had peered into surgical openings for nearly half a century: Grip got the sense that the retired surgeon had been important in his day but now faced medical advances that he hadn't fully mastered.

"It'll be fine," the doctor said, already moving away from the nurse, who closed the cabinet with the same indulgent expression as before. "Grip, wasn't it?" he continued, without looking back as he walked down the hallway. He was used to being the one who led the rounds, making the others keep up. "Here, you'll see."

They left the sick bay's well-scrubbed hallways and took a few ladders down to the harder worn areas. Streaks and scratches marked the floors and the bulkheads, and the peeling paint seemed to have sustained heavy impacts. The air blew moist and thick, once they'd left the *Sveaborg*'s air-conditioned compartments. Again Grip sensed he was in a labyrinth; inside the large open bays, their views were blocked by crates and bulky equipment that didn't require protection from moisture and heat. Cans of chemicals, spare parts for machines. Steel beams, planks, and buoys. A track ran above the floor left over from the Cold War, when the ship laid thousands of mines. They zigzagged quickly, the doctor sure of his steps. Grip felt the sweat dripping inside his shirt.

"Here."

At the very back in the stern, beside one of the big mine gates. Like something from a spaceship, rather than an old vessel like this one, and made of stainless steel—a morgue.

The doctor anticipated his question. "Brand-new, brought on board only a week before we cast off from Karlskrona. Mandatory, you know. Admirals and generals expect to lose a few men during a little adventure like this. It's a matter of dignity, and preventing bad smells. Six compartments." He opened one and pulled out the stretcher, which ran on rails.

Goddamn, what a thing to send home, Grip thought, imagining the relatives seeing what he was seeing.

"No, a shot through a skull is never tidy," said the surgeon, sensing his reaction. "Especially when the exit hole is in front."

"But," continued the doctor, "maybe that's not important. The key factor is the difference between left and right."

"Left and right?"

"It's his right eye that's missing, among other things."

"Yes . . ." said Grip, who saw mostly a muddy hole.

"You said you wanted angles, bullet angles," continued the surgeon. "I'd been told that Slunga was shot from behind, and it's true. Diagonally from the back, left, the entry hole is distinct. Here!" He took hold of the back of the head and twisted. "That means the bullet took out the right eye with everything behind, and projected it straight out onto the desert sand."

Grip only humphed in reply.

"To give you a more precise answer, I'll need to do some calculations. We cast off tomorrow, but as soon as we leave the dock, I'll have more time. I made some notes, basically just a surgeon pressing a pen into a bullet hole and then calculating the sine and cosine, but that should be pretty accurate. Also, I took some samples and sent them to the French hospital. They'll email me the answers, so I'll compile everything and send it to you."

"You do the calculations," Grip said. He hadn't taken his eyes off Slunga. As if in a steam room, the humid air of the third deck had started to condense on the cold body. Water pooled in the wide-open wound, and drops had begun to flow in rivulets down over the dead lieutenant's skin.

"What happens to him now?" Grip asked.

"The body will be removed tomorrow before we cast off, then loaded onto a Hercules that will fly him home to Sweden." The surgeon pulled the stained white sheet over the dead man's head and pushed the stretcher back in again.

They were climbing back up through the ship, and the surgeon was talking, but Grip wasn't listening. Impatient. All he'd seen was a dead body, and the clock was ticking. For Abdoul Ghermat and Milan Radovanović. Ideally, he wanted to let Radovanović stew in the loneliness of his soul one more day, but he might be running out of time. Grip was barely half a step behind the doctor, and now he was the one pushing to go faster. Per-Erik Slunga had been shot from behind, that much he knew. Meanwhile Abdoul Ghermat was probably hanging naked and once again losing control of himself, experiencing spasms and involuntary erections as the jolts shot through his body.

Grip had come aboard the *Sveaborg* without running into the men who'd left messages on his phone, and now he walked back down the gangway. Just a short nod to the ship's dock guard and then he disappeared again.

Handing a dollar to the boy who'd guarded the car for him outside the port, he escaped to the other side of the city and found a new boy, and again left him squatting in the shade next to the car. Grip left his jacket in the backseat. He rubbed down his shirt and cast an eye over his surroundings.

Almost two o'clock. Djibouti was, as usual, languishing in the afternoon heat. On the street, there was a little business being done in counterfeit clothing and knickknacks; women walked by, two by two, while the men sat. The Hotel Mirage rose a floor higher than the buildings around it. A family-owned place, not many rooms, even fewer guests. A European with a crew cut in sunglasses and a tight T-shirt sat under a parasol on the shared balcony that ran along the top floor. Still as a lizard on a wall, he looked down at the street, a bored but alert French military police officer.

Grip got up, exchanged a few words, and went into the room.

This time, Milan Radovanović didn't gaze down at the floor but, frightened, stared straight at Grip as soon as the door opened. He sat on the sloppily made bed, with the other MP in an armchair opposite. Frenchman Number Two didn't even nod, but just rose and walked out.

It was cool, and the air-conditioning was on. Good. They could have tormented Radovanović with the heat, but this wasn't about making him suffer, it was about amplifying his solitude. This kind of questioning always worked best without distractions, when basic needs were met: a pleasant temperature, a bed, enough food. Then the loneliness and doubts reigned undisturbed. On the latest tray from the hotel kitchen, the chicken curry sat practically untouched. The French never ate with him, taking their meals while off-duty. In the room, there would be only stillness and silence.

If the treatment hadn't gotten to him, Radovanović would have said something right away, as soon as he saw Grip. But he sat silent, looking self-conscious and caught.

What did he think, that he'd been arrested? Grip wanted to keep up the illusion. Two uniformed MPs had arrived at Radovanović's room at the Sheraton the night before, asked him to come with them immediately, and then paraded him past everyone in the hotel, one in front and one behind. They led him outside to the two other MPs in civilian clothes, who identified themselves and then drove off with him. A kind of ceremony, a ritual—perfect. The French were pragmatic, and they hadn't asked Grip about the legalities. It was simple: there were none. There were no grounds for holding him. If Radovanović wished, he could have just gotten up from bed and left. Yes, the French would probably have given him a rough time if he tried the door handle because they didn't know any better. Grip wouldn't have any other choice than to step aside. But Radovanović wouldn't try anything, because he was completely caught up in the illusion. He'd done what Grip wanted him to do, putting himself under the interrogation lamp. The gaze from the bed didn't show defiance, it only asked anxiously how it could get out of there, when the door was not an option.

At the meeting aboard the *Sveaborg* with the whole MovCon

group, his purpose had only been for them to get to know each other. The group had tasted Grip and spat him out again.

"Mickels's report says you accused Abdoul Ghermat."

Radovanović stopped biting his lower lip and took a nervous breath. There was a little chess game that needed re-creating, one with just a few pieces. It was Radovanović, Abdoul Ghermat, and Fredrik Hansson. These were the three who'd been standing in the back, when everyone else walked up to tape over the holes in the paper targets.

"Hansson says he fired," began Radovanović. "Fredrik Hansson says he saw Ghermat fire the shot."

"And you confirmed it. And now Ghermat is in a cell at the police station just a few blocks away. What do you think they do to a man who murders a foreign soldier here in Djibouti?"

No answer.

"Ask him to finish his chicken curry . . . or attach car batteries to his balls?"

Radovanović rubbed his mouth.

"What were you doing before the bullet hit?"

"I had my gun, and I was changing the magazine."

"And Ghermat?"

"He was behind me. I had my back turned when it happened."

"Did he have a weapon?"

"I'd just loaded one and put it on the ground in front of him."

"At his feet?"

"More or less. Maybe a little in front."

"And then you turned around, to do something with your own weapon?"

"I told you, I was switching the magazine."

"And the others went up to the targets and taped, while Ghermat waited for his turn to shoot."

"Yes, that sounds right."

"Sounds right?"

"That's how it was, I mean."

"So he hadn't yet fired a shot."

"No, it was his turn."

"When I asked you on the *Sveaborg* yesterday, you said he'd already fired at the targets."

"I did?"

"Yes. Definitely."

"Your questions were so confusing."

"Probably, if you have too many versions to keep track of. As you've probably figured out, you're not here by accident."

Radovanović's lie, if he even was aware of it, was insignificant. Yet he seemed to come unhinged.

Grip had already moved closer to the bed. "So, the shot that killed the lieutenant, that was the only shot that Ghermat fired that day."

"He picked it up and fumbled with the weapon, what do I know?"

"Well, what do you know?"

"I heard the shot."

"So did everyone else at the shooting range. But did you actually see Ghermat holding a gun?"

"I told you he was behind me."

"This room seems to have an echo."

"Okay, but the shot was fired, it was." Radovanović was upset. "Slunga is dead, okay? I heard the shot, and Hansson saw Ghermat fire. What more do you want?" His voice had risen to a falsetto, as if he could start crying at any moment.

"The report says you accused Ghermat."

"It was only reasonable."

"You saw nothing and guessed. It was only reasonable . . . ?"

He broke. Radovanović's eyes filled with tears as he gazed at the floor, utterly defenseless. A bubble popped when he opened his mouth. "I switched magazines. I squatted down and switched magazines. I don't know . . . it could have been mine."

Absolute stillness.

"It could have been your . . . you mean, your own shot?"

Radovanović nodded, his face buried in his hands.

Grip drew a mental picture. Radovanović, obviously an insecure young man, squatting and getting his gun ready, while Ghermat, high on khat, stands behind him with a loaded rifle at his feet. Too young, too impressionable, too many small blunders—*bam*. Hansson, that quick-witted bastard, standing alone some distance away, sees everything and thinks fast. Self-preservation mode. Check.

"An accident?"

He nodded again. Radovanović sniffled. "I think so."

The dam was bursting. There was only a trickle; he needed to force open the cracks to get the flood. He needed details, something clear, not just a sniffled "maybe." Grip had to give the impression that he knew more than he did.

"What'd you expect, that guys named Hansson, Jondelius, and Fritzell would protect a Bosnian Serb when the shit hit the fan? Once the lie about Ghermat was exposed?" Grip was running out of time, so he twisted the knife again. "What do you think your buddies have already confessed to me? Why do you think you're sitting here? For God's sake, think about your own version now, and think about it carefully."

Radovanović was at the bottom of his own pit, slumped and shaking silently next to the bed. Grip looked around the room, checking for ropes and knives. The kid was fragile, he'd spill everything now, but not if he killed himself first.

Geometries. Two Swedes and a Djiboutian. Who was standing and who was sitting, who was holding a weapon and who wasn't. Now there were two versions. Grip got impatient again. He couldn't hold Radovanović indefinitely, and Abdoul Ghermat wouldn't survive much longer. Grip opened the door, and a military police officer came over.

"Be careful," he said to the Frenchman. "We don't need any more Swedish corpses right now. All it will take is a broken drinking glass in there, and he'll slit his wrists. Make sure that he writes—writes down his version of what happened. A pad and a pen, can you take care of that?"

Grip headed out, the street even quieter now, as he went back down to his car. The squatting boy, curled up against one of the tires in the shade, got his dollars. Grip started the engine, cranked up the air conditioner, and sat for a minute, sorting out his thoughts. He checked his phone, still on mute, and saw two missed calls from Mickels and the first officer. Then, feeling the air start to cool off, he turned into the street.

He saw a taxi in his rearview mirror do the same, half a block behind him. White with green stripes, like all the taxis here, but this one with a blue flag on its antenna. Hadn't he seen the same one at the taxi stand outside the Kempinski, or was it just that one company put flags on all its antennas? Djibouti swarmed with taxis. He dropped the thought.

Grip wanted to get ahold of Fredrik Hansson quickly. Not many places to look: aboard the *Sveaborg*, in the Swedish offices on the French base, and of course first, at the hotel.

Direct hit. Grip found Hansson at the Sheraton, where they served drinks from the bar in the lobby, at low round tables. Early afternoon, a mix of uniforms who'd decided they were done for the day, beer glasses, a low murmur above black marble floors. Grip studied Hansson for a while at a distance. Relaxed and loose, alone with a few Germans he seemed to have met before. He gave them directions on a map, drew some lines. Then he caught sight of Grip, who nodded: Get over here! Hansson took a sip of beer before he stood up. He was in no hurry, without being flippant.

"Yes?"

"A quick question. Did you see Abdoul Ghermat fire the shot?"

Hansson let a few seconds pass, without giving the impression he needed time to think. He smiled and didn't even try to hide his own irony. "Yes, as clear as you're standing there."

Then there was silence.

"Anything else?"

"No, nothing at all," said Grip.

"I think Mickels wants to get ahold of you." He turned and walked back toward the Germans.

Hansson hadn't asked what had happened to Radovanović, what Grip was doing, or what would happen next. Grip stood there, watching Hansson sit down and slowly drink his beer, not even glancing over his shoulder. The man had no need to know, Grip thought, annoyed. Unflappable, he'd made the cold calculation that no matter what Radovanović had said, Hansson would be able to push his own version. Grip had seen it in his eyes, in the timing of his response. He didn't even care that he'd given away the real answer—that Abdoul Ghermat hadn't even fired. Hansson wouldn't be affected in the slightest, while Radovanović was willing to confess to everything.

Yet another hotel lobby, but now the roles were reversed. Mickels, expecting him at the Kempinski, locked his eyes on Grip the moment he got inside the door and started barking at him across the lobby. Every other sentence started with: "What the hell do you . . ." Most of what he said was absolutely true. Grip was rude, headstrong, and disrespectful of military rank, "which even a freaking maniac like you has to honor." The officer's ruddy face blazed with anger. The time for excuses had passed, so now he had to stand and take it. Then came a tirade about how things should be done: "Tomorrow the *Sveaborg* goes back out to sea . . . it would be best if you . . . it would be expected for you . . ." Grip had burned Mickels, and he felt bad about that.

But in his ramblings, he ignored the fact that if Grip had followed protocol, kept the captain informed, "relied" on people, and absorbed everything "that was already clearly documented," then Abdoul Ghermat would still be the one who shot Per-Erik Slunga.

All those formalities were just for show. Mickels was basically a good guy, but an MP's job wasn't so much about defending the truth as it was about keeping the machinery running. The captain wanted nothing more, and people like Hansson counted on that. Grip knew it, and that's how things had been with the security police, and among the princes and princesses at the royal court, and it was just as true among the ships and shooting ranges in Djibouti.

"You goddamn ungrateful . . ."

Grip let the insults slide and just tried to keep track of the essentials.

Which for him meant the question of what Mickels actually did or didn't keep track of.

Mickels went on and on about Radovanović. "What the hell have you done?" He raised his voice even more when he couldn't quite make his case. Mickels wasn't the cool prosecutor kind, with all the right legal terms; he was more of a bumbler. Mickels was the one who made sure people drove back sober, steered them away from the wrong kinds of brothels, and kept sailors and soldiers out of the hands of the local police. Grip understood that this time, he'd been forced to ask for outside help.

"The legal staff will return . . ."

He meant the lawyers at military headquarters; they would apparently come tell Grip what he could and couldn't do with suspects. Grip already knew. He assumed that the lawyers at headquarters were like lawyers in general: precise and very slow. So, while Mickels waited for the fancy formulations he couldn't come up with himself, Grip would get a few days to milk the Bosnian Serb for details. Mickels wouldn't call his bluff on Radovanović. Mickels still believed that Ghermat had fired the shot. Mickels would keep track of all the papers that said exactly that. And when Grip asked about the six automatic rifles from the shooting range, he replied, "Damn right, I still keep them in my safe."

Tommy Mickels was everyone's useful idiot. Even Grip's.

The military police officer swore one last time and left the Kempinski.

16

TRANSCRIPT OF RECORDED PHONE CALL, TS 233:6754

Recording requestor: Bureau Director Thor Didricksen

TOP SECRET UNDER CHAPTER 2, SECTION 2 OF THE SECRECY ACT (1980:100)
OF HIGHEST IMPORTANCE TO NATIONAL SECURITY

Persons present: Thor Didricksen (TD) and police officer
Ernst Grip (EG)

EG: Good evening, Boss.

TD: Good evening. You're an hour or so ahead, so I gather
it's after midnight there. Is this the only time the air could be
called pleasant?

EG: Something like that.

TD: I see you're not interested in small talk. So, what's
happening with the investigation?

EG: Slow-going.

TD: I hear your hesitation. Is the military stonewalling?

EG: They have their machinery, their own way of doing
things. They want this over and done with.

TD: Who wouldn't? I did get your message.

EG: Yes, I need backup. I don't have enough time to do things
right.

TD: Have you made yourself unpopular with the military?

EG: That too. I suggested that you send von Hoffsten or Skantz.

TD: I heard you.

EG: So when will one of them arrive?

TD: You need someone who understands uniforms, their way of seeing the world.

EG: Von Hoffsten was in the reserves.

TD: More than ten years ago, yes. He was probably the officer in charge of cocktails.

EG: No shortage of those. But I . . .

TD: Don't worry, you'll get someone, as soon as I figure out who's right for the job. But first I want to hear more about the military. What are they withholding?

EG: Not withholding, exactly. More that they're satisfied with their own version of things, as they've already written it.

TD: A shooting accident. One person has been charged, right?

EG: Yes, a Djiboutian. The problem is, he didn't do it.

TD: Really.

EG: The thing is that . . .

TD: I can do without the details. That's why you're there, not me. I trust your judgment.

EG: Got it, Boss.

TD: But this Djiboutian remains a problem?

EG: Right, he was accused by our Swedish soldiers. Now the local authorities think they have a terrorist on their hands, one who murders foreign officers. I've visited the man in jail. I don't think he'll last much longer.

TD: So you want him released. Why?

EG: The prettiest explanation is that, well, he's innocent.

TD: I appreciate your candor. But give me the real reasons.

EG: It was us—Sweden—who put him in jail. A tabloid journalist could take that story and run with it.

TD: You mean our government gets nervous when the words *prison*, *Horn of Africa*, and *journalist* appear in the same sentence. Yes, you're right, and if we can we should fix this.

But tell me, why are you so sentimental about a beat-up Djiboutian?

EG: His name, by the way, is Abdoul Ghermat. And if he gets released, I think the momentum will help my investigation.

TD: You mean, certain people down there will get nervous?

EG: Yes, Boss. The ones in Swedish uniforms.

TD: The military—don't ever surrender to their smugness. Anything else?

EG: Not for the moment, Boss.

TD: I'll speak to the foreign minister as soon as possible. I know that time is of the essence here, but that's all I can promise.

EG: I think it's the government that will be scrambling—not me—if Abdoul Ghermat doesn't get released.

TD: I'll pretend I didn't hear that. Good night.

17

At some point after the funeral, when most of Ben had been swept away like a sandcastle hit by a wave, Grip realized that he had insomnia. He imagined it would go away when he returned to Stockholm and went back to work. But only after he got home did the true grief hit, and one night he was caught off guard by his own heaving sobs. For half an hour they went on, as he stood completely alone, in the shadows on a deserted street. He'd seen where his life really stood, how with the distance, other kinds of holes had opened up.

One thing he never guessed would disappear so quickly: friends. Their mutual acquaintances had in fact been mostly Ben's. It was in New York that they'd had their life together, Grip being the one who came and went. But Ben was always there; he was the anchor. During the final year, their closest friends helped out when Grip had to return to Stockholm and his job. From some unthinking comments, he gathered that a rift had opened; they couldn't understand why they were expected to care for a vomiting and trembling Ben, while Grip was off escorting a Swedish princess in London. The better off the friends were, the less they seemed to recognize that someone actually had to earn money to pay for what Ben needed. Grip realized that some saw him as cowardly and irresponsible.

Despite all the dinners and trips they'd shared over the years, after the funeral it all dwindled down to a few dutiful emails. It was Ben who'd been the social genius—the one who'd snag a case of champagne from some patron that they'd uncork at an after-party in his kitchen, the one who could get a table for eight at an impossible restaurant half an hour after he got the whim. In all that, Grip was just his lover from Stockholm. That's what the others saw. When, after closing time at the gallery one Friday, they sat at a long table on the wide-plank floor, and Ben claimed the center of attention as they raised glasses with one of his long, subtle monologues, they didn't perceive the true closeness. They didn't see Grip's comforting embraces later that night, or hear their completely open and soul-baring talks. They didn't realize that Grip was the only one who could make the fear of dying—always lurking behind Ben's crooked smile—fade away for a few hours.

Grip hadn't been back to New York since the funeral. It had been nearly a year. And no one had come to visit him in Stockholm.

He'd become a person who defined himself by what was missing. But finally he realized there was an emptiness needing to be filled, and it occurred to him that he should do something about his loneliness. Have someone to talk to, share things with, touch. He'd been faithful to Ben through it all, when mortal illness brought another kind of closeness. But now, a year later, he was human again—yes, he could look at people and allow the thought. Ben was gay, had been all his life. But Grip had fallen in love with a certain type, that was the best way to describe how he understood himself. What mattered wasn't whether it was a man or a woman, but that the person conveyed something both seductive and incomplete. So that, if you took a sharp look, you saw the contradictions along with the fantasies. Seemingly self-aware, yet not entirely conscious of the scent they gave off. Ben didn't have rock-star looks, yet he could conjure up entire universes. People saw it; Grip saw it. And if they had created something together, he and Ben—it was their very own world. Others could see parts of it, even believe that they were near its center, but they'd never come close to imagining the whole.

Grip had always liked women, and had been with several men, but he'd only ever been in love with Ben. And now, barely a year later: insomnia, the walls at home pressing in on him, the sense that he'd betrayed Ben by not keeping the old feelings alive. He detested the lies cultivated by Ben's family in Houston, but now he began to see his own fabrications more clearly. How he'd depended on Ben for the good things in life. He saw how he'd made his own choices. That he had cut himself off, by not allowing himself to be with anyone else. This perfection that he'd had with Ben, was it really so perfect? And if it was, did the laws of nature say you could only feel this with one person, and only for a few years over a lifetime?

These thoughts had freed Grip from grief. But he still had insomnia.

Alone in his hotel room, late at night. Nothing to do, no one to call, not even an appointment to keep the next day. In his solitude, one thought kept turning around and around in his head: if anything happened to him here in Djibouti, if he suddenly just disappeared, who would look for him? Who would even miss him? Grip gave up on trying to fall asleep. Instead, he headed to the Kempinski's nightclub. To take the edge off, change the scenery.

The nightclub was on the top floor, half under the roof, the rest on terraces under the stars. He ordered a rum on the rocks, just because it felt right. A band played restrained cocktail reggae, the singer and the bass player tossing their long dreadlocks. Otherwise, hair was carefully styled at the Kempinski's pretend-savanna, for those who wanted to hunt, using cash and credit cards as weapons. The usual predators stalked: Chinese in suits, Russians with gold chains, and high-ranking officers disguised in civilian clothes. But there was only one kind of prey. Carefully chosen women from the Horn of Africa, dressed up and available, right there in the nightclub. Bare skin and low cuts that were a world away from the hijabs of Djibouti's mosques. The girls drew hungry glances wherever they passed. Still, the atmosphere was restrained, more *Vogue* than Amsterdam.

Laughter and warm smiles, nods of recognition and little inviting waves, fruit drinks, one for her and one more for me—the Russians drank only clear liquor from small glasses. Grip had another rum, at his end of the bar.

"Hi, I'm Nadifa." Grip said nothing, just gave a quick smile. She understood, moved on. The band played a slow cover of "Red Red Wine."

The spell was broken by a handful of loud Germans on the terrace. They looked like pilots. One of them thought he knew exactly what services were offered and what they cost. A burst of raw laughter, some bargaining, a wolf whistle to one of the girls. A bouncer with a bull neck took one firmly by the elbow, and after some brief instructions, they dropped their crude slang for the proper etiquette.

"Hi, I'm Penona."

Grip felt that he radiated loneliness. She put her hand on his.

Grip stood up and walked away.

He rode the elevator down, still restless. There was a piano bar behind glass walls by the pool. Quieter, lighter, no bad-ass bouncer, just a lonely old bartender and the woman at the piano. There was no heat in the air, and no hotel guests with moist, wandering eyes. "Moon River." Grip sat down and ordered a beer but left it untouched. He felt invisible and had a moment of peace, listening to the murmuring and the music. The buzz in his head died down, as all his thoughts flowed together, out and away.

The woman at the piano smiled. Not a fake nightclub smile, but just because their eyes had met. Nothing more. He was still invisible, and the calm reigned. His gaze caught little impressions—the way someone lifted his glass, a well-groomed beard, a hand gesture—but always returned to the piano. She wore her hair in a high ponytail, with a hint of something European, though she looked mostly Horn of Africa. Sometimes she let slip a few notes from a classical piece, while she decided on the next song. Sometimes she sang too. Although some guests sat by the piano, a few leaned forward to make requests. Red dress, bare shoulders, nothing more revealed than that.

After breakfast the next day, Grip went down to the harbor. From a distance he watched the HMS *Sveaborg* cast off and pull away. Already, the helicopter rose from the deck and shrank to a dot, drawn to something urgent beyond the horizon. For almost two weeks the *Sveaborg* would be out at sea, searching and boarding suspicious vessels in the hunt for pirates, before she came back again. Grip stood there and let the cannons, cranes, masts, and rafts merge until they became just the gray silhouette of a warship. Barely two weeks. *Tick, tock.*

Again, Grip saw a taxi with a blue flag in the traffic behind him as he left the port. He'd seen the flag parked outside the Kempinski earlier that morning. He took an extra turn in the road along the bay, went through a few roundabouts, came back in the opposite lane. No flag. Enough to convince him that the taxi with the blue flag wasn't following him. It was just a phantom, and he'd enough of those already. He continued on as planned to the Hotel Mirage.

Radovanović was sitting on the bed, the sun hot despite the closed curtains, and on the table sat another meal that only fed the flies. The French military police pointed to some papers and left the room.

It was a short, handwritten confession. Grip sat down on a chair. In blue ink, he absolved Ghermat of guilt and took responsibility for everything himself. But he gave no details, in his broken Swedish. He had the handwriting of a child. Ernst Grip should have pressed him to make the picture clearer—exactly where, exactly when, exactly how—but hesitated. The man on the bed was broken, his eyes redder every time Grip glared at him. Why push him? An accidental discharge wasn't murder, it was an accident.

"What will happen to Abdoul Ghermat now?" Radovanović said quietly.

"I don't even know if he's alive," said Grip sincerely. His own feelings of guilt took hold. He was getting impatient; why was he wasting his time here? "Please eat" was what came out, as his thoughts headed off in other directions—to the useful idiots and Hansson.

"Eat!" Grip took the papers and left. The two Frenchmen looked unshaven, posted on the walkway outside. "Make sure you take care of him for a few more days," Grip told them. "Then it will be over."

On an impulse, Grip drove to the jail, showed his ID card, pointed to his passport, signed the page, spat out the formulas, but wasn't admitted. "Ghermat?" Wall of silence. As if they didn't understand a word he said; as if they had no idea that a man was being held behind the whitewashed walls.

"Is Abdoul Ghermat still alive?" The answer was a wave that told him to get lost, while the other hand held tighter to the smooth-worn automatic rifle.

The sun stood at its zenith. The khat stalls had opened along the main routes, while street life everywhere else dwindled in the heat. Grip drove to the French base, out to the loading zone for transport planes. He found the all-white barracks where MovCon did its work in the daytime, opened the door without knocking, and stepped inside. An air-conditioned sanctuary. An island in a world of heat, exhaustion, and sand.

There they sat, the four who were left. The original MovCon had shrunk, now that there was one dead and one kidnapped. The room had two beat-up couches around a table, packing lists, schedules and orders taped to the walls, a small desk, stacks of bottled water.

"I'd love some water," said Grip, walking up to the little fridge. He got not a word in reply, only four pairs of eyes following him. Two and two, they sat on the couches, looking to kill an afternoon.

Grip drank a few sips. "Ah . . ." He rolled the fogged-up bottle against his forehead. Straightened up. "Yeah yeah, Radovanović." A sip. "He's confessed now, says it was an accidental discharge from his own gun that got Slunga."

To three of the dead lieutenant's former colleagues, this obviously came as a surprise. Two of them glanced at Hansson. Fritzell, the powerfully built one, leaned forward. "That sounds weird." He was puzzled, didn't understand at all, and was about to ask something when Hansson jumped in.

"I saw what I saw. The rest of you were up by the targets."

"That sounds about right, Fredrik Hansson," said Grip. "Something you saw for sure."

Grip put down the half-empty bottle on the edge of the desk. "Thanks for the water." And then he left.

Their reactions inside that barracks were worth more than Rado-vanović's confession. He stood by the car for a moment and looked out over the airport. A big four-engine transport plane had just started up, and on the far side, on the American half of the field, an unmanned drone taxied out slowly, like a huge sinister insect.

Grip slept away the rest of the afternoon in his room. He woke up after sunset, checked the phone. No missed calls, no texts, no emails. The silence amplified the feeling that time was slipping through his fingers, and he waited impatiently. After dinner, he put on a freshly ironed shirt, got it sweaty just walking to the beach and back, and then headed to the piano bar.

Grip had been thirsty, his mouth almost sticky, the whole day. "Rum with lime, and don't skimp on the juice," he said to the bar-tender, and then sat down on a bar stool facing the grand piano.

He sat near, watching her hands and the keys. Her ponytail was a little lower today, and she was dressed in cool blue. As night fell, she played distracted classical passages between the bar standards. His eyes stared at a small mole on her shoulder, a black pinprick on the dark skin. Something to hold on to while his other thoughts drifted. He was surprised to find that his shirt felt dry again. His drink had been replaced with a new one and half emptied again. An hour or so must have gone by. A drunk Chinese man came up to her with a request. The man wrestled with English, tried to say something that sounded like Gershwin. Holding a drink, he switched hands, she nodded, he patted her on the shoulder with his hand wet from the steamed-up glass. Only when the Chinese man turned away did she dry herself off discreetly with a napkin. Grip didn't know much Gershwin, but the song that followed definitely wasn't that. It was Piaf. She sang in French.

A tingle in his pocket, as his cell phone rang on mute. Grip got up and walked out to the lobby.

The call was from Frères, the French colonel.

"Good evening. I know it's late, but I think this may be of interest.

Your country's foreign ministry has been involved, and we have of course done what we could. Abdoul Ghermat was released by the Djiboutian authorities an hour ago. Cleared of all charges."

"How is he?"

"Let's just say that he's alive. His family came and picked him up, and my guess is that he'll be fine." Grip was quiet. Frères continued: "My men . . ."

"Only a few more days."

"I was going to say that they're yours for as long as you need them."

Grip returned to his bar stool, putting his cell phone back in his pants pocket as he sat down.

"Good news?" she asked, running her fingers over the keys before the next song.

"For a worried family, I'm sure it was," he said.

"Someone born?"

"No, someone permitted to stay alive."

"What do you want to hear?"

"More of that," he replied, with a gesture toward her hands.

"Debussy, no, not here. But Gershwin is a possibility."

"I don't know any Gershwin."

"Of course you do." She started playing, the notes immediately familiar.

"'Rhapsody in Blue,'" she said, without looking up at him.

When Grip finally got up, he glanced at a framed photo hanging outside the piano bar. The nighttime pianist, a portrait in black and white. With the small dot on her shoulder. Ayanna was her name, that was all the information it gave.

Grip walked through the lobby, then, on a whim, went out for some fresh air by the entrance. He stood there for a moment, seeing the lights of the city between the palm trees, the drivers hanging out by their taxis, and a few smaller groups farther away. He turned around, leaving the night sounds and the quiet behind him, and felt, for an instant, someone's eyes following him up the steps and back inside.

When he opened the door to his room, he found an envelope on the mat.

Inside was a handwritten note in English: *Mr. Lieutenant Slunga's death was not an unfortunate accident. Too many people liked the money.*

18

"They still want ten million," said Carl-Adam, when he got back to the room.

"What does it matter, whether it's twenty, fifty, or a hundred million?" said Jenny. "What matters, Carl, is who Darwiish is communicating with. About us being missing. Who is he talking to, back home?"

Carl-Adam collapsed on the cot, in what had become his corner. Every second or third day, they pulled him into the outer room, where Darwiish threatened and yelled. Darwiish was obviously frustrated. Carl-Adam had been beaten a few times, but that scared Jenny and the children more than it did him. To Carl-Adam, the waiting before they came for him was the worst part. Then, he was like a frightened animal. Carl-Adam would fall fast asleep after a beating from Darwiish, even when Darwiish was at his worst. As if the rifle butting came as a relief. And he was a changed man. He rarely spoke and found it hard to relax around the children. The only topic he ever raised with Jenny was the ransom, as he tried over and over again to find a strategy for dealing with Darwiish. He seemed unable to care about anything else—as if his survival instinct came down to a single hope: that a clever idea could transform their house on the sand into a place where they could bargain on equal terms.

"He's negotiating with the Foreign Ministry," said Carl-Adam, glancing toward the bucket of water.

"Did he say that?"

"It makes sense."

"Does Sweden ever negotiate with kidnappers and pirates?"

Carl-Adam took a while to answer. "We're not just anyone. Our family, our friends, of course they're pushing. Obviously they'll try to save our goddamn lives."

"Our friends, you say. What do you usually do, if you haven't heard from people in a few weeks? Call the police? And your parents . . . ," Jenny silenced herself; she was tired. "Sorry."

"Darwiish is under pressure," he said in an attempt to smooth things over. "We need to pressure him back."

Jenny got the feeling that he'd started to see his beatings as little victories. That he scored points, that Darwiish lost, and that he himself emerged stronger. But no one was getting stronger, and Carl-Adams's imaginary victories only shielded him from thinking about their real needs. Jenny closed her eyes and said, "Water, Carl-Adam. That's what we need." She took a deep breath.

"And Sebastian has to get his meds."

Something had always been a little off about Carl-Adams's son. Late to talk, late to walk, upset by tiny problems. "You know, at six months, Milla could already . . ."—Jenny's mother-in-law made statistical comparisons to all the cousins, knowing exactly how to turn the knife. At birthday parties in the Scandinavian Capital circle, he was always the one who smashed his cake, or screamed. No one really understood when Sebastian spoke. Faced with Aryan imperfection, they brought in doctors and second opinions in private clinics. He had educators and special programs in talking and playing, an eight-hundred-kronor-an-hour this, and a thousand-kronor-an-hour that. The Filipina nanny was quickly exchanged for a Swedish one with a degree.

Sebastian did catch up, almost, enough for it to work. They no longer needed to make lame excuses for avoiding parties.

Until he was almost five. Sometimes, when he was really tired, he'd be almost unreachable for a while. "Hey, Sebastian!" Someone would put a loving hand on his shoulder but still get no reaction. Blank, for long seconds, and then release. Jenny didn't think much about it. There was no yelling or screaming, and now they always understood what he said. But sometimes he just sat quietly.

A certain kind of silence can be telling.

One afternoon, they heard a little crash, while Sebastian was playing with Legos on a coffee table upstairs. Something he'd built had fallen on the floor. It happened all the time. The sound of Lego pieces falling was always followed by a reaction, some kind of movement. One floor below, Jenny unconsciously noticed something missing.

She was absorbed in a newspaper, but on autopilot she said: "Sebastian." She went back to her article. Then, a little louder, "Sebastian?" She wasn't even thinking that something was wrong. There was just a vague feeling, hardly even ominous.

"Do you want something? Mommy's getting hungry." She put down the paper, stood up. "Sebastian." Still, she was calm. Thick soft carpet on the stairs all the way up. Down the hallway, past the paintings. Into the TV room.

The human eye is highly sensitive to detecting motion, perceived as a break in an expected pattern. The wide white sofa, the table behind it, only half visible to her, the Legos scattered everywhere. But that she barely noticed; it belonged to the familiar, the expected. It was the movement she saw. The tiny foot sticking out on the floor between the couch and the table. How it twitched. In uncontrolled spasms.

She leapt and threw herself down, not even calling his name.

Without the couch to shield her, now all she saw was blood and his seizures. In her desperate embrace, she felt his little body twitching in her arms, against her chest. They didn't stop. She broke into sobs.

An eternity.

Then the ambulance arrived, with the soothing touch and big medical bags. Sebastian was breathing as they carried him out on a stretcher.

"He bit his tongue, that's all. It's over now."

They went to the emergency room. Not until an hour after Jenny had called from the hospital did she hear back from Carl-Adam. "Miriam said you wanted something?"

Then came two months in limbo. MRIs, EEGs, a lot of white coats at the Karolinska Institute. Carl-Adam annoyed them by trying to impose his own diagnoses. He was in an almost manic state of work. Scandinavian Capital was buying a health-care group, and he had to get the answers to everything; it all spilled over. Jenny tried to distract herself, waiting for the results: she cooked dinners and hired a landscape architect to draw up plans for the backyard. They would receive the results on a Thursday, they'd had the date set for two weeks. That same morning, Carl-Adam called from a taxi on the way to Arlanda: "Zurich. You'll need to handle this one. I have to go."

She sat alone with the doctor for an hour. She didn't raise her own concerns or ask any questions; she only listened. A woman physician who smiled the way they all do when trying but failing to find compassion within the harsh objectivity.

The next day, the phone rang twice—Carl-Adam—but she didn't answer. That evening, she tucked Alexandra and Sebastian in, and went back to their rooms a little later, to make sure they'd fallen asleep. She tried to watch a movie, then turned off the TV and listened to the house go quiet, without glancing at the clock. She sat in the kitchen, looked around, and felt like a stranger in her own home. All that extravagance—the cast-iron gas range with its brass fixtures, and the sink made from a single piece of Italian marble, transported across Europe as the only cargo on a flatbed truck. A carpenter in Värmland had carved flowers into all the cabinet doors, a different one on each. He'd identified every flower when he came to install them, and described what each one symbolized. She didn't remember. Life was happening somewhere else.

She waited.

Then she heard a taxi roll across the gravel and stood up.

The front door closed. He was fumbling with something. She was waiting for him. The single dimmed light left the kitchen in shadow. He still had his overcoat on when he came in and held out the little oblong package.

She stretched out her hand. She tried but couldn't do it. She brought her hand to her mouth, sat down on a chair, and couldn't look at him.

"I had to," he said.

She cleared her throat. "Yesterday, at the doctor's." Her voice broke, she took a deep breath. "Sebastian has severe epilepsy."

He stopped looking at her. "Well, we suspected as much." Then there was the need to explain himself again. "It couldn't wait, I had to get the endorsements. If this deal goes through, it means fifteen million kronor for me alone. For us."

She said nothing.

"Jenny, I had to."

She shrugged. "The doctor says she's a hundred percent certain. He'll need to take powerful drugs for his entire life."

"You got the prescriptions, I guess."

"Of course. For all kinds of things, but nothing that will cost close to fifteen million."

"You don't have to be mean," he said.

"I'm not being mean, just honest. There are a lot of people who need you, I know that. But Sebastian's medications can only suppress the symptoms, and there's no guarantee. No one knows now how effective they'll be. Yesterday I was sitting opposite a doctor who calmly told me that at any moment, our son could have a seizure that's too much for him. Yes, one that kills him. And when that happens, he'll be in my arms, while you'll be sitting at a meeting in London or Geneva." Jenny was calmer now. "I won't put up with this." She glanced at the unopened package he put down on the bar, then turned back to him. "Do you understand what I'm saying?"

Carl-Adam just stood quietly. He reached for the package and left the kitchen. The house was as quiet as before the taxi rolled across the gravel. You could barely hear the sound of his steps going up the stairs. She'd already decided to sleep downstairs in a guest room.

The next morning, it was as if nothing had happened. All four of them ate breakfast together. It was a regular Saturday: a little playing outside, a bit of don't-bother-Daddy-in-his-study, then driving

Alexandra to a birthday party. That evening, Jenny and Carl-Adam were invited to a dinner party. They hadn't said much to each other during the day, and when Jenny brought it up casually and somewhat late, he said that he'd already called to cancel.

The children fell asleep.

She came to him in his study. He had two things to say. That he no longer felt anything, and that he wanted out.

But he wasn't talking about the marriage. He was talking about the path that his father, himself, and all the others had mapped out for him. It was over.

Getting Carl-Adam to say what he wanted to do instead was like trying to get a blind person to describe his favorite color. He simply couldn't. Finally, Jenny started talking about happiness. She herself didn't believe in it, not as an eternal state—it was a fiction, like God. Something that drove your hopes and desires. Maybe you could find a little along the way, little glimpses of both happiness and God. When Carl-Adam couldn't come up with anything he wanted to do, she asked what made him happy. He said that he still loved her. She believed him, but it was a cheap evasion, a shot that missed the goal. Because love clearly wasn't enough. He had to be pushed off his safe and narrow path. So she got angry and made it clear that love couldn't be the only thing that mattered, and also confessed her true feelings about the bracelets from Zurich. Once the air was cleared, she asked when he'd last felt happy. He managed to look beyond the clichés and say that it was two summers ago. When they'd gone out sailing not just for a few days, but stayed out for two full weeks. Jenny remembered it well.

It had begun there. The path that had led them to the ocean.

That evening in the study ended with the easy decision that he'd resign from Scandinavian Capital—the decision made even before she came into the room. The rest unfolded over the next evenings. While the children were asleep, they flipped through *Yachting World*, and she showed him the most traveled routes. If Carl-Adam were to leave, it would be easiest to do something grandiose. He—King

Carl—would still get to amaze. Circumnavigation. Sure, she was sneaky, sure she was conspiring against an easy target, but what did it matter? If Jenny had her dramatic side, she wasn't foolhardy about money.

"Sure, you'll still be gone a lot, but on the trip we can all be together, all the time." There was no reason to cut ties with Scandinavian Capital until the deal with the medical group had gone through.

Jenny knew exactly what a real boat would cost, if you wanted to sail around the world in style. She was from the west coast of Sweden, and there were only two choices: Najad or Hallberg-Rassy. With Carl-Adams's bonus, the choice was simple. But ordering a boat and waiting for it to be built would take too long; the die was cast, and they wanted to leave as soon as possible. Through an old contact, Jenny found a German willing to sell them his sixty-two-foot Hallberg-Rassy. A couple of months in dry dock, and the *Mary-Ann* wasn't just like new, she was state-of-the-art. She let Carl-Adam have the limelight, standing at the helm in a few sailing magazines.

They kept the house but sold and spent everything else. They had no safety net. Parents swore: "Are you really . . . ?" unable to keep from making comments. Sebastian had some minor seizures at the beginning, but they'd fine-tuned his medication. For Alexandra, there'd be home schooling on board via the Internet, and eventually the same for Sebastian. Two and a half years at sea—so they'd told the newspapers and their friends. People could follow along through their blog.

Finally that weekend in Sandhamn, with pink champagne, *chin chin*, and *kaboom*—first the Baltic Sea, then Kiel Canal to the North Sea. There they met their first gale.

As the *MaryAnn*'s bow hit a wave, and the wind sent the salty foam arcing over the deck, it splashed over her face like rain. There was nothing more refreshing, and she found herself laughing straight into the wind. She wore her old silver bracelet on the boat; all her other jewelry had been sold.

Now she sat with the desert around them, and what had happened to the bracelet was far from her mind. Under the strain, the weakest link started to break: their son had started to have seizures again.

Jenny gestured toward Sebastian, but Carl-Adam simply repeated what he always said: "Let's try to keep him cool, and we'll give him a little more water later." The first attack had been minor, the next one more serious. They were living in a sauna, and Jenny, who had a constant headache, couldn't cut back any more on her own ration. She feared that she'd pass out and then be unable to protect the children. She still followed them when they went to the toilet, and she counted the few tablets they'd brought with them from the boat for Sebastian. They'd run out of one of his medications, and of the second, there was only a week's worth left in the bottle.

19

Ernst Grip received a short email from Didricksen. Help was on the way. He was given a flight number and a name: Simon Stark.

Shit, a complete noob. The guy had just joined the bodyguard detail, and Grip had only worked with him once or twice. He'd done a couple of routine jobs for the royal family, but beyond that, Grip had barely exchanged three words with him. He had nothing special against Simon Stark, but that was the problem: the guy was a blank slate. Grip didn't know whether he'd be getting a deadbeat or a dynamo.

Didricksen must have known that his choice wouldn't make Grip happy. In his email, he closed with a comment that was unlike him, something probably meant to justify his decision: *Good guy, understands uniforms. But don't ask him to run errands, he can't.* Grip had no idea what it meant.

Simon Stark landed in the afternoon. Grip was waiting in the small arrival hall, just as Mickels had done before. He carried a big shapeless duffel in one hand, and he looked pasty from the long flight and the wall of heat.

"Welcome. The car is right outside."

Stark had wavy blond hair and the short, stocky build of a welterweight boxer. His hair was a little long for Grip's taste, but he was handsome. And there was something restless about him. His cheek muscles bulged like plums—he must grind his teeth in his sleep, Grip thought. One shirt pocket looked like a miniature office, holding his passport, a stack of notes, and a pen.

They'd only been driving for a minute, and the car had just begun to cool off, when Stark rubbed his face as if he'd just woken up in the morning and said: "Right. So I was up with this Didricksen yesterday, and he said you'd annoyed everyone in the military down here."

Grip laughed. "He told you that, huh. What else did he say?"

"Well, not much more. That you needed my help. This is about the lieutenant, right, the one who was on the news about a week ago?"

"Exactly, that one." Grip waited a few seconds. "Didricksen, was that the first time you'd gone up to see him?"

"I'd never laid eyes on him before."

"And how long did you say you've been with our bodyguard detachment?"

"I didn't say, but three months."

"And how long total, as a police officer?"

Simon Stark turned and looked at Grip. "It wasn't my idea to come here. But if you really want to know, I've been on the police force for a year and a half." He leaned back again. "When I left the military, I was a newly appointed captain in the army."

"Okay, great. Just so you know, out here, we don't call Didricksen by name. He's just the Boss."

Police—Säpo—bodyguards: an ascent that took little more than a year. Possibly a record. Someone probably had their eyes on Simon Stark, and he didn't even realize it himself. Grip had seen the way Didricksen singled out and stole officers for the bodyguard detachment, which could spare people for his improvised missions. He wouldn't be tearing someone away from a high-level investigation, only replacing a guy who herded ministers with a yawn, wearing sunglasses and an earpiece. No fucking way Didricksen had just mumbled something about angry soldiers and tossed Stark a plane ticket with a few instructions. Grip needed help, but in return the Boss wanted total control, now that the foreign minister had his eye on Abdoul Ghermat, and some general had come from headquarters complaining about Grip's rampage.

Grip already assumed that the Boss recorded and saved their

phone calls. Now he'd probably be sent reports as well, and it would all be done behind Grip's back. That was the way things worked. If von Hoffsten or Skantz had come down, they would have mostly followed Didricksen's instructions but still done what Grip wanted. Didricksen knew that, so instead he'd sent Simon Stark, a new guy who'd trade total loyalty for a career move and some adventure. Grip couldn't object; he'd been exactly like that himself. And he knew that for Didricksen, Grip himself was still the man whose ass was on the line, the one expected to make things happen. His confidence wasn't shaken; Didricksen just wanted more information. That's how it was, and that was Didricksen's personality. Simon Stark was as much Grip's badly needed backup as he was the microphone in the room. He was an added variable in the equation, and also, for Grip, a reminder to watch his back. They'd left the downtown and were driving along the coast up to the Kempinski.

"The Boss said that I wasn't supposed to use you to run errands," Grip said, after a moment of silence.

"Didn't he say, to run in general?"

"Maybe, but what would that mean?"

"Run, literally."

"I'm not exactly tracking your exercise routine, so why would the Boss mention such a thing? Are you lazy or something?"

"I can't run. I can barely jog. My legs are shot to hell."

"But you made the bodyguard unit?"

"I told them about it, when they asked me to apply for the job."

Didricksen, Grip thought. He would give a guy in a wheelchair the job, if he thought he offered something valuable.

"An accident," Stark explained. He held his chin in his hand and leaned his elbow against the side, as if tired of the question that always came up. "A few years ago, before I joined the police force."

As they passed through the gates of the Kempinski, he lightened up and whistled.

"Oh yes," said Grip, "this is where we live. *One Thousand and One Nights.*"

Simon Stark checked in, took a while to get settled in and shower after his trip, and then met Grip in his room for a crash course on Djibouti. Stark was thrown right in: Slunga at the shooting range, the Djiboutians high on khat, Mickels's report, the arrest of Abdoul Ghermat, and everything that had happened since Grip arrived. Hansson's word against Radovanović's confession, and Grip's sense that something else was going on. Grip showed Stark the note that had been slipped under his door.

"So you did something ballsy," Stark said. He meant the kidnapping of Radovanović.

"We have the right to question him, that's what we're doing."

"Trapped in a hotel room for more than a week, isn't that . . . a little much?"

Grip shut his mouth before shooting back something stupid. Just arrived, and the guy had the nerve to say something like that, sneering. He figured Simon Stark still could afford to play the moralist. And if he'd zeroed in on the most vulnerable part of the investigation, from the short time they'd been talking, well, at least he wasn't stupid. The situation with Radovanović was just that—a little much.

"It's what was needed," Grip said, adding: "The alternative was a bunch of women shrieking when Ghermat was carried out from the jail covered by a sheet, and then a lot of headlines in Sweden. Would you have liked that better?"

He got a shrug in reply. Maybe Simon Stark would decide to wait a day or two before calling the Boss, giving his first report on the reality of the situation.

Colonel Frères had called that morning, again. Polite as usual, but now also slightly uneasy. Grip got it exactly, that although the colonel didn't object, both his police officers were sick of sitting on the balcony of the Hotel Mirage, babysitting for the Swedish police. It was time to act, before the French also started questioning the arrangement.

"Tomorrow morning, you'll head over there and stay until noon, so the French can get a day off," Grip said, and Stark nodded. "We can't keep him there much longer."

"Sounds reasonable," Stark said. He sat and leafed through the documents Grip had left on the table, not least the files on the MovCon members. "Hey, Philippa Ekman, I know her," he said, after looking at an open file for a while. "We were on the same rotation in Affe."

"Affe?"

"Afghanistan. We were in the same unit."

"So now I have one on my own team. Did you have the beard and shit as well?"

"I only grew a beard the first time. They live at the Sheraton, huh?"

"Do you want to see her?"

"I wouldn't exactly mind looking her in the eye—to see if anything has changed since last time. She's tough, though."

"They all are," Grip said, "except Radovanović. They're in their own little world. We can head out there tomorrow after you're done at the Mirage."

"Why not now?"

This was the impatient Simon Stark that Grip had already seen at the airport.

"Sure, why not," Grip replied, giving in. He looked at the clock.

But Stark had already made his own plan. "I can go to the Sheraton after we've had lunch. It can't be that hard to find." He looked at Grip, who was thinking he'd drive over and have a beer at the bar while Stark sized up the situation.

Then he understood. "You're thinking that Ernst Grip has crossed lines and pissed off everyone in uniform, and you can't risk being seen with him when you show up as an old friend?"

"Something like that."

"Go solo, then. You might as well relive old memories and tell some war stories on your first night in Djibouti. No, it's not hard to find the Sheraton. Show them your stuff."

20

"Check your in-box," said the text message from Simon Stark the next morning. He was guarding Radovanović at the Hotel Mirage while Grip went through his notes at the Kempinski.

Grip logged in. Stark's note read: "Take a look at this," with an email he'd forwarded. It was a photo of everyone posing for the camera, that day at the shooting range. The jumble of soldiers, Djiboutians, and weapons.

"Notice the laser sight," it said under the picture. Yes, one AK-5 had a laser sight mounted on the barrel. Not much bigger than a cigarette lighter. It was the only weapon that had one, and it was held by a Djiboutian looking proud. A laser sight projects a little dot showing where the bullet will hit, so you don't even have to lift the weapon to aim. Just by watching the little dancing dot, you can place a 5.56-millimeter hole precisely where you want it.

The laser sight email was signed by Philippa Ekman. From the time stamp, Grip could see that she'd sent the picture to Stark an hour before. So Simon Stark must have gotten somewhere when he'd sat and reminisced about Afghanistan with her the night before.

Philippa was in the photo herself, her braid hanging over her shoulder. She was the only woman there.

"Whose weapon was that?" Grip texted back to Stark.

"I asked, got no answer," he replied.

"Better if it goes through you. But can you arrange for me to meet with her?"

"I'm on it."

Early in the afternoon came the reply: "Tonight at 8—Kempinski."

At first, he didn't recognize Philippa Ekman. Stark was walking with her in the lobby, that's how he knew it was her. Her hair was down, and she was wearing jeans—that metamorphosis women soldiers undergo when they change into civilian clothes. The baggy uniform gone, and always something about the hair.

"Hi," he said.

She nodded in reply and looked around cautiously. In the lobby of the Kempinski, a blond young woman would automatically attract a dozen glances. That she could handle, but he saw that she was afraid of being seen. Someone might notice her talking to the police.

"Follow me," Grip said, and headed out back toward the pool. It was dark and nearly empty, just the comforting light of the still water, and a lonely figure putting away the last things for the night. Grip nodded to Stark, who put an extra bill on the counter and got three glasses of beer. Stark took a seat at the bar, and Grip and Philippa sat down across from each other, on wooden deck chairs. Grip drank his beer, but Philippa hesitated. He waited her out.

"The laser sight was on Fredrik's gun," she said, taking a sip.

"Hansson?"

"Yes." The only sound was the humming of the pump, sucking in pool water. "He had it when I went out to the shooting range with him the first time, to calibrate it. That was the week before we went with the Djiboutians and . . . yes."

"Does anyone else in your unit use a laser sight?"

"No, didn't you see the photo? Just him."

"How come?"

"In Afghanistan, almost everybody uses them, at least in the platoons out in the field."

"Ah," said Grip.

"But here," she said, "we're part of MovCon, we keep our AK-5s in a cabinet. You work on the base, you live in a hotel. In Djibouti, it's not exactly about ambushes and rapid response, in case you haven't noticed. Off the base, a gun is good enough. A laser sight is overkill."

On the other side of the pool, the bartender pulled down the last of the shutters and walked away. Simon Stark had turned around on his stool and was gazing out toward the lights down the beach.

"Why are you telling me this?" Grip asked.

"Fredrik calibrated his laser sight, and no matter what anyone says, he was the one pushing Slunga to arrange that idiotic excursion."

"Why did he bring you along the first time? Why didn't he just go himself?"

"Ask him, he always plays his little loyalty games. He pretends to be your friend, but he's really up to something else."

"Okay. But maybe you and he have been more than just friends."

"What makes you say that?"

"Just a hunch, and maybe the fact that you call him Fredrik, not Hansson."

She looked back over her shoulder toward Simon Stark.

"He can't hear us," Grip said.

She drummed cautiously on her beer glass before she answered. "A few months ago we were. It's a mission, people find each other and then they drift apart again. It works. Maybe not everyone understands."

"I think I have a pretty good idea. Something about love and war."

"Love, not so much. It's more about having someone there, a body to hold at night."

"And now?"

"Like I said, people drift apart. We haven't been seeing each other for at least a month."

She gave Grip a long look. "And now you're wondering why I'd rat on my lover?"

"A natural question—maybe jealousy?" he asked. She shook her head.

"It was Fredrik who got Slunga to arrange the excursion. But you seem to have locked in on Radovanović." Philippa Ekman was obviously annoyed. "Why did you take him in?"

"Radovanović confessed, saying he fired accidentally."

"Right, that's what he's saying now. But I'm wondering why you detained him in the first place?"

"Is Hansson trying to protect Radovanović?"

"Fredrik just does things for his own advantage," Philippa said. "And he kept pushing to make the shooting range happen, and to let the Djiboutians come along, and for Slunga to arrange it all."

"Okay, but Radovanović still says he fired by accident."

"You think that Fredrik and Radovanović cooked something up together?" she said, laughing artificially. "Jesus, you've seen Radovanović, you've been with him, he has zero self-confidence. Fredrik would never get mixed up with him." She was going to take a sip of her beer but stopped. "Now I've given you something. So, why did you take in Radovanović, just like that? I don't get it."

"You might as well answer the question yourself."

"Why, then?"

"You people in MovCon have hung out together for a long time, in your own little world, doing things exactly the way you want. I needed to shake things up and get something besides the stories you rehearsed."

"And now you've got the confession you needed. You hit his weak spot, and he caved."

"So, what do you think really happened?"

"I stood there at the front, taping over a couple of holes, and then, *bam*. No, I don't know, I didn't see. But if you'd been there, you'd have noticed the strange atmosphere, and that was long before a single shot was fired. Something was going to happen, everyone felt it." She looked away. "Sure, maybe I didn't care as much about Abdoul Ghermat as I should have, but Radovanović deserves better." She fiddled with her bracelet and stretched her back, as if she wanted to stand up after saying a little too much.

Grip felt he should encourage her and try to get more. But he didn't really know what to say. He realized he had to pick sides.

"Please stay," Grip said, at the same time realizing how awkward that would be, "or else have a beer with Stark at the bar here. And no matter what he says, charge it to my room, 804. In the meantime, I'll just . . . go check on something."

21

Grip's hunch was right. Mickels was the type who often spent evenings at his desk. He took a long look at Grip when he came in the door of the military police barracks, as if measuring him up before a showdown. No one else would be in the building.

Mickels was still impatient. A short breath, then in a loud voice: "Was it you who got Ghermat released?"

"It was the foreign minister who made it happen, but he certainly heard my opinion."

"But it's Radovanović that you're detaining? The legal staff . . ."

"If it matters," interrupted Grip, "you should know that Milan Radovanović confessed to an accidental discharge."

"What do you mean?"

"I have a written confession that he shot Per-Erik Slunga."

The MP froze. "Impossible," he said.

"It's true."

Mickels sat quietly. He bit his lip and then he let slip: "That little shit."

The last time they'd seen each other, Mickels had attacked Grip without getting the slightest pushback. Now Grip had scored.

"That's not the only thing." Grip was cool. He smiled disarmingly, and his tone wasn't mocking but still. "You missed some forensic evidence."

"The hell I did," said Mickels, no longer roaring with confidence.

"The six rifles from the shooting range . . ."

"No one has touched them since I collected them from the

shooting range. And I've had them here since. You want to see them?"

"Sure."

Mickels rose slowly from the desk, keeping his eyes on Grip. He held a pen between his fingers.

"Missed?" he said, turning his back on Grip and walking toward the gun cabinet.

The lock to it beeped, and the bolts slid back with a muffled metallic sound when Mickels turned the handle. "Here, all six guns."

Grip stepped forward to peer into the cabinet.

"Yes, I've checked the numbers on them," said Mickels, no doubt pleased that all the rifles were still in the cabinet, despite Grip's hint, "and each one checks out as the personal weapon belonging to MovCon personnel."

Grip looked at the gun rack. "All six, identical."

"Exactly." Mickels, still on his guard, was struck by a thought. "Checking the fingerprints would be meaningless, when there were so many people . . ."

"That's not what this is about." Grip unfolded the printed-out color photo he'd brought along. The one from the shooting range that showed the whole group—the swarm of people and guns. He handed it over. "Spot the difference," he said. "You'll find it on the picture, not in the cabinet. Something happened between the time the picture was taken and when you collected the weapons. Yes, beyond the lieutenant getting shot."

Mickels looked baffled.

All six weapons had clean barrels. Someone had seized an opportunity and then carefully removed the evidence. "It starts with laser and ends with sight."

Mickels had turned away from the photograph and was looking into the cabinet when suddenly he understood.

"Radovanović?" he asked.

Grip was a little amazed that this was the only possible connection Mickels could make. But why change it? "Maybe," he replied.

Above all, Grip needed to protect his bluff and keep Radovanović for a little while longer. Also, he didn't want to risk Mickels asking Hansson awkward questions.

Mickels closed the cabinet. He turned around, stood in his normal position with his legs apart again. "Besides," he began, "what does a missing laser sight prove, really?"

"Well . . ." but then Grip stopped himself. He resisted the temptation; he wouldn't strike again now. Mickels could only stick to his preconceived ideas. ". . . Only that it's missing."

Mickels stayed firm, but he was puzzled. That was enough. Maybe he'd cut Grip some slack. At the very least, he wouldn't yell at Grip the next time they met.

22

She was an unlikely vision of impeccable style: very overweight, her hair in a smooth gray pageboy, always dressed in black, and always announced by the click of her high heels. Yet she never seemed to sweat a drop.

"You realize that Djibouti wasn't my top choice," she said, the first time they met. That body of hers, in suits that fit so well—Grip thought they must have been hand-tailored. Also, no one had ever seen her wobble on her high-heeled pumps. She had a built-in radar for the cracks that made the Djibouti sidewalks a minefield for those heels. She radiated neither class nor cool but more that she was a controlled force of nature. Under her patronage, no one felt completely safe.

Judy Drexler, that's what it said on the business card she'd left at the Kempinski's reception. It had a gold eagle, with UNITED STATES EMBASSY embossed in one corner. "Call me" was the short message, written on the blank back. They were meeting at La Mer Rouge, an upscale seafood restaurant located on the outskirts of the city. Someone had gone beyond the usual attempt to dress up a pizzeria as a British pub, in their efforts to extract money from the Europeans and Americans. Instead, there was an open floor plan with black wicker furniture and tasteful touches in beige. Not quite the French Riviera, but a good try.

"You shouldn't eat every meal at the Kempinski," Judy said, as soon as they sat down. She was the one who'd chosen the place.

"The Djiboutians call this the best fish restaurant in Africa. Let's just say that in the Horn of Africa, there isn't a lot of competition." She laughed, but to make sure Grip wouldn't judge before he'd tasted the food, she added, "It's good here."

Around sixty, Grip guessed. Old enough to be getting a pension, but she liked the game too much.

"Coordinator of Consular Affairs," she replied when he asked, rolling her eyes as if the title was necessary but, in some obvious way, also a lie.

To order, they approached a counter where fresh seafood was artfully displayed on a bed of ice. The waiter gave a short lecture on which was which, the various accompaniments, and how each would be prepared. Grip didn't recognize any of the names, except tuna and lobster. "We'll just have it grilled," Judy said, halfway through the list of sauces, pointing to a couple of fish and returning to the table.

They made small talk while waiting for their food. They chatted about the heat, the chilled pool at the Kempinski, and the question of who could possibly be paying for the containers full of brand-new Chinese trucks in the port.

"So, I got in touch with you," she said, placing the cloth napkin on her lap. "You're the police officer who's investigating what happened at the shooting range."

"Right."

"Flown in from Sweden, I understand." He nodded.

"How's it going?" she asked, directly.

"Fine, thank you."

She laughed out loud. "I didn't invite you to lunch at La Mer Rouge to hear that everything is going fine. All investigations are going fine. That's what everyone says, anyway, until the day you have to present your conclusions."

"I'm not there yet."

"And I'm not looking for a written statement."

"Written or not, why are you even interested?"

"The accident occurred at an American shooting range. It took place on our turf, and we just want to follow up."

"If the American base commander, General So-and-So, had sent me an MP carrying a stack of neatly filled-out forms, I would have believed his version," Grip said.

"I'm sure he'll show up in due time, as soon as he gets his papers arranged. But I can also keep him out of your hair."

"Is that a threat?" Grip asked.

Grip smiled. Drexler smiled back.

"We can exchange threats some other time. My job is to gather gossip, you know that."

The waiter appeared behind Grip's back. He bumped Grip with the plates he was carrying, and then there was some confusion over who was having what. When he left, Grip touched his neck below one ear and found what looked like tomato sauce on his fingertips. He turned around to see the waiter, but now there was no one behind him. Grip took his napkin and looked at Drexler inquisitively as he wiped off the dark red from his neck and hands.

"So, what's the word on the street in Djibouti, for real?" he asked.

"About the shooting range?" Judy said, chewing, having already started in. "A remarkable event in which a Swedish lieutenant was shot, and a local worker named Ghermat was charged and arrested."

"And then released."

"Yes, I heard that too. But why?"

"It was a matter of one person's word against another's, and also the credibility of the witnesses."

"I understand that. Still, was it so wise to release him?"

"At the jail, the police were going to beat him to death."

"People can withstand more than you think." There was silence for a moment.

"Have you been in contact with Colonel Frères, by the way?"

"Yes, we've spoken."

"You see, I told him that you'd probably need his help, when I heard about the shooting. I guess he's the one who contacted you?"

Grip nodded.

"Good, he does what he's told," she continued. "The French can

159

sometimes be difficult, but the man owes me a few favors. Please let me know if you need anything more from Frères."

"I think I've gotten what I need."

"But the colonel failed to convince you that Ghermat should remain in jail? You realize that once he's released, you'll never get him back."

"I never spoke to Frères about it. But it doesn't matter, Abdoul Ghermat is no longer a suspect. He didn't fire the shot."

"You have other theories?"

"Yes, a few."

"May I ask you, Ernst Grip, how long you've been here in Djibouti?"

"Just over a week."

"Three years, that's how long I've been here. For three years, I've listened to the chatter, gossip, and tips, read the surveillance reports and the interrogation transcripts, and watched people come and go under every imaginable circumstance. One thing you learn quickly is that if you have someone in your sights, you don't take your eyes off them."

"He didn't shoot the lieutenant."

It was as if Judy Drexler didn't hear him. "A month ago, we received a tip that a certain Abdoul Ghermat was loading and unloading goods on transport planes controlled by Al-Qaeda. You don't want that type getting near your planes, so we checked it out. The report said he was a local worker with close ties to the unit's lieutenant. They sometimes went out for coffee together, or at night to the downtown dives, and so on. We might call it inappropriate, fraternizing that way, but hardly more than that, so we dropped it. But then a week ago the lieutenant dropped dead on our shooting range, and Ghermat was arrested."

Drexler lifted her fork, just as Grip was about to answer. "No, he might not have shot his friend, but Abdoul Ghermat is mixed up in something. And you know, he'd probably have been willing to tell you a bit about it, to avoid ending his days in that cell. The Djiboutians could have done that for you, but you gave him a free pass right back onto the street." She cut another piece of grilled fish, and smiled. "Don't be softhearted. You can't afford to be in a place like this."

Grip shrugged. "Softhearted, maybe. But what bothers me is that you spied on the Swedish MovCon unit. On us."

"Who said anything about spying? I simply listen to what people say."

"And what about this source? One little tip, and you do all that work?"

"I'm not terribly interested in what goes on in Djibouti. Ultimately, it's all about Somalia. My job is to collect information and analyze it for the machinery that determines whose car ends up in the drone sights, and whose doesn't. And the source who pointed to Abdoul Ghermat has been very reliable—at least, up until now—I can tell you that. But this time the source was wrong. No Al-Qaeda or Al-Shabaab."

"Couldn't the source be out to hurt Ghermat?"

"That can't be ruled out. But it doesn't matter now. The lieutenant is dead and we'll never see Abdoul Ghermat again. I thought you might want to know. You might need a crash course in the myths and facts of Djibouti."

"So what other advice do you have, while I'm so far from home?"

Judy put down her fork and pointed to Grip's glass. "They usually make the ice out of bottled water, but . . ."

". . . you never really know where the water in the bottles comes from," Grip said. "All right, so nothing is what it seems in Djibouti. And maybe I released Ghermat too soon. But not long afterward, someone slid a note under the door to my hotel room. Cryptic, but very interesting. Who knows, maybe it was a kind of thank-you? Maybe there's more than one way to get to the bottom of things?"

Judy Drexler stretched. Her whole being signaled that she could lower the temperature between them to subfreezing in a millisecond.

But that wasn't what she wanted with Grip. She laid a few fingers on his hand. Not in a gentle way, but well intentioned. "I didn't come here to lecture you, Ernst Grip. I wanted to tell you that we missed something important, only that. And I think you're about to make the same mistake."

23

The bottle hit the bottom of the bucket. This was an early end to the day's water supply, not even three o'clock. Jenny dropped it, postponing her drink, and looked at her children. Sebastian was half-asleep, his sweaty hair standing straight up, while Alexandra played with a lone ant on the floor next to her mattress.

The only part of their life that remained normal was Alexandra. She was weak, of course, but not sick. Moreover, she kept to a schedule: she got out of bed every morning, making a point of it, and did the same when she said good night. In the rush to leave the boat, she'd grabbed two books: a math book and a random paperback. In the morning, she did math—she'd taken a pencil too—writing microscopic calculations in the white margins of the book. But she solved only a few problems at a time, never more than five, saving them like candy.

Then in the afternoon, when the worst of the heat had passed but the darkness hadn't yet begun to fall, she read her novel. But if Jenny had patted her affectionately on the cheek, seeing how carefully the math problems were measured out, her daughter's regimen with the second book made them anxious. Alexandra read three pages, exactly three, not a sentence more. Jenny had taken the book while Alexandra and the others were asleep. It was a 520-page-long mystery, with a small dog-ear on page 63. Jenny herself hadn't managed to keep track of how they'd been kidnapped and held in their oven of a house for twenty-one days, but her daughter had. And her daughter had calculated that they might remain there for at least

150 days. In the dark that night, Jenny wept silently for so long that, in the end, she couldn't even taste her own tears.

Soon after the jeeps arrived one afternoon, a man wearing pleated pants and a white shirt came into the room. He simply looked around and went back out again. Jenny positioned herself to watch him in the front room, through the half-open door. He was a Somali like the others, but he made a very different impression. Darwiish stood and spoke to him, in his usual intimidating way. But although this other man looked younger, he talked back, and appeared both forceful and self-possessed.

He looked cool, that's what Jenny thought, as if he'd just drunk his fill and put down the empty, misty glass. All the pirates were affected by the heat, with their half-closed eyes, but this gaze was different. He took everything in and kept his distance. This godforsaken place was just dust in the sand he walked through. His shoes had lost their shine, that was all. This was someone who would return to a city. To some kind of civilization. There, he'd wipe the dust off the leather, and then the place, the buildings, and the heat would simply be left behind. But wouldn't he make something happen, wouldn't he talk to someone?

Jenny felt ashamed about her appearance. She was a victim, not him.

They came for Carl-Adam and closed the door. But the door was only made of thin boards, and Jenny got up and put her ear by the hinge, where there was a crack she'd used before.

A few words of Somali, then steps going away. It seemed that Carl-Adam was left alone with the man in the outer room.

"Do you understand the situation that we face?" The man's English was not what Jenny had gotten used to hearing. It flowed smoothly, sounded educated, and there was something familiar about it.

"I and my family have been kidnapped by pirates," said Carl-Adam. He made an effort, trying to sound angry when he said it.

"And is that all?"

"Yes."

"Pirates, that is one version. Another is that these are fishermen, and you have shot and killed one of them."

"But . . ."

"What happened to your hand?" the man interrupted.

"They . . ."

"They shot you, in return. You were lucky. That way your entire family escaped being massacred, and you yourself have escaped with your life." A long silence followed, before the man continued again.

"Of course, they are pirates, and you can think what you want about Darwiish. But now he has the upper hand—he has you. Therefore, it is his way of looking at things that is valid here. Not your way, not his men's way, and not mine."

"Why are you here, then, if you have no say in the matter?"

"I am here because I do not belong to Darwiish's gangs. He has hired me because everything has stalled, and because he, you, and everyone else need someone independent to solve this. I am not on anyone's side. I negotiate, I resolve conflicts. I bring you good advice."

"Why?"

"So much in this world is lost through misunderstandings."

"And this good advice comes absolutely free?"

"I have expenses."

"I forgot my wallet at home."

"It is not you who will pay."

"So what would your best advice be?"

"I do not think that you are truly in need of good advice right now."

"No?"

"You need another voice, someone to talk with people at home. Do you understand that Darwiish has nothing to lose? He can simply shoot me when I come out here, and it means nothing. It would have not the least consequence for him, and I'm a Somali. Out here, the lives of you and your family are worth less than that."

"Ten million dollars."

"Wrong. You are only worth the trouble of keeping you here if Darwiish believes there is someone willing to pay."

"He says ten, I tried . . ."

"Darwiish can come in here and suddenly change that to hundreds, or just three. And then that's the way it will be. Or he can come in here and say that he has gotten tired of the whole thing. Then he will send your cut-off fingers in the mail, or maybe he won't even have patience for that. But ten million US dollars—don't you think that is reasonable? Does the sum surprise you? You are used to dealing with acquisitions, you must deal with shareholders who resist. Ten million can't be an unusual amount to pay, can it?"

"What does that have to do with anything?"

"Answer the question. Is it an unusual amount?"

"It depends on the value of the buyout."

"Of course, the value. How many shares does the person own, and what liabilities would the shareholder bring to the new operation? Here, where we sit, in this deal, you need to be ransomed out. Also, you have killed a man."

"This . . . Where . . . ?" Carl-Adam was breathing heavily.

"Yes, you are tired. It is hell being here, and the wound in your hand does not make it any easier. But if you and your family want to have the slightest chance of surviving, you must try to grasp why you should never even *think* about defying Darwiish. The money that can solve this is not here, it is far away. And this is not where the negotiations take place. You and I cannot negotiate. You and Darwiish cannot negotiate. In this place, the very best outcome is that nothing happens, because anyone at any moment could decide to take out his frustrations. I can perhaps get someone to look at your wounds, but I cannot do anything about Darwiish's temper. Someone has translated online articles for him, and he has been told that those at Scandinavian Capital, which is your business, earn hundreds of millions each."

"That . . ."

"Well, what, then? That . . . ? Say something."

"I resigned. I quit my job at Scandinavian Capital. The deals people wrote about . . . the profits, that was for the partners. Not me, I never came near that kind of money."

"What do you think is easier, explaining that to Darwiish, or asking Scandinavian Capital to make an exception to its profit-sharing policy? Facebook and Instagram are full of pictures of you and your colleagues—parties, dinners, ski trips. Darwiish belongs to a clan, one that stands at the center of his life and that will protect him, if necessary. As he sees it, your clan is Scandinavian Capital."

"But I . . ."

There was the sound of a hand slapping the table. "Be a man!" A chair scraped. Jenny sensed his movement through the crack, imagining the smooth white of his shirt as he jumped to his feet. "A man! And let us hope that your Swedes stop thinking that their silence sends a message."

24

Djibouti was so damn full of eyes and ears. Every time Grip walked through a crowd and turned around, someone was watching him. The note under the door, Judy Drexler's card at the reception desk, the spilled sauce at La Mer Rouge. And now this waiter at the hotel, hovering over Grip's table every time he took out a scrap of paper.

He sat there now in the late-afternoon quiet, at a cool table inside the Kempinski by a window overlooking the pool, with a pile of printouts in front of him. "No, thanks. I told you, I'm fine!" That same waiter again. The man looked as if he'd failed at something.

Beyond dealing with all the eyes and ears, Grip feared he was back at square one. Earlier in the day, the old surgeon, somewhere out at sea on the *Sveaborg*, finally sent his report about Slunga. Grip forwarded the email to Stark (who was once again pulling a day shift at the Mirage), and then started reading. The doctor at the French hospital had found no trace of suspicious substances in the blood samples he'd received. The trouble was the shot itself—its geometry.

Grip was just getting into it when Simon Stark called his cell.

"Who's going to say it first?" he said.

"Okay, you start."

"Our problem isn't dealing with a suicidal shooter. Our problem is that Radovanović simply didn't do it."

Grip was quiet for a moment, enough to show that he agreed. Then he asked: "Where are you right now?"

"Standing on the balcony, looking at him through the window," Stark said. "Don't worry, he can't hear me."

"He still thinks he did it?"

"Totally convinced. And I agree with you, normally you can't dismiss a confession. Only now we can, on technical grounds. Or, well, I don't understand the entire page that the doctor covered with math. But I do know right from left. It's impossible."

"No, it's not impossible . . ." Grip began, but got interrupted.

Stark sounded judgmental. "Didn't you see the body in the ship's morgue?" The doctor had sent some pictures along with his file. "Couldn't you see that Slunga was shot from the left?"

"There was a big goddamn hole in his skull. I didn't really understand about the angle of the shot." Grip had begun to sketch on paper. He drew a picture, and then compared the surgeon's calculations with the witness statements from Mickels's report. He saw who'd stood where at the shooting range. In the sketch, Slunga was at the front, with Ghermat and Radovanović behind him, and Hansson alone, a little to the left.

"Sure," Stark said. "Of course, Slunga might have turned his head and looked backward when the shot was fired, but that doesn't match the statements from the witnesses standing up by the targets. The shot came from the left."

"Yeah, that makes sense. I can see it."

"Makes sense . . . Damn it, Grip, Hansson fired the shot! The laser pointer, the note under the door, this isn't Radovanović's world, it reeks of Hansson. We'll confront him. We'll contact the prosecutor and do this right."

"No, we won't. We still have to deal with Radovanović's confession. What we have is an email with a lot of math we barely understand, the word *left*, and an angle pointing to Hansson. If Hansson doesn't talk, all we can do is implicate him in an accidental discharge. We need more on him. And we need to find a way in, because obviously he didn't act alone."

"And Radovanović?"

Grip was quiet. Frères called every day now, so often that Grip didn't even answer when his phone buzzed with the colonel's name.

Meanwhile in Stockholm, the generals' lawyers were hitting the law books, underlining all the relevant rules. Could he and Stark hold out, without help from the French? But Grip didn't want to set foot in the Mirage again.

"You're scared of what you've done," Stark said calmly. He still hadn't gotten a reply to his original question. "And you're scared of what he'll do."

Grip kept silent, breathing a few times. "We'll release him," he said then.

"Now?"

"No, tomorrow, when the *Sveaborg* is back in port."

The conversation with Stark had been hours ago. Grip gazed at the pool and returned to his stack of printouts. He'd requested help from Stockholm earlier, getting some background information on Fredrik Hansson. There were mostly military files, but other things as well. Grip turned the pages. First came Hansson's service record. Not even thirty-three years old, he'd already been on nine foreign missions. Hansson was what Stark had called an ax. He led a kind of double life, alternating odd jobs in Sweden with international military missions. Hansson often worked as a guard, and he preferred nights at any hour, it seemed. Grip also asked them to check on Hansson's spending habits, triggered by something else Stark had said.

The first evening when Stark was at the Sheraton looking for Philippa Ekman, he'd caught a glimpse of Hansson at the bar, or rather, of his watch. Black and masculine, like that worn by so many others in uniform, so it mostly went unnoticed. But it was a Hublot Black Magic. A few days later, when Stark realized that it was actually Hansson he'd seen wearing it, he brought up the matter with Grip. He explained how international forces soldiers often blew their money on expensive watches. If they couldn't find it at the duty-free shop of Camp Bondsteel in Kosovo, or in Kabul, they turned to a few retailers in Sweden, who'd even delete the VAT tax if they were shipping to an international forces address. They sent Tag Heuer and Breitling by bulk mail. But a Hublot Black Magic—that cost far more than a soldier could save up from six months as a turret gunner in Sheberghan or Mali.

Grip flipped through the pages.

Hansson lived in Stockholm in a two-bedroom condo on Kungsholmen, so obviously he had money. Had he bought it himself, or inherited it? There was no way to be sure, but in any case Hansson had no mortgage to speak of. He rented three parking spaces in the basement but had only one registered car, a sporty little Mazda. Why did someone need three parking spaces for one car? Grip read over the list of his foreign missions. Congo, Sudan, Kenya, Djibouti, some of them more than once. But never to the Balkans, and only once to Afghanistan. Most axes were hooked on Afghanistan missions, Stark had said. Not Hansson. For him, it was all Africa.

One document concerned an investigation following a tour Hansson did in South Sudan. Apparently he'd been held hostage for a few days, seized by crazy militiamen, who'd beaten him up and threatened to kill him. The thing had ended peacefully, but Hansson came out in rough shape. Grip understood the fear that dogged people in uniform—that they'd be taken hostage and end up on their knees in an orange jumpsuit, their picture all over the Internet, while people holding swords shouted death sentences behind their back. Apparently, Hansson had been through it, and he was certain he was going to die. He got prescription meds afterward, Stilnoct and Oxazepam, and he'd been on tranquilizers for six months.

Then he was back in Africa, not even a year later. Grip could picture it, the way someone would dutifully ask how he was feeling, then send him right back to work. "Good to go," Hansson had said, repeating it a few times, and so the medical opinion was ignored. After all, the military didn't exactly have hordes of applicants. Grip underlined the word *hostage* and moved on.

He read for a good hour but found nothing more of interest, so he got up, walking past the empty tables to give his brain some oxygen. He gave the waiter a look to say he was still watching over his documents, and gazed into the piano bar. There she sat, with a shaft of late-afternoon light falling across the grand piano. In her first set of the evening, she played for only a handful of jet-lagged Chinese sitting at one of the tables. Ayanna, right, Ayanna was her name.

"You're here."

Grip turned around. It was Stark, back from the Hotel Mirage for the evening. He glanced into the piano bar, looked back, and nodded in a knowing way.

Then he said: "I couldn't resist. I stopped at the Sheraton on the way back and made sure to bump into Hansson. Played at being interested, then asked him bluntly where he'd bought a Black Magic and what he'd paid for it."

"He told you to fuck off?"

"Something like that."

"Hey, that's not how we're going to get him."

"No, but now he knows we're watching him."

"Who's watching whom remains to be seen. Do you want to shower before we eat?"

Stark was already walking away, a sign that he'd probably head to the gym first.

Grip returned to the papers. He took out his little notebook and listed three basic points:

- Too many people liked the money—note under door
- Hublot Black Magic—around $15,000
- Three parking spots—why?

Earlier that day, a Hercules from Sweden had landed, bringing supplies, mail, and spare parts. It would leave again some hours later, taking Per-Erik Slunga's body back home. Then the HMS *Sveaborg* would dock in Djibouti the following day. Grip realized he had an opportunity, and he had to get organized before the Swedish authorities closed back home. He had an hour to himself. To start with, he'd need to get ahold of someone high up at Customs.

25

"At work, people say that you're gay," said Simon Stark. His eyes narrowed as he said it. Grip had stopped counting, but they'd each had at least three drinks and as many beers. They were sitting upstairs in the nightclub.

After dinner, once they'd agreed that Radovanović was innocent and should be released, they stayed and hung out, instead of returning to their rooms as they had the night before. Letting down their guard, they'd both ordered a drink. They joked and made small talk as the restaurant emptied out, while the waiters started clearing tables and setting up for the next day.

When the place felt too deserted, they decided to change scenery and head to the nightclub terrace under the stars. A beer, to start with. They kept drinking, and after they dismissed a few "Hi, I am . . ." approaches, the girls understood that the two men hadn't come for them. They talked about sports, and then about why people moved to certain neighborhoods in Stockholm. They had another beer. When they started talking about Stockholm bars, Grip ordered an old-fashioned, and with that, they switched back to liquor again. That theme led to movies, which were really Stark's thing. They had a White Russian and a screwdriver, while Stark did lines from *The Big Lebowski* and *Jackie Brown*. Their laughter made the people at the next table turn around. Grip stared back and ordered another round. They were both getting drunk.

A comment about an event at work, and then that line. The

statement was really a question, and Stark's gaze said he wanted to test his power.

Warily, Grip picked up the gauntlet. "What if I'm gay?" He said it so that nothing would be left unclear. And then: "How often do you jerk off?"

"What does that have to do with anything?"

"Only that it's also a very personal question. So?"

Stark leaned back without blinking. "I might not put a dot in my diary, but I'd say . . . every second or third day seems about right." He tried to look mischievous about it, feeling confident from the alcohol.

"High testosterone, you have to work it off," said Grip, looking at him as if he'd been watching Stark pleasure himself. And it worked. "Who says I'm gay?" he asked.

"C'mon, when you're the new guy, it doesn't take long before people start telling you what's really going on. Who stole whose wife, and who's into what."

"And people say I'm gay?"

"Well, that you have someone in New York. A lover."

Grip took a long look at Stark. No one had ever confronted him point-blank like that. Never. And yet Grip was sure that Simon Stark was 100 percent straight.

"Do you know anyone who's out?" he asked.

"Of course I do, but that doesn't mean I'm completely comfortable with it."

"So why are you asking me?"

"People talk in our office, but no one seems to know for sure. It's the elephant in the room, right?"

"A homophobe who dares to ask." Grip gave him a nod. "Benjamin Hayden, that's the name of my lover in New York. But he's Ben, to me."

"A colleague?"

The question sounded funny, and Grip laughed. "No, no. Owned an art gallery in Manhattan, knew everything about Tom Friedman and Damien Hirst. To him, police officers have mustaches and direct traffic at intersections, or are the guys you'd dress up as, at a costume party."

"Damien who?"

"That's not important. What matters is that Ben was thin as hell."

"Was?"

"He had the virus, the one gay men wore like a caste mark. It was pneumonia that finally took him, a year ago."

Stark got up some courage.

"Did you love him?"

"Shit, Simon, look at you. You're so uncomfortable, even after all the alcohol."

"Yeah." He tried to say something more but stopped short.

"Oh fuck, it's okay. Go ahead, ask me the question you really want to ask."

"Which?"

"All right, when you ask if I loved Ben, I'll tell you he was all I had, all right? And if you're wondering whether I have to get my T cells counted and take antiretroviral drugs, the answer is no."

"Okay, I admit . . ."

"I realize what you were thinking. But you know they test us every year for the job, and I wouldn't have been allowed to stay for a single day if I'd been positive."

"Do von Hoffsten and the others know that your artist buddy is dead?"

"Ben wasn't my buddy, okay?"

"Sorry." Stark raised his glass in front of him.

Grip brushed it off. "We don't have to make a toast to Ben, but he wasn't just some dude. For von Hoffsten and the gang, it's enough that they imagined Ben existing, even if he was nameless—which he might as well remain. Why should I talk about it? Why should I make them uncomfortable when I step into the sauna next time: legs crossed, and that look of 'what new thing will Grip want to get ahold of now?'" Grip raised his glass to take a drink.

"Nothing but ice," Stark said with a grin.

Grip looked into the glass, feeling its effects. "Yes, I'll have another one," he said, "and you, you also need a refill."

They got another round of the same. A few sips and they were back on track. Stark hadn't yet finished his interrogation.

"Sure, I'll sit with you in the sauna next time, clench my ass, and be terrified that I'll get a hard-on. But regardless of my hang-ups— yeah, I get the urge to punch something in a feather boa when the Pride parade goes by—I won't tell the boys about Benjamin. It's just that . . ." Silence. "But," he began again, "you haven't totally convinced me."

"No?"

"I stood and watched you for a little while in the lobby today. Before I said hello."

"Are you spying on me too?" Grip laughed.

"It just happened."

"You could have asked the annoying waiter to tell you what I was reading."

"You weren't reading. You were standing there, looking into the piano bar."

"I remember."

"Just that"—Stark waved his finger at Grip—"no man who likes men would look at a woman that way."

"Hey . . ."

"Uh-uh, no 'hey.' Yeah, I get uncomfortable and don't know where to look when I see men holding hands. But from where I stood, with her over there, I know it wasn't the Chinese men in business suits you were watching."

"I was just about to say," Grip said, "that before Ben, I slept with women, and then I lived with a man. You can choose any label you want. Cut and paste it yourself."

"Oh, I get it."

"No, Simon, you have no fucking idea.

"Cheers," said Grip, clinking his glass, but Stark left his drink on the table. For a moment, Stark sat lost in thought.

"So what's your secret?" Grip asked, after he swallowed. Stark looked up.

"Barely been to a strip club. Not much in my life matches up to yours."

"Well, a bodyguard who can't run, that story has to begin somewhere too."

"Right. Well, it all starts with one of those desert uniforms that every Joe Schmo around here wears. You already know I got my police ID in a box of cornflakes. So I started out as an infantryman, the ones who have to walk a hell of a lot." Stark laughed. "At least, mine are still good enough for that," he continued, jiggling his legs. "Two tours in Afghanistan, altogether almost a year around Mazar-e Sharif, on the plains and in the valleys. Always with the peaks of the Hindu Kush in the background. It's beautiful there, you know. I could find my way on the roads around Sar e Pul, Darzab, and Sheberghan without a map. I was damn good."

"So that cockiness of yours hasn't changed," Grip said, smiling.

"No. But my hair was shorter." Stark pulled at his bangs.

"Go on."

"Right. It was often rough, but never really scary. I thought I knew how things worked. I tried to teach myself some phrases in Dari, so I'd know if the interpreter was sticking to the script or if he had his own agenda. I followed the local customs, didn't mind eating sheep liver when the village elders invited me in, that kind of shit. On my final tour, I helped to train a new Afghan battalion. That was when northern Afghanistan went from being a quiet backwater to something very different. Bombs were exploding on the roads, but this was before people began driving around in armored vehicles. No respectable politician or general wanted to admit that everything hung in the balance. War hasn't broken out until someone says it has.

"With the Afghan army, most projects were hopeless. We tried to get the gunners to use their weapon sights, and to get the truck drivers to shift past first gear. Equipment was missing or lost, all the firearms had to be locked up overnight, and from one week to another, a third of the company would desert. The Swedish forces would pretend to trust them, but we were suspicious of everyone, especially the local Afghan police, those bastards who play under the table with everyone they can.

"One time I was going to a meeting at a village police station south of Mazar-e Sharif, a little off the beaten track. You know how they always come as a surprise, the brief moments in life that are truly decisive. The ones when you get to know yourself and how you're seen by others. Right?"

"Maybe," said Grip. "What happened?"

"We had just two cars, with the dust swirling around us, yet the worst of the heat had passed after the summer. We were climbing into the mountains, through a landscape of hills and ravines. Obviously, everyone was armed, and I spent the whole time staring at the surroundings, looking for movement or places where someone could hide.

"Just before a curve, there were shots—automatic fire. I still remember, it's so strange, the sound of a single bullet hitting the side of the car, yet there must have been hundreds of shots fired."

Stark didn't look at Grip as he talked. He'd put down his drink to concentrate, completely absorbed by his story.

"It was an ambush, and in the first few seconds there was only confusion and screaming. We jumped out of the car and looked for protection. Trying to see the enemy, to get a glimpse of a head somewhere, and to make contact with the other car. From the screams, we realized that someone was injured, and it seemed like they were taking most of the fire up front. There were four of us in my car, all unhurt, unbelievable. We had to make a counterattack. I was panting like crazy and yelled something as the shots hit the ground in little clouds of dust all around us. Then we scrambled, and then I found myself with another guy on the other side of the road. I followed a dry streambed and went up over a crest. I had a little plan.

"Bingo, I was right, they weren't expecting it. Two men, kneeling, tried to aim down at what was happening on the road, but we'd come at them from the side. There were maybe thirty meters between us. One of them yelled and tried to shoot, but had they ever learned to use their gun sights? The Afghan who was closest got off the first shot, I'll give him that, before I got my own rifle ready and the red dot in the optics danced across his chest. He got two bullets in return, and I felt the two quick recoils. I don't know whether the second shot hit, I just saw a twisted body lying still when I lowered my rifle and at the same time started looking for the other guy. I didn't realize that he'd been shot by Tärnsjö, the reserve lieutenant who was with me on this side of the road. But Tärnsjö had done his part. He too had killed a man for the first time.

"We probably should have stopped right there, when we saw a bunch of other guys running from their positions, trying to escape. But we were pumped, now that we'd had a taste of these fuckers. I fired off a few shots, and then my rifle jammed. An empty shell was stuck in the chamber, so I cocked twice to get the next bullet in place. When I looked up again, I caught a movement in the ravine, much closer to me than the men who'd fled across the hills. I got a glimpse of someone and went after him, without checking for Tärnsjö.

"I'd gone a hundred meters when I stopped at a bend down in the ravine, where the shape disappeared. In the dry ditch, it was impossible for me to see anything ahead. I stayed close to the steep, sandy bank and tried to calm my breathing so I could listen. Then I heard cautious steps over the dry stones, and I thought they were just a little farther out than I could see. This wasn't the sound of someone running or crawling, but exactly the sounds someone makes when he's waiting. All I could think of was the jammed empty shell, how that had happened to me in a training exercise just a few days before. Suddenly, I didn't trust my rifle.

"So I let the rifle drop to the back of my belt and instead pulled my gun out of the holster on my leg. I held my breath and cocked it as quietly as I could. I heard a stone move, as if someone had the weight of his foot on it, and somewhere far behind me I heard single shots. I was amped up from the ambush we'd been in, and once you get a chance to counterattack . . . I took a few quick steps forward.

"I can't say I was surprised—in that situation you don't have that kind of thought—but it wasn't what I'd imagined. A man was waiting there, crouched on a rock. Maybe he was injured, something about his foot, or maybe he didn't know there was someone behind him. He looked more surprised than scared, with no more than six meters between us. He held his rifle with one hand on the barrel, while I kept my gun in a two-handed grip.

"But despite my racing pulse, and all the adrenaline, something stopped me. I thought he recognized me. The way he looked at me, when he saw my face. What the hell was that about? So I stood there, with my gun half raised in front of me. Where would he and I have . . . ? I searched through my memory, where?

"There'd been a meeting, a week earlier, with a handful of local police chiefs and their guards. A meeting about who would do what. Whether the man looking at my gun was a chief or a guard, I didn't remember, but he'd been there. That was it. He'd heard the plans for when and where we would go that day, and he knew we'd be alone in two cars on a bad road.

"I was looking point-blank at a traitor, and he was just waiting, knowing that I'd figure it out. I kept approaching, and now there weren't even three meters between us. Over the radio in one ear, I heard that the medevac helicopter was coming in for our soldier who'd gotten injured.

"And then, he moved. Damn it, I've thought about it so much, how it happened when there was no distance at all between two people. I didn't know it then, but Tärnsjö had run along behind me, following a little ridge that gave him a good view. He saw both of us, me and the man crouching on the rock. Whether the man tried to do something with his gun maybe wasn't that important, but Tärnsjö saw me shoot a Taliban member twice at close range and then just walk away. I had no idea what a big deal this would be. From the cars, the other men had seen the shoot-out with the first two men, but Tärnsjö had also seen this other thing. These stories travel farther than you might think."

"Did they give you any crap about it?" Grip asked.

"No, no, not at all. On the contrary, people were talking around me, but I didn't notice a thing. There was a strange sort of admiration. Afghanistan, you know, for a while there was fighting everywhere, but there were still very few who'd actually done the deed. People are preoccupied with the question: what's it like to actually kill someone? Do I have it in me? But no one asked how I felt. Maybe they asked about the duel on the ridge but not about the shots in the ditch. I guess they felt there was something cold in me, something calculating. In the story they told, there was nothing about the man making a move, because Tärnsjö never saw it. To him, I just shot and walked away. If they'd asked me, I would have said that the Afghan expected those two shots. He reached for his gun to get it over with. But as I said, no one asked."

It was as if Stark had just come out of that ravine when he looked up at Grip. "Have you ever killed anyone?"

Grip shrugged.

"I won't go on about it," Stark continued, "but it's liberating. Because then you no longer have to wonder."

"And your legs?"

Stark looked down at them. "They're still shit."

"It feels like something's missing here."

"Right. But everything is connected, an Afghan in the ravine and my legs, my fucking legs. A month after the firefight, I was a passenger in a convoy on Ring Road 5. We'd just come out of Sheberghan when the jeep I was in shuddered.

"I don't remember much from the rest of the day, only little pieces. No, it wasn't a remote-triggered roadside bomb, it was a rocket-propelled grenade that slammed right into the side of the truck. I got shrapnel from the grenade in my calves, but the guy sitting next to me lost everything below the knees. And that's why I was sent home a month early.

"It didn't take long before I could walk fine again, but the problem is running. See for yourself." He pulled up one pant leg. His calf looked as if it had been attacked by a tiger. "I can take strides, and it doesn't hurt, but I can't get up to speed. Something in there never healed, but the doctors can't find anything wrong. 'Of course you'll go back to work,' everyone said. And for the first time in my life, people looked at me with pity. It's not like the strange admiration you get for the shots you fired, talked about behind your back. It's right in your face.

"And then, one day just before Christmas, I found myself in the cobblestone courtyard of the Army Museum in Östermalm. The snow was really coming down, and everyone in my unit had come home from Afghanistan and gathered for the medal ceremony. Do you know what one of those is like? It's all pomp and circumstance, and yet you know, at the same time, that somehow you're being covered up in a certain way. A few stood in little clusters of families, but many had come alone, and there were some military trumpeters assigned to ceremony duty. It wasn't just that the air was chilly—something about the atmosphere felt wrong. A minister gave a short speech, the usual stuff passed around from one speechwriter to another. He couldn't even pronounce the places we'd been to. He said he was proud of what we'd done, but what the hell did he know about what we did or didn't do?

"Someone had gotten the idea that the injured vets should stand together. So I ended up next to the guy who, the last time we'd been together, had been totally functional, sitting next to me in the jeep. Who was on the right side of whom was as random now as it had been in the convoy. But I was standing, and he was sitting in his wheelchair.

"It took forever to hand out the medals, but finally the generals came over to our unit. They said a few words to each of us, as we stood at attention, the ones who could, and saluted as the medals were pinned on our chests. Sure, there's a little pride in that, but it's nothing so special. And for my part, it was mixed with something else, in their eyes. Not toward me, but toward the man in the wheelchair beside me in the snow, with the blanket over what was missing below the knees. It's difficult to explain. I had as hard a time not staring as anyone else. It was like we were all embarrassed, and some of that shame came from my hearing— 'Of course you'll go back to work . . . ,' said with the best intentions.

"So when it was time for the next round of defense cutbacks, and those who wanted to were allowed to apply for the police force, it was a no-brainer. I wanted out.

"The qualifying rounds for the police weren't really a problem, between the written exam and the interviews. But then there was the day we had to show up in tracksuits, at the indoor gym in Bosön. Bench presses, pull-ups, push-ups—no sweat. The problem was doing three kilometers on the track, under the time limit. I was like one of those girls who'd cut herself with razor blades, and I hid my calves in running tights that whole day. When it was my turn, I gave it all I had, you can't even imagine the pain, but I was still on the wrong side of the line.

"And here's the thing. Earlier in the day, I'd said hello to Tärnsjö, the reserve lieutenant from Affe, who as a civilian happened to have joined the police. He was there interviewing some of the other applicants. I didn't think about it then. When the tryouts were over, and it was time for us to receive the news a week later, I sat alone with a man from the commission. My application lay open on top of the table, with the results from Bosön.

"'Forty-eight seconds too slow,' said the police officer. He could have woken me up in the middle of the night, and I would have spat out the number. I knew exactly how many seconds over I'd finished.

"'Thank you,' I replied, 'I understand.'

"'I don't think you do. Sit down.' He liked putting on his little show. 'I think you have other things that we might need.' And with a stroke of the pen, he cut my time by two minutes. He showed me the new time, looking serious, and then he said: 'I heard . . . heard you're a good shot, and that you don't think twice.' The police officer was much older, a classic bully, but damn if there wasn't a look of admiration in his eyes. It was only then I realized Tärnsjö hadn't just seen me in the ravine but also told his version of the incident. The stories had spread."

"There are different rules sometimes, for those who've killed," said Grip, who'd just put a few pieces of the puzzle into place.

"Yeah, I understand that someone wanted me. But why this silly drama, crossing out my time on the page?"

"Not just anyone, the Boss wanted you. Those stories, as you call them, had probably reached him too. He's always looking for risk-takers."

"Still, they could have just mailed me a letter saying I'd been accepted."

"No, no—they let you trade two shots in a ditch for two minutes off your time. This way, you're in debt to them, that's the whole point, and you know exactly why they wanted you."

"I know I'm drunk, but killing changes everything in a human being."

"No, it doesn't, it's everything around you that changes," said Grip, who didn't like it when people oversimplified. "How long did you say you were on the job before they asked you to apply for a different division?"

"Not even a year. Then I went over to you at Säpo and the bodyguard detachment. 'Plenty of overtime, and a dark suit for the royals,' they said." Stark laughed.

But something was making him uncomfortable.

"During an interview for the bodyguards, that ravine came up again," Stark said. "'What happened to the Taliban guy?' he asked me while I was sitting there, trying to look tough and make it sound as if he'd done the same thing many times himself."

"Come on," Grip said, "how many Swedes do you think have shot someone at close range, without a moment's hesitation? Most who have are probably inmates at Hall, not officers in Säpo. And who wouldn't want to have a man like that among his bodyguards, even if he can't run like a gazelle?"

26

The HMS *Sveaborg* had come into port at nine in the morning, and an hour later, Mickels was at the front desk of the Kempinski calling Grip. When he came down, the MP looked both freshly showered and authoritative. Grip had a nasty hangover from his night with Stark, one he felt behind his eyes and tasted in his mouth.

"The captain would like to see you before lunch."

Grip popped two pieces of mint gum into his mouth and went down to the port in Mickels's car.

The captain's cabin again: wood paneling and coats of arms. The long mahogany table where they'd dined that first night was now bare and gleaming, as if it sat in the boardroom of a bank. At one end, Grip saw a stack of documents. There sat the captain, and, behind him as usual, the feline first officer, too impatient to sit still. Mickels also came in, closing the door behind him.

It was like being called into the principal's office at a boys' school.

"We have a few irregularities we need to clear up," the captain began unceremoniously.

Grip gazed out through a porthole at the view over the bow, as if he weren't the one being addressed. "Yes . . . ?" he said, after an excessively long pause.

"The legal staff has issued an opinion. The situation is untenable."

Grip looked uncomprehending. The captain pulled out a page, and the first officer couldn't stay quiet any longer.

"It's a matter of jurisdiction. We are Swedish soldiers and sailors here, governed by Swedish laws and regulations. You cannot just come in and arrest people. The legal staff is adamant about this."

"All arrests must be sanctioned by a prosecutor." The captain had found his phrase and pointed to it on the page. Mickels moved behind Grip's back, as if he'd gladly add something to the accusation.

"Are we talking about Radovanović?" Grip asked.

There was a moment's pause, seeing he'd gone straight to the heart of things.

"The law says this is criminal," replied the first officer.

"Yes, and that's why I'm here, to determine whether a crime has been committed."

Silence.

"It is a criminal act to arrest someone on a whim."

"Who was arrested?" Grip asked. The captain was red in the face, but he stopped short.

"Radovanović, for Christ's sake," the first officer broke in. "He has . . ."

"Radovanović is sitting in a taxi on his way back to the Sheraton, if he's not there already." Grip smiled mechanically. "I took him in for questioning," he said, as if explaining a common misunderstanding. "That's all. If he was away from his duties during this process, that is my fault. I'm sorry." It was hollow, hollow as hell. "It's complicated, what took place at the shooting range. Swedes and foreigners, and an awful lot of weapons." Grip nodded to Mickels, who moved dejectedly. "It took a few days to sort things out. But now I think we have a clearer picture."

"So Radovanović has been released?" asked the captain.

"He's been returned," Grip corrected. "If you have concerns, take them up with Colonel Frères. Djibouti and the base are first and foremost under French military jurisdiction." In reality, the relationship between Grip and Frères was about as solid as whipped cream, but the captain would never impose on a high-ranking French officer. Not this sailor. "Call the French base and they'll transfer you to him."

The captain's expression didn't change.

"So what is your assessment now?" the captain said, taking a different tack. "Mickels here says this Abdoul Ghermat person was released a few days ago. Was that necessary?"

"Yes. He was innocent."

It was apparent that the captain was considering his options, as someone still had to take the blame.

"Mickels also tells me that Radovanović has confessed. Is this true?"

Grip felt the ice beneath him get thinner again.

"Apparently there's a written statement from him," the captain continued.

"We don't think he did it," Grip replied.

"This has gone on long enough now, this fiasco with Ghermat and Radovanović. You seem to keep inventing procedures and legal maneuvers out of thin air. An officer is dead, obviously someone has done something—why else would you be here? Has he confessed or not?"

"He has acknowledged an accidental discharge, nothing intentional. An accident. He's not in good shape, and you need to get him some help."

"An accidental discharge," said the first officer in a confident voice. The captain leaned back in his chair like a judge.

"I'm afraid that Radovanović might harm himself," Grip tried.

"You see, an accidental discharge, that is no accident," said the first officer, "it's a violation. We have rules, after all."

Mickels chimed in: *"Treat every weapon as if it were loaded. Keep your finger off the trigger."*

And Grip saw how the grenade he'd hoped to keep the pin in had already exploded. Too fast, too soon. The uncontrollable force, triggered by someone's death.

"We'll need to see Radovanović's statement," said the captain, with renewed confidence.

An accidental discharge. It was a godsend for the trio in the room. At first, it seemed a Djiboutian had shot a Swedish officer, a sad story under the circumstances, and no officer with any ambition wanted that blot on his files. But now the African was released, so who did the deed? This new situation was not only tragic, it reeked of scandal. But a stray bullet—that meant no conspiracy, no larger implications, no debt that might cross legal and geographic boundaries. No one could be held responsible. Well, one man could be, but after all, Radovanović had broken the one rule carved in stone: *Treat every weapon as if it were loaded.* The train had left the station—and it was heading straight for the poor bastard.

"It's manslaughter," said Mickels.

"You could look at it that way," Grip said.

"Could?" Now the captain had a plan. Nothing would stand in his way. "Has anyone else confessed?"

Grip could probably refuse to hand over the confession, claiming it was part of an ongoing investigation. But Milan Radovanović was already a quivering mass of self-loathing, and now the mob smelled blood. It was Grip who'd dragged him into this mess. At the very least, he'd try to spare him a hearing with Mickels bending over him, yelling and threatening.

"I'll get you a copy," Grip said, nodding.

"Well then."

"But he needs help," Grip repeated.

"He gets to stay at the fucking Sheraton," said Mickels. "That's good enough."

Ernst Grip was struggling.

"So we'll be getting a copy later today," said the first officer.

"As you know, the foreign minister will be here soon," added the captain, "and it would be best for everyone involved to get this wrapped up by then. Nice and neat, right?"

They wanted the investigation and the visiting police officers gone. They couldn't get rid of him fast enough. Grip felt he'd been badly beaten, but he wasn't going to just take it anymore.

He nodded, some kind of assent. And then Grip changed tacks. "I was at the air base last night. When the Hercules landed."

The captain looked pleased; they could move on to other topics. "I couldn't get there myself," he said, "as we were still out at sea. But do you think it was handled well?"

"I only watched from a distance. I didn't want to interfere. There were some other things getting loaded as well, but a coffin draped with a flag, everyone paid attention. They loaded it last. Six soldiers carrying it up the ramp, very dignified. They did a good job."

"We got the message a while ago that the family would be meeting the transport plane at the base in Uppsala," said the first officer. "A nice, short ceremony, and the media can be kept out."

"That's one of the benefits," Grip said. The first officer looked blank.

"Of a military compound, I mean. You can shut out the world."

"You make it sound like . . ."

"No, no, I think it's good," Grip said. "That they landed there, I mean, on the base. Because you can keep track of what's coming and going."

The first officer had a cat's instincts. His look said something was wrong. Grip went on.

"Things like letters to families back home, broken equipment, and everything else that gets flown back on a Hercules. Just now, I received a message from Uppsala. From the Customs Enforcement office. When the ceremony was over, they went in and searched the cargo hold. I was the one who sent them. No, no one had tried to send home a smoke grenade or hashish from when you stopped in Salalah. They did, however, find a package containing fifty thousand dollars in cash. Fifty thousand. It wasn't in the mail, it was marked as spare parts. Someone had thought about it. It's virtually risk-free to send something by military transport— only this time it wasn't."

Grip looked over his shoulder toward Mickels. "People who don't treat every gun as loaded aren't the only problem on this mission."

"One thing at a time," said the captain. "First, we'll close the file on this accidental discharge and tie up everything with Radovanović. Then we can deal with the money changers, down the road."

27

Ernst Grip and Simon Stark spent the afternoon by the pool at the Kempinski. Grip swam laps in the chilled water and then went down for a stroll along the hotel beach, which always looked empty, far from the sun worshippers and the well-watered lawns by the pool. Down there, he found a shed with snorkels and masks for rent, along with posters of diving trips to the reef, and a couple of catamarans whose wires chimed gently against the masts in the breeze. The outbuilding was dirty and bare; the Kempinski's elegance hadn't made it out that far.

That night, he and Stark would meet with MovCon, questioning the whole group once again. Grip stood by the water's edge, stayed there a long time, but saw not a single sign of life. Too close to the industrial port? For the first time, he felt it might be best to go home. He could finish up his assignment from there. Something had happened in Uppsala, and that package of cash was real. Shouldn't he be there instead? Here, the heat and his fucking insomnia would continue to destroy him. The intimate conversation with Simon Stark the night before had stirred up long-buried feelings, and suddenly the slightest glimmer—an unshaven face with a crooked smile, or noisy groups drinking champagne at tables, or a painting in the lobby—reminded him of Ben. The old pain had returned. Contrary to what Didricksen had said before he left, he couldn't escape from himself, he never could. Shouldn't he just go home?

Then he was back in the pool chair, after getting beers for Stark and himself, letting his feet poke out in the merciless sun beyond the shade of the umbrella. Stark sat and typed Radovanović's handwritten confession into his laptop. He was struggling, trying to find a comfortable position, irritated that it was too bright not to wear sunglasses—but then when he put them on, he couldn't see the screen. Annoyed, he got a grease stain on one of the lenses, but when he tried to wipe it off with the corner of his towel, he only smeared it more. Fumbling angrily with the towel, the documents, and the computer, he dropped his sunglasses on the ground. They didn't break on the grooved concrete, but now there was a scratch across the middle of one lens. Although they were just a cheap pair, now he swore as he put them on and discovered the damage. His reaction seemed out of proportion. He sat for a moment, writing with the sunglasses perched on his forehead, but then he stood up, snapped them in half, and threw them in the trash.

"I'm going up to my room to take a shower," he told Grip, and off he went.

Half an hour later he was back again, with damp hair combed back, wearing long pants and a shirt. He sat on the end of his deck chair.

"Going somewhere?" Grip asked.

"I'll finish writing that shit later, I can't relax. And since I felt only semi-human after taking a shower, I was thinking about taking the car to get a new pair of sunglasses."

"Give me five minutes, and I'll tag along. I can fill up the tank while you do your thing."

At the market in the city center, vendors were selling knickknacks, fresh fruit, and counterfeit goods. There were whole tables covered with watches, sunglasses, and Louis Vuittons. They stopped the car on a vacant lot beside the market, where it was crowded with people. A boy who wanted to guard the car claimed it by grabbing the antenna, but Grip waved him away.

"I'll go get gas and call you when I'm done."

"Sure," said Stark, putting two fingers on his chest-pocket office, where he kept a wad of bills and his phone. "Later." He got out and, looking purposeful, disappeared into the maze.

Grip backed out and was about to turn onto the road when something smacked against the car. There was a crowd around him, so it took a few seconds before he realized that someone was pulling on the back-door handle, trying to get in. Out of habit, Grip had pushed the power lock when Stark got out to go shopping. He hit the accelerator, and the man disappeared without Grip seeing his face. But then something hit the car again—a rock, which left a web of cracks the size of an apple on the side window. Grip flinched behind the wheel, and people turned around to see what was happening. The crowd was looking at something, but Grip couldn't tell where the rock had come from or who had thrown it.

Simon Stark passed tables covered with little bananas, dried fish, and household odds and ends. He bumped into someone and mumbled an excuse. The crowds moved in unpredictable waves. On one table stood a mountain of Lacoste and Tommy Hilfiger shirts with crooked seams. He found a table with sunglasses, but they had oversized frames and too much gold, the kind only Russians would bring home. He tried on a pair, looked in the mirror—no way. The salesman pretended to be upset when he didn't try on any others. Stark kept going.

Someone came toward him walking fast, then he stepped aside as Stark moved out of the way, so that they only bumped shoulders. It was hard to see more than a few stalls away because of all the people. Stark stood on his toes and looked for reflections from the glittering sun. He stretched up again and saw what he wanted, a couple of tables away.

Heading there, he felt a vague wave of vulnerability wash over him, maybe because the crowd had opened up more than usual, as if people wanted to avoid him or had seen something coming.

A movement in the corner of his eye made him turn. Someone passed him, close by, and an empty space opened up around Stark in the crush. The man, wearing a baggy brown shirt, came back toward Stark. Wrinkled pants and leather sandals. The knife in his hand said something, but his eyes said more. This was a man who knew exactly where he was and who had chosen his moment. He controlled the space, and he didn't worry for even a second about anyone in the crowd. He stood with his legs apart and held the knife low. With his mouth half-open, he took a couple of breaths, and then he struck. Stark made an awkward swipe that broke the path of the hand wielding the razor-sharp blade.

And again, like an arrow, but Stark was saved by his reflexes, meeting elbow against elbow. The score was 2–0, brute strength beating malice and agility. Or almost. Stark's entire back stung. The knife had sliced through more than air when it swept behind him the first time.

The man moved sideways, keeping away from the foreigner's powerful reach. A moment of hesitation, but then a new dodge, and a strike from the side. Stark was ready this time, but he winced from the pain in his back and didn't have time to get his leg out of the way. He felt the knife slash through the fabric of his pants, and tried to grab it, but could only get a hold of the arm that held it. He gave it a sharp twist, but overcome by another stab of pain from his back, he lost his grip— still, the knife fell to the ground. The man grabbed the knife again, yet the look in his eyes revealed that he'd lost faith in a good outcome. He turned and backed off a few steps, and Stark went after him. Now Stark felt an explosion of rage. He'd give this story a whole new ending.

But Simon Stark had those bad legs he'd brought home from Afghanistan. No one thinks about that, not when rage is flowing through his veins, and although the man's first steps were slowed by fear, then he turned on the speed. The white man behind him couldn't throw the switch the same way. He only saw the running man's back, and his dusty steps that landed like drumbeats. Stark tried to follow the baggy shirt into the crowd. He felt his steps falter. The stab wound in his knee ached. And something about his back didn't feel right. He tried again. He could still see the shirt, through the tunnel of anonymous bodies.

Everything hurt, everywhere. He fell to the ground and saw his money and his phone slide across the dirt in front of him. His vision darkened.

A few moments with clouded senses. A humiliated giant, lying in the dust. Blank, strange faces looking down at him. His mouth tasted of gravel and iron. He groaned and tried to get his phone, but it was out of reach.

28

"It's just a game," said Carl-Adam without looking at Jenny, as he sat slumped in his corner. "Just a game."

"I still think we can trust him," she said. They were back to arguing about the negotiator, whether their hopes were rational or irrational.

"Fine. I'd say they found some random guy who speaks decent English," Carl-Adam snorted, still not looking at her.

In the back room, the late afternoon brought some relief, as the worst of the heat began to die down. Jenny got up to give Sebastian a drink, while Alexandra read her daily ration of novel.

"I don't know," said Carl-Adam, after a moment. The question of trusting the negotiator hung like sticky flypaper between them. "But Scandinavian Capital will help . . . They have people."

"Those greedy trolls, won't they do the bare minimum? You were like that yourself. Everything was about mine and yours, and what was written in ink. Never a penny more."

"They . . ."

"No, Carl, they won't. Despite all the money you made for them. They used you for years—we've talked about this a thousand times. You always thought you were next, but then they picked someone else, never made you partner. And now that you've quit your job—it's over."

Carl-Adam replied with a shrug. Was he disagreeing, or simply resigned? Jenny didn't care anymore. She filled the bottle from the bucket for Sebastian.

"That negotiator you think so highly of says Darwiish still wants ten million," Carl-Adam began again, after a moment.

Jenny coaxed Sebastian, lifting his head and getting him to drink.

"What if we could get it down to seven."

What Sebastian couldn't finish, she poured back into the bucket.

"Seven million dollars," repeated Carl-Adam. Alexandra made a dog-ear and put down her book.

"The house back home and the yacht," continued Carl-Adam.

"Whether they're worth seven million?" Jenny asked with forced calm.

"Six, guaranteed."

"And how exactly would they get sold?" Jenny touched the last half-empty compartment of Sebastian's pills. She got another shrug in response. Her fingers trembling with anger, she flattened the plastic of every little empty bubble.

It was Friday, the only day of the week they could reliably keep track of. The guards delayed their khat-chewing by an hour, abstaining while a few gathered for simple Friday prayers over at the other house. Jenny couldn't see much, only that the men who usually stayed in the outer room disappeared, sometimes followed by a quiet call and what sounded like perfunctory prayers.

Then silence. It was the same thing every week: for about an hour, no one kept an eye on the family. But escape wasn't much of a temptation, not with the landscape around them shimmering in the heat. It was the time of day when Jenny had the hardest time resisting the urge to drink all the water in the bucket, and when Sebastian mostly lay gasping.

Later on Friday afternoons, there was always a shift in the mood, and the guards found excuses for being with the family. There was expectation in the air. They searched for things supposedly hidden or tried to make jokes. It had started the same way, this Friday. Shortly after the discussion about the negotiator, a couple of guards came in, but they hadn't just poked around. The look in their khat-high eyes, as they stared at Alexandra's body, cut Jenny like a knife. A hand reached out tentatively to Alexandra's arm, pulling her to him. When she resisted, the man pulled harder, making the Kalashnikov on his back smack against him. And Carl-Adam pretended not to see.

"Be a man!" Jenny hissed at him, the second time they'd come inside, when a hand caressed her daughter's hair.

"She's a child," he said, defending himself by adding, "they know that."

"They don't see her as a child!"

And then, that shrug from Carl-Adam again.

Eventually, darkness would fall. At least two jeeps would show up, with several pirates joining in. Darwiish would also be there; he always came on Fridays. Darwiish, holding court over his kingdom of chaos, with all the liquor he brought. Khat and cheap gin all night. Panting, their mouths reeking of liquor. Jenny would wake up in the middle of the night to see Darwiish standing and swaying in the doorway, before he'd either shout something or stumble in to give Carl-Adam a kick.

This time dusk fell, but no jeeps came; there was some kind of delay. She heard the guards' excited conversation in the dark outside, felt the energy building. Their loud laughter, in anticipation.

They came in again. Jenny couldn't stand it, so she slapped one of them when he tried to get Alexandra to sit on his lap, hitting his arm as hard as she could. He winced and let go, giving Jenny a brief glance before he snorted, as if to say it was just a bad joke that caught him by surprise.

Eventually, the cars arrived, and with them the shouts of welcome, the clinking, and sounds of partying getting started. When Jenny heard steps in the outer room, she thought it was the new bucket of water being delivered. This was always associated with the jeeps' arrival, and she'd just made sure that Alexandra and Sebastian drank what was left. But Darwiish was never the one who replaced an empty bucket, and now he stood there, with another man close behind.

"We need help," he demanded, while pulling at his red beard as if considering something. Jenny could already smell the gin on his breath.

She hesitated for a moment, before saying, "I'll do it."

But Darwiish was already looking in the other direction. "The girl will serve us."

"Carl!" Jenny yelled.

Alexandra understood nothing at first, but the guard behind Darwiish pulled her to standing from the mattress.

"No!"

There was a brief struggle: Alexandra fought back, Jenny tried to get to her, but finally her knees buckled when they dragged her daughter out.

Self-hatred, loneliness, and Carl-Adam's empty platitudes. Jenny didn't say a word, listening to every sound through the walls. The rest of the evening and throughout the night: the men firing their guns into the shadows, piling onto each other in drunken wrestling matches, playing at being violent, or fighting for real, so that eventually someone had to break them up. Jenny yelled Alexandra's name a few times. She winced at the sound of shots, and tried to distinguish voices, moods, and movements in what was happening on the other side. She tried to avoid imagining everything that sounded like evil, or crying.

It was dark when Alexandra returned and impossible to tell what time it was. She came in alone, without a word. Sebastian slept, and as to what Carl-Adam was doing, Jenny didn't care. She moved toward the rustling sound on Alexandra's mattress. In the pitch dark, she perceived only her daughter's breathing and realized she was already lying down. She knelt and lowered her hand with infinite gentleness, afraid of what she would find. Feeling her daughter's hip, Alexandra didn't shrink from the touch as she lay on her side. Perfectly still. Jenny embraced her and then slowly touched every part of her with her hands. In the darkness, she was like a blind man who, after many years of its being lost, has found his prized possession. Her movements were restrained, as when someone fears the worst. But there were no tears, no sudden movements, just very still breathing. Later, in the glimmer of dawn light, she saw that despite one rip, the dress was still mostly intact. Jenny tried to solve the riddle of the dirt stains on it, but hadn't they been there before? They'd all been filthy for weeks.

The next day, when Carl-Adam tried to sit next to Alexandra, she immediately moved away from him. As if she could no longer bear being next to her own father. No one said anything, and no one asked anything. She did her math, but she didn't read her book. They heard voices outside but didn't see guards the whole day. Only once when the new water bucket was brought in.

They drank. The bottle floated high in the bucket.

"Do you want to wash yourself?" Jenny asked. Alexandra nodded.

29

Simon Stark, bloodstained and pale, sat leaning forward on a bed in only his underwear, aboard the HMS *Sveaborg*.

"You know, we'd been planning to head out to sea tomorrow," said the old surgeon, as he sewed up his back. Grip was also there, in the ship's small operating room. "You're lucky, in other words," continued the doctor. Stark said nothing; it was Grip who carried on the conversation. And he had no idea what the lucky part was—that the ship would remain in port, or that although Stark had a long slash across his back, it wasn't deep enough to damage a vital organ.

"You know, a small delegation has arrived from Stockholm to review trash sorting on board," continued the doctor, as he stitched. "There are always a few of these types at every port of call, examining something: kitchen hygiene, the Band-Aid inventory here in sick bay, or the onboard lighting. They get a trip down to the sun, play at being officials for a few days, and then go home and say that they've been there, done that. War tourists." He snipped. "This time it was a matter of examining the compost, I think. They're keeping us in port for that. The truth is, no matter how we sort our garbage, it just ends up in the same mess, in a truck going God-knows-where . . ." The doctor looked up at Grip through the magnifying glasses on the tip of his nose. "I guess they have to draw a line somewhere, between Sweden and Africa."

He seemed to be waiting for something from Grip. "In any case, it seems that for trash, the pier marks that line."

It was Grip who'd found Stark at the market after the stabbing and driven him to the *Sveaborg*. The trip had been chaotic and bloody, and Stark didn't speak much because of the pain, but Grip had understood enough. When the doctor cut open Stark's shirt and washed out the wounds, he'd begun to ask questions and thought they should notify the police. Grip was reluctant, to say the least. "I *am* the police, aren't I?" He'd tried to change the subject, and then said, "Just a failed attempt at a robbery," dismissing the whole thing. Clearly, the old surgeon didn't buy it, blinking like an owl, nor did Simon Stark. Thirty-three stitches, so far.

Afterward, Stark avoided looking Grip in the eye. His cut-up clothes lay in a dirty, bloody heap on the floor. The bundle of notes he'd had in his breast pocket had disappeared, but he still had his phone, which now lay in a kidney-shaped dish made of stainless steel, along with the knife that the perpetrator had dropped. Grip had spotted it when he picked up Stark. It was a switchblade, a mean little black one.

When they'd reached the *Sveaborg*'s gangway, both men were covered in blood. Grip yelled for the watch officer and helped Stark out of the backseat, where he'd been lying down. If they gave off anything, it wasn't a sense of control.

The doctor picked up something from the tray that held his instruments and looked at Grip over his glasses again. His calm was contagious, like a grandma who'd keep embroidering through any kind of crisis. Ernst Grip didn't want it to end; he would have been happy if there'd been a hundred stitches, if only he could stay.

Of course everyone was talking about it now, on the ship and throughout the whole Swedish contingent. The watch officer and others on deck had not only seen them but helped them get aboard. Now they were swabbing up the blood and talking. "Just a robbery," Grip had told them, as they helped Stark up the gangway, while someone ran ahead to alert the medical staff. Stark hadn't said a word about a robbery when he was in the backseat of the car, moaning and trying to explain what happened. On the contrary. But Grip had stooped to denying the obvious, to the people who'd seen them. "A mugger ran up from behind—no way to see what was coming." He'd made it up. He'd stooped that low.

Everyone knew that he and Stark had flown in to find out who had fired the shot at the shooting range, and by now nearly everyone knew that Radovanović had done it. The captain and his cohorts had pasted up a convenient answer for all to see. But Radovanović wasn't exactly the type who'd hire a local man with a knife to take on a two-hundred-pound white security agent. Something had happened, someone had gotten angry, and Grip had been publicly challenged. An investigation that ended in a crappy stray bullet wasn't good enough, not as long as Grip and Stark were still operating in Djibouti. There was something else going on, something they'd gotten too close to. And now Grip bore the weight of that. He'd tried to whitewash it on the gangway, and now the doctor revealed that Grip was fucked. Whoever was behind the knife in the kidney-shaped dish would soon learn that he'd backed down. That the fierce and fearless Ernst Grip could be humiliated.

"Just a robbery." And now it was Stark who looked away, with equal parts of surprise and disgust.

The surgeon began washing out the smaller cut. The knee wound was a minor thing, needing just five stitches; the fabric of the pants had gotten the worst of it.

"May I ask something," he said as he put a compress over the wound. "Slunga's body and the shot angle, how did that turn out?"

"Led to speculation, nothing more," Grip said.

The old owl looked at him. "Like the trash sorting, then. People do the right thing, up to a point."

Stark bent and stretched his patched-up knee. The surgeon continued. "They say it was the young Yugoslav who did it."

"You mean Milan Radovanović?" Grip asked.

"Milan, right. Imagine having to live with the guilt for something like that."

"All you can do is offer your condolences," Grip replied, without looking at the doctor.

It was time to go home.

30

TRANSCRIPT OF RECORDED PHONE CALL, TS 233:9865

Recording requestor: Bureau Director Thor Didricksen

Persons present: Thor Didricksen (TD) and police officer
Ernst Grip (EG)

EG: Good evening, Boss.

TD: I was just about to call you, when Eva said you were trying
to reach me. Do you want someone sprung from jail again?

EG: Not exactly.

TD: From what I gather, you don't have any trouble detaining
suspects yourself.

EG: What do you mean?

TD: The legal office at HQ is making a stink over a soldier.
Don't worry, I'll take care of it. I just wanted to know, are the
rumors true?

EG: In essence, the phrasing can be . . .

TD: Leave the phrasing to me. But what about the soldier in
question?

EG: He confessed to firing the fatal shot.

TD: Intentionally?

EG: No, an accidental discharge.

TD: Well, that's what we call a happy ending. I'm sure the captain down there is delighted. Say what you will about the military, but when someone accidentally kills themselves or others, that's business as usual.

EG: The soldier isn't doing too well.

TD: That's a completely different issue. We take no responsibility for individuals, only for the whole.

EG: I'll try to keep that in mind.

TD: So you've wrapped up your investigation, but I hear the hesitation in your voice. Is something else going on?

EG: No, nothing. Just small things along the way. I wanted to talk to you, because I see no reason to stay down here. If the Boss doesn't mind . . . Simon Stark and I can be in Stockholm tomorrow.

TD: What about the *Sveaborg*, the helicopters, and all the personnel they have down there? Don't they capture pirates?

EG: Excuse me, what?

TD: Have they taken any?

EG: I don't really know. The foreign minister's visit and trash sorting seem to be the priorities right now. Air France has a flight tomorrow afternoon, through Paris to Stockholm.

TD: Let's stick to pirates for a moment. Booking plane tickets isn't our biggest challenge. A principal called the police in Kungsholmen last week.

EG: A principal?

TD: Yes, she runs a school here in town, some kind of international program, using online classrooms. You know, a manager at ABB wants to flex some muscle, so they send him to a factory in Uruguay for a few years. But they're afraid the kids won't have read *Pippi Longstocking* when they get back, or be able to calculate the area of a circle. So Mom becomes the teacher, and the school sends assignments over the Internet for the kids to complete and send back. Very ambitious, international diplomas, the whole thing. Now, one of their students hasn't been heard from in nearly a month. She's never turned assignments in late before.

EG: This family isn't in Uruguay, is it?

TD: No, on a sailboat. One of our investigators called around a bit. It turns out that their family friends haven't heard from them in a while. They haven't answered their email, and their last blog entry was outside the Horn of Africa. Think about that for a moment. No one in their whole circle of friends and acquaintances reported a thing. You wouldn't believe this, Grip, what I was just reading: "We didn't think it was our responsibility to notify anyone. They've always valued their independence." I happened to see their addresses, Lidingö and Djursholm, some of these people are even sailing types. No one has heard a peep from a boat in the Indian Ocean, in over a month . . .

Anyway, had it ended there, I wouldn't have gotten involved. But three days ago, a strange call was made to a private equity firm here in town. The contact followed up with pictures. Mom, Dad, kids, they look miserable, and they seem to be in a place they absolutely shouldn't be. Apparently, the family is named Bergenskjöld. It seems someone Googled the father, who used to work for Scandinavian Capital. So now there's a, let's say, very insistent voice, demanding ten million dollars or those two children will never read *Pippi* again. It's a real shit show. Any day now, the media will get wind of it and the cameras will start flashing. The government is already saying they won't negotiate to pay the ransom, and the Foreign Ministry is, as usual, trying to point in another direction. Who knows where this is all heading. In any case, I think we should keep a joker in this game.

EG: We?

TD: Let me worry about the wording—didn't we mention that we'd hit a little snag with the generals and their legal staff?

EG: I appreciate you sweeping up the pieces I might be leaving behind, but I really thought, isn't it . . .

TD: I know exactly what that hotel room you're staying in costs per day. Take advantage of it. Indulge, by all means. No one is closer to the Horn of Africa, or more familiar with the lay of the land, than you.

EG: But what do you want me for?

TD: I'm sure you will find ways to pass the time. Just be available.

EG: As the joker?

TD: In case something comes up.

EG: And Simon Stark?

TD: Him you can send home. [Three seconds gap.]

TD: You went quiet, Ernst. I told you to send him home.

EG: I think I'd rather keep him here, if that's all right by you.

TD: Well, you have your reasons.

EG: Yes, Boss. I do.

TD: That's good enough for me. I'll be in touch. By way of apology, let's say that once this is all sewn up and you're heading home, it will be Air France, first class.

EG: I'd be happy with a cheap seat, leaving tomorrow.

TD: I'll pretend I didn't hear that. Good night.

31

"You're staying, then?" Mickels couldn't hide his disappointment, talking to Grip on the phone.

"A formality," Grip said. It sounded hollow, but he couldn't think of anything better. Sure, that hijacked family was the reason, but he wasn't involved and didn't want to advertise any kind of connection. He'd been put on retainer by the Boss, no more and no less. Nothing to be proud of, so he'd call it—a formality.

"For how long?"

Grip avoided the question. As soon as he'd hung up, Grip sensed the ripples starting to spread in Djibouti. People would whisper: the security police officers are staying. What's Ernst Grip really up to? People would ask the question. Wasn't it enough that his sidekick got knifed across the back? Everyone knew Simon Stark had been stabbed, but no one had brought it up, not Mickels, not the captain, no one. It would all quiet down now, that was the wordless agreement. Grip had been cornered, and Stark got the worst of it; when something like this happens, it's time to go home. He was down for the count. If they weren't leaving, then they'd have to sell people on a whole new concept, and Grip needed something up his sleeve. Something powerful, so he'd be able to move without fearing another knife in the crowd. Some kind of no-holds-barred provision that said Ernst Grip could get to them, as easily as they could get to him. Not an amateur move, but one that would stop them from even thinking about sending out more knives, because they'd know the consequences.

He'd lost all credibility on the gangway. Not because Stark was stumbling and bleeding, or even because he hadn't caught the assailant who had stabbed him, but because everyone had heard Grip's denial. It played like a movie in his head, over and over again: getting out of the car, going up the gangway, step by step; how they'd brought Stark in and attended to him, and then Grip couldn't stop himself from exposing his underbelly: "Just a robbery." He obsessed over it.

And now he and Simon Stark were afraid. They stayed inside the Kempinski, in their rooms. Stark mostly lay in bed, but it wasn't just his injury that was dragging him down. Only once had he asked Grip: "Why the fuck did you say it was a robbery?"

"To buy us time," Grip had answered. He had no idea what that meant, but Stark hadn't asked again, just glared at him. Grip clearly saw that Stark was engaged in a battle between anger and fear.

Stark took all his meals in his room, and once as Grip was walking by, he found himself right behind the room-service attendant as he knocked on the door. Stark opened up, wearing only his underwear and clutching the knife that had stabbed him. More exposed than ready to charge. He looked troubled when he saw Grip and fumbled with money for the tip while the cart rolled in. A tragic figure. Making a futile attempt to fight back.

Meanwhile, Fredrik Hansson appeared to be more than just a phantom. He could shoot his boss and keep on happily doing his job, sending and receiving through MovCon in Djibouti. Fifty thousand dollars in a package labeled spare parts. That required an organization, not just a single ax. The money was made somehow, then received, and forwarded once it reached Sweden. In dollars, nothing else.

So Hansson did whatever he wanted, while a half-naked security police officer stood in his hotel room holding the knife that was supposed to stop him. Surrendering to fear, that's what leads to defeat. Grip had seen it just as much in himself as in Stark, as he stood there in his underwear—the fear of fear, the kind that breeds self-hatred.

"Mr. Grip," said one of those overly helpful women at the front desk, as he passed by on his way up to his room. She got his attention. "Now you have stayed with us so long that we would like to invite you to receive a free massage." She handed him a card with squiggly writing. The hotel had a huge spa on-site. White buildings with glass, like an ascetic temple. "If it is convenient for you, perhaps this afternoon at two o'clock?" Grip looked thoughtfully at the card without actually reading it. "If not, we can arrange another time that would be suitable."

His hesitation wasn't about the time but some kind of lingering fear. "A one-hour massage?"

"Yes, we thought . . ."

Would he avoid even this?

"Thank you, that will be fine."

Open and spacious, with few people around and everything echoing off the stone, the Kempinski's spa felt like a medical facility. She introduced herself as Sarah, and he guessed she was from Malaysia. The entire facility seemed to be staffed by Asians dressed like nurses in sober gray. While he undressed and lay down on the massage table, she read over the health form he'd had to fill out. The room was larger than he'd expected, with a couple of comfortable chairs and a table holding snacks—as if people came to sit and watch someone get a massage. There were niches for candles in the wall, which was tiled in Moorish mosaics. Ambient music was playing, mostly the sound of waves and rippling water. It wasn't the gentle sounds, the warm light, and the scent of essential oils that made him feel calm, as much as the comfort of being within four close walls. She touched and then gently squeezed the long surgical scar on his shoulder, asking him about it. No, nothing that hurt or limited him, not anymore.

With the oil, skin against skin, soon her hands grew warm. Under the steady, familiar movements, his own muscles at first resisted but then let go. He rocked as she dug into them, and then his conscious thoughts drifted away, as her kneading turned gentler. Even when she walked around to change sides, she always kept a couple of fingers touching him. Never breaking contact.

Grip regained his conscious thoughts again, hearing the sounds of the water, but wasn't aware of her presence. He moved his head slightly, feeling the towel covering the headrest against his face. The body's pleasant weight. Had it been an hour already? He opened his eyes and squinted. Saw only the floor.

Then Grip heard a movement. It sounded impatient; maybe it was a sigh. He raised his head and was going to say something, but Sarah was gone. Instead, there was another woman in one of the two chairs, sitting with crossed legs, and a gaze that awaited his reaction to the surprising situation.

"Ayanna," she said, reminding him, after he looked at her for a moment. As if she knew that he'd looked for her name on the poster outside the piano bar. Grip propped himself up on his elbow, glancing at the towel over his hips and then toward the door.

"Sarah is not coming back. She has finished, even if there are thirty minutes remaining."

Grip was trying to decide something.

"Take a bathrobe, by all means," she continued. There were several in a neat pile on a low table by the head end. She was wearing makeup but didn't wear that "available" face she always did at the piano bar. Nor was she wearing any of the dresses he'd seen her in, but instead a more everyday cotton. She gave the impression of being herself.

"You arranged this so we could be alone for a while," said Grip, and stood up.

"That was my plan," she replied.

Grip stood with his back to her as he reached for the robe. "So actually, the Kempinski didn't treat me to a massage?"

"Many amenities can be arranged for guests at this hotel, but no, Sarah's hour was in fact on me."

Grip let the towel around his hips fall to the floor. He was in no hurry to cover himself up like a schoolboy getting caught, but quietly put on his robe before he turned around. She sat quietly, her legs still crossed, her hands folded. A wide golden bangle on her wrist.

"Is this based on me wanting to meet you, or you me?" He poured himself a glass of water from a transparent pitcher containing slices of orange and lemon.

"It is a strange way to meet, I understand if you feel that way. Perhaps the wrong kind of questions might arise, so let me answer some. My father was Somali, my mother Russian, from Ukraine."

"Should I interview you?"

"No, but if you are a light-skinned black person, as I am, white people are always wondering, and they get no rest until I explain the details of my mixed-race background."

"I wasn't really thinking about it."

"Soon enough, you would have, trust me."

"Fair enough. More questions then. Are there Somalis in Ukraine?"

"In Kiev. In the eighties, the Soviets paid for some Somalis to be educated at the university there. I have seen pictures of my father, he was very handsome. He and my mother were drawn to each other, there were some sparks, and I came into the world."

"You have no contact anymore?"

"Not with my father."

"And your mother?"

"She is still color blind. She does not understand why I left Kiev."

"For Djibouti?"

"Not so much for, as away from."

"I thought Russians and Ukrainians liked colored women."

"One could summarize the problem exactly that way."

"And the piano?"

"Mama is a music teacher, I got it from her." Her fingers trilled a moment on invisible keys in her lap. "In Moscow and Saint Petersburg, no one would buy a ticket to hear someone they considered a nightclub girl interpret Rachmaninoff. But on a grand piano in a hotel somewhere in Africa, they cannot get enough of Bacharach and Gershwin."

"That bitterness doesn't come through, when you're sitting there."

"There used to be a lot, below the surface, but now . . . I have no trouble finding work, and that helps."

"Well," said Grip, and thought for a moment. "I am Swedish."

"I know."

"What else do you know?"

"That you seem lost," she replied.

"I'm sorry, but was it Colonel Frères who sent you?" She seemed indifferent to the question.

"Colonel Frères prefers men but will do anything to keep that a secret. When he stayed here at the Kempinski, he was careless enough to ask for the same room several times. What he was doing was captured on film. With his uniform on, he is an influential person here in Djibouti, but those images make him weak. No, Frères did not send me."

"Is it true that in Djibouti, as they say, it is the French who maintain order but Americans who make the decisions?"

"On the surface, or just below, that is so. But there are Russians and Chinese here too, and they do not care much about which flag is flying."

"Maybe they're more interested in money."

"In Djibouti, that is all anyone is interested in." She nodded. "The money is the reason why the whites and Asians come here, and the Africans need their money in order to get out of here."

"Personally, I came here to investigate an accident."

"Then I understand those who say that you are lost. Whose toes have you stepped on?"

"What makes you say that?"

"I heard about your colleague, the one who was cut across his back." She paused a second. "Was it a robbery?"

He smiled.

"No."

"Do you know how hot it is today? One hundred fifteen degrees in the shade—one hundred fifteen! No one in Djibouti bothers with principles of justice. If you are injured, it is because you have gotten in the way of someone else's happiness. Principles weigh lightly, but money represents the chance for a different life."

"Now we're getting somewhere, to what I want to talk about." Grip took a sip of lemon water, then pointed with a slightly exaggerated gesture around him. "First, I want to know whose charity I am benefiting from here, without deserving it."

"Someone who is worried about you."

"Well, I hadn't even been here for a week, when Judy Drexler at the US embassy said she could help me out. Among other things, Colonel Frères owed her a favor. Now I'm starting to believe that this involves her knowing about his male lover."

"Judy even has a copy of one of the videos," Ayanna said, without a moment's hesitation.

"And she received it from you."

"I ordered a copy from the hotel."

"You work for Drexler."

She shook her head. "I provide her with information. For payment."

"And why do you think she wanted to get Frères's people to help me?"

"She could stay informed about what you were doing, while keeping her distance."

"And now this?"

"She suggested that I contact you. She thinks you need help."

"And you will help by providing information?"

"All that I can give you, about life in Djibouti, both inside and outside the walls of the Kempinski."

"And you know people?"

"Yes, that is why Judy occasionally comes to me. I have access to different people from the ones she has in her court."

She got a shrug in response. Grip was thinking.

"You have ten minutes remaining," Ayanna said.

He leaned against the table. "Tell me three ways that people earn dirty money in Djibouti."

"It is hard to say if any clean money can be earned here, but I will give you two ways that are dirtier than others: refugees and weapons.

That truth applies to the entire Horn of Africa, but it is here in Djibouti that many of the deals are made."

"And if people have taken to using a knife against a . . ." he began but then stopped.

"Then how do you make them think twice before doing it again?" she said, completing his thought. It sounded sympathetic when she added: "It is not very easy."

But there still was a reason why she had sought him out. She knew something about how one plus one could add up to something immense. "I have a morality tale," she began. "Here at the Kempinski. No matter what anyone says, it is owned by Saudis, with a select staff of Swiss running it—they have an eye for detail and discretion like no others—but where they need an especially firm hand, in the casino, they use Russians. No sane person behaves badly inside such a place, not when facing that type of Russian. Right?"

"Their reputation is pretty well established."

"And they care very much about their reputation. There must be order, it must appear spotless. They get enormous sums of money from the Saudis to keep it that way. But this casino is located in Djibouti. You've seen the Legionnaires?"

"The French ones?"

"Yes. A large base, thousands of people. Imagine the people needed to enforce discipline on the soldiers recruited from South America, Eastern Europe, and Africa. Not to mention the assignments they do for France . . . The officers, of course, are exclusively French. They are often here, the officers. One of them, a lieutenant, came to the Kempinski to spend an evening. He drank a little too much, and he gambled away even more. The roulette ball took a bad bounce, it landed not on black but on red. It has happened before, it happens every night. But this fellow started to make a big scene, he shouted that the roulette wheel was rigged and grabbed a croupier so that the shirt buttons popped. He was thrown out. Very gently, but out.

"Two weeks later he was back again. In the casino run by my

Russian friends, who do not take orders from anyone. Yet the Foreign Legion officers believe they answer only to God. And so he was admitted.

"This time, he put his hands on the head croupier. Valeriya, you should see her. Men have all kinds of thoughts about her. But in there, thoughts do not turn into actions, not when she is the head croupier. The worst thing was that those who watched thought they were giving him a free pass. A hand touching where it should not, by someone who is drunk and thinks he owns the world. There was no scene, Valeriya finished whatever she was doing and disappeared. But he stayed, and it was a shift in power for everyone to see. You cannot have this, not at a casino in Djibouti. It could have been enough if one of the Russian bouncers had made a little stop on the road between the casino and the parking lot later that night, and the French lieutenant would never have been the same, and everyone would have known why. However, this presented a dilemma. No French captain, major, or colonel would say that their colleague's behavior was acceptable. They probably despised him, but if someone had really roughed him up . . . it would make the entire officer corps vulnerable. That can never be tolerated. It was two thousand Foreign Legionnaires in Djibouti against twenty Russians at the Kempinski, so the lieutenant could drive off that night without incident.

"But a few nights later, two Senegalese who had never before set foot in the Kempinski were assaulted, and their hands were crushed. They will never again be able to hold a gun, a terrible fate for a Legionnaire. They are, or were, the lieutenant's soldiers. Not a hair was touched on the French officer's head, but he could not protect his own soldiers from his actions. Four black hands, in exchange for his two white ones. Whenever an officer sacrifices his soldiers for his own sake, then his soldiers lose respect. The lieutenant's leadership was weakened, and soon destroyed, and he was moved to a different post. He was never seen at the casino again. And now we never have problems with officers here, getting drunk and gambling away more than their entire salary."

Ayanna opened her hands as if to give him something and said, "So, it can be done."

The door opened and Sarah came in. She seemed completely at ease, as if neither Grip nor Ayanna were in the room.

Ayanna continued. "You have stepped into a hornet's nest, where there is money involved, correct?"

"Yes."

"Do you know any of the players?"

"I think so."

"Well then, it is high time to decide on a plan."

Sarah pressed massage oil from the pump and rubbed her hands together, looking at him. "Legs?"

"Sorry?"

"We did not do your legs. Would you like me to . . . ?"

He looked at the clock as Ayanna rose.

"Will we meet again?" he asked her.

"That is entirely up to you. But then you must reserve a time with Sarah." The door swung shut behind her, and soon Grip heard only the gentle sound of lapping waves in the background. "Thank you, I'm all set," he replied to the Malaysian. "But maybe I'll be back."

32

PIRATES KIDNAP MILLIONAIRE WITH KIDS

Not until Ernst Grip saw the photo of the sailboat under the headline did he realize how big it was. The newspaper went for the money angle, showing the customized Hallberg-Rassy with all its add-ons, along with the mansion in Djursholm. The other evening paper went for heartbreak, that this was a family with children: a girl's face circled from a school picture, and next to it, her brother looking puzzled in his passport photo. Both papers ran bland quotes from the government spokesperson at Rosenbad, and a flimsy statement from the Foreign Ministry saying its website had warned people not to sail those waters.

The Bergenskjöld family. Poor bastards, thought Grip. But what did all this have to do with him? He hadn't heard back from Didricksen, Simon Stark had a nasty slash across his back, and Grip was trying to avoid his coworker's disgusted looks while deciding what to do next. Although the Boss was laying low, and Grip hadn't left the Kempinski in several days, he hadn't been completely idle. He'd gotten in touch with a security police analyst. An old acquaintance—one who had experience, paid attention to detail, and understood deadlines. He'd gotten her interested, and she'd sent out a few feelers. Grip had told her about the money hidden in the Hercules in Uppsala, and as much of the backstory as he knew.

The next day, she called back. Apparently, there were detectives working on the case, even if their time clock wasn't ticking at the same rate as Grip's. The question was: who would have picked up the money in the spare-parts box once the aircraft landed? Five civilians handled spare-parts deliveries to the military in Uppsala, two women and three men. When they looked more closely at the records, they discovered a thirty-year-old man who'd worked there for over a year. A few red lights flashed: driving without a license, bad credit history, and a lot of complaints from an ex for not paying child support. Moreover, he'd done three tours with the international forces. An ax who'd lost his footing. That's how far the detectives had gotten. Astrid Süss, the analyst, had contacted them and forged ahead, and that same day she'd gone to Uppsala with two criminal investigators. They'd spent a few hours with the deadbeat dad, sitting on wobbly chairs inside the old echoing repair shop on the air force base.

"Nervous type," said Süss on the phone. "When the investigators asked questions, he frowned and sweated. If they'd been using a polygraph test, the needles would have gone nuts every time they mentioned this Fredrik Hansson in Djibouti. He rubbed his face and turned bright red, but he didn't utter a goddamn syllable. Clearly, he's smart, he wants to rat and get out of this mess, but he knows he'll be in deep trouble. We told him he'd never get to serve on a foreign mission again if he didn't cooperate. Then he really lost it. He was so scared he nearly shat himself."

"Believe me, I know how that looks," replied Grip.

"Anyway, given his behavior, this is certainly our guy."

The rest of Astrid Süss's report detailed the list of goods that the suspect had recently sent from Uppsala, according to the detectives. Most of the addresses were for the military and obvious subcontractors. But every other week, a package arrived from Djibouti addressed to Swiftclean Co. in Åkeshov. The package was always marked: Kretskort-MFD.

"That's some kind of helicopter maintenance service. But Swiftclean doesn't have anything to do with aviation. It's a cleaning business fronted by a bald Swede with a BMW, who hires a few hundred immigrants to clean offices in the city."

"Who handles Swiftclean's mail?" Grip asked.

"It could be anyone there."

"Check them out?"

"The backgrounds of all the people who work there?"

"Exactly."

"There's the guy with the BMW, Sven Rydén, and about two hundred people named Amadayo and Caydiid. A slew of people, some with residence permits and others who are undocumented, each with their own story, all thinking they have something they need to hide. To get to the bottom of it . . ."

". . . will take weeks," Grip said, interrupting.

"That's time I don't have. I'm just doing this on the side for you."

"Try another round with that sweaty guy in Uppsala."

"He won't talk. No matter what we dig up on him, we can't twist his arm hard enough to make him feel it. It's Fredrik Hansson he's scared of."

So there was a whole assembly line. It seemed they would go to extreme measures to protect something so profitable. And they knew who'd come after them. Grip couldn't stop thinking about the story of the French lieutenant and the Russians. What they did to restore the balance of power. He thought about the man sweating in Uppsala, and he thought about himself. His own fear. It hit him every time he sat by himself, eating at one of the hotel restaurants, while Simon Stark still stayed in his room alone. They were both prisoners at the Kempinski, and they weren't getting anywhere. Just for a little while, for an hour or so before dinner, he allowed himself to escape. He sat in the half-empty piano bar, but he never got a glance of recognition or a comment over the keys from Ayanna. Was this coming from her, or was he just wallowing in his own self-hatred?

Grip watched the TV news in Sweden over the Internet. A piece on the evening news. Scandinavian Capital had held a press conference;

apparently the pirate's negotiator was still talking to them. A clean-shaven man without a tie, identified as the company spokesperson, appeared on the screen. He said: "Carl-Adam Bergenskjöld is not employed here, and he has not been for a long time." The man tried to look sympathetic. "We want to support him any way we can, but this situation is not our company's responsibility. The Swedish government must take this on. This is not about an employee, it's about a family of Swedish citizens." The man was surrounded by microphones and flashes. He nodded when someone asked if the ransom was still set at ten million dollars.

From updates in online newspapers, he learned that Carl-Adam had been known as King Carl among venture capitalists, and that his specialty was mergers of medical companies. *Dagens Nyheter* had a link to an older article on ScandiCap, as they called it. Through its real estate operations at the UK tax haven of Jersey, the company had minimized profits in the previous year to a few tens of millions, but they gave virtually tax-free dividends to their partners, in some cases as much as several hundred million kronor each. The tabloid *Aftonbladet* latched on to this, adding up the totals from prior deals, and came up with a "Billionaires Club." There were pictures of houses all built on the same cliff overlooking the sea at Antibes. One partner collected absurdly expensive wine, while another snatched up every painting he came across by Anders Zorn.

Inside a fact box, the morning paper *Svenska Dagbladet* stated that on average, hostages were held in Somalia for six months, but some had sat there for more than two years. Others were never heard from again.

33

The negotiator arrived unannounced. His shirt was as smooth as ever, with his cuffs rolled up. This time he brought along a short, nervous man in rumpled clothing, who carried a cloth bag over his shoulder marked with a red cross.

"Come here. Now," called the negotiator to Carl-Adam, motioning for him to walk over to the table. "They say that you are weak. Dar-wiish understands something about protecting an investment." He smiled, gesturing to the guard to leave them and waving quickly toward Carl-Adam again. "Your wound."

The doctor, if that's what he was, set his bag on the table and put on his reading glasses, while Carl-Adam dragged himself over. Experienced hands cut through the dirty bandage, washing and cleaning out the opening.

As he examined the wound, the man asked: "Do you have enough to drink?"

"It's difficult," said Carl-Adam after a moment's hesitation.

"It is impossible," said Jenny. She'd stood in the doorway, watching. "One bucket per day, for the four of us. They treat us worse than animals."

The man looked at her, surprised at first, from behind the glasses. Then he looked at the negotiator over the top of the frames. "They need to drink!" he said, adding something in Somali.

The negotiator made a dismissive gesture, not entirely convincing, and spoke in Jenny's direction: "You can economize better."

She rubbed her arm. "If this continues, we will die."

"Water," said the man, as if he was thirsty himself, rolling a clean white bandage around Carl-Adam's hand.

"It's not just water we need," said Jenny, after a brief glance over her shoulder toward the children. "Our son, he . . . he has epilepsy. He needs Lamictal and Zonisamide, or he will die from the seizes he gets in this heat. What we brought with us has almost run out. Do you understand?"

The man had left a couple of fresh bandages and gauze on the table.

"If I understand?" he said, looking at her. He picked up a small white bandage roll and stood up, next to the other man. "This is what I can do," he said, pointing to his bag. He snorted, with contempt that seemed directed at himself. "Your son . . . you must understand where we are?" He pulled out two boxes of tablets and put them next to the bandages. "Antibiotics, it is a miracle just to obtain these. Your husband needs them, for his wound. Three packages of bandages and clean gauze to swab with, those I can spare. But Zonisamide, here? Everyone deserves to live." He pointed apologetically toward his bag again. "What do you want me to do?"

"We have a supply, on the boat," said Jenny, looking at the negotiator. "On board, we had enough to last for several months, but we weren't allowed to bring it with us."

He didn't reply.

"He needs it every day, but now we're down to giving him one in three. I've stretched it out as much as I could, but soon it will be gone. His seizures come more often, and they are increasingly severe. Soon all I'll be able to do is pray that somehow my child's life will be saved."

The man closed the straps on his bag and asked the negotiator something in Somali. Jenny had only learned a few words during her time in captivity. One of them was the word for water—*biyo*.

The next morning, they received a new bucket of water, and then another came as usual in the afternoon. After a few days, they even dared to set aside a little for washing.

One evening, while Jenny was dressing Carl-Adam's wound, he said in an annoyed way: "Did you see that ring he was wearing?"

"Who?"

"The negotiator."

"Well, what about it?"

"You didn't notice? Very valuable. He makes money on this."

"Could be," she replied, fastening the bandage with a safety pin. Jenny tried to muster some resentment toward the negotiator, but all she felt was simmering contempt for her own husband. Sebastian's eyes rolled upward at least once a day.

A few days later, a guard came in carrying two hoods. "The women," he said.

"Why? Where are you taking us?" But after the initial terror subsided, Jenny understood that Darwiish had finally agreed to let them go back to the *MaryAnn* for the medications. She and Alexandra were the only ones in any condition to move, and this time, the daughter was allowed to accompany her mother.

They sat in the backseat of one of the two jeeps, bumping into each other, for what seemed an eternity under their hoods.

From a distance, it looked like some kind of strange colonial outing, as they got out of the cars and onto the beach where the big sailboat was anchored, a little ways out. Two white women and a half-dozen African men—but the illusion was broken by the men's weapons, the women's sticking-up hair, sweaty from the hoods, and their clothes, which were turning into rags.

The *MaryAnn* looked the same, standing there in calm seas. They heard an engine, and soon a skiff appeared, coming from a village on the horizon. Half the men stayed on the beach, while Jenny and Alexandra got into the boat.

Aboard the *MaryAnn*, the first thing Jenny noticed was the piles of bird droppings on the deck. Even after the hijacking, she'd felt it was critical to maintain order on board. After the first days of chaos, she'd shown that she was the one who took care of the yacht. She kept everything stowed and clean, and she'd washed away Carl-Adam's blood from the cockpit. She never left loose ropes, but now she saw that the ones she'd coiled so neatly when they anchored were missing. Who would need sailboat lines out here, she thought, without dwelling on it. Then she understood a little more. The door to the cockpit was smashed, split in two by powerful blows. On the floor of the salon lay scraps of paper and wood chips. Everything that could be moved was gone: cushions, boxes, cutlery, gas stove, mugs— everything. All the locks had been broken, and someone seemed to have gone looking for hidden compartments behind the teak panels with a crowbar.

Alexandra hurried off to the children's cabin, while Jenny went to the one she'd shared with Carl-Adam. There lay the spinnaker, yanked out and left in a heap on the bed that had no mattress. At least there was one sail left, but there were no lines left on deck to hoist it. For a moment, she put off looking for what she was seeking, in the closet, in the little steel safe. It was meant for valuables, and she'd kept a few things inside. But after she'd been forced to open it for the pirates, on that first day, and they'd grabbed what little jewelry was there, it had been the storage place for Sebastian's supply of meds.

Jenny sat down on the spinnaker, which sank beneath her. The familiar feel of the fabric against her hand. She stretched out her foot and nudged the closet door open, so she could see all the way in. Where their clothes had once hung, now there was nothing. The steel safe hadn't been smashed open, it had been ripped right out of the wall. There were a few black marks, and empty holes from the bolts. Her hopes dissolved into thin air.

The *MaryAnn* could float, that was all.

Jenny sat for a while, eventually becoming aware of the sailcloth under her again and hearing the sounds of Alexandra farther aft. She stood and then, with her daughter, climbed back up. The pirates waiting on deck didn't seem to care that their hostages left the sailboat as empty-handed as when they'd arrived.

When the skiff approached land, Alexandra took her hand. Jenny let out a sob but held herself together. She thought the real tears would come when the jeep drove off, under her hood when no one could see, but nothing came. She just felt Alexandra's head against her shoulder and then she fell asleep.

Jenny didn't say much when they returned to the back room. Hopelessness shaped into a few words. She just said that the safe was gone, nothing more. Then there was the usual silence, with exhaustion and boredom. The day's movements were all so familiar that when Alexandra started to read her book and some plastic rustled, both Carl-Adam and Jenny turned. A familiar sound that they nonetheless couldn't place.

She held up her hand. "At least I got this." The bright yellow of a bag marked Zoo, full of little red gummy monkeys.

"Where did you keep it?"

"They would have taken it if I hadn't hidden it on me."

But Jenny meant aboard the boat.

Alexandra's eyes had a touch of defiance. "You told me and Sebastian that we weren't allowed to eat candy on board, except on Saturdays. So I had a hiding place." She opened the bag.

"Is today Wednesday?" Carl-Adam asked, as if someone mentioning a day of the week had reminded him of something.

"No, Dad, it's Thursday," said Alexandra, stretching out her arm, so Sebastian could take some without having to get up.

When the pirates changed guards a few days later, they seemed to forget about the new orders. Jenny yelled, trying to explain that they needed more water to survive, but the new guards were indifferent, and the morning bucket never came. Two buckets meant life; one was pure misery. The first time Jenny forced herself not to drink was unbearable.

34

"That apartment Fredrik Hansson has in Kungsholmen . . ."

"Yes?" replied Grip, on the phone.

". . . it's a two-bedroom apartment, and he also rents three parking spaces in the basement." It was Astrid Süss who'd called him.

"I checked out that basement," she continued, "in the garage. His Mazda was sitting there. Low-slung, nice condition, just waiting for him to come home, so he can go out trawling on a warm summer night."

Süss cleared her throat and continued: "The spot next to the Mazda is empty, and then there's a white Passat, around five years old, unremarkable."

"In one of his three spots?"

"Yes."

"In my files, it says only the Mazda is registered to him."

"Mine say the same," said Süss. "The Passat is registered to one Khalid Delmar."

"What do you mean?"

"The VW Passat in Hansson's spot is registered to a Somali. I asked a neighbor, and the Passat is almost always there."

"Khalid, you say?"

"Khalid Delmar, thirty-one years old, has lived in Sweden since the early nineties."

"And where is this Khalid now?"

"No clue."

"And his background?"

"There's nothing, no criminal record. Only that he owns a white Passat."

"Damn."

"But guess what, his uncle also lives here. And his uncle is the owner of Swiftclean."

"Swiftclean?"

"Yes, Swiftclean, the place that receives a box of aviation parts from Uppsala every two weeks. Or did."

"Wasn't there some bald Swedish . . ."

"He's just the CEO, owns ten percent. The uncle has ninety. It's about having a Swedish front, a familiar name, and a voice without an accent on the phone, if you want to do business."

"Go nail the uncle."

"Deep breath, Grip. There are more than a hundred employees, so it's not just a front. Sure, people come and go, and certainly some are undocumented, but their accounting is in order. This is not about his uncle. The Somalis seem comfortable talking about him—he's respected, finds them jobs. But they get nervous when asked about Khalid. They only give evasive answers, if they remember anything at all."

"So what do you have?"

"That he worked at Swiftclean, but it was a few years ago. Among those who know him, he seems to go by the nickname 'the Jew.'"

"The Jew?"

"Yes, something like Yuhuudi in Somali, which apparently means just that—the Jew."

It took Grip a few seconds to sort out his memories.

A bedroom in Husby with a closed door, the sound of rushing water, and screams from the bathroom. A young man trembling and mumbling in his grasp: "It's the Jew you want."

"Hey, you still there?" asked Astrid Süss. More silence. "If you move ahead with this, you're going to need people and time. I can't do any more on the side. This requires resources. Real ones."

Grip knew exactly. He needed support from higher-ups, a written report, prosecutors to authorize searches, a wider circle that knew the full context. But no senior manager at Säpo wanted to—or even could—go near anything having to do with the raid in Husby. A total failure, with adrenaline-pumped henchmen playing Guantánamo in a bathroom. To base an investigation on confessions made under the threat of water boarding—it wasn't just useless, it was collective suicide. He stood alone; the dice had been thrown by others.

"Thank you, Astrid. You've done what you can."

"But? Shouldn't we . . ."

"That's fine, thank you."

"And this thing about the Jew?"

"I don't know, the name doesn't ring a bell. And whatever's happening in Stockholm, it's a major hassle to work on that when I'm in Djibouti."

"That sounds kind of thin, you know. But I guess you have your reasons."

"See ya."

Grip sat quietly, thinking about Radovanović. The sad figure sitting in his room at the Hotel Mirage—it got Grip in the gut. The fatal shooting of the lieutenant in Djibouti might be another way in. The excuse he needed to look under rocks, search houses, and bring people in for questioning. But he'd lost that justification, thanks to none other than himself. The report had been written. Radovanović would go down. The case was closed.

Fredrik Hansson and Khalid Delmar? Grip didn't have a clue. But he'd come up against something, and it didn't give him a good feeling. He was solo here, on the brink of a much bigger game. The image of that man being interrogated in Uppsala, not just some hardened type who sat stony-faced, but a man in a cold sweat, terrified of what would happen if he said a word. To be able to create that kind of fear in someone. All Grip could think was: Give them as good as they gave. And he'd give them so damn much, so damn fast, that they wouldn't have a chance to pull their knives on him before he made his move.

"Could I get a massage this afternoon? One hour, full body?"

The spa receptionist scrolled through her computer.

"You'll book this for me? I want it with Sarah." The woman looked at a list.

"It's important that it be Sarah."

"I'm afraid she is fully booked."

Grip already had a hundred-euro bill in his hand. He pushed it forward, with one finger, across the counter.

"But I can change you to another treatment, here," she said, pushing the bill back toward him.

Grip backed off, realizing the associations were all wrong: Kempinski, women, money. "Sarah helped me last week. My back . . ."

The woman at the front desk nodded. "It must have been painful. One must ask for help."

Grip crumpled up the note in his hand.

"Come at four o'clock. I will tell her."

The day went by, and soon enough he was lying in that room again. On the low table. The sounds of the sea, the lit candles, the scents.

"Does this hurt?" For lack of anything better, he'd gone on about his imaginary bad back, and Sarah felt cautiously.

"That's good, right there." The charade made him impatient. But it was still a real massage: pulling, kneading, knuckles going in deep. And soon Sarah found where the real tension had set in—his neck and shoulders. As if at the push of a button, and despite his resistance, he grew drowsy. But he didn't fall asleep, or at least he thought he didn't.

Now she softened up his legs. Thighs, calves, cautious on one side where the knee bore old surgical scars.

"What happened here?"

It was the voice he responded to. Caught by surprise, he flinched and turned around. The fingers slipped off the back of his knee. Ayanna.

Sarah was no longer there. Whose hands had those actually been, massaging him?

"Just relax. This is not terribly dangerous." Ayanna, feeling the back of his knee with one hand, turned and looked at him. "Do people often come after you?"

"It was my partner who got cut. That scar is from a soccer thing, a long time ago. I had some bad luck."

"Bad luck? Do you even believe that yourself?" She seemed to be in a good mood, as she took a towel from a high shelf and rubbed the massage oil from her hands. "So . . . ?"

"So what?" Grip asked. This time he was not as confident, unnerved that she could so effortlessly get to him, and that he had only a towel around his hips, while she was fully clothed.

"The scars on your knee and now this back pain, does it say something about who you are and where you come from?"

"I played soccer, that explains the knee. And the back, well, I had to come up with something to get a last-minute appointment."

"So that is how it works." Ayanna tossed down the hand towel. "You concoct a lie, and through it we meet again." She sat down in one of the armchairs.

"I am sorry," she said then. "I meant no harm. You wanted to meet, and that is good."

Despite his desire to talk to her again, the atmosphere in the massage room made him feel insecure. He had the sense that they were hiding from someone. Ayanna carried herself with obvious self-assurance, but she still gave him the sense that her loyalties were unclear.

"How's Judy?" he began.

"Judy Drexler? She is doing wonderfully, I am sure. Did I not say that the last time? It was she who suggested I contact you, but that is all. What is it that you are so worried about her discovering?"

"Nothing, for now."

"But . . . ?" she asked, and got no response. She wiped something imaginary off her cheek, as if his uncertainty had spread to her. "Because this is not about Judy," she said then, "it is about me. You are wondering where you really have me?"

"We find ourselves more in your world than in mine, yet it is difficult to define what you are actually doing here. I'm trying to in-vestigate a murder, while you, yes, do more than play the piano . . ."

She looked away for a moment. She was about to say something but changed her mind. "The first time you came to this town," she said then, "what did you see?" He shrugged, and she continued: "The first thing you noticed was the khat stalls, and men chewing with clouded eyes. Admit that you felt contempt. You only had to look at them, to take in the musty smells and the drunken eyes, and you could distance yourself from the misery. It became obvious to you that the way people live here is partly their own fault. Then you don't have to feel the guilty conscience of staying in a place like the Kem-pinski.

"Here I am, I share this world with you. Night after night, I dress up and sit behind the piano. But I cannot just turn my back on what is out there, not because I think differently than you, but because I am always in danger of ending up there. My life can fit in two suitcases, and I go from job to job. I can make the rounds of luxury hotels in Africa and the Middle East, because I play the way I do, and I look the way I do. But it is just jumping on icebergs, and ultimately . . . I call it the curse of passports. I have two, one from Ukraine and one from Somalia. When I can no longer sit at the piano bar, where will I go? If I have a family, where will my children grow up? Returning to Kiev would be impossible, and living in the real Somalia or Djibouti would be my downfall. I would not survive it, the daily life would destroy me."

She was quiet, still looking at him.

"Have we reached the point where you've let me know exactly where I have you?" he asked.

"I, myself alone, I am truly the only one who cares about me, and I have to do what I can with what I have. Just as the pirates, they also want a different life. They are trying to grab a piece of the world that they see floating by . . . that dream. But they do it by trying to make their own rules, and then they are met by warships and armed he-licopters. My idea is to swim with the current, be an ally, end up on the right side, and offer what no one else can. As you said, this here, it is more my world than yours, and I can move freely. I can be Judy Drexler's eyes and ears, because when people see me, they do not think of the CIA and Washington, or Moscow, or even Stockholm, for that matter. I charge for my services, and once in a while I get a stamp in my passport that allows me to go somewhere a person from Somalia or Ukraine cannot otherwise go."

She smiled again. "You see, it is not dangerous to talk about yourself. The last time we met, you played at being surprised when I explained my background, but when one is a black among whites, one must always explain where you come from and where you eventually intend to go. You never have to, even when you are alone among blacks. And there you have me. I am not just playing the piano, because I cannot afford to wait for what the world might possibly give me. On that score, I have nothing to hope for."

Grip felt ashamed. In five minutes, he'd been told more about her essential self than he'd learned after years spent side by side with his colleagues. Still, there was a part of him that wasn't satisfied, that felt she was hiding something, and that sensed something was missing. What could he expect, what else could she say that would move them forward? Sometimes, real trust can only be built on action. After all, he was the one who badly needed to move forward.

"Black or white," he said, "you say you can't afford to wait. Right now, I can't either. You told me about the French lieutenant, at the casino."

"The Legionnaire who was taught a lesson?"

"Yes, you could call it that."

"And you want to make something happen?"

"I need help with my investigation."

"What do you need: a chauffeur, or a bartender who can listen to a conversation?"

"I want to get in touch with the police officers who arrested Abdoul Ghermat."

"Abdoul Ghermat?" She sounded surprised.

"He worked for the Swedes on the base, probably loading and unloading the planes that landed there. He was accused of killing the officer at the shooting range."

She laughed. "I happen to know who Ghermat is. About a month ago, Judy Drexler asked me to check him out. There were no leads, and I did not have much to tell. I think he turned out to be an ordinary Djiboutian who occasionally had a beer with that lieutenant. But who is this Ghermat to you? You would hardly need to try to bribe someone for a massage appointment at the Kempinski regarding him. Now you would like to talk to the men who questioned him?"

"Something like that." Grip stood up, put a rolled towel around his neck, and held on to the ends.

"Why do you not just go to the police station? Can that be so difficult?"

He shrugged. "As Judy knows, it's not always an advantage to be seen. And you speak Djiboutian better than me."

"Do you need an intermediary?" She was quick, she got it, and she didn't need more than a second to fill in the blanks. ". . . For the local police to twist the arm of a white person?"

"If they accept my proposal, it won't be so much about arm-twisting as about conjuring up a very unpleasant memory. I need to scare someone, and the best way to do that is to use someone's own demons."

They met twice more, in the room with piles of towels, Moorish mosaics, and the sound of the sea. One day between each meeting. Ayanna spoke to the local police officers, brought him their questions, and Grip supplied the answers. She came by with an offer, and he gave a counteroffer. He knew it wouldn't be cheap. Finally, he passed her one evening at the piano. She nodded.

35

Grip had to stay agile. Not so much physically as in decision and thought. He didn't want to watch over anyone when it was hard enough to protect himself. Besides, he knew that the rules of morality could be bent more easily when there were no witnesses.

"What's up?" said Stark, when Grip came into his room the next morning at six a.m.

"Pack your bag. The *Sveaborg* leaves in a little over an hour."

"Are we going with her?"

"Not we. You."

Stark was still drowsy. "You're kidding."

"No, you're going with."

"Why the . . ."

"You're going to sit down with the doc to figure out the angles and math, so we'll have crystal-clear evidence to prove Radovanović's innocence."

"We can do that at the next port stop."

"We owe him this, clearing his name. You're going."

Stark looked at Grip. "Why are you doing this to me?"

"We need to get this wrapped up."

Stark raised his voice. "Why are you getting rid of me?" Grip didn't answer, and Stark continued: "You said the knife thing was a robbery, not me. Yeah, I'm scared, but I'm no coward."

"Pack up."

"Is this Didricksen's idea?"

"The Boss has nothing to do with it, and I'd appreciate it if you didn't mention this to him."

"What the hell are you planning to do?"

"Don't tell the Boss. That's important, okay? Just focus on getting an airtight explanation from the doctor."

"It's Hansson, isn't it?"

"You'll get your own cabin on the *Sveaborg*. It's all arranged," said Grip.

"You want to be alone with Hansson, and you don't think that I . . ." Stark stopped himself. He walked to the dresser and yanked out a drawer. Stood with his back to Grip.

"I get it."

"We both know I was the one who caved," Grip said.

"Yeah, you need to do something." Stark picked up socks and T-shirts at random and threw them in. "And you want ten days on your own?"

"The *Sveaborg* will be out for twelve days this time."

"Twelve then." Stark opened the closet and pulled out a bag.

"The Boss . . ." Grip began.

"I know," Stark snapped, "not a word. But promise me one thing, if I'm going to be humiliated on a ship for two weeks, make damn sure you get revenge on that asshole."

Grip kept silent. Stark still had his back to him. "Hansson isn't working alone, that much is obvious, but you want to be alone with him." Stark yanked some shirts from their hangers in the closet. He turned and reached for something.

"Do me a favor," he said. "Take this." He held out the knife that had slashed him. "It only gives me nightmares."

Grip took it. He spun it slowly around in his hand and put it in his pocket. "Pack up."

36

The sun had set long before, but Friday-night anticipation still hung in the air. A few new warships had arrived in the port of Djibouti. Khat-fueled taxi drivers and drunken sailors came together in symbiosis: choppy conversations, loud laughter, crumpled bills, and impatient hands waving for more.

Fredrik Hansson had primed the pumps with pre-party whiskey and was now shepherding the flocks between the bars and clubs. Bullshitting with the bouncers, high-fiving, and ordering the first round on the house. He was the man who knew everyone, had all the contacts, and was everybody's golden boy.

Himself, he stayed sober.

He'd just left a bunch of Germans determined to see some nudity, and checked for texts from other hunting parties who'd been sent the wrong way. He jeered at Mickels when he drove by in his white Land Cruiser looking grim—he and the MP were polar opposites. Mickels sat in his field uniform and chased sinners, while Hansson found sin for them, wearing an untucked shirt and jeans.

Hansson turned the corner and checked his messages again. He headed behind a bar, where he'd parked the VW van he used for rescuing those who'd gone astray and, in their excitement, ended up outside the city limits.

A taxi drove up. "Sir!" Hansson shook his head as he typed a new message. The driver leaned across his seat and hit the latch, making the passenger door slide open. Fredrik Hansson, still looking at his screen, kneed the door to make it close again. He pressed send, looked up, and gave a wolf whistle. There were a bunch of small boys at the back who always guarded the van for him. The van was there, but the boys he'd spoken to a moment before were gone.

"Hey!" he shouted. They were probably sitting in a corner somewhere, a little stoned. He only got an echo back; the back lot was strangely still. As if abandoned. But the taxi remained there, idling in front of him.

The passenger door swung open again, forcefully.

"I told you—no!" Hansson said impatiently. His phone pinged again. He leaned down to look inside the taxi, saw the driver's empty gaze, looked at his phone, and then saw something move when someone who'd been crouching farther away rose to his feet. Hansson turned around to pay the boys, but then two men came at him in the stillness, knowing exactly what they wanted.

Hansson had dropped the ball. He'd never imagined it would be like this. Not here.

At first, there was only exhausted breathing, but eventually he made out, despite the poor image quality, a figure sitting on a stone floor with his arms extended. The shape held a strange pose, balanced there, as if constantly struggling not to fall over to one side. He had some kind of cloth hood over his head. One foot was bare, and on the cement a meter away lay the other shoe, which had fallen off. The camera was filming from behind. A man's shape came into the image and stood in front of the figure on the floor.

"Can you hear me?" the man said in English. He was wearing a police uniform. He got no noticeable reaction back. He took a step forward and grabbed the man's shoulder, and the figure winced as if he'd been woken up in the middle of a dream. They heard the sound of chains rattling; those hadn't been visible before.

The hood was pulled off.

It had been three days since Fredrik Hansson tried to turn down a taxi, behind a bar in Djibouti.

The police officer waited until the man's eyes could focus on him.

"Yes, it is hot as hell, and everything stinks," he said. "But this is how it is, when you are sent to a place where no one can see or hear you."

Once again, he heard the sound of metal being pulled up and falling back down onto the stone floor. Now he could see that each arm was held by a chain that ran a few meters out, to a ring in middle of the floor.

"You cannot stand up and you cannot lie down. I have heard people say that despite the terrible pain and fatigue, the worst is when you are unable to scratch insect bites. Perhaps you have found a thought that helps you bear it, but that does not matter, because that is not the point. You are estimating how long you can endure, but you must let that go. You know, we have been acquainted with you since you tried to make Abdoul Ghermat into a murderer. Surely, we went at him hard, but in return he gave us a lot of useful information. So this is not about how long you can hold out but about what we are going to get from you now."

The police officer squatted down.

"Abdoul told me about your interest in the black market, concerning liquor and more. That is illegal, both here and where you come from. But most likely, we can live with it. We are more concerned about the other things that Abdoul talked about, all the packages of money that appear and disappear in planes that fly out of the base. That interests us." The officer leaned so close that they were cheek to cheek. He whispered in Hansson's ear.

"I will say that the way we posed questions to Abdoul Ghermat, and the way he answered them, makes us confident that he had nothing to do with it. The money being flown out from Djibouti on Swedish planes, that involves you and you alone." The officer pulled one of the chains, making Hansson tilt sharply toward the ring in the floor. "Such an important activity must be protected, and we here at the police have few resources but many expenses. Think about that for a while. You have plenty of time."

Hansson just sat quietly, rocking. So the hood went back on.

Grip put the USB stick he'd been given, the one with the video on it, in his hotel-room safe. A little while later, he called Mickels. He sounded distracted and said he'd launched a full-scale manhunt. Fredrik Hansson seemed to have disappeared that Friday evening.

A few days later, it was just past midnight. Grip drove his car slowly into the zone by the port where livestock were transported outside the city. He passed the big pens packed with goats and camels. There were a few scattered houses and structures for shunting the animals. The building was hard to find, given the darkness, the few lights, and all the fences and nervous herds obscuring his view. On the second lap around, he saw what he'd been told to look for—a policeman standing guard at a house. Grip stopped the car, got out, and was instantly hit by the noise and stink of livestock packed close together. And in that same moment, despite the darkness, he sensed the swarms of flies and other biting insects. He thought: thousands here were suffering. The house he approached seemed to serve some practical purpose; from its porches, long chains and ropes hung from hooks. Grip went inside, and the roar was muted. Another man in uniform got up from his chair, nodded, and started walking toward him. Grip recognized him as the police officer from the video. They didn't exchange a word but simply followed the agreement that had been negotiated in several stages.

They came into a room where a large lamp shone on the figure who sat chained to the floor. The lamp was low, holding the man and the insects circling him in a bubble of white light that didn't reach either the walls or the ceiling. The sounds from outside could barely be heard, but the stench was intense, more from human excretions than from animal ones. Grip heard the man's slow, strained gasps.

The policeman crouched down in front of Hansson and pulled off his hood. He let a few seconds go by, until he became fully conscious again, before he said: "You are winning, but you have misunderstood the game. We do not have much time left. Keeping your mouth shut—that we know you can do."

Grip was standing behind Hansson's back, but he could see that the police officer had Hansson's full attention. He shifted one of the chains uneasily.

"Who is with you?" he asked. The voice was hoarse.

"Who?" the officer said impassively.

"There's someone behind me." Hansson leaned over, tried to turn around, but his body didn't obey and the chains stopped him. He was more worried about what would happen next than about who was standing there. Even if he could turn around, the light shining on him and the darkness beyond made it impossible to see.

"Now listen to me," the officer said, "your time is up. Your options are running out. Abdoul Ghermat knew what you were doing—and surely others at the airport did—and we know too, from the gossip on all the bases in Djibouti, that you have been running big operations. Such a person easily can become a victim of circumstance, or disappear altogether . . ."

After the days on the stone floor, the chains, the exhaustion, the insects, now his thoughts followed their own logic. "Are you going to sell me?" Something about the stiffness of his neck told Grip everything. Terror had begun to course through Hansson's veins. Memories from when he'd been taken hostage in Sudan were playing tricks on him. He felt the terror of someone who truly believed he was going to die.

A throat cleared, and then: "A call. I need to make a phone call." Hansson's hair lay like ooze over one ear and his neck.

The police officer picked up the loose hood, glanced at Grip, who made a sign, and then looked at the figure on the floor again. "There will be no phone call. A phone call, that is what foreigners who have been officially arrested can make. But you have not been charged with anything."

The hood was put back on, and Hansson shouted something unintelligible. Grip headed for the door, and heard that it didn't stop.

37

It had been two days and two nights since Grip heard the screams from under the hood. Two days and two nights that he'd mostly spent in his hotel room. He slept late and woke up under the lingering fog of a sleeping pill. All that time. A grinding eternity. He was too anxious to do anything, other than wait and read the Swedish news online.

"Zorn Painting Worth More Than Friends' Lives." The evening papers kept hounding the partners of Scandinavian Capital. *Aftonbladet* had gotten ahold of pictures inside the home of one of them, and an expert calculated that if he'd sold four paintings hanging on the walls, it would be enough to pay the Bergenskjöld family's ransom.

While the Djibouti police let Fredrik Hansson stew a little longer in his pen, Grip tried to find out as much as he could about the Bergenskjölds. He found their blog about their trip around the world, whose last entry was posted from just past the mouth of the Gulf of Aden. He looked at their photographs of dolphins, got to know the children's faces, saw Jenny's clear gaze, and noted the posturing of Carl-Adam, always posing as the one at the helm.

"We can't be sure that they are still alive." So said another expert, in an interview. Six weeks before, a dotted line had stopped short in the middle of the Indian Ocean. A voice with an accent had shouted over the phone that they'd been hijacked, and no one had heard from the family members themselves. How reliable was that information? The government and the Foreign Ministry seemed strangely silent.

Ten million dollars, that was what the pirates wanted. Grip

thought about it, asking himself what he'd do if he were on the receiving end. He'd often thought this was a crucial way of defining yourself: what you'd do if you suddenly had a vast sum of money. The thoughts you'd think, and the choices you'd make. But with ten million dollars, everything would be within reach—there wouldn't even be a game. What about just one million dollars, then? You couldn't get everything, you'd actually have to make choices. Just for the hell of it, Grip surfed the auction sites; he knew exactly what he wanted. He wasn't the type to buy a fancy car or a boat, or who'd retire and live frugally off the interest. It would be one thing, one that most people would walk past, without even noticing. Just a few streaks of charcoal, on paper that had turned yellow with age. It would be up for auction in a month in London, with a starting price of just over $200,000. Edward Hopper's *Night Shadows*.

The last time Grip had walked past Ben's gallery, the windows had been whitewashed, making it impossible to see in. Life with Ben had been a life of art. Now that was gone. Everything that came with the gallery, the people they'd surrounded themselves with, the talks, the exhibitions—gone. At home in his apartment in Stockholm, Grip had hung up some paintings, but they were mostly reproductions. They had come to life before, when Grip went to New York's major museums to see the originals. He'd stood for half an hour in front of an oil of a brutal boxing match by George Bellows at the Metropolitan Museum of Art. The boxers were so powerful and realistic that you felt you were there in the ring. You felt the pulse, the sweat, and the impact of the opponent's incoming fist. Standing there, Grip experienced it: two men in a fight to the death.

Another time, Grip had wandered through an exhibition of preparatory studies for some of Edward Hopper's most famous works. There were several drawings of the couple at the bar in *Nighthawks*, and some quickly sketched lighthouses on Cape Cod. Some were of places he'd visited. He was fascinated by the way ink could so precisely capture the atmosphere of a deserted yard, or a couple who'd become strangers to one another. Moods that Grip himself knew so well. And being there left Grip with a sweet craving to feel that, again and again. But with Ben's death came the end of museum visits and trips together along the New England coast, and then what hung on his wall at home were just posters that had no meaning.

The sketch being sold at the London auction was a study in light and dark. From a bird's-eye view, you saw a solitary man hurrying down a deserted road. It was so late at night that even the bar he passed by had closed. There was no life, except for the man. But from a few floors up, the observer became more than just an observer—he turned into a witness, although to what remained unclear. From outside the scene, just beyond it to the left, a single streetlight cast a long, ominous shadow across the picture. It was an evil deed the man had committed, or one just about to befall him.

The scene was better known as an etching, one of the few Hoppers that existed in an edition of several hundred. You could snap one up for around thirty thousand dollars; they showed up regularly at auctions. But Grip didn't want one of these, he wanted Hopper's preparatory study. The page where the idea had been created in charcoal, before the needle ever scratched the plate. Charcoal on paper, this was still the essence of everything that was Hopper: melancholy and loneliness tinged with hope. Grip wouldn't hesitate for a second, if he had the cash.

As Grip passed the reception desk, a porter stopped him and handed him an envelope. While it looked completely anonymous, he assumed it was from Judy Drexler. But he was wrong.

Inside was a color printout of a photograph. A man and a woman held up a newspaper between them, while in the background, a girl sat on the floor, and another child's legs stuck out on the mattress. Only the faces of the man and woman were shown, and they looked miserable. There was something familiar about the pose of the girl on the floor, and then it clicked. The Bergenskjölds. Carl-Adam looked so defeated and Jenny so exhausted that at first he didn't even recognize them. Between them, they held the *Daily Nation*, Kenya's largest daily newspaper. Four days old—to show that the family was still alive. On the back of the printout, someone had written: "If you want more, buy a new mobile phone with a prepaid card, and give the number to the taxi waiting outside the entrance at Kempinski at 15:00."

That gave Grip four hours. He went into town and did what he needed to do, then came back with two hours to spare. He debated whether he should inform Didricksen, but decided to skip it, and instead sat and Googled for a while, without finding anything he hadn't already seen on the Bergenskjölds. He got an email from Simon Stark, saying he'd sorted out the surgeon's report and everything looked good. But now Stark was wondering what the hell he should do with the rest of his time aboard the *Sveaborg*. At three o'clock, Grip went down to the lobby and out the door. There were two taxis parked there.

"Yes?" said one of the drivers, taking a few steps toward him. "I am supposed to pick up something for delivery," he added, when he saw Grip hesitate.

"Where are you taking it?" Grip asked.

Still smiling, the driver shrugged his shoulders, tucked the folded piece of paper with the number into his breast pocket, and left. Grip stayed to watch the taxi disappear behind the bushes by the Kempinski entrance.

Three hours later, the phone rang.

"Is this Ernst Grip?" asked a voice in good English.

"Yes. And I assume I will not get your name, but you represent the pirates?"

"I am trying to find a solution to this terrible situation. That is my role, only that."

"It's easy, then. Simply let the Bergenskjöld family go. They have suffered enough."

"I do not think your government understands . . ."

"My government does not negotiate with terrorists."

"If you are going to interrupt me with platitudes, we might as well end this right here."

"I'm sorry," Grip said, after a moment's hesitation. "Can we go back a couple of steps?"

"I can probably agree to a couple."

"Where did you get my name, and why are you contacting me?"

"Someone told me that you were sent to the Horn of Africa by the Swedish government."

"By the security police, and for a different case, but all right. And you have been in contact with my government?"

"All the lowest officials, and their receptionists. My calls are only getting transferred from one to the next. No one wants to listen."

"It's more of a policy, as I mentioned before, against terrorists."

"These are pirates, not terrorists. They simply want to make money. I am in touch with their leader, called Darwiish, several times a week, and I have been to see the family a handful of times."

"So what do you want from me?"

"You've seen the pictures, how bad they look."

"Let them go."

"Let's accept the fact that I cannot make decisions for Darwiish." There was silence.

Grip waited.

"Neither you nor your government seems to understand how time passes here," continued the voice at the other end. "The conditions of their captivity are destroying them. The boy is ill, and the last of his medicine is running out."

"I have nothing to do with that."

"I did not call to tell you that Darwiish wants ten million. Everyone already knows that. I am calling you in search of an entirely different solution."

"One that means the family will go free?"

"Yes."

"Without paying the money?"

"Yes."

If Grip had expected anything from the conversation, it wasn't that. "Let's hear it."

"Not over the phone. I will get back to you." The background noise disappeared.

"Shit," said Grip aloud, into the silence of the phone.

The timing was bad. Not this, not now. Grip postponed the inevitable, but finally, a few hours later, he called Didricksen.

It was late at night in Stockholm. The Boss listened, without a single question or comment, to Grip's description of the connection made and the phone call. Finally, he gave only one instruction: "Set up a meeting as soon as possible, and establish a personal relationship. But don't go yourself. You should save that move for a while. Send Simon Stark."

Apparently, Stark had kept his promise and not gone behind his back to tell Didricksen that he'd been sent out to sea. Keeping some distance was a good idea, but Grip figured he'd go to the meeting and then keep his mouth shut about it to the Boss.

The next morning, when Grip read the Swedish newspapers online, they all led with the same story: "Pirates Send Pics!" It was the same photo Grip had seen the day before, plus a couple inside the house where the family was being held. There were also details about their condition, that the father had been shot and that the boy had epilepsy. Apparently, Grip's caller had also been in contact with Swedish newsrooms. In fact, the pictures were worth a thousand words: dirty bandages and haggard faces, the filthy mattress the boy lay on in an unnatural position. In response came a constant stream of articles, comments, and posts. The old contempt for the partners at Scandinavian Capital was still there, and now everyone from bloggers to editorial writers began questioning the government's lack of action. The prime minister offered yet another "No comment at this time" outside the entrance to Rosenbad, but he looked uneasy. The foreign minister was as usual shown with a government plane in the background of an international airport, but he had little to offer in response to the aggressive questioning, and his usual banter was softened. "We are looking into the situation," he tried. When a reporter said back, "But the pirates' representative claims that you are not looking into anything at all," he had nothing to say.

So smart, thought Grip, so damn smart. If you want to open the valve, first you must build pressure in the boiler. At ten, he got a text message on his regular phone: "When is the meeting?" It was from Didricksen, who'd never done that before. No doubt under pressure from the government.

At lunch, the other phone rang, the one Grip now took with him everywhere. It was the negotiator.

"When can we meet?" Grip opened, to get to the point.

"Tomorrow, late afternoon."

"Obviously, you know that I'm staying at the Kempinski. Do you want to meet here, or would you prefer somewhere in town?"

"No, no, not in Djibouti."

"What do you mean?"

"We are not meeting in Djibouti, we are meeting in Mombasa, Kenya." Grip was quiet.

"There is a flight that leaves tonight," said the voice.

Grip was battling with his anger, feeling he was being taken for a ride. He held back when he said, "Is that necessary? That takes a lot of time . . ." He couldn't find the words. It would mean at least three days away, and that was impossible, not now, not with Fredrik Hansson chained to the floor of the police dungeon by the port.

"I need to rearrange my schedule," Grip said at last. "I will confirm this evening."

He didn't even get an answer, the noise just disappeared. It disturbed Grip that this player could end a call so casually. For a player he was.

38

Grip didn't have to go through spa booking anymore, as he and Ayanna had established a faster system. They still met in a massage room, but without Sarah working on his back first.

He sat. She stood. "Is everything okay?" she asked. In ten minutes, Grip had given her the whole story: the Bergenskjölds, the mobile phone, the voice who'd called him.

"So, you would like me to leave for Mombasa tonight?" she filled in, before Grip had given her the last pieces of the puzzle.

He fast-forwarded. "You know I've got something going with the police here. I can't just let that slide. Not now."

"But an innocent family of hostages, that you can ignore." She wasn't upset, she was teasing him.

"Two small children, you said, right?"

Before Grip arranged the meeting, he'd thought Ayanna would give him a flat-out no. "One of them is sick," he replied.

"I am not surprised."

Grip saw it, how she said one thing and thought another. Considering the pros and cons. She twisted a strand of her hair. She was already made up and dressed, ready to do the first set at the piano bar in an hour. The Kempinski wasn't the kind of place where you could walk in and ask for a few days off, without being punished.

"I would like five thousand dollars, if I go."

All she wanted in life was not to play Gershwin in a bar.

"You'll get six," he replied.

"You will pay all expenses. Two nights. And I will choose the hotel."

"You're familiar with Mombasa?"

"Yes. I know my way around, and what is available."

"I see where this is leading."

"Just a nice place by the water. It is not you who will go eye to eye with my boss, ten minutes from now."

"I'm sorry. You should stay where you want." He looked at her hand, still twisting the strand of hair. "I mean it."

"And where will I meet this . . ."

"Probably, we'll find out right before. That's the way it usually works."

She nodded. For the first time during their meeting, Grip saw that Ayanna was not entirely at ease.

"No big deal. You get coffee, you sit down, you listen to what he has to say. You will not react, and you will not disagree. You will not be carrying a proposal."

"I sit, like a good little girl?"

"You'll just tell me what he has to say."

She let go of her hair. "What can happen?"

"In the best-case scenario, the hostages will go free."

"I mean, to me."

"Nothing will happen to you. He's the one who wants something."

"Does it state anywhere that I actually represent Sweden?"

"You will not go as a diplomat, if that's what you mean."

"I have heard of people being held hostage for years in Somalia."

"That's what we're trying to avoid. Those two kids . . . the boy would not survive."

Ayanna's gaze wandered thoughtfully around the room, then back to him again.

"And if I had said that I wanted a visa to Europe?"

"I would have told you it's impossible."

She nodded, as if yielding to something. Then she said, "Certainly, you are paying me well. But this is really about Judy Drexler wanting me to help you. It is for her sake that I am taking on the job and skipping out of work like this."

"Let's just say that I owe you one."

She didn't reply to him, saying instead, "The hotel and the rest, you can reimburse me for that, but the flight, already tonight . . . ?"

"Here," Grip said, shifting so he could reach his back pocket, "is the booking confirmation. The flight leaves at six o'clock."

"It is already booked, under my name?"

"I bought it a while ago. You will be back on Thursday."

She made a gesture, not of surprise, but as if he'd taken an improper liberty. "So from the moment you came in here . . . you expected this?"

"Not at all. But I had no other way out."

Grip got a call on his new phone when Ayanna was already sitting in a taxi on the way to the airport. The man had no problem with someone coming to Mombasa in Grip's place; he almost seemed to expect it. Just as Grip had expected that he'd get a text message about the exact time and place of the meeting about an hour beforehand. Details that Grip, in turn, would convey to Ayanna. It was a short conversation that the man ended with a demand: "Do not use this mobile phone except to contact me."

"I wouldn't even think of it."

"Good. There are so many who would like to listen in."

39

Time had done its work. There at the house by the livestock port, down in the dungeon, with the thick walls that muffled the bellowing of the livestock, the rings in the floor, and the chains. Grip stood at the side of the room, with four police officers. One held a large bundle while another began pulling off Hansson's pants.

"What the fuck." The hood came off. The exhaustion showed in his voice and his movements, yet still he kicked.

"What is that?" When the other two policemen grabbed him, he resisted even harder. He writhed like a worm, but with chained arms, it was useless. The officer who'd been handling him before just stood and watched.

They had a uniform for Hansson, who'd been wearing civilian clothes since they brought him in.

"You're going to sell me, you bastard!" Hansson shouted. They got him into the pants, then the jacket, by unchaining one arm at a time. Hansson did everything in his exhausted body's power to stop them. As if the last thing he could stand was putting on an ordinary Swedish desert uniform, which he'd otherwise wear every day. He screamed, as if his skin burned from touching the fabric.

Finally, he sat fully clothed, with his arms handcuffed behind his back and his head defiantly turned away from the police officers.

"Would you like something to drink before we go? You have a long journey ahead of you."

At first, he answered only by breathing. Then: "How much are they paying for me?"

"Now that we have you in your original packaging, they will pay more. The price is a matter between them and me."

"Let me make a call."

"We have already spoken about that."

"I can arrange the money."

"You did not seem very interested in cooperating before. Now, it is a whole new game."

"Don't tell me . . ."

"Would you like something to drink?" interrupted the police officer.

"Khalid Delmar can offer ten percent of what he handles," Hansson said instead.

"Khalid?" Silence and then a quick sign from Grip, standing in the shadows. "The one you're working for?"

"Yes."

"Right now you are willing to offer us anything, and your word is worthless. Would you like something to drink or not?"

It was like offering him a cigarette before the firing squad. Something broke in Hansson, something that didn't have anything to do with him having sat for almost a week in chains on the stone floor. It was that thing, whatever it was, that had happened to him in Sudan. The thing he could never let happen again. That makes a man willing to sacrifice his own children. Grip saw it again, some movement in his body, the skin splitting to reveal an utterly naked soul.

Hansson cleared his throat, hesitated for a moment, and then confessed.

"Abdoul Ghermat figured out that I sent money, how I did it, and how often. He and the lieutenant were tight. They tried to blackmail me and get a piece of it. I had to do something."

"The lieutenant, the one who . . . ?"

"Yes, the one who got the bullet at the shooting range. I tried to stop them, but they wouldn't give in. In the end, Slunga threatened to reveal everything and send me home."

"Khalid, this Khalid. Is it worth so much to him, to have you here?"

Hansson didn't answer.

"One shot, and the lieutenant was gone. And then you only had to point your finger, and Abdoul Ghermat was out of the picture as well."

"It had to be done."

"Obviously, Khalid deals with big money, and here you are."

Silence again. Hansson was wrestling to fill it with something. He was exhausted, cornered, and terrified by the thought of people who wanted nothing more than to lay their hands on a man in a Western uniform.

"I fired the shot," he said at last.

"We do not care about Ghermat," said the police officer, "and we do not care about the Swedish lieutenant. We get nothing out of prosecuting you. Would you like something to drink, or not?"

"In the hangar, there's a hundred thousand dollars hidden— take it!"

"Bullshit."

"Send someone to the hangar where we prepare the cargo loads for the plane. At the far end, there are stacks of used air filters from the Swedish ship, big ones. In the back row, by the wall, there's a box marked with the number fifty-eight in yellow. You'll find $142,000 inside, wrapped in waxed paper, like ammunition."

Silence again, but the mood had shifted.

Hansson didn't realize that both the police officer in charge and Grip had heard him.

"The money's there," Hansson added, writhing on the floor. Swallowing, feeling the fear inside him, he forced the words out: "Al-Shabaab, or whoever wants me, they can't offer you that kind of money."

"What do you know about them?"

"They are the kind of people Khalid makes his money from, and he knows how much they have to spend and what they pay in other situations. I just send the payments along, but I hear a fair bit. No blacks in the Horn of Africa have that kind of money. Around here, you can't get more than thirty thousand dollars in ransom, not even for the most beloved person, one who is badly missed."

"But you are not black," said the police officer. "You are white. In addition, you are wearing a uniform."

"But it's still someone black who will buy me. And you types never have anything to give, at least not $142,000 . . ."

A short burst of bravado. The police looked at him with a mixture of disgust and wonder, but Hansson's gaze didn't match his words; it was broken. He looked despairingly back at the police.

Ernst Grip closed his eyes tight and only opened them again when he got out of the building. That's enough, he thought. If Fredrik Hansson was going to confess anything else, it would only be once he was cleaned up and in a normal place.

On the stone floor, Hansson would soon have spent his seventh day. The knife that had cut Stark's back was in Grip's pocket, its blade closed. In another pocket was a notebook that said: "Khalid?" After seven days, he'd gotten an identity and a name. And a gaze that said Hansson wouldn't be hiring anyone with a knife for a long time to come. Grip crossed out the question mark after the name and added: "Delmar."

Khalid Delmar, who had a white Passat sitting in Fredrik Hansson's parking space in a garage in Kungsholmen. Who'd worked for Swiftclean. The one Hansson wanted to call, when everything fell apart, on a stone floor in a room in Djibouti.

Did Khalid Delmar make money working for Al-Shabaab or whatever it was? He had no time to formulate the questions, not now. Other things were more urgent.

Grip was focused on the hangar; that was his top priority. He didn't completely trust the hired cops. The French would never let them in to poke around on the base, but there was always someone willing to look the other way. So far, Hansson was probably right: that kind of money could trump all types of contracts and loyalties.

Grip held up his card, slipped past the guard, and headed down to the airplane hangars. The gates to the Swedish buildings were closed. One, however, had a small door in the middle, with a Swedish flag. Grip parked in front, then got out and tried the handle. Just as he expected, it was unlocked. He looked over toward the MovCon barracks—there were two cars parked outside but no sign of activity—and went inside.

From the blazing lights of the airport, he entered absolute darkness. His eyes had to adjust; for a few seconds, it was like being in a coal mine. Then the trucks, pallets, and shelves began to emerge. He saw the huge air filters from the *Sveaborg* that Hansson had talked about and, in the back row, small boxes made of familiar military-green plywood. He found the number fifty-eight, marked in yellow. Grip had to break the seals. There was nothing written on the packets inside, which looked like three bricks wrapped in waxed paper. In the heat, the wax stuck to his hands. Grip opened his jackknife and cut through the paper, the smell reminding him vaguely of gingerbread. There was a thin layer of cardboard inside the paper, and then the bills. He riffled his thumb along the edge, all hundred-dollar bills. He did a rough count; it seemed right.

Something vague was becoming concrete. He was the police officer, and now he stood with the knife that had stabbed Stark in one hand, and the money that the assassin's deed was meant to protect in the other. But oddly enough, he felt no sense of satisfaction.

40

The police in Djibouti held Fredrik Hansson one more day and then left the exhausted Swede on a rocky field a few kilometers outside of town. They'd left it to him to take off the hood. He'd completely lost track of time; when he pulled his head free, he found himself under the stars. There were city lights on one side, and on the other, the taillights of the truck that had dumped him, disappearing down a lonely road.

It took him a while to understand that nothing more would happen. That it had all been a bluff. And that he should start walking.

When he passed through the lobby of the Sheraton six hours later, people turned around, terrified by both his ravaged appearance and his smell. Some soldiers on their way down to breakfast recognized him and spread the alert.

He was pampered all morning: a shower and then a bath, a medical examination, a breakfast he declined, and so on, until Mickels's kindness toward the victim was replaced by: "What the hell is this supposed to mean, anyway?" People said Hansson had been sitting in Mickels's office, dressed in a new uniform, drinking bottle after bottle of cold water from the refrigerator, without saying a word. Nothing more than, "I don't remember."

"But where the hell have you been? Obviously, you got here from somewhere?"

He shrugged in response and kept looking at the clock on the wall. "Can I go now?" His watch had gotten lost.

"We organized one hell of a manhunt here. We thought someone had kidnapped you. Did you just take off?"

"Can I go now?"

The angry MP had set up another appointment for the next morning, and he shouted so loudly about MovCon and gangs of robbers that people heard far beyond the white walls of the barracks after Hansson was escorted out.

The day went by, and that night, Hansson was back at the Sheraton with the rest of MovCon. Crisis management would be kept within the group, as someone in Human Resources had advised. Still, no one knew the slightest thing about what had happened; they could only guess based on how he looked and smelled. In any case, Mickels had been proactive and said that Hansson wasn't allowed to leave the Sheraton without being accompanied by two others from the group. Obviously, no one in MovCon would dare to challenge Hansson if he decided otherwise—that's the way Ernst Grip saw it. So he'd had a little talk with Philippa Ekman.

The sun had set when she called. "He just took off in one of our cars."

Grip was sitting alone in the café on the French base. It wasn't much more than a metal roof supported by poles, where people went to have a coffee after lunch or, at this hour, to sit a little longer with something cold, now that the sun was down and the people could actually be outdoors. Grip left a tip on a cocktail napkin and headed out. He drove down to the hangars and sat there to wait, with his windows open.

Not even ten minutes later, Hansson appeared. He parked outside the MovCon barracks and walked toward the hangar. Grip had parked among a bunch of other vehicles. Hansson didn't even look in his direction, just headed toward the small door in the gate, whose knob Grip himself had turned the day before. Now it was all about tying up loose ends, moving beyond what Grip knew but couldn't use—and building a nice, clean airtight case against Hansson. Saying good-bye to the accidental shot, giving Radovanović his life back, and serving up Hansson on a silver platter. On his side, Grip had the Customs findings from the Hercules in Uppsala, Philippa Ekman's testimony about the laser pointer, and the surgeon's report about shot angles that didn't add up. Solid stuff that pointed away from Radovanović, but not enough hard evidence for a prosecutor to charge Hansson. Grip needed a confession. He'd already heard one, but now he needed one without the rattling chains. Not least, so he could face himself in the mirror.

He couldn't stop thinking about the look in Fredrik Hansson's eyes as he finished confessing to the police chief, while Grip stood in the shadows, watching. The way he looked totally exposed. There weren't many like Hansson, who could withstand that type of treatment. He could have died from the heat and stress, in that agonizing position on the stone floor, but he held up. It was his old fear of being bound up for sacrifice by religious fanatics that made him crack. His gaze in that moment revealed not what he'd endured but what he needed to be saved from.

Confronted with his worst terror, only his reptilian instincts remained, and all he could do was protect himself. Only then did he crumble and spill his guts. Once Grip had used the trick of conjuring fundamentalists' spinning swords, he couldn't try it again, not to induce a clean confession. Faced with the thought of having his throat slit like an animal, Hansson had still managed to control himself. He didn't give up everything. He'd confessed to the murder he committed, but he continued to hide his motive. He hadn't shot the lieutenant or hired someone to stab Simon Stark in order to protect the deliveries of cash. He might even have thought so himself, but in truth he'd acted out of a primal fear of abandonment. This made him the most dangerous type, afraid of losing something larger than himself. He'd been released from his chains, but he didn't feel free. He was still vulnerable, and very dangerous. It didn't bother him that people in his way might have to die.

The hangar door opened, and Hansson came out again. Grip surprised him, standing perfectly still just a few meters away, but Hansson didn't even flinch. He just stopped and stood there, eyeing him, shaking and breathless. He was soaked in sweat, looking like a man who'd just lost $142,000 that he owed someone. Money that now lay tightly packed in the safe of a hotel room at the Kempinski.

"Sweating out all the water you drank in Mickels's office?" asked Grip.

Hansson made a face but didn't go back to his car. He stood there and tried to make sense of the coincidence.

Exhausted, lips cracked. Every thought and feeling showing on the surface. He turned and looked toward the hangar door.

"Whatever is in there will be fine overnight," said Grip.

Hansson couldn't put his thoughts and doubts together.

"What time do you have to report to Mickels tomorrow?"

"Ten, I think," Hansson said.

"You think?"

"Ten." He nodded.

"Now, let's move on to another matter," Grip continued. "You and Khalid Delmar share an apartment in Kungsholmen. Yeah, it's in your name, but you own it together. Three parking spots in the garage, and a car each sitting there."

Direct hit. He watched it sink in.

"The money that Customs seized in Uppsala would have been picked up by Swiftclean. The company owned by Delmar's uncle. Does he even know that you launder your money there?"

That look again, lonely as much as desperate. Hansson had one second left before detonation. Did he understand that Grip had been there, while he sat chained on the stone floor? Had he seen him, after all?

Grip had the knife he'd got from Simon Stark in his hand, hidden and ready, but he remained completely cool on the surface, as if he'd just asked about the weather. An ounce of contempt in his eyes or his tone, and Hansson would have ticked the last thousandth down to zero.

"Ten o'clock, you say. So let's you and I meet at eight tomorrow. Eight o'clock. I'll come to the Sheraton, and we'll have a chat there."

Hansson turned again toward the hangar door.

"You need to get some sleep," Grip continued, in a voice that could easily have been mistaken for caring. "Head back to the hotel, and go to bed. That's what you need to do right now." That was the plan, a night without chains for Hansson, still prisoner of his own anxiety. In the morning, he'd confess to the murder, to distract Grip from Delmar and whatever else he was up to. At least, that was what Fredrik Hansson thought he could get away with. Grip had already asked about a small conference room at the Sheraton. They'd sit there, and this time it would all be recorded. He'd made a checklist of what would follow, starting with the call to the prosecutor in Sweden, so the arrest would be done right. Mickels, who didn't know it yet, would have a real criminal to deal with, while the National Police sent down a couple of men for quick transport home.

"Eight o'clock," Grip repeated. "Set your alarm, to make sure you wake up."

Maybe it was a nod he got back. Hansson got into his car and drove away. Grip closed the blade and put the knife back in his pocket.

As Hansson's car disappeared, Grip heard the engine throttle of a drone taking off on the American side. A barely discernible silhouette that rose up under the lights of the runway. A red navigation light at the wing tip, an anticollision light flicking angrily somewhere at the back. First the engine noise died away, then the lights faded, and finally the pilotless craft disappeared into the night.

It was an evening with a very special schedule. Grip's first ball was in the pocket, and the next was rolling in. Ayanna had landed half an hour earlier, on her Ethiopian Air flight back from Mombasa. Late at night, there'd be no massage room available at the Kempinski, but they wanted to meet as soon as possible.

Grip had just received the address from her in a text, but he had no idea where the place was or what kind of a place it was. It turned out to be on the outskirts of town, in a crowded residential area. Behind the walls and tall iron fences leading from the street were views of small courtyards and low houses. Everything was run-down; the car's wheels rattled over the rocks and potholes, despite its low speed. Grip tried to find the street number among the scattered lights and randomly lit entrances, when an elderly man stepped out into the street and waved him in.

"Here," he said, when Grip stopped, motioning for him to leave the car where it stood.

The man led the way in through the wooden door in a wall, and then down a wide path past a house where the light of a television flickered inside a window. They turned the corner, and the space opened onto a small paved terrace. A handful of trees obscured the surrounding walls, and their branches formed a sparse archway against the night sky. A gas lamp hung from a branch, above a table made of stone. There were a couple of chairs, and Ayanna sat on one of them. Her hair was gathered in a bun, so that her neck was bare, and she was wearing a loose, comfortable cotton dress. The man who led the way made a gesture of delivery and disappeared again.

"Who . . . ?" Grip said, as he sat down.

"These are just some acquaintances of mine."

"Of course." Grip watched a moth bump against the glass of the gas lamp. "So, what did you find out?" he asked. There was a pitcher of something on the table. Seeing that Ayanna's glass was already half empty, Grip poured one for himself.

"You already know that I met the negotiator at a hotel," Ayanna began.

Grip drank; it tasted of mint and citrus. "What did he look like?" he asked.

"Clean-shaven, well-dressed, good English."

"You didn't sneak a picture of him?"

"He asked me to turn off the phone as soon as we said hello."

Grip nodded. "Was he relaxed or stressed?"

"He was eager, if you understand what I mean."

"Not exactly."

"He gave me these." She handed over a pair of paper tabs torn from packages. Grip read the few printed words on them but didn't understand. "The medications," Ayanna explained, "two different types, for the boy."

"The ones that have run out?"

Ayanna nodded. "The pirates do not care, and even if they did, there is no way for them to obtain them."

Grip twisted and turned the pieces of paper. "The idea is to supply the drugs, which he will bring to the family?"

"Yes."

"A nice gesture, but what does he want in return?"

"He said that your Swedish family will not survive much longer, and he sees a way to get the hostages released."

"That's what we want. And what did he want?"

"He said that in return, he wants immunity from prosecution."

"What?"

"If the hostages go free, then afterward there will be no investigation and no charges filed against him."

"But he wasn't there when they were kidnapped, right? He's not the one out there in the desert, pointing at them with a Kalashnikov. He is their negotiator."

"He said that the West is resentful, and that they will find and kill scapegoats at any cost."

"So he said that," replied Grip. "Well, who can blame him?"

"Do you think it sounds too good to be true?"

"Freeing the hostages without paying any ransom? Yes, I'd say so." Grip fiddled with the pieces of paper.

"But you cannot simply dismiss him."

"No, I can't. He's in direct contact with the pirates." Grip leaned back, trying to think. He emptied the glass in a few gulps. "A phone number and the vague promise of an impossible plan, that's what I have."

"Everyone wants that little boy to survive," said Ayanna.

"In that case, he needs to get the drugs immediately."

"I can go back tomorrow." She didn't look at him when she said it, trying to make her own wishes sound like an offer to him.

"What do you mean?"

"It is clear that you are busy here in Djibouti, but you are the one who must obtain the medicines. That I cannot do. Only white men have access to proper medications in this town. But I can take them down to Mombasa tomorrow."

"You'd go straight back?"

"The negotiator said he would remain for a day or so. You can call him to schedule a meeting. Another text message, a new meeting place. This will show your goodwill and also prove that you can get things done. This way, you will keep in touch with him."

"What about the Kempinski. Isn't there an empty grand piano at the bar?"

"I said that my mother has become very ill, that things must be arranged. That it might take a while."

"Was that the lie that got you time off?"

"Yes. Timur, the Russian manager of the casino, put in a good word for me." She closed her eyes and turned her face up toward the trees. "So have we agreed that I will go?"

Grip put the paper tabs in his breast pocket. "I'll try to contact him tonight. But you should arrange the plane ticket and the hotel, as I'm busy with other things."

She nodded. Grip leaned forward and pulled an envelope out of his pocket—a withdrawal from the war chest in his hotel-room safe. "You asked for six thousand for this trip. How much were expenses?"

"Another three?"

"For a hotel room and food?" He sounded dubious, and she nodded. "Dollars?" A nod again. He laughed and began to count the notes.

"Here are ten." He handed over the stack.

"So I do get a tip, after all?"

"You've got a sick mother in Kiev, don't you?" She smiled.

"Anyway. From now on, the rate is a thousand dollars a day, plus five hundred for expenses. Do what you want, that's what you're working with, but make sure that this man keeps talking to us. Then there's this matter, too." Ayanna looked bewildered at a new bundle of banknotes, thick as a paperback. "It's fifteen thousand," he explained. "For the police officers you persuaded to work with me, here in Djibouti. They should be paid for extra night shifts, the cost of chains, and whatever else. I'm sure they will bitch and moan, trying to squeeze more out of me. What's here"—he pointed to the pile in her hand—"is more than we agreed on. You're going to make sure that they're satisfied with what they get. I don't want to hear a word back from them. Do me that favor, in exchange for all your extra expenses and your tip. Agreed?" She hesitated.

"So are you going to Mombasa or not?" he asked.

She absentmindedly played a few piano notes on her thigh, before she looked up at him and said, "The police in Djibouti thank you in advance for your generosity. I will be leaving tomorrow, and they will be more than satisfied before I do."

41

Recording requestor: Bureau Director Thor Didricksen

TOP SECRET UNDER CHAPTER 2, SECTION 2 OF THE SECRECY ACT (1980:100)
OF HIGHEST IMPORTANCE TO NATIONAL SECURITY

Persons present: Thor Didricksen (TD) and police officer
Ernst Grip (EG)

EG: I'm sorry, Boss, it's already past midnight, but I thought . . .

TD: No problem. The problem is what's in the newspapers
here at home—have you been keeping up?

EG: I've had other . . .

TD: The media are like vultures. Some government secretary
calls me from Rosenbad at least once an hour, and I'm the
one expected to come up with a solution. People think the
government is doing nothing. Basically, that's right—but the
photos of the Bergenskjölds looking miserable shook everyone
up. The prime minister can hardly go anywhere without being
called cold and heartless.

EG: And just because I happen to be down here, I'm supposed
to solve this?

TD: Something like that.

EG: They shouldn't expect a major miracle.

TD: What counts as a miracle is no longer determined by our government. It's mob rule. What have you got?

EG: Contact with the negotiator has been established.

TD: What happens next?

EG: He wants to be granted immunity from prosecution if he brokers a solution.

TD: But what can I tell the government? Granting immunity to a pirate isn't much of an opening move if we want to show decisiveness.

EG: It's the negotiator, not the pirates, who'd be granted immunity.

TD: Never mind who. I need something that looks like a victory for the prime minister, even in the tabloids. That boy, for example. Finding something to keep him from dying.

EG: His drugs are on their way. The doctor on the *Sveaborg* handled the prescriptions, and I just went to pick up the package.

TD: Never mind the details. How are you going to get the pills to them?

EG: The negotiator assures us they'll be delivered to the family.

TD: When did you last speak with him?

EG: An hour ago.

TD: But you haven't met face-to-face?

EG: The Boss wanted me to keep out of it, remember?

TD: Okay, very good.

EG: Delivering drugs to the boy makes everyone look good, but I still have to ask. What is my real position in the negotiations?

TD: The government won't pay a single krona. We're just like any other country, refusing to put an official price on the heads of our citizens. No one would be safe if we did.

EG: So . . . ?

TD: So what?

EG: I've got to have something.

TD: It sounds as if you're fishing, to put it bluntly.

EG: We have no reason to go after the man who contacted us, and immunity from prosecution costs us nothing.

TD: Then he'll have to prove he has something to offer. He's pulled you in, but he'll need to lay some cards on the table before you say anything about a guarantee. Make sure you get the man's name. After all, you're working in intelligence here.

EG: I'll do what I can.

TD: You might have to do a little more than that. Good night.

42

"Don't tell me . . . ?"

When things don't go the way you expect, sometimes the hardest part is believing that what happened really happened.

At just past eight in the morning, Grip stood with Philippa Ekman in the Sheraton and discovered that Fredrik Hansson had thrown in the towel. But not exactly the way Grip had imagined.

"He went to bed early last night. That's what we thought, anyway," she said. Ernst Grip had a sinking feeling.

He found a maid to open Hansson's room. Most of his military stuff seemed to be there, but his civilian things were gone, as Grip discovered when he pulled open the drawers and searched the closets. The maid stood with her arms crossed. When Grip handed her a twenty-dollar bill, she reluctantly agreed to wait in the hallway. Once he was alone, he gathered up all the papers, magazines, and notes he could find, stuffing them into an empty gym bag. He even grabbed the half full trash bag and took everything with him.

Then he sat in the lobby, his thoughts spinning. At ten, Hansson was supposed to meet with Mickels. At quarter past, the MP barged into the hotel, shouting Hansson's name and barking orders at any Swedish uniform he ran into. The search for the missing sergeant was on. Fredrik Hansson hadn't just left Grip up shit creek without a paddle, he'd fled from everyone.

Barely two hours later, Grip walked through the tall gates of the US embassy. Judy Drexler had called him. He was relieved that she'd made the first move, as it seemed to give him an advantage. He'd asked if they'd be meeting at La Mer Rouge, but she replied that waiters and other curious ears were an unnecessary risk, considering what they had to say to each other. It sounded promising. And unlike him, Drexler had an office. With its bulletproof glass, Marine Corps guards, and marble floors, the Americans' newly built complex was as much fortress as embassy. Once Grip had picked up his watch and wallet and put his belt back through the loops, past the metal detector, he heard Drexler's heels hitting the floor. Dressed in black like the last time, she greeted him with open arms and an expression intended to excuse the initial indignities. Above all, she was welcoming. An ambassador sat somewhere in that complex, but this was Judy Drexler's castle.

They walked along, chatting. She pointed and said a few words about the artwork, made from thousands of ceramic tiles, that covered a vast wall. Drexler's own office was drabber, filled with bookshelves but very few personal effects. She was what defined the room, not some object on the desk or walls. There were no distractions—perhaps it was deliberate. She provided the energy.

"It sounds like you were also planning to call me," she began. "But I blinked first, so I'll start. You seem to be facing a problematic situation, involving MovCon?"

Grip wasn't going to play games; he needed all the help he could get. "Yes, things have deteriorated."

"Let me see if I have the situation clear in my mind. It all began when a man died at the shooting range. That led to a soldier being sent home, right?"

"Radovanović. Once he knew that the evidence against the Djiboutian was nonsense, he got the idea that he'd fumbled and fired an accidental shot. And I fell for it."

"Colonel Frères's military police were helping out?"

"Yes, but I can't blame them."

"Blame them for what?"

"I pushed too hard. And once he'd written his confession, it couldn't be taken back. I underestimated the military's need for a scapegoat."

"It's in their nature. There isn't much glory to go around among the men and women in uniform these days, so they mostly focus on keeping things clean."

Grip hesitated, then said, "Radovanović was sent home anyway. They left it at that."

"But you remain here in the sand."

"They found a lot of money getting smuggled out in MovCon's shipments, and my partner . . ." He was interrupted.

". . . was stabbed in the marketplace, of course I know that. And the one behind this thing was Sergeant Hansson?"

Grip nodded. There was silence. Then he said, "Ayanna almost managed to convince me that she wouldn't run to you with my little troubles."

"Oh, it's harmless. You fill her time with your cases, and I'm convinced that we both win. All I noticed was that her piano at the Kempinski stood empty. Then she said you were interested in this Hansson, and it's only a matter of loyalty, of course she has to feed me things now and then. And actually, that was all she said. So this sergeant, he is and has done what?"

"He's behind everything: the murder, the smuggled money, my partner getting stabbed."

"And now he's gone."

"Ayanna is on her way to Mombasa on my behalf. She doesn't know that Hansson has disappeared."

"She wasn't the one who told me."

What did he expect? Judy Drexler had a whole intelligence service working for her. It was quiet for a moment before Grip said: "One thing struck me early, here in Djibouti. At hotels, people are always sitting with drinks. And out in the barracks and hangars, no one ever seems to get enough bottled water—they're always holding a cup of mountain spring in their hands."

"Thirst unites us, that's old news. And you believe this has an effect?"

"Yes, it leads to all the damn talking. I do it too."

"Can I get you something?" she asked, seeming to mean it.

"That said, I'm always thirsty." She reached for the phone.

Grip continued. "You made the first move, but so far, I'm the only one who's talked about my situation."

"I couldn't stop you," she replied, with her eyes on the phone.

"Hansson, MovCon, the tips you received that someone there was Al-Qaeda. It's obvious that something is going on. Something you're involved in, and that's why I'm here. No matter which one of us called first."

Drexler raised a finger, to pause him. "Send up a tray, with ice and glasses." She hung up the phone and drummed on the desk pad with her fingers. "Drones, do you have those in Sweden?"

"The ones that fire missiles? As far as I know, we've stayed away from them."

"In western Europe, you seem to put drones in the same category as dumdum bullets and nerve gas."

"Obviously, you've seen that on the signs of people marching outside your embassies."

"Your protesters can yell and scream, but for us the drones are the logical consequence of what had stumped us before."

"Because no one sits in them?"

"Because we were faced with an enemy willing to make the ultimate sacrifice. Our mind-set was based on the idea that human life is sacred and on the premise that everyone has a fundamental desire to live."

"But you have the death penalty."

"Exactly. The very worst crimes, we punish with death. You can say what you will, but it's based on the idea that the state instills fear, to discourage people from committing terrible crimes. But how do you deal with people who use themselves as human missiles, or who wrap themselves in layer upon layer of explosives and nails? Sometimes, there are hardly molecules of them left afterward. As a consequence, it makes no sense to threaten a suicide bomber with death. We still had the mind-set that no person chooses to die voluntarily, so when we were subjected to this—we were perplexed."

"We were all perplexed. Even in Sweden, people at airports have to take off their shoes and hand over their toothpaste."

"And then you waited, wondering what we were going to do next?"

"It's always that way. We always wait for the US reaction. So the countermove was the drone?"

"Yes, if terrorists are willing to make the ultimate sacrifice, our drones can reach them everywhere without any risk. Their willingness to sacrifice themselves was met by us attacking without risking our lives. It wasn't the answer they'd imagined. The battle has been taken to their backyard, and now we don't even need to be there. Before, they could randomly detonate a bomb in a subway or a shopping mall, and now they're the ones who can't feel secure, no matter where they are. They have to be on the alert around the clock. It has made Al-Qaeda and ISIS both frustrated and furious; it leads to lots of rash actions and mistakes."

"The drones gave you back the advantage."

"Absolutely. Not so many jihadist bombs exploding in American squares and subway stations. And let's be real, we've even targeted bomb-makers who were eyeing you northern Europeans. With our pilotless aircraft and good intelligence, they barely have time to think about attacks on us anymore."

There was a knock on the door, and a young man wearing a button-down shirt and chinos brought in glasses and a pitcher on a tray.

"Just put it there," Drexler said, pointing to the corner of the desk. She began to pour, and he went out again. "I grew up in Georgia," she said then, "in the interior, a place where we didn't have an ocean or a river to cool off in during the summer. Here, the desert's dry heat burns everything in its path. There, the humid heat eats the soul. Here, people die of thirst. There, they go insane first. That's why in Georgia you don't just drink water but iced tea. You need something for body and soul. Here you go. I've even taught them to make it right, slightly sweet but not cloying."

"Is that one way to define a person—those who drink water versus those who drink iced tea?"

"That's how you recognize the ones who can really stand the heat. But where was I?"

"You were probably about to say something about pilotless aircraft and intelligence."

"Right. We can hit precisely what and who we want, but the ones who control the drones are not the people who identify the targets. Others do the painstaking work of figuring out who's actually sitting in the car. From an infrared camera a thousand meters high, we all look pretty much the same, regardless of our intentions."

"So who identifies your enemies around here? Not you. You're mostly behind these walls and fences all day."

"Exactly. The world hasn't become as cosmopolitan and interconnected as many would like to think. On the contrary, it's more and more 'us and them.' Thirty years ago, I was able to move freely in Kabul, Mogadishu, and Aden, on the other side of the bay here. That's impossible today."

"On the other hand, now you can put a reconnaissance satellite on any building on earth, and there's not a cell phone call that you can't listen in on."

"Sure, but somebody has to say whose house we should be interested in, and whose phone is worth listening to. It's impossible otherwise."

"Having someone on the inside has always been priceless."

"Now you're getting warmer. More tea?"

"I'm fine for now," Grip said. "First, I should find out a little more about that shot fired at the shooting range."

"We have an excellent source for Al-Shabaab and Al-Qaeda, in and around Somalia. Three weeks ago, we were able to eliminate five men from Al-Shabaab's top leadership. A single missile—*poof*—all thanks to information from him. And through this same source, we've found out about many others who've marked world destruction on the calendars. He's very reliable, he knows who's who in the organizations we are looking for, and where they are, and when. The opposite applies to himself. Due to his extreme caution, we don't know much about him as a person. Through intercepted telephone calls, we've learned that other Somalis call him the Jew."

"Go on" was Grip's only reaction, even though the synapses in his head had begun to flash.

"The Jew, if we can call him that, gave us a tip about a Djiboutian with the wrong ideas, who worked for you in MovCon. I told you about him, it was Abdoul Ghermat. We checked him out, it didn't lead anywhere, so we let him go."

"Your source tipped you off, and you released him. Fredrik Hansson did the job for him instead."

"I'm missing some of the steps here, Jew—Hansson?"

"Your source is named Khalid Delmar. Born in Somalia but a Swedish citizen. He and Hansson have some kind of business together, God knows what, but they use our military transport to move their money around, in cash. How do you pay him?"

"In cash."

"And how much is it, roughly?"

"Not more than ten thousand dollars a month."

"I thought he was priceless."

"It's easy to overpay. But we've learned that the informants most likely to survive over time are driven by conviction as much as by greed. Those who are only ideological tend to take too many risks, and those who are too greedy start reporting anyone and everyone. So we're happy to keep the banknotes flowing."

"I intercepted one shipment of fifty thousand dollars that reached Sweden, and then I came across a stash down here of more than one hundred and forty. I'd say that, all told, they're sending a hundred thousand a month, probably more."

"Nope. Obviously they're not just working for us."

"My guess is that it's Khalid who makes the money, and he uses

Hansson to make sure that it gets out of here." Judy Drexler shrugged. Grip wanted to get everything out on the table and continued: "And Abdoul Ghermat, he and his friend the lieutenant figured out what Hansson was sending along with the spare parts, and pressured him to get a cut. Hansson talked to Khalid, they're used to playing in the big leagues, and they don't just start paying the first guy who asks. Khalid did his part by giving Ghermat's name to you. The idea was that when he suddenly disappeared one morning, it would scare the lieutenant into silence. But you didn't buy it, and the lieutenant threatened to expose Hansson and get him sent home. Had that happened, he'd never have gotten a job with the international forces again. So instead—*bam*." Grip nodded and then looked down at his empty glass. "Now I'll have a little more."

"You see," said Judy Drexler as she lifted the pitcher, "it was just like I said." She went on, as the ice cubes and tea poured into the glass, "That Djiboutian wasn't completely innocent after all."

"Everyone's trying to get a piece of the business here."

"That sounds like something Ayanna often says," Judy said. "But we shouldn't lose the thread. You need to understand that Khalid Delmar has become key to US security interests. Neither you nor I can identify the next generation of leaders in Al-Qaeda or Al-Shabaab, but he can. And I'll make sure that he's protected, no matter what. He shouldn't be alarmed or threatened. He should just continue to do what he does so well."

"But his wingman murdered someone," Grip objected. "And of course, he tried to make Ghermat disappear."

Drexler leaned forward from her desk. "We didn't do anything to that Djiboutian. It takes more than a scribbled-down name for us to send the drone out into the night. It was this Hansson who stepped out of line."

"So you're saying that you don't mind if I go after him?"

"I guess it's inevitable. And I might have information that can help."

"In exchange for Khalid remaining untouchable?"

"He is not just any informant, he's my main source and essential to my work here. How he earns the rest of his money, and how he sends it out, I don't care. In any case, my bosses don't want to know anything about it."

"And I'd like to get Hansson. That's enough for me."

"Well then, we agree. Sergeant Hansson left Djibouti on the Ethiopian Air flight down to Mombasa this morning."

"You keep track of him?"

"Once it became clear that you'd gotten interested in him, then I did too. Ethiopian Air is one of the few lifelines in and out of this country, so naturally we check the names listed on the departures."

"Thanks."

Drexler looked at Grip as if she expected something more. "I understand that Sergeant Hansson had been missing without a trace for some time," she continued, "but since he showed up at the Sheraton yesterday morning, he has called the same number nine times from his private cell phone. But no one picked up."

"Who did he call?"

"The number is unknown to us, but we can safely assume he was trying to reach Delmar."

"I think it's time for you to contact Khalid Delmar and tell him that he has to give up Hansson."

Judy Drexler jiggled her glass. "That's not the way our partnership works. He's the one who contacts me about things I need. I can reach him, but only in an emergency, to protect him. Not to make demands."

"Is that his explicit privilege?"

"More, that our relationship is fragile. He has to decide what the personal price for his actions will be."

"Then we'll draw a line, and leave Khalid Delmar on the other side of it."

"I'd appreciate that."

"Am I right in believing that now you owe me a favor?"

"We're doing more for each other than just an even exchange. What else have you got?"

"You've probably read about them—the sailing family that got kidnapped?"

"Of course. What a nightmare."

"The pirates have a negotiator, and my government won't deal directly with him, so now he's going through me."

"This has become quite a cottage industry along the Somali coast, all these innocent negotiators filled with goodwill."

"Anyway . . . you have access to different resources than I do." Grip held out a piece of paper. "This is the cell phone number he uses, probably with just a prepaid card. Maybe you can find out where he goes, who the other callers are, even who he is."

"Have you met him?"

"I haven't, but because you're keeping an eye on the passenger lists, you already know that Ayanna is on the same flight as Hansson to Mombasa."

"Yes."

"She's going down there to meet with this negotiator."

"Is there a risk that they'll recognize each other on the flight, Ayanna and Hansson?"

"As far as I know, they've never met."

"Good!" said Drexler and continued. "You should know that she's important to me. You have to be careful with her."

"Of course."

"No, not just *of course*. I put you two in contact not only because she knows a lot of people."

"It's obvious that there's more to her. She's good."

"Good—she's more than damn good at what she does. You've seen for yourself, with her background, her looks, the way she carries herself, outward grace combined with inward talent. And I don't mean playing the piano, but the fact that people confide in her. People see her as harmless yet interesting, and so they talk to her openly, thinking they can get close to her. Too close, that's where they want to get."

"I've noticed that."

"Of course you have. There are things that can't be taught by any program in intelligence work. But it also means that she's outside the system, and she's unschooled. She's useful in many ways, but she also misses a lot. Think about it."

"So what drives her?"

"Oh, that's easy. She wants to find a way to get out of Africa on her own terms."

"And you haven't given her that?"

"I've given her a lot, but obviously not that."

"And you never will."

"I want to keep her with me." Drexler thought for a moment, then said: "I am a woman, you are a man. Ayanna's way of working requires certain reins. Watch out."

"I'd say, I'm the right man for the job."

"Well, now it's been said. Take my gentle advice, and I'll do what I can with this negotiator." She looked down at the note Grip had handed to her. "And this?" She pointed. "What's this—Darwiish?"

"Apparently, it's the pirate leader, and that's his name. I wondered if you had anything?"

"There's a name I don't even have to look up. The French sent some missionaries down here, maybe, what, five or six years ago. Religious fools who thought salvation would solve the Somali chaos. They were taken hostage as soon as they got to shore. Colonel Frères let me read the report. Darwiish, that's an easy name to remember—the French reported that he was the leader of the kidnappers. There were never any negotiations, time just went by, and Darwiish didn't want to be seen as weak, so it seems he shot them all. They never had the chance to save a single soul."

"Well, now his hostages are bored rich people without a real reason to be here."

"If they haven't prayed to God before, they'd better start now."

43

"On behalf of the government, the Swedish military mission off the coast of Somalia has today carried out operations to bring Sebastian Bergenskjöld lifesaving drugs. The hospital aboard the HMS *Sveaborg* has . . ."

The press officers at Rosenbad had inflated a bulletin about the prescription being sent from the ship to the French hospital into something newsworthy. Grip surfed the online headlines. The prime minister sounded impressive, and even the tabloids took note of the long-awaited victory. It was as if they'd beaten an African epidemic that threatened the whole world.

The French hospital—Grip—Ayanna—Mombasa: a few packets of pills had leapfrogged for more than a day, on their way out to the desert. "Delivered," Ayanna had texted. And as a kind of acknowledgment: "I'll get back to you in a few days," from the negotiator.

Some of Jenny Bergenskjöld's childhood friends had started a private fund to collect ransom money for the family. It was now up to $350,000; it was, in other words, still more than $9.5 million short. Two of Scandinavian Capital's senior partners issued a statement from a board meeting: "We are hereby pleased to announce that we will match all donations to the Bergenskjöld Rescue Fund." With that, Scandinavian Capital succeeded, for the first time since all the publicity began, in getting a few positive comments from journalists.

But then another partner made the mistake of agreeing to a lengthy interview on a morning TV show, and, too tanned but unprepared, got blasted on social media for lying about his art collection. Soon the tabloids started sniping again. Grip grew annoyed reading about it, feeling he was lost in a storm of details and impressions whose real meaning he couldn't gauge. Judy had touched base: "Hansson didn't use his cell phone when he got off the plane in Mombasa, so we can't follow him. We've lost him." The satellites at the top of the food chain were useless. Grip had sent a picture of Hansson to Ayanna, but she hadn't seen him on the flight.

It was like a wound that wouldn't heal. Couldn't heal? Where the hell had he gone? Grip was surprised himself that he couldn't stop thinking about Hansson.

"You have to stay longer in Mombasa," he texted Ayanna.

"Then I will need more clothes." She'd only packed for a quick trip back and forth. "How much can I spend?"

"Don't disappoint me," Grip had replied, just to say something, but a few hours later, she began sending photos taken in front of fitting-room mirrors.

"Satisfied?" Grip didn't know at first if she was being vain or just teasing him.

"Aren't you the one who's going to wear this, not me?" And soon the game was on. A few minutes of images and comments sent back and forth, then a break of an hour or so before the next store.

Meanwhile, Grip went through the gym bag he'd taken from Hansson's room. He flipped through the sports and car magazines, and found a dog-eared page about diving in Mozambique. His pocket calendar had a spread for every week without a single note, only dots in blue and red ink, obviously a code. There were business cards from foreign militaries and African firms around the continent, often marked with only a company name, a phone number, and a vague note saying "Services" or "Transportation."

Judy texted again. "Hansson paid someone named Zaruba more than $1,500 using a credit card a few hours ago."

"Zaruba, who would that be?"

"I don't know. That's all we got in the transmission we intercepted. I thought . . ."

"Thank you."

While Grip picked through Hansson's meaningless papers, he started thinking about something the ship captain had said that first night, at the dinner for diplomats aboard the *Sveaborg*. He'd described how ransom payments were actually delivered to the pirates, for their hijacked vessels.

"The money is dropped from the air by parachute . . . There's a legitimate airline in Kenya that does the job using small planes." And soon, Grip sat with the stack of business cards in his hand again. He laid them out on the hotel-room carpet in a fan—there. What he noticed was the stylized drawing of the plane, with the spinning circles of propellers viewed head-on, more artistic than the other cards. Zar Air. TRANSPORT IS OUR BUSINESS, THE CARGO IS OUR CUSTOMERS' BUSINESS. And in one corner, above the phone number and the web address in small print: ZARUBA AIRLINES INCORPORATED.

An air taxi company in Mombasa with twin-engine propeller planes. On the website you could book tours, safari flights, trips down to Zanzibar, and other more specialized excursions. A short video showed them delivering money by parachute to a merchant. They were proud of what they did—We Go the Extra Mile. They could arrange everything from taking tourists to see the lions in Mkomazi National Park, to packing and moving perishable goods.

Fifteen hundred dollars, that was the last sign that blinked on the Americans' screens from Fredrik Hansson, who'd begun to fade out and soon would disappear altogether from the radar.

"Now that's enough," Grip texted back to Ayanna when the image of a hand lifting a designer suitcase appeared, "whether it's a cheap fake or not."

"That is out of the question. Everything that I bought must be packed in something." It was after eight in the evening. He called her. Not to discuss the suitcase, or any of her other purchases, but only to ask: "So where are you staying?"

She told him the name of the hotel; it was on the beach. Grip searched on his computer and looked at the pictures.

"I have played here, entertained in the bar a few times."

"Is it better, being there as a guest?"

"You can avoid the rooms next to the parking lot when someone else is paying."

It was Fredrik Hansson's bundles of hundreds, which Ayanna knew nothing about, that were bankrolling her ocean view. Grip sat on the floor of his room at the Kempinski. Ayanna knew Hansson's name from playing the go-between with the police in Djibouti, but no more. So when, earlier in the day, Grip had sent her the picture of him, he told her that Hansson killed a Swedish officer and now had fled.

"Tomorrow morning, I need you to go out to the airport," he said now. "Zar Air, an air taxi company there, they have a few planes. Hansson seems to have sent something through them."

"Zar Air, tomorrow. I will do it. Have you eaten dinner?"

"Didn't have time."

"Order room service. I will."

"If you say so."

There was silence for a moment.

"Good night," she said then.

Zar Air, epilepsy medicine, Mombasa. Almost exactly one day ago, Grip had been standing face-to-face with Hansson at the hangar. He'd had his knife hidden, ready in his hand, and yet the world had seemed so much simpler. Twenty-four hours ago: no Zaruba, no politician's inflated pride about a few pills. And now he faced the possibility that a few bad decisions would have infinite repercussions.

Grip called and ordered up two hamburgers. He ate only the meat and fried onions, and then, obsessively, went back online. A hotel baron had donated $1 million to the fund, while his staff smiled and applauded. Now they were just $8.5 million short. Grip watched his auction site, the one with Edward Hopper's works in London. There were links to some articles, and the *Night Shadows* drawing was mentioned but not the main feature. The focus was on a major oil painting of a classic Hopper house that, according to the amped-up writer, would go for the annual budget of a small country. Grip figured the sketch—the one he couldn't get enough of—would go for somewhere around the starting price. A little more than the fund collected so far for the Bergenskjölds. They'd been held hostage for sixty-five days now. The auction would be in about three weeks.

It was well after midnight, and Grip was still awake. He hadn't taken a sleeping pill, afraid of getting addicted. He wrestled with unruly thoughts and a nightlong pain in his stomach: he was homesick, missing Ben.

Longing for meaning, and longing for someone.

44

On the mattress in the stone house, they'd lost track of time. But their fear of Darwiish, and the party he threw every Friday night, gave them a reference point for the days of the week.

In this way, they knew for certain that Sebastian died very early on a Tuesday. Jenny would always listen for his breath when she woke up in the middle of the night, but in her exhaustion, she often slept straight through the last hours before dawn. It must have been then that the life flowed out of him.

There were no scenes; she didn't even wake up Carl-Adam. Instead, she cried softly to herself, for a long time, filled with sadness that at first felt like a confusing kind of relief. Her frustration had given way a long time ago, at about the same time as she lost hope that something would save Sebastian. She had no idea how many seizures he'd had. The last time she'd looked at him, she'd been searching for warning signs of more seizures—a twitch of his mouth or an involuntary movement of his eyes. Only now could she see what he looked like, actually see her son, not just his illness. She saw Sebastian as he lay there peacefully—the child who was no longer part of the dirt, or the soiled mattress—saw the serenity in his face, and how thin he'd gotten.

Alexandra had heard something and woken up earlier than usual. She'd crept over without a word, sitting down to lay a hand on her brother's feet. So they sat, mother and daughter, and though the tears came in waves, it was the silence that let them shut out the world.

Carl-Adam sobbed and coughed for a moment when he woke up

and realized what had happened. Then he sat as usual, unresponsive and apparently weak.

Two guards appeared in the doorway, whispered and pointed, and then disappeared. After that, everything continued as usual. Even the water bucket arrived without a single comment.

A day later came the changes: the swollen body, too many flies. Alexandra sat facing her novel, with her back toward Sebastian. Jenny saw that she wasn't reading.

"They have shovels," she said.

"Here?" Jenny asked.

"That night." Alexandra meant the Friday night she'd been pulled away by the guards. "They have shovels in the other house."

She was the only one in the family who'd been there.

They had to dig the grave themselves. The ground was baked hard by the sun, so they mostly used loose stones. Carl-Adam broke into sobs, and only calmed himself by swearing, as Jenny put the last stone over the sheet that covered Sebastian's face. They kept adding stones until they'd built a knee-high mound.

That same evening, a guard came in with the four boxes of pills. He held them out toward Alexandra, as if she were the one who needed the medications, and he stood for a moment before Jenny took them out of his hands. She sat the rest of the evening with the boxes in her lap.

Someone must have said something to the negotiator, because he showed up the very next day.

They'd seen the jeep coming; Darwiish was one of the passengers. They heard loud voices and arguing, and it was impossible to tell who was accusing whom. A shot rang out.

Then steps in the outer room, and the fluttering of the negotiator's neatly ironed white shirt. He sent the guard away with angry gestures, as if he never wanted to see his face again, and then called for Carl-Adam, who dragged himself out. The door between the two rooms was closed; Jenny sat as usual by the gap.

The negotiator bit his lower lip, hard. "Enough is enough," he said, drumming on the table, as if searching for what to say next. He didn't mention a word about Sebastian—Jenny had seen through the little window that he'd been to the grave—but instead he went off about Scandinavian Capital. Although Jenny could hear his every word, she realized she didn't understand what he wanted next. Carl-Adam got hung up on the details, trying to counter with his usual agenda: the ransom money, whether it could be reduced, and what he imagined the *MaryAnn* was worth. The negotiator didn't bother with him, and continued his monologue about partners and sales. He got up and paced the floor a few times before he went up to the front door, opened it with a jerk, and looked out.

Jenny realized then that it hadn't been about anything; his only purpose had been to fill the air with words, until he could be sure that he really was alone with Carl-Adam.

"Maybe we can cut it to seven," said Carl-Adam, when he sat down at the table again.

The negotiator met his submissive gaze.

"Don't you understand?"

"Seven million might be possible."

"Nothing is possible." He reached down for something in his bag on the floor, and when he sat up again, there was a gun on the table. A small thud on the dry wood of the table, and it lay there, like something totally unfamiliar. "Six bullets, that's all you get," he said.

Carl-Adam looked as if he'd just been ordered to kill himself.

"But it doesn't matter," the negotiator continued, "because you'll never get the opportunity to reload."

Jenny felt nauseous. Being held hostage was itself a curse, and now she faced a violent end. Did what lay on the table represent hope, or was it the ultimate symbol of impotence?

"How . . . ?" Carl-Adam couldn't find the words to formulate his question.

"Do you know how to use it?" said the negotiator, with a look that said this wasn't the time to hesitate. "You shot and killed one of them."

Carl-Adam nodded awkwardly. "And when . . . ?" he managed to say.

"When is something that you must decide. But not tonight, and not tomorrow."

Alexandra had patiently managed to make a hiding place in the back room. Sitting on her mattress, she'd removed a stone from the corner of the wall using the handle of her spoon. Loosening the stone wasn't hard, as the mortar was barely more than dried mud.

But carving out the space behind it took time. Jenny and Carl-Adam had seen her working on it in the evenings, and often in the middle of the day, when the guard in the outer room mostly slept in his chair. They'd let her have her way, seeing it as a way for her to kill time. It was harmless enough, as they didn't have anything that needed to be hidden. For a while, she kept the candy that she'd brought from the *MaryAnn* there. Once in a while, she'd wiggle out the stone and take a couple of pieces for herself and Sebastian, before returning the bag and gently putting the stone back in place. It was a kind of ritual, a tiny gesture of victory before the day's last light disappeared. But time had run its course, both for the zoo candies and for her brother.

The loose rock meant nothing, until suddenly there was something that needed to be hidden.

"Don't touch it!" Carl-Adam said, after Alexandra had shown him how to remove the stone, and stashed the gun behind it.

45

Judy Drexler called him again: "The cell phone that your negotiator uses has been active in Mogadishu. The people who do my monitoring say that he's in contact with some very interesting numbers. They followed up, but now it seems the phone has been dead for a couple of days."

"You mean, something happened?"

"I don't mean anything."

"He'd make sure the family received the drugs," said Grip after a few seconds' hesitation. "He probably turns off his phone when he goes out to where they're being held."

"Maybe. Have you gotten anything more on Hansson?"

"Nothing."

That wasn't quite true. Ayanna had gotten in touch with Grip after her morning visit to the airport in Mombasa. They'd spoken for quite a while, and she'd described everything in detail. Grip could see the whole scene: how she'd headed out to the Zar Air offices, well-dressed and confident, entering the hut between two hangars. She'd slipped in as an important customer with many contacts, yet without supplying any full names. She talked nonstop, asked questions about everything, been both friendly and incoherent. She'd created uncertainty by trying to get the order for a goods transport confirmed, an order that naturally wasn't registered anywhere. She played at being upset, and worried; she started talking about imaginary friends, dropping both made-up and real names. At some point, Fredrik Hansson entered the discussion, as a seemingly minor character. Yes,

yes, she'd been told, they knew him well, a loyal customer over the years. Soon one thing led to another.

Fredrik Hansson hadn't used Zar Air to send a package—he'd sent himself. He'd left Mombasa and flown to Lamu Island. During peak periods, Zar Air flew there several times a week.

"Lamu Island?"

"Where the rich people go," Ayanna explained.

Grip had a vague idea; he'd heard the island described as a kind of East African Ibiza. When he Googled, he got images of a historic town with fancy villas owned by actors, along with fruit drinks, white sand beaches, and bars with views of the sea. The island was a fair distance north of Mombasa, but just an hour's drive south of the Somali border. The wealth was provocative, so near to the lawlessness—Grip found a strange mixture of ads for two-story villas with custom pools and articles about Kenyan police engaged in shoot-outs while trying to stop gangs from reaching the island. Only a narrow channel separated Lamu's northwest coast from the mainland.

"I can go tonight," Ayanna told him.

He owed her, Grip knew it, and he was indebted for more than just money. But now he had a lead on Hansson, and he couldn't go there himself. There on Lamu Island, in Kenya, he couldn't make a move. Hansson would recognize him and disappear again. He couldn't let him get away, not now.

"Do not be difficult," she continued. "After all, you want nothing more than to get your hands on Hansson."

"How will you get there?"

"With Zar Air, how else? And your money."

Wrong, Grip corrected her in his head—Fredrik Hansson's money. And then he added, "Get on the first plane you can."

What would he really do if Ayanna found Hansson on Lamu Island? Grip tried to stop thinking about the problem by distracting himself with another. He texted the negotiator: "How's it going with the medicine? And how is the family?" He got no answer.

Already the next day, Ayanna was on the island. Her reports

sounded like posts from a blogger on holiday. There were photos with short captions: a local woman buying fruit at a market, elaborately carved wooden gates, Ayanna's lunch on a plate, the view down from the lush hillside to the sea. Grip deleted the silly messages as they arrived. It was like watching a fishing bob float hopelessly on the surface, for hours. Every time the phone pinged, it was another meaningless tug on the line. "I am talking to people." . . . "They party everywhere, and some fear raids from across the channel." Then a picture of military officers looking solemn down by the harbor. Ping. "Have met a broker." . . . "The place is full of hustlers and plainclothes police officers." The bob moved, but only because of the wind.

Then suddenly, the bob dove. Ping. It was her second night on the island, and there he was, Fredrik Hansson, in a jerky video, secretly taken with a cell phone. Drunk, it appeared, in the crowd at a bar. Grip felt his anger mount, just seeing the man's grin. He was yelling, toasting with his beer bottle toward the camera. Was Ayanna, with her phone, just a face in the crowd?

A moment later, she sent a new video; now they were sitting down, just the two of them. Hansson was so drunk he didn't even notice that she was filming. Snippets of video kept arriving, so Grip assumed Ayanna sent them when she held her phone under the table, or when she excused herself and went to the bathroom.

Hansson was out of his element, and in pretty rough shape. It was just after midnight, and Ayanna was no mere pickup, but a stranger he'd decided to pour his heart out to. He was committing hara-kiri, in the corner of a bar near the port in Lamu's historic district.

"What should I have done?" He slapped his forehead, running his hand through his hair in a gesture of frustration, repeating the phrase over and over again: "What should I have done?" A drunken, sniffling monologue. "It's over." Obviously, he had betrayed someone. But why had he chosen to escape to Lamu Island, Grip wondered.

"Ask about Khalid Delmar," Grip texted back to Ayanna.

A half hour later, another short video arrived of Hansson, who was now so drunk that he leaned against the wall behind him or propped both elbows on the table, whenever he really wanted to say something. "We get thirty thousand dollars for each one. Take them out of the fucking desert, send them back home to Mom in the suburbs. He's good, he's good, he gets them home. But me, shit, what a fucking mess I made." His saliva spattered. He lifted his glass halfway and put it down again. "See, I've got a passport, but now I can't go anywhere." Hansson looked lustfully at Ayanna and continued to stare for a while.

"Where do you live, anyway?"

Ayanna had rented a bungalow. If someone asked, she said she was on Lamu to buy something bigger. She dressed up and met with real estate brokers. There was an insane amount of money in a very small place, and still too many who only pretended to be multimillionaires—but the local brokers knew who actually owned what and what kind of money lay behind it. They loved to butter up potential customers with gossip, as long as they promised to keep it to themselves. So Ayanna browsed the fancy brochures, and, amid the chitchat about floor plans, collected the pieces she'd been entrusted with, until a complete picture took shape.

Soon it became clear that Khalid Delmar owned a big sand-colored house not far from the harbor. Newly built, it had walls and terraces designed by an architect playing off the forms of a desert fort. Even in Lamu, various people knew Delmar as the Jew. Grip looked at the pictures Ayanna took from the outside; it wasn't his two-bedroom apartment in Kungsholmen that showed the profits from Delmar and Hansson's business deals.

Ayanna rented a place not far from the house where Hansson had apparently taken refuge, and she ran into him, as if by chance, again at the bar that evening. She'd sat with him, until nonstop drinking turned his words to mush. Ayanna had declined to go home with him, but the next afternoon, she knocked on the door of the desert fort.

Probably, he didn't remember much from the night before, but he let her in. He felt that all mankind was about to turn its back on him.

A face bloated from his hangover, and a thousand-mile stare. They made a little small talk, mostly Ayanna killing the silence before the pressure of Hansson's inner Armageddon began building again. Ayanna didn't question the confused world that Fredrik Hansson had started to describe. She wasn't trying to connect the dots, only to send back unfiltered information to Grip.

Khalid Delmar and Fredrik Hansson, two very different lives intertwined in the same Swedish suburb. Fredrik Hansson gave Ayanna every detail.

46

Khalid Delmar came to Sweden in the early '90s, after the situation in Somalia went to hell. His father had owned a grocery store in Jowhar that was looted, little by little, until nothing remained. With the future increasingly bleak, the family left Somalia—his parents, his brother, and himself. Their escape was awful but in no way unique. They shared their thirst, their fear, and the experience of being ruthlessly exploited with millions of others. They were a very small part of the mass of dust-covered flesh and blood that had for decades been moving up and out of the Horn of Africa, but one detail of their flight stood out from the rest. Nine-year-old Khalid, terrified of the sea, threw such a tantrum that the smuggler refused to let them onto his boat. As a result, the family was stuck in a makeshift refugee camp for weeks on end. There, his older brother got sick and died. His father never forgave Khalid for being difficult, and the father's contempt eventually led to the surviving son's good luck.

They ended up in Tensta, a crowded immigrant neighborhood in Stockholm. Entering school, Khalid became the only one in the family who learned Swedish. His father never really settled into their new country—with its high-rise apartments, its trees, and its endless social welfare paperwork—and he spent much of the next two decades in an echoing room they called a café, along with others who, like him, were reduced to nothing. He smoked and cultivated his disgust for what he saw around him.

From early on, he felt his son had become too Swedish; he even tried to beat that knowledge into him. Khalid helped his mother fill out the paperwork, but he told his father that a real man did this himself. Finally, given Khalid's disrespect, and his father's sense that his son had lost all Somali ways, his father saw no alternative but to ship him off to relatives far out in the Somali countryside. This would teach him a lesson, and then he would understand. He'd be dumped there, not just over the summer but forever.

His mother refused to go along with the plan. The rift between the parents that became obvious that day went beyond this incident alone. It was the mother's relatives who'd made it possible to escape, using their money. They'd never asked to be paid back, but the father's pride had been pawned forever. It was her family in Sweden who'd given her a job, and they'd also offered one to her husband. But he would never put on rubber gloves and go to work cleaning for others, not after having had employees of his own. So he kept on sitting and smoking, now supported by his wife. The father didn't want his son to watch his inexorable downward spiral, and this was no doubt another reason why the father wanted him sent away.

But his mother wanted something else; she didn't even ask, just presented his father with a fait accompli. It was the summer between seventh and eighth grade, and instead of getting sent down to Somalia, Khalid moved to Bromma. Not to a mansion, just to a small row house on the corner—but still, it was Bromma. His uncle lived there with his family. The uncle knew exactly what was possible and what was not, in this country populated by white people in their apple orchards. One thing he learned was that when you clean up other people's dirt, neither your unpronounceable name nor your skin color matters, so he started his own company. Another thing he realized was that if you wanted your kids to go to a good school, you had to have the right address, and then no one could refuse. That meant Bromma, and the admission ticket his own children had was now also available to Khalid. His mother visited occasionally; his father, he never saw again.

Now his uncle was in charge. He was the one who earned the money, and he said that money bought respect. Khalid soon realized that he too wanted money and respect, but he also wanted something else. He wanted to be an insider—and he had it easy, incredibly easy, in school. In Tensta, it wasn't hard to impress people, but that got him nowhere. In Bromma, he could play in a whole different league. A couple of his teachers went from exaggerated responses of "Hey, nice job!" when he did well on tests, to actually taking him seriously. They encouraged him and invited him places. And Khalid was 100 percent in; he wanted to become so completely assimilated that he and those who saw him could look beyond his being black. Not that it would be denied, it could never be. He was still and forever Somali, but he wanted to be able to express himself like everyone else, and be seen as one of them. If an exam requested two synonyms for apathy, he wouldn't hesitate to give three: indifference, dispassion, and unconcern.

Khalid was still a teenager, and he hadn't yet discovered the term *glass ceiling*, in all its crudeness. His high school class was completely white, and he was as much a curiosity as a part of it. His uncle didn't mind his Swedish ways, and accepted everything as long as his nephew brought home good grades. He had only two rules for Khalid: (1) party, but don't come home if you can't walk straight on our street; and (2) if you make out with a Swedish girl, never do it where other Swedes can see. He obeyed only one, and never threw up where his uncle could see, after they'd emptied the wine bottles stolen from the parents of his friends. It went well, he was full of energy, he partied in the apple orchards and radiated self-confidence in panel discussions at school. An irresistible Mr. Diversity for the headmaster to parade, when otherwise there would have been too many white faces on the stage. Khalid wasn't totally blind to the game, but still he played it with enthusiasm, and reaped the benefits. They would get him inside.

Despite his successes, only one kid ever got past Khalid Delmar's own door. He and Fredrik Hansson had met in a high school class. Fredrik was an afterthought, but his mother hadn't remarried until he was in high school. There was something sad about her plunging necklines, and although his stepfather had cash, the new kid in the house never really meant much. Fredrik Hansson was the one who always got the cool new gadget—a year too late. And he hated that. The two didn't understand it then, but Delmar and Hansson were vulnerable in the same way: don't ask questions about our backgrounds, and don't ask to come over to our houses.

And the real sticking point was money. Getting some. For Hansson, it meant fighting for what he didn't have, and for Delmar, money meant getting as far as possible from everything his father represented. Hansson was tough; Delmar was smart. When they came together, everything clicked. Hansson brought girls to Delmar, and in return, Delmar never cracked jokes about his mom. One knew black people, and the other white. Hansson had his eye on what people wanted in the suburbs, and Delmar knew where to get it in the projects. Not drugs—there were others working that side, willing to take the risk. Delmar and Hansson focused on the next level, making contacts and ensuring that goods and services flowed smoothly from A to B. They arranged the right DJs for parties and got the hottest young rappers to perform at improvised gigs, so that those hosting got street cred, if that was what they wanted, and the lines stretched all the way down the block, and those who sold alcohol and small items in Ziploc bags got more handshakes hiding rolled-up twenty-dollar bills.

Delmar always dressed in white, and Hansson fed the myth that he always carried a knife. Some people began to call Delmar "the Jew"—straight-up nastiness, based on his love of money. No matter how anyone twisted and turned it, there was always some way, some reason, for him to take a percentage. Together, they skimmed off the cream, and it was other people's parents who got the phone calls from the police, about someone selling weed at the parties they'd organized. There were no incidents with blue lights for either Hansson or the Jew, and nothing in the police files. These were good years, instructive years.

Soon, it was time for them to decide on a future. Hansson had little ambition and no head for books, but when he put on a uniform, everything fell into place. He went on a mission right after basic training and wanted to become an officer, but naturally they found out that he had trouble with authority and following orders. So there would be no officer training school at Karlberg for Hansson. But the military always struggled to find fresh meat for their missions, people who'd actually do the work in the desert or on muddy roads: move, dig, patrol. And handle logistics. This was second nature: getting things done, getting systems in place, managing the fucking impossible Lebanese, Kurds, or Nigerians. He'd learned a hundred times more from what he'd arranged in Sweden between Bromma, Hagsätra, and Tensta. Hansson was cut out for the job and soon could choose among the missions he wanted or didn't want. He could come and go. Six months out, then back to Stockholm to live life and take care of business. His childhood friends kept doing their thing when he came home to visit, while Delmar moved ahead with his own plans. He studied law at the University of Stockholm, his uncle smiling wide every time he said those words. His mother was more of a proud skeptic, gently asking every time she saw him why he couldn't switch his major and become a doctor.

He worked hard, learned the lingo, and was encouraged to get a law degree. Never in his life had he dreamed of working at a law firm. In one of those offices in the city, where his fellow students got part-time jobs because they knew the right people. They told him about the offices on Strandvägen: sky-high ceilings, oil paintings on the walls, and sixty-five-hour weeks. As if that was what he wanted, when it was really about earning money and respect, and being an insider. During his last year, Delmar exchanged his permanent resident status for Swedish citizenship and stepped out into the world with flawless qualifications. He'd built his résumé, had everything in place, had done everything he should, dressed and moved with the restrained confidence of someone who knew the value of education and humbly wanted to learn more. That was the man who came to the interviews. But that was not the man they saw. It wasn't about his coffee-colored skin, which was offset by all other boxes he'd checked and his academic honors. Senior partners in the firm had long since decided that someone like him would only be an asset.

There was something else, some slight nuance. After thirty applicants had been whittled down to two, Delmar found himself defeated by the fact that he'd moved to Bromma a few years too late. There was something about his intonation, something he could never shake. He had the words, every single one; he could write the briefs, the opinions, the summaries, anything, and no one would have had a clue. Nothing of the Somali from Tensta showed through. But when he spoke exactly the same words—a foreign accent, that they could handle, it could even be exotic. But when they heard wrong-side-of-the-tracks, they got nervous. It had to do with values; they feared that he didn't share the opinions that never are spoken about.

So the bright future Khalid had imagined turned into something else. He spent a year on this Via Dolorosa, going from firm to firm, a lengthy execution every time. What hurt most was that they always put him through several rounds of interviews, nodding approvingly, giving him a fraternal pat on the back. But then when it came time to make the decision, which was never explained, he was never better than runner-up. It was never really close; he was a world away.

He sank and for the first time understood his father's shame. He not only understood but felt in himself the rise of bitterness. But unlike his father, he took the job his uncle offered. His mother cleaned offices for Swiftclean at night, and Khalid did their paperwork during the day, meeting and getting to know many new Somalis. Some he could use in his services as the Jew, while others were good to keep in his back pocket, just in case—people who told him things, and who kept their eyes open.

A cousin was getting married in Mogadishu, and his uncle took him along so he'd get a chance to relax and recharge. When his uncle went home to Sweden, Khalid decided to stay on another month. But he didn't so much relax as start things moving. At that time, Mogadishu was like a never-ending Stalingrad, with endless wars between

Al-Shabaab and whichever country's troops had been lured into the trap of being stationed there.

For most people, it was just background noise while real life consisted of other, far more pressing feuds. In an old office building near where he lived, a family ran a simple construction company: naturally, given the circumstances, cement and plaster were in high demand. Another family insisted that the building was theirs, and they wanted the company out, or at least paying rent. In Somalia, there was no longer an official archive: the deeds and titles had been burned, or scattered to the winds during the looting. Claims of ownership were based on thin air. And whenever a feud spread beyond families to involve entire clans, it was hard to find a mediator who could be seen as neutral. There weren't many elders left, and people no longer had the same confidence in them. The construction company feud was on the brink of turning violent, when somebody told somebody that somewhere in the neighborhood, there was a lawyer.

Delmar was brought in to find a solution. Although at first they didn't know whether to trust him, both parties realized that the alternative was an outcome that neither would find acceptable. Hours of glaring with crossed arms followed, but now there were negotiations, not just escalating threats. Sometimes, a Western approach to justice had its appeal. Eventually the suspicious looks stopped, and instead they began to imagine possibilities. Finally there was a handshake, and a sum of money changed hands. Ownership, access rights, contract law: the sale of plaster and cement could continue, compensation had been paid, and soon there were rumors around town about what had been achieved.

He'd found his calling, and he opened an office. It was very simple: all he needed was a phone. His specialty was mediation—arbitration where laws no longer existed—and he took a percentage for himself. The Jew was back. The demand was endless; it was like being the only pharmacy with antibiotics during a leprosy epidemic.

That is how Khalid Delmar and Fredrik Hansson moved more and more of their lives down to Africa. Hansson had already been there, wearing a United Nations beret, and he'd thrived, so he already knew he did well with Africans. He did mission after mission, while Delmar untied knots in Mogadishu. Whenever they had time, they lived the good life in Kenya, Mozambique, and South Africa. Of course, there was also a practical advantage to having Hansson in Africa. Everything Delmar earned from his business was paid in cash, and soon this meant major amounts, and the lack of a banking system was causing problems. He didn't want to keep the money in Somalia, he wanted access to it in Sweden. The money was legitimate, but it wasn't easy to convert bills stuffed in bags in Mogadishu into a number in a Swedish bank account. The problem wasn't so much moving money around within Africa, which wasn't hard; the problem was getting it off the continent. He'd been able to use the informal networks, Al-Barakat banks, and others. But Delmar didn't want other Somalis to know about the sums he was moving—which could make him vulnerable. The advantage to Hansson's being in Africa was that, with his military logistics connections, Delmar got his very own transport service in and out. Regardless of where he was living, he'd managed to maintain this link between Africa and Sweden for nearly ten years.

As Delmar's consulting business grew, Al-Shabaab was bringing in more and more armed hordes. From Sweden, they heard talk that young men in immigrant neighborhoods were getting sucked in. At first, these were just rumors, about lost souls trying to make themselves feel important, with lots of talk and little action. But then the young men began going off, leaving their families back home at wit's end. They'd be left in the dark: complete silence, or just a grainy picture of their child's face on all the wrong Internet sites, or a death announcement from some untrustworthy source.

Delmar's own operations had developed a widening network of contacts, even far out in the Somali countryside. He'd managed to track down some of the missing youths in what Al-Shabaab called a training camp: a dusty scrap of land in the middle of nowhere, without enough food or ammunition for anyone to be able to train for anything. After a few months of being bossed around by thugs whose only ambition was to destroy the world, the adventure would have run its course. The young men had thought they'd win respect by carrying a Kalashnikov. Their actual assignment was to bring glory to others by becoming one of the multitude, with a bomb belt strapped around their waist.

It wasn't hard to convince them to leave—they ached with homesickness—but it was a matter of getting the right leaders to look the other way while distracting the thugs assigned to guard the sheep. Two of the youths got home safely, and one died on the way. Still, the operation was considered a success. Again, there were rumors, now in cities with a large Somali diaspora: in Minneapolis, Ottawa, and Rotterdam, there were people who wanted their sons brought home. Delmar, who hated jihadists, was happy to sabotage their designs—and he also liked making money. Few people managed to do both at the same time. He set a price of $30,000 to bring a man home. Many of the families hated him for it; they saw only this huge sum and imagined his life of luxury They didn't see the bribes that had to be paid, the risks that Delmar and his sources ran, the escape routes that had to be arranged, the clan borders that had to be crossed, the machinery that could only be lubricated with a single tool—cash. Now, if ever, that name, the Jew, really stuck. It was rarely spoken with respect, but still, the boys came home.

Naturally, the business meant that ever larger sums of cash could be moved, and that was what Fredrik Hansson did for Delmar, both within Africa and between continents. Money flowed along one route, and the confused and often defiant young men along the other. These were youths who would otherwise have ended their days with a bang that took far too many lives in a marketplace, or in a senseless shoot-out in a shopping mall. Invisible to all, Delmar and Hansson had built up something that the West's police and intelligence networks could not.

There were many who were dependent on Khalid Delmar. And he, in turn, needed Fredrik Hansson.

47

Fredrik Hansson gave Ayanna a full confession. A whole day, sitting by the pool in the house on Lamu Island. And everything that he told her, Grip took in. He understood how it worked, what the Swedish soldier and the Somali were actually up to. On the cell phone voice memos that Ayanna kept sending him, when Hansson talked about his "friend," that meant Khalid Delmar. The more he laid out for Ayanna, the clearer it became who was the genius, and who the guy lucky enough to tag along.

Khalid Delmar ran a travel agency for jihadists, not for the ones buying a one-way ticket to hell but for the families who wanted someone brought home again. That paid much better, and that's where the real money came from. Dollar bills in bundles from his own compatriots, weeping over sons who'd left behind the housing projects of their adopted country. Some were taken home by force, which cost more.

Hansson gave the details in bits and pieces, but Grip already knew enough to start filling in the blanks. It wasn't just families in Sweden they helped, but Somalis worldwide. Money flowed in from the United States, Canada, and Europe, always in different ways, to different places. Their approach was to hide the money from others who wanted to get ahold of it, and also from the intelligence services eager to handcuff and interrogate whenever they found Muslims exchanging cash. Most of it ended up in Africa, as that was where the networks were, and it was always there that a beloved son would finally be traded for hard currency. Delmar had a whole

319

organization up and running, inside Somalia and in its neighboring countries.

But there was another dimension, the game that not even Hansson seemed aware of. The one that in Judy Drexler's world, was driven by greed as much as by conviction. Khalid Delmar knew everything about those who recruited and armed young jihadist adventurers. While looking for the young men he was bringing back home, he infiltrated operations, learning the names of leaders, their cell phone numbers, and the places where they'd built their bases and training camps. That's what he gave to Judy Drexler, and that's how he'd become her most valuable source. She in turn passed the information along, and then the drones did their part. Hansson was in the dark, Grip was convinced of it. Fredrik Hansson was just the guy who made sure it all got loaded and unloaded, the one who got the profits home. Only now he'd fucked up.

Grip took it in and spun it around in his mind; clearly the house on Lamu Island had a very specific function. When Ayanna tried to exchange cell numbers, Hansson had refused. The desert fortress with its swimming pool and shady terrace was a safe house with crystal-clear rules: no phone, no Internet. In his nearly stateless situation, Fredrik Hansson was trying to shut himself off from the world. He would ride out the storm, and then everything would be fine again. But for now, after the shipwreck, he'd cling onto anyone. So when Ayanna drifted by, he was grateful to be able to reach out and feel he could keep his head above water. Maybe he could get someone to believe that he mattered, that it wasn't over. He'd drag out the story as long as possible, so that she wouldn't look at the clock, excuse herself, and disappear. He'd tell more and more, it didn't matter what, just to keep from sinking. Anything to fend off the loneliness, the sense that he was being swallowed up and pulled down into the darkness.

"My friend is coming soon . . ." Eventually, Khalid Delmar would show up. This was the place where they both felt the most comfortable, their own secluded island. Within the walls of that house, there was luxury—a prosperity few in the world would ever know. But even if Fredrik Hansson had no place else to go, he also feared their reunion.

Grip listened to the latest voice memo Ayanna had sent. "He went apeshit . . ." Hansson sounded distressed. Even as he was spilling his guts, he sometimes spoke in riddles, but Grip realized he was talking about the incident at the shooting range. Delmar had been furious about all the attention it got, attention their business could have done without. The two hadn't met face-to-face in six months, Hansson busy in Djibouti and Delmar in Somalia, where he was needed most.

"My friend should just . . . He's put together a new group to be returned home. It's a hard trip, very risky, it takes time, but then . . ." Delmar would show up on Lamu Island, sooner or later. What was eating at Fredrik Hansson was that maybe Khalid Delmar would come to the island to say that their partnership was finished.

The sun went down on Lamu Island. An islander had arrived to cook dinner. She brought all the fresh ingredients she needed in a basket. The cook was the only other person Ayanna laid eyes on during that day in the big house. She stayed and ate with Hansson, a quiet meal. The only sounds were of the woman washing dishes in the kitchen, somewhere in back. When it was time to go, Hansson seemed to grow restless, like a nocturnal animal coming to life; the silence drove him crazy. He insisted that they get a dose of street life, at least to go out for a drink. Ayanna excused herself, saying that she had errands to run and needed an hour to herself. They decided on a time to meet later, at the same bar as the night before.

Ayanna went back to her bungalow and called Grip. She had a few things to add about Hansson's past history, but these were just small details. Really, it was an excuse to talk. Grip heard the anxiety in her voice. She wanted instructions. He said she should just keep doing what she was doing, building trust.

"He is scared," she said.

"Of course he is."

"He thinks that people are watching him."

"I'm watching him."

"Not only you."

"He's paranoid."

When they'd hung up, and Ayanna went to take her evening shower, Grip thought about his final dismissive comment. Was it meant to comfort himself, or Ayanna?

He called her back. "I just wanted to say that you're doing a very good job."

"You do not have a plan, do you?" she replied, and waited out his silence. "You have no idea where this is going."

"Not really."

"Okay. Just so I know."

Before she went off to the bar, she sent a picture of herself in front of the mirror wearing a blue dress she'd bought in Mombasa and wrote: "So that you can identify me in the morgue here at Lamu, if it comes to that."

Hansson had already been at the bar for a while when Ayanna arrived. He'd had at least one double Scotch so far, to kill the pain, and for a moment he looked like the old Fredrik Hansson, muscular and cocky amid the nightlife. He sat down with Ayanna but kept looking around and greeting people, and he was so wary that Ayanna could only record short snippets with her cell phone under the table.

"Who are you looking for?"

"People are watching me," he replied. "But you don't need to turn around, they've already left."

Another snippet Ayanna sent Grip was of her playing the real estate game. "Maybe I'll settle for something a little farther from the water."

"An ocean view costs money."

"An ocean view does, and a private beach even more," she said.

Hansson guffawed. "Everyone has dreams. If you don't go after them, then you settle for crumbs."

"That's life," she said, making light of it.

"Maybe, but with that attitude, you'll never get anywhere. If you want it, you have to grab it."

Ayanna excused herself. She didn't head to the bathroom but instead out into the street and called Grip. She'd sent another voice memo. "Did you hear that last part?" she asked, as soon as he picked up.

It had been hard enough to hear before, but this time he only got background noise, mumbling, and people walking across the floor. "No, not a word."

"He is speaking in riddles, but it seems he wants to use me as a courier."

"Carrying money from where?"

"From Lamu."

"To?"

"I do not know, Djibouti I suppose. With all the mess you've made, he's trapped. He's behind schedule, and Delmar is furious." There was silence for a few seconds. "Are you still there?" she asked.

"Say yes," Grip urged, in the next breath. He saw a chance to trick Hansson into returning to Djibouti. "What we'll actually do next is another thing, but say yes."

When Ayanna went back to Hansson, he seemed more troubled. He talked about other things for a while and then asked, "Well, what do you say?"

Ayanna had simply nodded.

There were some loud bangs on the recording that Grip listened to later. Then Ayanna's voice: "They're shooting?"

"No doubt out on the canal, warning shots." There was the sound of Hansson lifting his glass, and then he added: "Just the police chasing people, it happens all the time. No one even notices.

"Anyway," he said, and lowered his voice. "Under the table, I'm holding a key chain. By your right knee. Do you feel it?"

"Yes."

"There's a big key and a small key. Don't worry about the big key, it's for the house, but I have another set, I can get in anyway. It's the small key you'll need. You met Irene today."

"The one who cooked dinner?"

"Yes. She lives just outside of town here, she and her young son who's always sick, in a small house at the edge of the forest. At the back, behind their place, there's a storage shed."

"I cannot find . . ."

"Take the keys with you when you go. I'm leaving now. Tomorrow I'll tell you what to do and how to find Irene's shed." There was the sound of the chair scraping when Hansson stood up.

"Tomorrow?" asked Ayanna.

"Yes, yes, for lunch."

"Here?"

"Come when you want, after one or so."

Grip had listened to all the recordings Ayanna sent over. Pondered and listened again. When he rang at half past two in the morning, she answered in a sleepy voice, and after a brief apology, he asked, "Did you tell him where you live?"

"Here? You mean the bungalow?"

"Yes."

"I talked about the place, said something about the courtyard here. He knows the town, surely he could figure it out. Why?"

"And who else did you tell?"

"I pretended that I was looking for a house for him," she replied, now sounding more annoyed than sleepy. "To get gossip from the real estate brokers, you must be generous yourself. I do not know how many I told. Is it important?"

"No, but . . . tomorrow I want you to find another place. Do it quietly, don't go through the brokers you've gotten to know, get something . . . I am sure there are signs for tourists to rent on their own. Just get a room."

"Is this about how much I am costing you again?"

"Not at all. Just a feeling. Don't check out of the bungalow, and don't give them any reason to think that you're not there. Mess up the bed, but take your things out of there."

"So is this my last night here?"

"Yes."

"Why?"

"I don't tell you how to play Gershwin, so leave this to me."

"We have a plan, in other words?"

"It would be too much to say that. Just a little breathing room."

"I am starting to feel more and more like bait, both for you and for Hansson."

"You've borrowed a bunch of keys, that's all. Go to sleep now."

"You should hear the night here," she said. "It is not like the stillness of the desert. This darkness is alive. People, animals, sometimes you can hear the ocean." She was quiet for a second. "This is an island. It is not so easy to get away."

"What do you mean?"

"Do not abandon me."

"Try to sleep now."

48

It was after breakfast, and Grip was swimming laps in the Kempinski's pool. He'd done this several mornings in a row, feeling the pleasure of having some kind of routine in his life. A short, refreshing way to relax. When he came out to get his towel under an umbrella, he found a text waiting on the phone that was his only link to the negotiator. At first, he saw it as just a string of numbers, but then he noticed an S at the beginning and an E in the middle. Latitude and longitude. He'd been given an exact location for something. He responded with a ? but got nothing back.

He went up to his room and, still in his bathing suit, found an online satellite site and entered the coordinates. A point in the middle of the Indian Ocean. He typed the numbers again, got the same result. Went to another site, still a pin in the same place, just blue sea.

He stayed in his room, and soon the anxiety that the pool had eased was back. Too much uncertainty. He'd showered and dressed when it rang. The call could only be coming from one person.

"I did what I could," the negotiator began bluntly, as soon as Grip answered. "Someone in Sweden could have responded earlier to my call. You had every opportunity in the world to send that boy his medications."

"He didn't get them?"

It was quiet for a moment. "The pills got there. Darwiish let the family have them."

"Well then," said Grip, suddenly thinking that the negotiator felt pressured by something, which was good. He decided not to ask more questions about the boy.

"I do not think this will end well," continued the negotiator. "I want guarantees."

"You give us something real, and then we'll talk. The drug delivery worked in your favor, but it was just a way to buy us both some time."

"I'm not sure it bought us much. No one in Sweden is willing to pay. There is some kind of ridiculous collection fund, as I understand it, but Darwiish's patience and the family's health . . ."

"You need to give us something concrete."

"The coordinates I sent show where they're being held."

"I saw only ocean, on the map."

"They need to be adjusted a bit, but first I want guarantees."

"The government never negotiates openly about such matters. All you can have is my word. Now, give me the right numbers."

"Do not forget that I am, after all, representing the side that is holding the hostages. It would be all too easy to charge me as an accomplice. I want you to say it, that you will not come after me, that you will not try to kill me or imprison me."

"I promise."

"Reduce the first and the seventh numbers by one."

Grip typed in the numbers again. The satellite image on the computer relocated to a point where land and sea intersected, somewhere north of Mogadishu. He zoomed down to the brown desert sand and soon saw: a series of hills, next to the sea seen from space. Finally, although the image was grainy, two small houses. It looked to be about as hospitable as a distant, dead planet.

"The family is being held in the house on the eastern side," explained the negotiator, "and the guards live in the one to the west. Should you choose to do something, Friday would be a good option."

"Why Friday?"

"Speak to someone who understands Somalis. Also, Darwiish is usually there on Friday nights."

"And from now on, you will stop leaking details or photos to the Swedish press," Grip warned.

"I have your word. And from me, you now have the exact location. This is what we have agreed on. What I ultimately care about is how blame will be assigned, if you choose to do nothing. Is it me or the Swedish government who is truly acting in the family's best interests?"

"You represent pirates who kidnap innocent people and let them die."

"And now you have the exact coordinates. All opportunities lie with you, Mr. Grip."

Judy Drexler came walking across the marble floor of the piano bar at the Kempinski, where Grip sat with a drink. She and Grip hadn't set up a meeting. There was a new woman at the white grand piano, but Drexler didn't comment on that. She did, however, mention Grip's appearance when they met: "I see you've let your beard grow since you arrived in Djibouti. But you're still dressing well." Grip looked down at his own shirtfront. He'd even put on a jacket.

"One could mistake you for a sharp type from the Middle East," she continued. Her manner was unexpectedly lighthearted, and she laughed. "Straight out of Lebanon, even. Easy to imagine your background, your father a businessman who hit on a Scandinavian model in Paris in the mid-1970s. Barely forty years later, and here you are, with some Swedish in you anyway."

"Is that what you're doing at the consulate, inventing people's backgrounds?"

"Not just that. But you must agree that you Swedes often let yourselves go a little too much when you arrive in warmer countries."

"Another lecture on iced tea?"

"Under the hot sun, your appearance deteriorates. You don't think it matters anymore. How many of your aid workers and second-tier officers have I seen at the embassy wearing wrinkled shirts and unpolished shoes?"

"What can I say? We're basically a nation of peasants sitting with our backs to the sea. We'll always be insecure about the world south of Copenhagen."

"But you do dress well. I just wanted to mention that." She looked around without lowering her voice as a precaution when she said: "And speaking of insecurity, you were invited just an hour ago to talk to someone who understands Somalia."

"I didn't think you showing up here was a coincidence."

"You asked me to keep track of his phone, and obviously we listen in."

"So why did the negotiator drop that line about doing something on a Friday?"

"For the simple reason that there are Friday prayers, and for those who don't take minarets too seriously, it's party time. My guess is that late on a Friday night is when the pirates are at their most trigger-happy, but also their least accurate."

Grip spun the ice in his glass, looked at her, and then dropped his eyes to the ice again.

"Well, what?" said Judy.

The ice made one more lap inside Grip's glass. "I haven't yet told people at home that we know where the family is being held. There will be a lot to digest in Stockholm, especially for the politicians."

"Is this about you being peasants with your backs to the sea?"

"More or less. Sooner or later, the matter will come down to you having special forces here in Djibouti and us having a ship that sorts trash and chases after pirates. You do this kind of thing every day."

"Not as often as you might think. We often eliminate targets, but this is about getting the hostages out alive. Nine times out of ten, it will be messy. You can promise us twenty years of unconditional support for our resolutions at the United Nations, and we still won't do it for you. The hostages' home country has to take responsibility. The risks, and the headlines. Ask the French, they'll give the same answer. That is how the world looks south of Copenhagen."

"You don't owe me anything?"

"Plenty, I'm sure—remind me?"

"Khalid Delmar—a Swedish citizen who's implicated in the murder of a Swedish officer, and again in a hit man's attack on a police investigator. And you want me to lay off."

"I'm willing to go far to protect him. But there are only so many resources I can mobilize. Rescuing the Swedish family would require a decision by the president, personally, and that you will never get. Drop it—don't waste your time. You can get any other kind of support you need: high-resolution satellite imagery, signals intelligence, transports. But if you want to get them out, you must take responsibility for the part that hurts."

"Is that what protecting Delmar buys us—support?"

"Something like that."

Grip took a long look at her, then at the new pianist. She played the theme from *The Godfather,* and Grip smiled. "I know how Delmar and Hansson made all their money," he began, "and in that business, they also hide the money they earn from giving you tips."

"I don't know that," replied Judy.

"And I have an eye on Hansson now—he's in hiding in a safe house down in Kenya. Delmar seems to be on the way there."

"I'm impressed. Ayanna's handiwork?" Grip nodded. "She's become more yours than mine now."

Grip ignored the comment and asked instead: "You've never met him, huh?"

"Who?"

"Delmar."

"No, he gives me the names and places, and I make sure that he gets paid." It was as if she was about to say more but suddenly changed her mind. "Hey, just so that we have our ducks in a row here. Hansson"—she made a dismissive gesture—"we've been successful with our drone attacks, but they create a thirst for revenge. Now we've received reports that informants are being ruthlessly pursued in Somalia. I'm worried about Delmar, who's deep into this—that he might disappear or suddenly decide to quit."

"You want me to just turn around and let Hansson off the hook?"

"I don't want anything special. I'm just saying everything is so damn volatile down here."

"Should I proceed with caution?"

"We have different agendas. You do what you need to do." Drexler started walking away.

"Wait," said Grip. "The Swedish family, if we do the part that hurts, going there and carrying out the attack, running the actual mission, can you . . . polish up the story?"

"Now you're talking in riddles again, but as long as you assume all the physical risks, everything else is possible. Just take care of my best interests."

"I'll let you know."

49

TRANSCRIPT OF RECORDED PHONE CALL, TS 233:10123

Recording requestor: Bureau Director Thor Didricksen

TOP SECRET UNDER CHAPTER 2, SECTION 2 OF THE SECRECY ACT (1980:100)
OF HIGHEST IMPORTANCE TO NATIONAL SECURITY

Persons present: Thor Didricksen (TD) and police officer
Ernst Grip (EG)

TD: Don't say anything yet. If you're calling, that means you
were in touch with our negotiator yesterday?

EG: That's right, Boss.

TD: Is the news good or bad?

EG: Depends on how you look at it.

TD: Let's view this through the government's eyes, and then
I'll decide what they get to see. Well?

EG: The family received the meds.

TD: That's a victory we already won in the media, and while it
may be true, it's already old news. How's the boy?

EG: I have no idea.

TD: In that case, the boy is fine. How did this negotiator seem
when you saw him?

EG: We didn't meet, we talked on the phone.

TD: At first he wanted a meeting, but now the phone is good enough?

EG: I think he feels pressured, and he doesn't want to waste time.

TD: Then time is on our side.

EG: He doesn't think so.

TD: Don't forget whose side you're on.

EG: Not for a moment, Boss. But he was supposed to give us something concrete, in exchange for us agreeing not to prosecute, and now he's given us the exact location of where the family is being held.

TD: I see.

EG: Sometimes when you open a door, it can't be shut again.

TD: The government doesn't know anything about this yet, so for now it's just you and me. Every nation practices self-deception. We deploy Swedish soldiers so that little girls can get to school and food aid can get to ports, not for any other reason. It's only soldiers from other countries who kick down doors.

EG: So we'll just let things be?

TD: The medications have been delivered, the money's pouring in, everybody's happy.

EG: And if someone dies, the pirates will be the only ones who get blamed?

TD: There you go again, Grip. Your tone.

EG: With all due respect, Boss, I don't think the negotiator will be satisfied with that decision.

TD: It's our decision to make.

EG: He's the one who got the Swedish public to pay attention, with those pictures of the family. He was the one who sent them. He's the one pushing the government to act.

TD: What are you trying to say?

EG: My guess is that he'll wait a reasonable amount of time, maybe a week, maybe two, and then he'll call the newspapers again. These days, he's seen as the most reliable source.

TD: And what will he say to them?

EG: He'll send worse images, probably when everyone is dead. And then he'll reveal that the government knew exactly where the family was being held but chose to do nothing.

TD: That's unacceptable. You have to stop him.

EG: I've just promised him that he'll go free.

TD: Only words.

EG: Whatever was said, he knows exactly what he started, and now he won't reply if I try to contact him. For him, this is about how blame will be assigned—those were his own words.

TD: But that's *not* what this is about. He simply wants to force the government to pay the entire ransom, which isn't going to happen.

EG: It's not our only option.

TD: You mean, special forces.

EG: For example.

TD: The pirates are poor fishermen, and we'd be shooting them to save a venture capitalist. This is Sweden—we don't believe in violence.

EG: But we have special forces.

TD: We have bombs on our Saab Gripen fighter jets too, but they're not supposed to be dropped.

EG: The family will die, and it will come out that we knew exactly where they were being held.

TD: I haven't said anything yet to the government. They know nothing.

EG: So they can continue their little show, and Sweden will at best pursue quiet diplomacy?

TD: That's the picture we need to preserve. We'll see how things develop.

EG: Damn it, Boss! I can't do any more, I won't do any more for this family. I have my hands full just keeping track of Hansson and dealing with the Americans down here.

TD: Clearly, we're done with this game. Call me when you have something else.

EG: No, nothing is done. And for the Bergenskjölds, there won't be another chance. Now it's in your hands—it's up to the government. I'm in a good position with the Americans. I have something they care about.

TD: I don't need the details. But besides knowing where the family is being held, there's also a third party who's willing to help create . . . ?

EG: . . . a smoke screen. But this isn't some shadowy third party—we're talking about the Americans here. Our people have to kick down the door. Then the Americans can make it look like something else. But first, you and the government have to respond through your channels. And no matter what the answer is—I'm done.

50

"Damn, you grew a beard," said Stark, when Grip picked him up early in the morning at the gangway. The *Sveaborg* had come into port, the gangway had descended, and Simon Stark had stepped ashore as the first bags of sorted trash hit the dock.

Grip felt relieved to see him. The feeling of being two again, he needed that. And Stark didn't seem to harbor any bitterness; he was mostly quiet in the car on the way to the Kempinski. Not without pride, he held up a red folder: "A complete report from the old doc." The surgeon on board had given them everything they needed to exonerate Radovanović.

"I think I'll lie down for a while," Stark said when they arrived. "They started early in the morning, making a big fuss about getting the ship ready to return to port."

"Let's talk after lunch, then?"

A nod. There was time; this was no emergency. Grip could relax and do a few laps in the pool. Right at that moment, everything was looking pretty good.

The phone rang just as Grip was about to leave his room for lunch. He couldn't understand what she was saying. He knew it was Ayanna, and he understood individual words, but he couldn't get the context because the words said one thing and the voice another. She was terrified. While he calmed her down and tried to sort of whisper, the devil's advocate played in his head: She's not trained . . . Drexler had it right, after all, saying she needed a different kind of rein—it was you and no one else who pretended otherwise.

337

On Lamu Island, it had been a slow morning. After lunch, Ayanna had gone to the bar where she'd met Hansson the night before. She wasn't entirely clear on the details, and when he didn't show up, she took it as a sign that she'd misunderstood the meeting place.

Fifteen minutes later, she was back up at the sand-colored house with the gate in the wall. You couldn't hear the bell from the street when you pressed the button. If there was one thing that defined Ayanna, it was that she gazed straight ahead, Grip thought, once she'd calmed down enough for him to understand her story. She looked for opportunities and followed up on them, but she wasn't the type to have a plan B. He didn't blame himself, not yet, he thought, as he braced himself for whatever news would come over the phone. She had Hansson's key ring; she seemed to see that as an invitation to use it.

The gate had been easy to open and close. Behind it, a paved path led up to the terrace. If Grip had called her there, if he'd gotten ahold of her, instead of vice versa, everything would still have looked promising. If he'd just gone ahead with the plan he'd had for Ayanna ever since he'd met with Judy Drexler: Turn back, we'll let Hansson go. Leave Lamu and come back to Djibouti again. But she had walked up onto the terrace and looked at the pool. It was from there that she'd called. After she'd seen.

"Hansson is in the pool."

"Yes . . . ?"

"He is floating on his stomach, and a large black bird is sitting on his back."

"Is there blood in the pool?"

"Not that I can see. I want to get out of here."

"Wait just a minute. What else do you see?"

"What do you mean?"

"Does it look the same as last time?" There were some long seconds of silence.

"There is a chair in the pool as well." New silence. "And yes, there is a little confusion among the tables and chairs on the terrace."

"As if there was trouble?"

"Perhaps."

"Get out of there, and try not to be seen. You've moved from the bungalow to your new place?"

"Yes."

"Buy food and water on the way, enough so that you can stay inside for a few days."

"I have not done anything!" She was upset.

Grip had to raise his voice. "Go, and call me when you get to your room."

When Simon Stark knocked on the hotel room door to meet for lunch, Grip ushered him into the room instead.

"Sit down!"

"So serious, all of a sudden."

"Look. Hansson confessed, but it wasn't pretty." On his desk, Grip had set up his computer with a USB stick in one of the ports. "And listen, too."

Fredrik Hansson, in chains on a stone floor, writhing like a worm and screaming when a police officer forced him into a uniform. A moment later, the police chief voice said: "Would you like something to drink?" Then the horse trading, the broken gaze, and, not least, the confession: "I fired the shot." Fredrik Hansson, naked and completely exposed.

Simon Stark watched the video without a single comment or glance at Grip. He was like a sponge, sucking up every impression and every word, until the frame went black. A quiet moment, the silent confirmation of who'd been behind the events in Djibouti, and what Grip had been involved in, while he'd been at sea.

"Shit," Stark nodded, looking at the floor. "I had it wrong. I never thought you could get him to that point." He pointed to the computer screen.

"Because I called it a robbery?"

"Among other things. But now, fuck, I've got you breathing down my neck." Simon Stark looked up. "But regardless. You got him, so now we're even. Where is he now?"

"In Kenya," said Grip.

"What's he doing?"

"It's complicated."

"So, he's dead."

"You understand," Grip broke off, and then began again. "I had two assignments: to rescue the hostages and bring home Hansson with an airtight confession in the bag. You and I can't do anything more for the family, but now Hansson is lying dead in a pool, and I've sent in an innocent civilian who needs help getting out of there in one piece. And I need to ask you something."

"It sounds like I'm taking a trip again."

"Even if it's just the two of us down here, I need you in Stockholm. Officially, to go see the generals at HQ and explain the contents of your little red folder so Radovanović can start breathing again. You'll have that meeting, but you can do that afterward. The real emergency is that I need you to meet face-to-face with someone in Immigration."

"So there's a catch."

"There always is, when decisions should be untraceable."

"Decisions about what?"

"A permanent residence permit. The right to move freely and live in Europe."

"I can't do that. I don't know a thing about it."

"You don't need to, and it's not something you can learn by reading. Just go home and talk to Astrid Süss, an intelligence analyst for us, and she'll know who to talk to. Impossible things have been done before. You'll need to collect and drop off documents, actually transport them physically. We can't have any email exchanges that can be traced. And you'll probably need to find a few names whose signatures you can fake."

"But never my own?"

"You'll never have to use your own name. I can't tell anyone else about this. Absolutely no one can know."

They looked at each other, Stark more puzzled than Grip. "I'm going to Stockholm, and where are you going now?"

"A short trip to Kenya."

"In order to?"

"I need to scan someone's passport, and maybe arrange some photos. Things you might need."

"So who is it?"

"You'll recognize her, but keep it to yourself."

"Oh, her," Stark smiled. "What has she done?"

"She hasn't done anything. This is more about me and my own carelessness, and I have to tidy up afterward."

Stark shot a glance at the computer screen. "I'll say, you certainly have been cleaning," he said, looking back at Grip again. "Be careful."

"We're just rescuing an innocent person."

"If that's what you choose to call it, then fine."

51

Using the bundles of hundred-dollar bills that remained in the war chest, Grip was already in Mombasa that evening. After a night at a downtown hotel, he turned off both his regular and his negotiator phones and headed back to the airport.

ZAR AIR, read the big faded letters at the end of the hangar. Behind the open gate sat some of the airline's nimble little twin-engine planes and, farther down, the door to an unassuming office. Grip walked in and asked some basic questions. Sure, most things were possible, even when crossing borders. Lamu Island—Djibouti, one-way? Grip asked about the price for passengers, and also the cost for unaccompanied cargo. The pilot in charge of ground services that day, without even lowering his voice, told him the high-end prices. But as it happened, they already had a flight going to Lamu Island that afternoon, a group with four other passengers. That would make the trip more affordable. Grip had enough for a one-way ticket with the group but not enough to hire Zar Air to fly him back.

The plane followed the coast all the way from Mombasa. In the cabin, four businessmen with something to celebrate kept refilling their plastic glasses, which were too small for the task, from a bottle of whiskey, while Grip mostly looked out the window. It was a bumpy ride through afternoon showers, and by way of apology, the pilot made a pass over Lamu's historic district before they landed. Preparing for the trip, Grip had Googled the satellite images, but it was something else to gaze down from just a few hundred meters up, over the tropical maze of pools, lush gardens, and white coral-stone houses. The view mingled with his thoughts about why he was there. He thought about what he had to do and where Ayanna was now, amid the beauty of the place.

They landed at the small airport on the other side of the channel. There, he got a taxi and then caught the ferry that took him to the island, in the pleasant twilight breeze. They passed Lamu's port, mostly filled with small boats, some with their old-fashioned sails reefed for the night. Grip closed his eyes during the crossing, the wind and waves at the bow giving him a few moments of peace. Not until several days later would he be able to indulge his senses again, when the sky opened up in a nocturnal downpour.

As he stepped off the ferry, he was met by police officers checking IDs and passports. One of them asked to inspect Grip's bag. He ran his hand through the change of clothing and waved him through. If the police had gone through Grip's pockets instead, they would have found a jackknife, three new cell phones, and several SIM cards with cash balances. Grip lingered at the dock and watched the same security checks carried out on people heading back across the strait. Given the grumbling and comments among the passengers, this was not routine. Someone had recently decided to keep a close eye on Lamu's comings and goings.

Grip had no idea where Ayanna was staying, as he'd specifically told her not to mention the name of her new place over the phone. Once he got to Lamu, he assumed that she'd be keeping a low profile, staying at one of the guesthouses in the narrow streets of the historic district. For himself, he found a small, secluded hotel on the outskirts, probably intended for honeymooners, its bungalows scattered around a garden with privacy hedges, under the shade of acacias. Grip went to bed without contacting Ayanna. He wanted to have something concrete to tell her, and he wanted to put a few things in place first.

Sure enough, everyone sat in twos at the breakfast tables: all the talkative newlyweds, and a few middle-aged couples hoping to rekindle what they'd lost over the years. Grip finished his juice and started walking toward the city. Lamu drew much of its charm from being nearly car-free. There were paths, stairways, and cobblestone alleys, and mules not just for tourists but for items too heavy or awkward to carry on foot. In a town without cars, the squares remained intimate, and talks in a crowd weren't lost in the traffic noise. The public spaces felt almost transparent—a surprise could arrive only as fast as someone could walk, or maybe run. Nuances and moods could be sensed quickly, and conversations were easily overheard, more than what the person beside you was saying.

Grip walked around for a few hours. From drinking coffee while eavesdropping at a few strategic sites and making small talk in the quiet crowds, he got a sense of life in Lamu at its various levels. There were the tourists, who, outside of their hotels, often seemed restless—there wasn't much to do on the island. Then there were the rich newcomers who didn't want to be taken for tourists yet who never stayed in Lamu for long; and also there were the caretakers and maintenance types hovering around them, trying to skim off the cream. Finally, there were the locals, mostly recognizable by their patient gazes. The white faces on the street seemed more worried about the latest Somali terrorist raid across the border, while the islanders gossiped and asked each other about the man recently found dead in his own swimming pool. There were soldiers, the uniformed police, and the badly disguised undercover cops, in identical sunglasses, who insisted on wearing jackets in the heat.

Grip headed up to Hansson and Delmar's spacious villa and walked along the high wall, the one Ayanna had been standing behind when she'd called him the day before. A young policeman stood at his post outside the gate, and Grip passed by with a friendly nod. At the reception desk for the bungalow where Ayanna had stayed, Grip didn't need to ask many questions to grasp that everyone was talking about the police crackdown the night before, when the hotel had been searched. On her door hung a poster with a few paragraphs of print. Ayanna was being sought as more than just a witness. Fortunately, Grip was given several versions of what she looked like.

The civilian police, who were dozing at the reception desk when he arrived, said she definitely had short hair. They didn't even seem certain of her name.

Not until afternoon, once Grip felt he knew his way around the old city, did he pick up one of the new phones he'd loaded with a prepaid card. Given who might find a way to listen in, he didn't want to give away his plans too easily.

"Hello?" said Ayanna, picking up on the first ring.

"Yes, it's me."

"You are . . ."

"Just listen. I want you to go for a walk. Start by going to the Riyadh Mosque, then head down toward the water and follow the beach path in the direction of the harbor. While you're in the neighborhood, stop to buy fruit in the marketplace and look around in a couple of gift shops before returning to where you are now."

"Right this minute?"

"Yes. Dress like a tourist trying to avoid the sun."

Grip spotted her before she noticed him, on her way to the mosque. Sun hat and sunglasses, and lightweight baggy pants—she could have been anyone, among the afternoon's tourists out for a stroll. But at this time of day, not many wanted to visit the mosque. There weren't a lot of people out in the neighborhood, but Grip wanted to sift the sand to find the hidden stones. He found a spot with a view of the open plaza in front of the Riyadh Mosque, and he positioned himself in the shade of a colonnade opposite it. Only a few people were walking around, and when Ayanna emerged from one of the streets, she became a natural focal point. She moved carefully, her step a little nervous. And although he wanted just the opposite, the fox who was trailing her was easy to spot. She'd already passed the mosque when he came out from the same street, but then the man stopped in front of the plaza, as if the sunlight or the view might cause him pain. Grip found his restraint reassuring. Although the man was apparently following her, he displayed the self-conscious posturing that said he was doing something he shouldn't. Who was he working for? And was he alone?

As Ayanna headed toward the street that led to the boardwalk, the man at the corner started walking and crossed the plaza to catch up.

As they followed the route to the beach, zigzagging down to the neighborhood by the port, Grip saw no sign that the man had a partner. He kept his distance, not wanting to give himself away to Ayanna, only to keep track of where she was, without being too concerned about the details of what she was doing.

Grip had hired a messenger boy earlier in the day, an extra pair of eyes that no one would notice. He'd bought his loyalty with a little money up front, and the promise of much more later, from a kid who wasn't yet a teenager. Grip had carefully interviewed a few others, but Abdu seemed the smartest, and also his uncle in the village of Matondoni, less than ten kilometers up the coast on the west side of the island, had a few boats that the boy said he'd be happy to rent out.

When Ayanna, having bought some fruit as they'd agreed, went into a souvenir shop carrying her plastic bags, Grip sent a glance and a nod through the crowd. Ayanna's tail lazily kept his distance from the store, while the boy, cool and smiling at the challenge, made straight for his destination. The boy quickly left the shop again, empty-handed, and a small package wrapped in newsprint now sat with the fruit in one of Ayanna's bags. She had no idea it was there.

She'd come back out and was heading into an alleyway when Grip saw a signal between two people—her tail was no longer alone. A new guy wearing a striped shirt had joined. Grip wasn't sure he could stay out of sight of both at the same time, but he decided to take the risk and see where Ayanna went. He needed to know where she was staying and get a clear sense of her surroundings.

Winding along the streets and alleyways, Grip sometimes hung back, letting the men and Ayanna out of his sight, and looked at his paper map. He'd scouted out some possible addresses ahead of time, trying to make an educated guess, while Ayanna's tail behaved as if he already knew where she was heading. Sometimes he had to wait for a while, watching through the gap between a stone wall and a whitewashed building. There was always some obstacle, or people in the crowd blocking his view—there, wasn't that her going by?

Finally, in the honey-colored afternoon light, he saw the baggy cotton pants climb the steps up to Baytil Ajaib, a guesthouse with a plain entrance, and ten minutes later, the man in the striped shirt followed. Grip pulled himself away.

Three hours later, Abdu found him sitting in a restaurant. Grip had already learned that Baytil Ajaib was newly renovated and built around a courtyard: open stairways, nooks and crannies, palm trees in big pots, and odd-shaped rooms and suites. It was far from the cheapest place on the island, although it still marketed itself as a guesthouse. The boy could tell from his reconnaissance that the striped shirt stuck near to Baytil, waiting on the ledges above or just outside the entrance in the streets nearby. Ayanna couldn't possibly leave without her tail seeing her.

"Go get some food," Grip said to the boy, "but be back in an hour." He went out, and Grip picked up the last of the new phones. The first he'd burned when he'd called Ayanna on her regular phone and told her to go for her walk; the second she'd brought back with her from the harbor in her bag of fruit. Now there were two phones that had never been used, and never would be used for anything except a few days of staying in contact with each other. An isolated network, one nearly impossible to locate and listen in on, against the roar of all other telephones—even with the resources of a great world power.

"Yes." She sounded calmer when she answered this time, following the handwritten instructions enclosed in the package, setting the rules for using the phone. She would mostly just listen, keeping to yes-and-no answers. Grip described what he'd seen and heard during the day, and told her that the police were looking for her but didn't seem to know any details.

"I want to get out of here," she said, just as Grip was about to tell her that she was being tailed. He was silent, and he heard from her breathing that she was trying to regain control.

"We'll both get out of here, but there are a few things we need to organize first." She said nothing. "I need your passport, but you won't have to go for a walk again."

"Is someone following me?"

Perhaps Grip was silent a little too long. He sat looking at his messenger boy's quick sketch of the inside of Baytil Ajaib. Instead of answering, he said: "Is it correct that you're on the third floor?"

"Yes."

"When you come out of your room onto the balcony, there's a palm tree in a big pot, set on a ledge a little to the right."

"Sure."

"It's there, believe me. Find a reason to go to reception, ask them anything, but push your passport into the loose bark in the pot on your way there." Ayanna was quiet again. Grip looked around; no one could hear him. "I know," he began. "I wouldn't let go of my passport if I were you. A citizen of Ukraine, with your skin color. Without a passport . . . in Africa, you're nobody." He listened to her exhale. "But you must."

"I have nothing to hold over you," she said. A view of life as an exchange of debts.

"No, nothing," Grip said. "But I don't even have enough money to get myself out of here, and you have Fredrik Hansson's keys. Which are the keys to more than just the house he shared with Delmar."

He heard her breathe again.

"Make sure your passport is there half an hour from now. This is the only ship that's going to sail." Grip remembered the man in the striped shirt: "And put it there on the way down to reception, not on your way back up to your room."

She didn't answer, and Grip hung up. Like the negotiator, he knew when the other party had no alternative.

Shortly before midnight, Abdu walked up and gave him the passport. Back in his own hotel, Grip borrowed the scanner and attached digital copies of its pages to an email draft, along with an enlarged image of Ayanna's passport photo, using an anonymous email account. Simon Stark had the password to the same account, and now—without an email ever being sent—he had access to the information. Grip changed the SIM card in the phone he hadn't reserved for Ayanna and made a call.

Stark was in place in Sweden, and, with Astrid Süss's help, he'd started the immigration wheels turning.

"Things are looking good," he said, "but now that the passport has been scanned, I need thirty-six hours."

"And I need to get out of here," Grip said.

"Immigration still says thirty-six hours."

"Then the information has to show up in every database that allows entry into Europe."

"Someone has promised me that it's possible."

Grip checked some other formalities and was about to hang up when Stark said, "By the way, you remember Philippa Ekman, our tipster from MovCon? She called me earlier tonight, didn't know I was in Sweden. She said a big C-17 transport plane had landed in Djibouti. An American plane, but they unloaded it on the French side. A massive amount of equipment, enough for a small war, she said. Tight-lipped types wearing uniforms without a national insignia."

"Completely anonymous?"

"Not entirely. One of them swore in Skåne dialect when he dropped something, and the helicopters they rolled out of the aircraft had black emblems that looked like a cat's paw. Do you know anything?"

"What do you want me to say?"

"I'd say, it seems that Swedish Special Operations has landed in Djibouti."

"Seems like it. Did you run into them in Afghanistan?"

"Now and again. If you want, I can ask Philippa to keep us informed if she finds anything, and I'll put a note in our email account."

"Good thinking. Do it, and if you can pin down the time for any action, that would be great."

"I guess it's not you they're getting out of there, huh?"

"If only."

Ayanna had to take another walk in the morning, and just like the day before, the same tails followed her, while Grip watched from a distance and considered the possibilities. Why didn't they arrest her, and what were they waiting for? Were they corrupt policemen? Kenyan security? Some other country's agents or money-hungry jihadists? Or maybe they just had something against Khalid Delmar—no doubt many people did. Grip had a feeling he recognized the man in the striped shirt. Wasn't he one of the men who forced Fredrik Hansson into a uniform on the stone floor, in the house by the livestock port? Fuck knows what Hansson had confessed to, talked about, or tried to negotiate when Grip wasn't there.

Regardless of their reasons, they were in the way.

Grip made Ayanna take a short stroll after lunch, to test out a few theories. In fact, there were only two men. In equal shifts, they changed positions, one of them staying at or near the hotel and the other picking up the chase if Ayanna went out. The man watching the hotel would call the other, who'd take over following her. When she was walking around town, one tail was enough, but whenever she headed toward the outskirts, one tail would call the other, so there'd be two. That was the key: realizing that they were waiting for Ayanna to go to the storage shed. Probably they knew about it but didn't know where it was. Once she'd shown them the way, they'd make themselves known to her; or rather, something in the way they moved told Grip that Ayanna wouldn't get a chance to defend herself the moment she put her key in the lock.

They were sniffing at something, no doubt realizing that Ayanna had been hired as a courier. But Hansson's confessions before he drowned in the pool didn't extend to the little storage shed next to his housekeeper's garden plot. Grip had the housekeeper's name and a rough idea of where the shed should be. After asking around, he managed to locate it exactly and even considered breaking in after dark—it was isolated enough. But his plans kept getting derailed by the trinity: Ayanna—tails—shed. He was alone and so couldn't divide the parts into clear steps. Instead, he'd need to create chaos with a single blow. Everything had to happen in the same instant.

Grip figured the men were pretty tired by now, precisely because they were only two. They didn't have much chance to sleep, not when one of them always had to stay awake. Probably, they were heading into their fourth day, not so bad, but at some point people start to get distracted and frustrated, too eager to be done. Once they started to lose focus, they'd try to compensate by pushing things harder.

Grip had sent Abdu to buy the one last thing he really needed: a couple of strong nylon cable ties from a Lamu hardware store. Once that errand was done, he paid the boy for his services, gave him a good tip, and told him to go to Matondoni, the village where his uncle rented out boats, and stay there a few days. The boy only knew Grip as Mr. Bolzano, the name that he'd registered under at the honeymoon hotel, and the same name the police had seen when they checked his passport as he came ashore. A practical arrangement from long ago, having a passport that not even Didricksen could trace.

"One more thing," said Grip. "Give this to him when you get there." Another envelope with instructions for the uncle and all that remained of his war chest, except for two hundred dollars. He watched the boy's back disappear down the wide path that followed the coast north and beyond. Just as long as he doesn't fall into the hands of the police, he thought.

In his hotel room, he lay on his back watching the ceiling fan spin. He needed to kill time. Waiting until the sun sank and disappeared.

At nine, the night shift came on in Grip's hotel. Fifteen minutes before, he'd spoken to a young man who worked at the front desk, as he stood to one side picking dead leaves off a floral arrangement in the lobby.

"Well, I was wondering if you . . ." Grip began, as the man snapped something off, "you have rooms down by the water."

"Yes, they are nice, a bit larger than the others," the man said, turning to him. "Would you like to change?"

"No, no, but I thought there might be a possibility, could . . . could we . . . I'd like one of them, just overnight, you understand, and I'll also keep the room I have."

"Now?"

"You give me a key now, and I'll hand you two hundred dollars, what do you say? All you have to do is make sure someone cleans the room tomorrow morning."

With a mutually conspiratorial look, the man said to Grip: "And you will be out before breakfast?"

"As if it never happened."

"Wait here?"

Key in hand, and no record of it anywhere. Grip stashed a small bag under the bed in the extra room. Ten minutes later, the night staff at the front desk came in and straightened their collars. They smiled without a second thought, as Grip passed by and went outside.

For the first time in weeks, he felt the night air cool him off. He stopped for a moment and looked up. The stars were disappearing. There was a low rumble of thunder in the distance, and a breeze rustled like a premonition in the palm trees.

Grip had just checked the email account he shared with Stark. A new draft message was waiting. It said that Philippa Ekman had seen rubber bags filled with kerosene being loaded onto a transport plane, clearly preparing for parachute drops. It would be a long haul, with few places to refuel. An hour later, the helicopters she'd seen arriving took off from the airport. There was no information about what they were carrying, but the time was carefully noted: they left at 17:24.

Right, thought Grip, now it was Friday night. In Lamu, the bar crowd would soon be in a good mood, and in Djibouti, a group of helicopters had just taken off on a nice long flight, right before sunset.

Grip started walking again, taking a path toward Lamu's center. When he heard the sounds of street life getting closer, he texted Ayanna: "Fifteen minutes to go." He was traveling light: no wallet, no ID, just a phone with a prepaid card, a couple of cable ties in his pocket, and a jackknife. If something went wrong, he'd be one previously unknown, probably dead, Mr. Vincenzo Bolzano from Bari.

52

She'd heard it before, and even seen one once, when she was taking Sebastian out to the toilet—a helicopter. But it had always been during the day, far away, and it always seemed to be following the coast. Now it was in the middle of the night, and coming from the land. Something like a shift in the wind, just for a couple of seconds, and Jenny wasn't even sure it was a helicopter that she heard. Still, she sat up. The guards were still partying, but not as loudly as earlier in the evening. Even before the sun had gone down, a guard who was always unpredictable when drunk had come inside, and, while keeping one finger on the trigger, licked his other forefinger and stroked it along Alexandra's cheek. More predictably, Darwiish had stormed in later, completely drunk, knocked over a chair, and kicked Carl-Adam in the neck.

After the muffled sound pulsing in the wind, Jenny tried to hear what was going on with the guards and their buddies who'd arrived in jeeps. She tried to figure where the more laid-back ones were sitting and chatting, as the front door banged open and shut in the other house, and where the high-strung ones had built a fire and gone on with their binge. It was from there that she heard the voices of the men as they played with their weapons. The clanking of guns being sloppily cocked and magazines getting shoved in and out. Nothing careful or controlled, just the usual Friday-night male rituals. Jenny didn't so much as blink, but Carl-Adam flinched and gasped with every random shot. Then he tossed and turned a few times before seeming to fall asleep. Alexandra lay completely still, but Jenny had no idea if she was actually sleeping. There was shouting, and some kind of struggle. Then a crash, as someone had been hit or toppled over.

Jenny got up and looked through the peephole. She felt the night air against her face. The flickering fire beyond her view didn't give off much light, but there was just enough for her to make out the foot of Sebastian's grave. The head of it, and everything beyond, was swallowed up by darkness. She tried to imagine the hills in the distance and where the sound could be coming from.

Bam! Bang! A moment of confusion. The bullets must have flown right past her; she'd heard the sharp hiss before the cracks that followed. Two in quick succession. Behind her, Carl-Adam's violent breathing, and outside, although she still couldn't see anyone there, sudden chaos. Someone had been hit. When a voice shouted a warning, Jenny realized that the shots had come from outside, not from the guards' weapons. Then a blinding white light shone through the peephole. A supernova. Jenny turned back into the room, where the colors made a rainbow in front of her, and took a tentative step. Although she wasn't sure what all the shooting was about, she had one clear goal: "The gun!" she shouted to Carl-Adam. She couldn't see him, only the swirling colors, but she kneeled and grabbed his good arm while he half-sat, dazed. "Now! Get it!"

"What?"

The rush, the thought—Carl-Adam didn't get it. He yanked his arm from her tight grasp, as if he'd been unfairly punished. Jenny pushed him away and, guided by her fingers spread out and feeling along the wall, she took some low, fast steps to the opposite corner. Down by the floor, where the stone was wedged. She still couldn't see anything straight ahead, only the colors in their undulating forms, but in the periphery, the darkness had regained some of its shape. She made out Alexandra's mattress and saw her move.

Jenny dropped to her knees, feeling her way as if she were blind. She was surprised when her foot found the stone on the floor, and then she reached her fingers into the open hole. Her hand felt around, scraping her wrist on the sharp edges of the hole. Around and around, in the emptiness that couldn't be.

"Alexandra!"

A stray beam of light lit up the slit between the floor and the door for an instant, before the door to their room flew open. A flashlight, a rifle, and one of the guards. Blood glistened over his shoulder and side, splashing around him when he made a sudden movement. The flashlight broke through Jenny's blindness; she was the one he was looking for. He pulled her to him, trying to get her in front of him, as a shield against whatever was outside. He wrestled with her and his weapon, and then Darwiish came through the door, taking fast backward steps. The shooting outside was getting closer. Darwiish mumbled loudly, his attention completely focused on the outer room, while the guard behind him struggled to get a firm grip on Jenny, who put up a fight.

Too much was going on, and there were too many impressions in the darkness and noise outside for anyone to realize that a shot had been fired in the back room. No one flinched; not even the guard himself—who'd come up behind Jenny and gotten an arm around her—realized that he'd been shot. Crosswise, up through his stomach and out his chest. The power of his grasp flowed out of him, and in shock, he clung to Jenny for a moment before he fell like a puppet whose strings had been cut. His flashlight lay on the floor, shining a diagonal beam across the room.

The second shot had a much more immediate effect. Darwiish hadn't noticed what happened behind him, but stood crouching in the doorway and yelling threats into the room in front of him, when Alexandra stepped forward into Jenny's peripheral vision. She held her thin arms in front of her, her movements totally direct and focused. She was short, but Darwiish was crouching. Pressing the barrel against his neck, the girl had made sure the gun was cocked. The pirate leader had misjudged where the real danger lay. Darwiish fell face-first from the impact, as if starting a somersault, part of his head splashing over the floor in front of him.

Much later, Jenny found it difficult to understand what had actually happened after Darwiish went down. Her impressions contradicted each other, and her senses were confused because she couldn't see. There were explosions, she was pretty sure, and soldiers pouring in from all sides. She didn't know exactly how they could do this when the walls were still standing, weren't they? There were flashlights, shouts, and gloved hands that held her down. "Alexandra!" she screamed again and again.

She remembered how she'd sat down and held her daughter. And then suddenly they were out. Under the night sky. No more shots. Clumsy soldiers, incomprehensible equipment. The only human part that showed was a bit of face. One had leaned down and asked: "Where is your son?" Jenny didn't understand. "Your son, Sebastian Bergenskjöld, where is he?" She had explained, pointing to the nearby stone pile. They'd spoken Swedish with her. They had, hadn't they?

Then came the lights in the sky. She'd been right, it was the sound of helicopters that she'd heard, and now several arrived, making a turn and landing in a row as they kicked up a cloud of desert dust. So much dust that two soldiers had to sit down and cover her and Alexandra. It was only once she was sitting inside the helicopter that she saw Carl-Adam, leaning against the wall in a seat. Unharmed, but a medic had given him some type of drip. The man she'd met in London and everything they'd once had—now he was completely foreign to her. They didn't look at each other once during the entire flight. The helicopter ride seemed like a long dream. Had they given her something, or maybe put a drip in her too? She knew for sure that Alexandra lay with her head in her lap the whole way, and that the rotors were spinning—that was what she recalled of the trip. They must have put something over her ears, but she didn't remember. But she did remember the little flags that each of the soldiers wore in the cabin. It was crowded, there were people everywhere, sand-colored coats, backpacks, and more. And those little blue-and-yellow flags, those she remembered for sure.

Ayanna had her phone on mute. "Go now," said the message on her screen. She opened the door to her room at Baytil Ajaib and, breathing fast, headed for the courtyard through the balconies, feeling she was going in slow motion. She walked with forced calm, carrying a cloth bag over her shoulder, wearing a scarf around her neck and her hair down. Down the stairs, across more balconies, past the front desk, and out. She'd been given a detailed description, in the previous text, of the route she needed to take, out to where the town gave way to fertile fields. People were out for their evening stroll, but she'd walk up to the hills above the harbor, where it was less crowded and she'd be easy to follow.

Grip watched the man in the striped shirt start following her near the hotel and then, after a couple of blocks, call his accomplice. Five minutes later, they made eye contact, and the newcomer gave a signal when he saw Ayanna, and the handoff was done. Striped-shirt was free, at least for a while. Probably he wanted to get something to eat, or just get a coffee, needing the caffeine. A short break without having to be on guard, and without having to worry about that woman.

The man who'd been sitting on a battered oilcan on the street outside Baytil Ajaib waiting for Ayanna started slowly making his way down to the harbor. Rubbing his eyes, as if the lack of sleep caught up with him the moment he no longer had a job to do.

He was alone in the street, alone at one of three different places someone had predicted he might go. From a distance, no one would

f you'd caught it out

have thought twice about him stumbl... out there, with only a
of the corner of your eye. After all, ...as surprised by something,
few lights on. It probably looked li...abbing his shirt from behind.
but in fact a hand had pulled hi...he hand pulled, the man had a
And just a tenth of a second... as if he was trying to steady him-
cable tie around his neck. ...nd, the grooves of the cable tie locked
self, when, with a whirr...antly, his air supply was cut off. The only
irreversibly into place...ble hiss. With one knee down and one foot
sound was a barely... did everything he could to get his fingers be-
in the street, the...the cable. According to the tie's specifications, it
tween his neck...east three hundred kilos. With a sharp jerk, he was
would hold... up to standing, and then he was dragged along. They
yanked b...und a corner and into a narrow courtyard filled with trash.
went a...

The man, still struggling with the cord around his neck, was getting dizzy. He didn't even notice the foot that made his knees give way, as he slid down onto his side. His arms had lost their strength, so there was no resistance when Grip took his hands and attached them to an iron railing using more cable ties. His feet had just started twitching in spasms, when the knife went in and, with one flick, his airway was free again. He gasped from the shock but moved like a tranquilized animal, and could only roll from side to side while his pockets were quickly emptied of their contents. He was conscious, but no more than that. It would take quite a while before he'd be able to cry for help.

Ayanna had stuck to her route and now headed on to streets with shorter walls and lower buildings. The man tailing her made another call from his cell phone but got no answer. Soon they weren't in the city anymore, but surrounded by dry sagebrush and garden plots. He wanted his partner with him, to follow her out into the darkness, and he swore quietly when he realized he'd have to go alone.

The housekeeper lived on the edge of the forest, with trees on one side and cleared land stretching more than thirty meters in the other. There were rows of mounded soil and seedlings supported by strands of vertical steel wire. Among some banana trees, at the other end, stood a shed. A powerful front lamp shone from the house toward the lot, presumably to discourage nighttime vegetable thieves. The light from there filtered through the banana leaves, casting shadows that danced in the breeze across the walls of the shed.

Ayanna had kept up a good pace on the lonely road beyond the city buildings, but now she turned cautious. Maybe it was the lamplight, or her sense that she was being followed despite the isolation of the place, that made her hesitate. She walked past the house, followed the she out into the darkness, turned around, and circled back. Then trees. The ligh... seeing the shed a little farther off, among the banana ... fell across her face revealed her for a moment, with her eyes closed. A ... a prayer, before she left the path.

She had no trouble getting the door open, as there was only one key on the ring that fit. She breathed unevenly as she entered, not really knowing what she was supposed to do. With the door left wide open, shadowy light entered from outside. There were pots, shovels, some sacks of fertilizer stacked in a pile, and, next to them, three elegant fabric suitcases. Packed and ready, as she'd expected. But maybe this was more baggage than she'd thought—she'd never be able to carry three suitcases. Or maybe that was never the idea.

She noticed the man when his body blocked the light at the door. She didn't step backward but instead clenched her fists over her chest, facing the inevitable.

He moved fast, using excessive force against a woman who showed no sign of resisting. As if he wanted to quickly get something over with. He held something in his hand, but in the darkness, it was impossible to know what.

Right there in the doorway, stepping in, he reacted instinctively when Ayanna took her eyes off him, and he raised his left arm in defense.

It was his arm movement that made the cable tie miss, even though Grip had jumped him from behind. In the shadows, Grip couldn't see, but he felt sure that the thing the man was holding was a gun. They both tumbled down in the storeroom, and then their bodies rolled apart. There was the sound of a shovel falling, and shoes scraping against the floor. Not a shot, not now, for a thousand reasons. The hand with whatever it was holding made a sweeping motion, and in a shaft of light, the barrel was revealed.

Grip didn't go for the arm; instead, he used all his strength to get ahold of the man's head. In a fraction of a second, faster than instinct, or even the idea of pulling the trigger, he forced the man's head back, exposing his neck, and cut. The knife sliced through everything that sustains life, just below the larynx. So that the air, while ing out of his lungs could form no more than a gurgle. But before the heart a few last heartbeats sent up fountains of blood, and then fell forward too surrendered. The man sank to his knees and then fell forward headfirst as Grip let go. With the heavy thud of a lifeless body, hitting the floor.

Grip had the metallic taste of fear in his mouth. He tore at an empty burlap bag to wipe the blood from his hands, then thought of the suitcases and keeping them unstained. Ayanna had gotten splashed only on one foot and a sandal, but his shirt and pants were covered. "We have to go," he said, taking an anxious look toward the house, through the wide-open doorway. But there seemed to be nothing beyond the banana trees and their leaves. As Grip walked up to the bags, he sent the gun spinning on the floor. It was a Glock—the man on the floor must have been some kind of cop or agent. The gun left there, in the midst of all the blood, would suggest that the one who'd killed him had acted out of self-defense.

But now Grip realized he had to deal with the money in a whole new way. He'd been quite sure about its being there, but he'd never imagined he'd take more than what they needed to get away from Lamu Island. The rest would be left to the men who'd been following her, so that when they came to their senses, they'd be happy to disappear, never to be heard from again. A way to buy silence. But now—one alive, and one dead. Cash in suitcases at a murder scene would serve as evidence, and Grip realized that the bags had to go.

"You'll have to take one of them." The bags were heavier than he'd imagined. They only had a few minutes to get out of there, he was convinced of it.

A gust swept like an invisible hand through the treetops, and the first heavy drops of rain hit the leaves. The thunder was still in the distance. Grip had carried the bags the last half mile by himself, going back and forth a few times to get all three, while Ayanna had set off with the key to the extra hotel room. She was presentable, her usual self, despite a few drops of blood on one of her leather sandals. Grip had heard loud shouts and what sounded like some kind of siren. He couldn't be seen after the fight, not with his torn pants covered with deep red blotches. Moreover, he was drenched in sweat.

A li[ttle]... bare body, the bloody clothes made him feel unclean. on a narrow, deserte[d]... [t]he hotel complex, a half-eroded concrete pier stood been cleared for a building, but w... Just above it was a glade that had once back again. There, Grip had made a hid[ing] place. He'd found an old plastic trash bag that he'd cut up and wrapped carefully around the suitcases, to protect them from the storm. He heard that distant sound again—a siren? It soon faded away, in the growing murmur from somewhere behind him, and then the real rain hit, like a wall from the sea. His hair, his shoulders— he was soaking wet in just a few seconds. He didn't even try to run and find shelter in the trees a short distance away but just stood there. Tearing off his shirt, he turned his face to the sky. There was a sharp bang, and a flash as lightning struck the island. The storm was close by. He figured there'd no longer be a risk of finding anyone outside. His cell phone and the knife had been ditched long before, and his soiled shirt lay like a shed skin on the ground. The water flowed over his chest and back, rinsing away the blood. He still felt repulsive and longed to get rid of the other garments too. He took off not just his pants, but everything. He stood naked in the downpour and let the rain flow over his body. He got goose bumps, but still he was too hot and amped-up. Soon they'd be after him— Mr. Bolzano or whoever they thought he was. He was breathing hard, his mouth exhaling vapor in the rain. He started walking.

He came in through the unlocked hotel room door that opened directly onto the sea. Even inside, he could hear the rain drumming on the roof tiles. The water poured off him, and he stood just the way he'd left the clearing, buck naked, and looked around the room as if it were new or something he'd never seen before. The dim lights, the earthy colors of the floor tiles and ceramic tables, the enormous bed with its mosquito-netting canopy. Above and outside, the sound of the rain. Wouldn't she . . . ? Then the gap of light widened from the bathroom door, and she came out. She had showered; she wore one towel wrapped around her body and another around her hair. Her step was cautious, tentative, not because of his nakedness, not because of their wordlessness as they met again. The even given it room, her going there ahead of him—yet nob~ . . . with water dripping all a thought, until he stood completely n~ ~ . . over the floor in front of her.

She pulled the towel from her hair and handed it to him; he dried off his face and then dropped it on the floor. His nipples were stiff from the rain. He took a last step forward and pulled the towel where it was held in place between her breasts, so that she was completely nude. All his wetness met her heat. Putting his hands around her back, he held her tight, and she took hold of his arms in his embrace and pressed herself against him. Then he took her and lifted her onto the bed. He was already hard. Relentless, unstoppable, the certainty that something had to be completed. They both moaned from tense throats when he penetrated her, thrusting from his muscular ass. Tendons taut as cords under the skin, his knuckles whitening as he held her. He couldn't wait to feel the tremors that lay in the borderland between life and death.

They lay, still panting in the aftermath, without a word having been spoken, when they heard a sudden noise outside and then the sound of people running. The direction was perfectly clear to him—it was from the main building, where he'd been staying. He was still holding her, but he stood up, noticing how she was listening, most of all waiting for his reaction. Another hotel room being stormed by police who'd picked up their trail. They were close now, and there was no other way out, so now he sat with his last card: the hope that the one person at the hotel who actually knew where he was had left for the day and was now huddling in the rain on some faraway part of the island.

The noise continued—shouting, boots stomping closer on a concrete path and then fading away again. The commotion outside grew uncertain. They wouldn't start banging on doors and breaking into one room after another. Maybe they had no sense of how close they were, or maybe they lacked the courage to upset so many white honey-

ers.

one was c..rder could be heard for miles. Without a doubt, some-Grip for the first tim/lusive ghost of Vincenzo Bolzano, while Ernst other than a man.   y years had found release with someone

54

At four in the morning, Ayanna and Grip left their room, heading out into the total stillness surrounding the hotel. Above them, the stars were coming out again. They made their way up to the abandoned concrete pier and soon heard the sound of an outboard motor shutting off and a boat gliding in, guided only by a flashlight. There they both stood, as if being picked up for an extravagant safari or a cruise: a man, a woman, and three fancy matching fabric suitcases. But there was also something shameful in the silence, and Abdu's uncle, who was driving the boat, didn't say a word, only returning to full throttle once he'd made his way out again, and then he navigated in complete darkness past the few lights that shone on the other side of the channel.

Their agreement, negotiated in only basic terms with their young messenger, reached the next phase when the uncle once again shut off the engine, seemingly without anything in front of them except the dark shoreline. But when the bow dipped and the water grew less choppy, some thin pilings, as tall as a man, appeared in the predawn light. These supported a narrow footbridge, and the man threw a rope over one piling and ran, without a word or a sign, alone over the creaking planks.

They heard low voices and then a lamp was switched on, lighting up a window like a square in the darkness. The agreement involved transportation in several stages, with the uncle getting help from a friend for the final leg. Once the bags, Grip, and Ayanna were ashore, they got into a car that wasn't exactly roomy, but it was a car. The motor was running, and there was more of the same silence between those helping and those being helped. Grip had taken out a few bundles of notes from one of the bags, and when the loaded car headed out, he made the first installment. The uncle counted the bills without embarrassment and then went back down to his boat, without a thank-you or even a backward glance.

The same thing happened out at the small airfield. Grip paid up, and then the car disappeared immediately. Nothing seen, nothing heard, no name given in the early dawn.

Zar Air had said they could do pretty much anything, but on the airstrip not far from Lamu Island, they requested some daylight, if the customer wanted the time between landing and takeoff to be kept as short as possible. They'd agreed on an amount and on payment in cash, but when Grip had laid out all the conditions over the phone the day before, the price had very quickly doubled. It was the law of supply and demand, and he had the smell of someone with very few options. When Grip had first spoken to them, he hadn't even had enough cash to buy a regular ticket back down to Mombasa. And now he'd scheduled not one but two planes, landing with only fifteen minutes between them. It wasn't just the cash payment that pushed up the price, but the fact that he would decide the pilots' destinations at the last minute. This wasn't just a safety measure; Grip simply didn't know what or who should go where, and he didn't want to limit his options before he knew exactly how things would unfold.

When he and Ayanna had been standing with the bags, waiting for the boat at the concrete pier, she'd said out of nowhere, "You know, a Russian running a casino can convert cash into numbers in a nice, clean account." Maybe it was really about trust, that she hadn't quite dared to believe that Grip would get her and the bags out of there, but then things had changed during the night.

"Who?" Grip had asked.

"Timur can."

Grip remembered the story of the Senegalese soldiers who'd gotten their hands crushed, in order to teach a Foreign Legion officer a lesson.

Ayanna had continued, as if to reassure him that this was care-fully considered and not just an idle thought. "We can call him. He answers, he always does."

The first plane landed just after the sun had half-risen above the trees, and it taxied in. Grip looked at the bags again. This was money he shouldn't be bringing with him, and yet it was money that didn't exist. The time for deciding had already run out. He had to move forward now; looking back would get him nowhere. When the cabin door opened and the stairs came down, Grip made a decision: "Call Timur." Ayanna was already getting out the remaining phone, with an unused prepaid card.

Maybe the man she called was in the habit of getting up extremely early, or maybe he slept very lightly, but Ayanna started speaking Russian after just a few seconds. No strong emotions, no long expla-nations, just a tone of sober objectivity and even a short laugh. She put down the phone and held her hand over it. "He says he wants a third." Obviously, more than just the owners of Zar Air lived off of people with few options. Grip shrugged. Behind his back, he heard Ayanna answer yes and hang up.

A pilot stuck his head out the door with an uncertain look.

"You'll fly to Djibouti," Grip said, "but only the three bags are go-ing with you." The pilot started climbing down to help carry the bags.

When he'd gotten paid and closed the plane door, Grip and Ayanna heard the next shuttle approaching.

"Timur knows that he has to pick up the bags himself at the air-port?" Grip asked, when the front propeller of the plane carrying the money starting spinning again.

"Someone will get them," Ayanna said, "but they probably won't go through customs as usual, if that's what you're worried about."

Grip took out the phone's SIM card and pushed it down into the dirt next to the tarmac where they were standing.

The second plane taxied in, shutting down only the engine on the cabin side. It was all done in a minute, and then Grip and Ayanna were inside the plane and heading back to the runway. As if they were in a taxi, Grip said "Nairobi" to the copilot, who took the neat bankroll Grip held out and went back into the cockpit. The destination was news even to Ayanna, but after thinking for a moment, she didn't have anything to say. When Grip turned to sit down, she gave him a puzzled and slightly hopeful gaze.

They were in the air when Grip asked her, "Did Hansson ever tell you how much money was in that shed?"

"No, never," Ayanna said with half-closed eyes.

There was no use pretending. He had a couple of wads of cash on him, but beyond those and what he'd taken from one bag to pay for the boat, the car, and the two airplanes, he had no idea how much was in them.

Maybe half an hour later, between sleep and wakefulness, she added, "Timur will count the money when he gets it. That's how you'll know." There were new layers of trust and dependence. Ayanna would be the one who'd handle the Russian casino operator.

The three suitcases of money that he'd sent off kept bothering him. Grip was tired but found it impossible to sleep. Finally, before landing, not wanting to leave things unsettled that he knew would come back to haunt him, he said, "Timur, you, and I—that's a third each."

Ayanna leaned forward, as if she'd expected it. "Do you mean, you seriously thought there was another option?"

In the international terminal at Nairobi, she'd bought a brush, a little makeup, a blouse, and a shawl as soon as they had gotten their boarding passes. Grip waited a few minutes outside the bathroom, and when Ayanna came out, no one would ever think she'd done anything but spend a carefree night in a hotel, and that she'd just arrived at the airport in a taxi.

"They might pull you aside when you get there," he said to her at the gate. "After passport control, it might take an hour or so, I don't know. They might make a phone call to check things out. But the permits are there, they'll come back to you again and apologize, and then you'll be able to travel freely."

She kissed him on the cheek and boarded. British Airways, to London.

Grip stood and waited until the plane slowly taxied out.

He had an hour to kill, and he regretted that he'd only allowed himself to book a domestic hopper to Mombasa.

Not until he reached the Mombasa airport did he finally try to relax. He sat down with a coffee and the boarding pass he'd just been handed for the flight up to Djibouti. A few minutes of peace, and he still hadn't turned on his regular phone. He'd seen himself in a mirror in the bathroom, red-eyed—anyone could see that he'd been working hard. When he'd finished his coffee, Grip finally turned on his phone and was surprised that he had only one missed call. It was from Didricksen, who'd called just a few hours before. On the answering machine was the familiar voice, as concise as it was impatient: "Ernst, make sure you're the one who does the debriefing." In other words, the hostages were free, and now there were nervous expectations and versions that needed polishing up.

When he turned on the negotiator's phone, it pinged as the messages stacked up, one after another. Five total, and a voice mail, but that was no more than a breath, and then the recording stopped. Grip immediately called back, but he got no answer. The hostages were free—what else had happened?

55

Grip behaved as if he'd never been away from Djibouti. No one asked where he'd been; no one missed him. The room was just as he'd left it at the Kempinski, and the HMS *Sveaborg* was somewhere out at sea. He'd tried to call the negotiator a couple of times but got no answer, and then he realized that the Bergenskjölds had landed in Djibouti that morning and were now being treated at the French hospital. A physician he got ahold of said they needed rest, at least one night's sleep before anyone started questioning them. The doctor was expecting pushback, but when Grip spoke to him on the phone, it was after ten at night, and he'd started his day before dawn on a crumbling pier with Ayanna and three bags by his side— so getting a night off was more than he could have hoped for. He just said thank you and hung up.

All he had the energy for was heading to his Thousand-and-One-Nights bathroom to shower and shave, but he ended up sitting on the shower's mosaic floor, letting the hot water pour down. As he sat there, in a haze, thoughts of Ben came to him. He felt the guilt that, up until now, he'd managed to fend off. What he'd done with Ayanna wasn't about love, it was about regaining control—about him being alive and Ben being dead. He was alive, and all he could do was set aside the past and try to move forward.

Not until morning did Grip shave off his two-week beard, and then he headed to the hospital. Apparently, Colonel Frères was involved, because the same two military police officers who'd helped with Radovanović were now in the hallway outside the hospital room.

ney looked down at a list and nodded. Grip had made an appointment, and they pointed to the door.

The Bergenskjölds. They looked freshly washed as they sat in their beds, and their hair was clean, but their faces were marked by another place. Grip felt it as soon as he stepped into the room, beyond the exhaustion and the IVs; there was electricity in the air from an ongoing drama. Jenny Bergenskjöld was tucked into one bed, and her daughter, Alexandra, lay on top of another, with just a blanket over her legs. The father, Carl-Adam, looked out the window.

"Is the boy very bad?" asked Grip, thinking that this was the mood he was reading.

"He's dead," said Jenny Bergenskjöld, without emotion in her voice.

"I'm so sorry."

Carl-Adam turned toward the room, his eyes strangely empty, and Jenny continued. "It was some time ago. We left him behind."

Grip introduced himself, explaining at length that he represented Sweden and that he wasn't looking to interrogate them. He simply wanted to see how they were doing and get a basic understanding of what had happened to them.

Jenny was careful to point out that they hadn't spoken with anyone except the hospital staff so far. And then that strange silence set in again, and Grip's gaze was drawn to the slender Alexandra, who hadn't taken her gentle gaze off him.

"How are you?"

"Good," she replied.

"What have the soldiers said?" asked Jenny. "About what happened and how?"

"They haven't said anything."

"What does it say in the newspaper?"

"Nothing. They weren't those kind of soldiers. It doesn't work that way."

"But they killed all the pirates?"

"You know more than I do."

Over the next hour, Grip tried to put together a picture of what had taken place, going back in time, making them begin at th[e] beginning, when the boat was hijacked, the shots, and what happe[ned] afterward. Carl-Adam held up his freshly bandaged hand, otherwi[se] he mostly answered yes or no to the questions directed his way. Jenny did most of the talking. There was Darwiish with his red beard, and the two houses surrounded by heat and dust. And her son's seizures, described without the slightest tremble in her voice. She broke down only when returning to the constant refrain of the water bucket. The desperate need. The thirst, the eternal thirst--her whole body seemed to tense up at the thought. Remembering, she closed her eyes and her words fell away. The daughter listened; the father seemed mostly to stare at the ceiling.

Then Carl-Adam got up to use the bathroom, with a nurse helping him, and Grip was left alone with mother and daughter. They'd gotten to the arrival of the negotiator, how he made sure Carl-Adam was reasonably well taken care of, how he tried to get drugs for Sebastian, and how, in the final stage, he'd put that gun on the table.

"You used the gun?" Grip asked.

"We shot two of them," replied the mother.

"We?"

Jenny Bergenskjöld looked over at her husband's empty bed and said, "I never want to see that man again. I don't want to have anything to do with him. And I don't want to talk to a bunch of journalists."

"Here in the hospital . . ."

"He can lie there for now," she interrupted, "but I'm talking about later. And we shot two of them. We shot Darwiish—will that do?"

Grip listened to her, but he looked at her daughter. There, in her gaze, he was reminded of something. He searched his memory, oh right--when they were drunk, Simon Stark's story. How one man had walked down into the ravine, and a very different man had come back up. His eyes as he described it. Knowing you had killed someone, that you were capable of it. And Grip saw that the girl sitting in bed with a blanket over her legs was no longer just a child.

o journalists," continued her mother, "but I want you to thank Swedish soldiers, the ones who actually took risks."

"No journalists, I promise you," said Grip. "As for the soldiers"—he stopped and started again—"they were someone's soldiers, it's not important whose."

"On the sleeves, I saw flags—they were Swedish."

The door opened, and Carl-Adam came back in. The nurse who helped him made a point of looking at her watch as she went out again.

"We just talked a little more about the negotiator, what he said, and when," Grip explained, to get him up to speed on what he'd missed.

"Oh him. Yes," said Carl-Adam.

"Did he have a name?"

"He just wanted to make money off us, but he didn't take the slightest responsibility for the situation." For the first time, Carl-Adam had something to say.

"But what was his name?" Grip continued.

"A goddamn scavenger, that's what he was."

"He didn't tell us," Jenny interrupted, "but the guards and Darwiish called him Yuhuudi, when they talked about him."

"What did you say?"

"Yuhuudi," she repeated.

Carl-Adam launched into a discussion about the ransom, but Grip was no longer interested in what he had to say. He picked up the negotiator's phone and looked: still no missed calls. And suddenly, he felt a sharp pang, because he'd left something undone.

"Excuse me." Grip got up and went out into the hallway. He tried calling the negotiator, but just as before, no one answered. He started pacing back and forth, with the restless steps of an anxious relative waiting for an operation to end. He stopped and shifted the phone in his hand. That was it, he had to up his game; indecision turned into something else. Judy Drexler—two rings, then an anonymous voice said he could leave a message. "Shit!"

Grip went back to the Bergenskjölds again but didn't sit down.

"I . . . you've described your ordeal and told me what you need. one from the Foreign Ministry will come see you over the nex days, to arrange your transportation home and whatever else mig be needed. I have to . . . I have to go." He made a move toward th door but stopped again, his thoughts too scattered, and turned to Jenny.

"Forget about the flags. Forget that the soldiers spoke Swedish," he said, with an eye on the blanket that lay over her daughter's legs. "Some things are better left unsaid."

56

The US embassy and its goddamn security. A marine shouted at Grip to calm down.

Finally, when he was in his stocking feet with his belt in his hand, a young officer appeared.

"No," said Grip, "I didn't set up a meeting in advance. But believe me, Judy Drexler wants to speak to me ASAP."

"Who should I say is calling?"

"Tell her it's Delmar. Khalid Delmar."

The young man looked disapprovingly at him but turned and disappeared.

It was only a few minutes before she came out.

"I was sitting in meetings and only just now saw that you'd called."

"Of course," Grip said, looking around as they walked through the embassy's grand lobby. Really, he was hoping for some privacy, as there were too many unauthorized types within earshot, but Drexler eyed him as the uninvited guest he actually was. "Your informant, he's my negotiator," he said, so she'd immediately know that this was serious, but she hadn't caught on.

"Khalid? What are you saying?" But the Somali's name and Grip's look convinced her to take him to a more secluded spot.

Grip tied the other shoe he'd had to remove going through security and stood up. "It was Khalid Delmar who led the negotiations over the Swedish hostages. It was Delmar who gave me the coordinates so that they could be rescued."

"Is his cover blown?"

"No, no, he was careful, he didn't utter a word in Swedish to either the hostages or me, the times we talked. They knew nothing, and I never suspected it was him. But now, when I spoke with the family here at the hospital, they said the pirates called him the Jew when they talked about him. That was when I understood."

"I'm asking you again, is his cover blown?"

"I don't know, but if it is, it wouldn't be because of him. I'd be the one who screwed up."

"How?" said Judy, straightening up.

"I gave you the negotiator's phone number, and neither you nor I suspected that it belonged to Delmar." He saw the look in Drexler's eyes, as the pieces started to fall into place. "Sure, fine," Grip said, "but you don't look worried enough to be thinking the thought that made me yell at your marine a minute ago. I gave you the number of someone moving like an insider in the world of pirates and God-knows-who-else in Somalia. That number, and the movements of the cell phone connected to it, would have put him on the top-ten list of every single one of your satellites and listening stations. People would have put two and two together and drawn certain conclusions. That number was used by someone with a few other phones as well. As he visited more interesting places, and met with more interesting people, his name would start to climb up the list. Maybe he met with Al-Shabaab, maybe he was connected to known money launderers, maybe he got close to training camps, maybe he even was in touch with truly vicious fanatics." Grip waved his hand. "But what no one here realizes is that the guy you just started following was your most valuable source on the entire Horn of Africa."

Judy Drexler stood silent. "You don't have to tell me," Grip continued, "it's the same in my own organization. It's just that yours is huge—sometimes the right hand arrests someone the left just set free. And Delmar's been a little too professional in protecting his identity, doing everything by the book. He's had one set of phones and prepaid cards when he's Khalid and your informant, and a completely different set when he's the Jew getting things done in Somalia:

he sniffs out goodies for you, and also flies back lost jihadist[...] me I'm wrong. You got his number as a hostage negotiator from[...] Tell me you saw this coming, say that you haven't already put thi[...] together and drawn certain conclusions." Drexler was still silent, a[...] much lost in her own thoughts as she was listening to Grip. "He tried to call me four times yesterday, but I was busy with other things. Now when I try to reach him, I get no answer. Say for God's sake that I'm on the wrong track."

"Wait here," said Judy. Her mouth was a straight line when she disappeared.

When Grip heard Judy Drexler come walking back, it wasn't with her usual sharp steps on the stone floor. And in the hesitation of the last step she took behind his back, Grip sensed that she was weighing how intimate she would dare to be with him.

"Yes?" he said, turning around.

"There has been a drone strike."

"Yes?" Grip repeated.

"Not a decision I was involved in, but one based on intelligence from cell phone eavesdropping."

"On his number?"

"Among others."

"You sound like a telegram."

"I was gone for ten minutes, that's what I can tell you. That kind of operation isn't directed from this godforsaken desert fortress."

"And what was the target, then?"

"I don't know."

"A crowd of people, a house, a car heading from point A to point B?" He threw up his hands. "Or does the left hand not interfere with what the right hand is doing?"

"You said it yourself, it's an enormous organization."

"The hell with enormous. This is about you and me, and how we screwed up. The hostages have been freed, but I've just been down in Kenya cleaning up after both of us. And now this, when intelligence and our own interests go different ways."

"...ou don't need to lecture, I know exactly where we stand." Judy ...ed right at him; it was clear that she'd made a decision.

"Don't look at me that way," said Grip, taking her by the arm and ...owering his voice. "He was your man, your most valuable source." Judy Drexler said nothing. Grip paused but finally said, "Besides, I promised him that no one would come after him if he got the hostages released." Dark thoughts floated in Grip's mind: the man in the shed with his throat cut, the gaze of the Bergenskjöld girl in the hospital bed. Worst of all was the memory of Ben—the loneliness of death that never let Grip go.

"What exactly is our obligation to Khalid Delmar?"

"To find him," Grip replied, without blinking.

"Why?"

"You could put it different ways. One is, our side of the world owes him that much. In return for getting so many people out of this place and back home, and for all the madness he prevented, both down here and at home. And he's a Swedish citizen, who did far more for the world than our rich sailors—and he was the one who got them the attention that led to them being rescued."

Grip fell silent and looked at Drexler.

"Or you just say it as simply as possible," he continued. "Someone should look for you when you disappear. At any rate, I need to keep that idea alive inside me."

"Put it this way," Drexler said. "I've never encountered a man lonelier than you, so I'm not surprised that's what you believe."

Grip looked out a window, catching a glimpse of a plane against the sky.

"I promise you," he said, after standing there for a moment, "that if I sit down on that couch in this air-conditioned oasis, and I stay there for half an hour, you could tap on the shoulder of someone who respects your seniority and owes you an old favor. And you'll come back with numbers that look pretty innocent, but that when deciphered will answer the essential questions of where and when something happened."

"Is this the way you do it, you peasants with your backs to the

"Sometimes, it is."

It took more than half an hour, but when she came back, she did.
have just one set of numbers on a page, but two, with markings on a
small map that had been folded up.

When he'd unfolded it and held up the image of Somalia, Judy
Drexler explained the red dot: "Thirty-five kilometers off the coast,
last night. A variety of interesting cell phones, all in the same location."

"Are there photos?"

"Of course. But the black-and-white footage from the drone with
crosshairs on it will be kept locked up for months. That's the way it
is. That's always the way it is these days."

"And the one in the ocean?" Grip asked, about the black mark.

"That's the last position of the HMS *Sveaborg*."

"Why do I need that?"

"Take a good look. They're not very far away from each other. If
you're serious, I won't let you down—I can shuttle you out to the
ship, that's as far as I can go. To get the rest of the way, you'll have to
make your own arrangements."

"When do I leave?"

"There's a V-22 on the base being refueled right now. Give them
two hours. The rest is up to you."

57

They winched Grip down just in front of the bridge. The helicopter deck of the *Sveaborg* was way too small for the V-22 to land on. A deck officer received him, under the thunder and wind of the rotors, then unbuckled the harness and led him inside. The Swedish warship was escorting a merchant ship bringing food and medicine up to Mogadishu. Half an hour earlier, they'd gotten the message from Stockholm, alerting them that the security police officer was on his way.

Grip had talked to the Boss beforehand, saying that he had a few loose ends to tie up and needed an excuse to board the ship. Didricksen harrumphed at first, explaining that for now he'd let the state and foreign ministers know that the Bergenskjölds were free. Just that much, and he'd kept the lid on the rest. Of course, there was a group of soldiers who knew more, but they belonged to a branch of the military that kept its mouth shut. At most, the navy ships down in the Indian Ocean could have picked up a few rumors. They agreed on the phrasing: "Sensitive intelligence regarding the Swedish hostages, requiring immediate follow-up action." It was sufficiently vague, yet precise enough not to be questioned. Before he let Grip go, he took half a step backward and started talking about what the newspapers said, how more and more people had donated to the ransom fund. The ministers, or at least the ones who sensed something was going on, worried about how their political supporters would react if it turned out that the armed action in Africa was premature.

"Premature?" Grip asked.

"Their words, not mine," Didricksen replied.

"With all due respect, Boss, I've seen the Bergenskjölds at the hospital. They wouldn't have survived."

"Popular opinion drives everything here, and a venture capitalist
can always sit for one more day."

"Anyway, the family is free. But if you can squelch the news about
the Bergenskjölds for one more day, maybe I can do something
about the ministers' concerns, regarding both the morning TV shows
and the voters' reactions."

"This has gone on long enough as it is. Now, get to the ship, do
whatever it is you need to do, and come straight home. You get one
day, and then you'll be standing here on the carpet in front of me."

Before Grip went out to the waiting V-22 on the US base, he'd
made sure to spend a few minutes on the phone with Simon Stark.
It was the first time he'd checked in since the night on Lamu Island.
Even if all they said was "You all right?" and "Good enough," Grip
could hear the relief in Stark's voice. Also, Grip wanted his opinion
on what was possible, or not, aboard the ship. Stark had, after all,
been the *Sveaborg*'s prisoner for almost two weeks.

"I need access to their helicopter," Grip explained.

Stark gave his knee-jerk response.

"The captain and the first officer have enough bad feelings toward
us as it is. Whatever you want, they'll oppose it. So don't give them
any details, they'll only dig in their heels."

His second piece of advice was more useful.

"I'd bet on the helicopter unit commander, though. He's a pilot
I met in Afghanistan. An unshaven, half-Finnish guy who has a
grudge against the first officer. I don't know why, but there you go.
Maybe it's because he's pretty loose about following the rules."

That was what Grip had to go on when his soles hit the deck of the
ship. Sure enough, the moment he walked into the operations room
and the first officer spotted him, he looked as if Grip were carrying a
contagious disease.

"Not now" was the first officer's immediate response. He pretended
to be frustrated. "This damn barge we're escorting can't do more than

eight knots. Loaded full of medicine, and if we leave her, she'll become a meal for pirates."

"The *Sveaborg* can stay on course. I just need the helicopter," Grip said. "Surely your machine guns and ship cannons give you adequate protection?"

The first officer knew there was muscle behind the message coming out of Stockholm, but said anyway: "It's up to us to weigh the request against operational risk."

"I just need a couple of pictures taken from the helicopter. You can live with that. Can I at least talk to the flight crew?"

The first officer was interrupted by something on a screen farther away, then came back. "Wait a minute," he said, lifting a headset.

It was a short conversation. Grip didn't hear a word of what was said, but he understood that the first officer was talking to the captain. Then they climbed up a ladder and turned a few corners, inside what for Grip was still an incomprehensible maze. Soon enough, they were in a large room with yellow walls and intense fluorescent lights.

"Yes?" said a man standing and bracing his arms on a table, looking at them as though they must have gotten lost. Grip saw the stubble, then the Finnish-sounding name on the flight suit, and realized who they were dealing with.

"We need to schedule a flight," explained the first officer.

"Right, the captain just called, some kind of reconnaissance, apparently." There were a few others wearing flight suits in the room, but they barely noticed the visitors, sitting in front of their bulky computers.

"Not a few passes, only one. And you will remain over the water, not go one meter inland from the Somali coast."

"I wouldn't even dream of it," replied the flight commander.

"Excellent." The first officer stood there for a while, until one of the other pilots looked up from his computer, and then he nodded and left. The unshaven pilot waited until the door had closed, and then said, "First the captain himself calls, and then the first officer shows up—so where do you really want to go?" Grip picked up Judy Drexler's

w somewhat crumpled page and pointed. "But you realize, this is
irty kilometers inland from Barawe. It'll be just a dot on the screen
if we stay on the coast."

"Of course," replied Grip, ready to start arguing.

"What's there?"

"I really don't know."

"But something happened on the ground there, and that's why the
Americans flew you out here in a V-22?"

"Yes."

The man with the decision-making power turned to one of the
others. "Olsson, you and I will fly this one."

With that, the sleepwalker atmosphere in the room instantly
shifted. They exchanged a few quick words about map data, location
intelligence, and weather that might develop. Grip's new host took
him down into the ship, and in a cabin labeled BOARDING TEAM, he
stuck his head into the semidarkness where a pair of bunks stood.

"Wallinder and Sandahl, now's your chance for a helicopter ride.
But make sure you're properly suited up. See you on deck in forty-five
minutes."

It was crowded in the helicopter cabin at takeoff. In addition to
Grip and the two well-equipped soldiers, the helicopter crew's mission specialist was on board too. As soon as they took off from the
ship and shot out across the sea, he opened the cabin door and let off
a short burst of machine-gun fire, then turned and announced to the
cockpit, "Now we're in business."

They passed low over the coast, barely more than twenty meters
up. They were far enough away from the ship, but still wanted to
make sure a lucky radar operator aboard the *Sveaborg* couldn't snitch
to the high command. Beneath them, sand and scrub.

With ten kilometers to go, they rose up higher, making an arc
around what was still just a dot on the navigation system. The mission specialist began scouting the area with the camera mounted
to the helicopter's underbelly. There was a road, barely more than a
rut edged by low vegetation, but still clearly making a straight line

through the slightly rolling landscape of gravel and sand. In a depression among some trees, they saw the square shapes of houses built of stone. After a few checks, they confirmed that the dot put them there. The image was blown up to maximum size, making everything look shaky, and still the infrared camera didn't detect the slightest sign of life.

"We have to go in closer," said the mission specialist, and the helicopter veered toward it.

"The big house," he said after a moment, pointing to his monitor, "it looks slightly burned on one side, and the sand next to it is blackened." When they came around on the opposite side, they saw that where the door had been, there was now just a hole. Part of the roof had collapsed, but it was impossible to see into the building from the air.

"But all this you already knew," said the voice from the cockpit into Grip's headset, while he looked out over the desolation through a side window.

"Yes, but I need more."

Grip and the two soldiers disembarked and crouched down together as the helicopter took off again, sending the sand whirling around them in a nauseating cloud that tore at their skin. It would circle above—twenty minutes, not a second more, that's what the half-Finn had given them.

Grip had only a borrowed pistol; one of the soldiers raised his automatic rifle and went first through the hole into the house. They'd already guessed what awaited them, from the stench that engulfed them once the rotor wind died down and the still air quivered again in the heat.

Grip tucked his gun back into the holster as he entered. There were no survivors. Stones and mortar were scattered everywhere, and an interior wall had collapsed when the missile exploded. The bodies lay there, less burned than Grip had expected; it was the shrapnel that had killed them—one was missing both an arm and a leg. Four bodies, parts of them swollen and parts sunken in. For almost two days, they'd been lying there. It was dark in the house, despite the light coming in through holes in the walls and ceiling, so Grip borrowed a flashlight and went closer, to get a better look at the men. The soldier who'd left the house shouted something from outside.

"There," he said, when Grip came out, pointing with his weapon. At first it looked like just a scrap of cloth in the sand, maybe a hundred meters away. But then Grip made out the shoe soles, and he walked up to them. The man lay in a way that suggested he'd leapt into the air at the moment of death. Now the wind was calm, but it must have been blowing hard earlier, as the body was mostly covered with sand. Grip began pushing it aside with his foot. He'd noticed that the men in the house were wearing sandals, but this one wore proper shoes. His shirt was white, stained with dried blood. Grip shoved hard with his foot, to make the sand fall away from the man's face. He lay with one cheek down. To make certain, Grip had brought a printout of his passport photo, but he didn't even need to take it out. The man's face was completely untouched. It wasn't hard to imagine the events that lay behind that leap across the sand. The man's instinct had been to get away from the house, away from the poor suckers inside. Somehow, he'd managed to avoid the first hit; maybe he'd just gotten outside and started running after the explosion. But against those with infrared and night vision in the desert darkness, he had no chance. He made it a hundred meters, a maximum of twenty seconds, then someone had fired again.

Khalid Delmar lay stretched out in the sand with a cloth bag over one shoulder. Grip felt around and took out four passports. Two American, one Belgian, and one Danish. All the pictures were of young Somalis, whose journey back home had ended suddenly.

Grip glanced up toward the helicopter's black silhouette high above and went over to the soldiers.

"We have to bury them."

"We didn't bring shovels, and we only have ten minutes left," replied the one who was in radio contact with the helicopter.

"The man over there," said Grip, pointing behind him, "he will get a decent burial."

When the helicopter landed to pick them up, all three were breathing hard. They'd done what they could, using their hands and feet. A pile of earth and sand rose up where Delmar had fallen, with a ring of stones as some kind of marker. Although it was strangely quiet in the helicopter on the ride back, and Grip felt the two soldiers' eyes on him, he said not a word. When they'd landed aboard the *Sveaborg* again, finished up, and were ready to leave the helicopter on the flight deck, the first officer came up.

He stood with his legs wide apart in the breeze and asked Grip, "Well, did you find anything interesting?" The pilot who'd led the mission stepped forward and said, "Nothing. Impossible to see anything from that distance," so that both his own crew and the two soldiers would be on the same page.

"Gravel and sand," Grip added. In his back pocket, he had four passports and a leather bracelet that had fallen off Delmar's wrist when he'd laid the body out, before they'd covered it up.

A few hours after the sun went down, Grip went out into the sea air. He stood alone on the quarterdeck. Above him was the helicopter, lashed down for the night, but the sides were open to the sea. He went all the way to the back and stood in the stern, gazing at the wake's white line out into the night.

He'd just been up in the radio room, talking with Judy Drexler over the satellite phone. On an encrypted line, the conversation had been short and devastating. He confirmed what they'd both feared.

"I'm sorry" was all she could say, and Ernst Grip couldn't even say that.

He'd also told her about the other four found at the same location and given her the names from the passports. They were all between nineteen and twenty-three. "But hardly completely innocent," Grip said.

"And not savvy enough to turn off their cell phones when they were brought together like that."

There had been a long silence, with only space speaking on the satellite channel, before Grip added, "He was just getting them back home."

Now Grip took the four passports he was holding and tossed them into the sea. Four dark flakes spinning in the white foam of the wake. Then, nothing.

The last thing Judy Drexler had said was "Anything else?" She knew. Of course, she did.

"I need something major to give my bosses," said Grip, who was far beyond tiptoeing, "so that everything that happened in Somalia and Kenya can be conveniently forgotten."

"Otherwise, things might get uncomfortable for us, concerning the death of a Swedish-Somali?"

"Not just for you, mostly for my own sake."

"Thank you, I just wanted you to say that, and not take this for granted. I've already prepared something. We'll get it out in time for the evening news."

Grip weighed the leather bracelet in his hand after the passports were tossed into the sea. It was strung with black wooden beads, like prayer beads worn around his wrist. It was just a reflex that made him take it when it had fallen off Delmar's arm into the sand. The need to have solid proof of something. But evidence was of no use, not now. What he needed was to cleanse himself, and then to free himself. The bracelet needed to go the way of the passports; that was why he'd brought it up on deck.

But it went back into his pocket again. The wake had swallowed enough, and for a while, he couldn't understand his own reluctance.

58

When it was still nighttime in Stockholm, CNN broke the news that while American special forces led an operation to protect vital national interests, they also rescued the Swedish hostages. And as usual when it came to special forces, nothing more came from the American side. The morning news shows on Swedish TV had to scramble to find archival images of helicopters and soldiers with pixelated faces, and someone from the Swedish Defense University played commentator, offering a few educated guesses. The evening papers took a harder angle, given time to write proper headlines and throw together a few feature pages. The boy's death had been leaked, and in a short statement, the foreign minister was forced to admit that the Swedish government had been informed of the family's release. The opposition party complained that they "certainly hadn't been informed we were fighting a war in Africa," and the comments from celebrities who'd lent their faces to the ransom fund looked slightly disappointed, as if they'd been cheated out of something.

Didricksen, being old-fashioned, still had paper copies of the major newspapers on his desk.

"We'll see if this holds up," he said, flipping through the *Aftonbladet*, while Grip stood on the carpet in front of him. "But it's good," he said, looking up over his reading glasses.

"It's damn good. We Swedes didn't have to kill a single person. As I understand it, none of the pirates survived."

"They fought back, so that's how it usually goes." Didricksen looked down at a picture that had been blown up to a half page in the newspaper. A grainy cell phone photo from the airport in Djibouti, where Jenny Bergenskjöld walked hand in hand with her daughter up an airplane stairway. Her husband was nowhere to be seen. "This family then," he said, drumming his fingers on the newspaper, "what do we think about them?"

"They're dealing with a lot. Believe me, that's one hostage who won't go on a book tour."

"Yes, we'll see. So far, the illusion has been preserved. I'll say thank you for now, and then I guess I'll reprimand you when it gets shattered."

"What are the ministers saying?" Grip asked.

"Nothing. It doesn't get better than that. I understand that the foreign minister canceled his visit to Djibouti and the navy mission down there."

"I'm sure the captain of the *Sveaborg* is bitterly disappointed. It was that visit and trash sorting that took up most of his attention."

"I don't know how much the foreign minister cares about recycling, but when our own soldiers are shooting each other, and epilepsy medications don't get where they need to go, you can be sure he'll keep it at arm's length. And that applies not just to the ship but to the entire Horn of Africa, for some time to come." Didricksen put down his glasses and looked at Grip. "And when the country's leaders choose to look the other way, it's an invitation for others to do the same."

"Yes, Boss," said Grip, when the silence lasted too long.

"Did you let Simon Stark take part in actions I don't know about?" The old man looked straight at him.

"You mean, when I sent him home to Stockholm?"

"Not so much that, as that he suddenly went quiet. You know as well as I do that I sent him to keep an eye on you."

"And you know I sent him home to reassure the generals. The daily operational decisions you tend to let me handle myself."

"That's the way we usually do it," Didricksen went on. "But through some unusual channels, I've ended up with information on my desk about an unpleasant event on Lamu Island in Kenya. Chaos, a man with his throat cut, and an Italian who died long ago showing up on Interpol lists. A source suggests we were involved."

"Uh-huh. And what kind of source is that?"

"A police chief in Djibouti, apparently."

"A very credible witness."

"Maybe not, and he's demanding money, but after all, someone has been murdered. And these events on Lamu Island are pretty important, for the Kenyans."

"How much do you want to know?" Grip asked.

"Neither I nor anyone else needs to know more, right now. The hostages came home, and no Swede was involved in a killing. Well, that Hansson was, but now he's dead himself. So if anyone suggests otherwise, we just shake our heads and put it aside. Right?" His words were not a rebuke, nor were they intended to put Grip on the defensive. Despite the desk between them, and one standing and one sitting, it was the first time the two had met, for just an instant, on exactly the same level.

"To me, letting things lie seems quite sensible, Boss." Didricksen sank back in his chair again, like a dog returning to the house after checking the fence around his property.

"I do believe in keeping things at arm's length, as a principle," he said then, still careful.

"I'm returning to the bodyguard group tomorrow," Grip said. "At the moment, aiming at cardboard figures and wrestling in a basement is all I could wish for."

"You're not . . . ?"

"No, no, not guarding any ministers. You said it yourself, arm's length. I'm planning to return to the princesses again."

"Back to a life in Haga Park." Didricksen smiled at the thought.

"Well, you do get to go places," Grip objected. "The one who shops nonstop, I think she's gotten a place in London."

"No risk that she'll travel to Africa, and you'll be recognized?"

"For her, I'd say that's simply out of the question."

59

It was just over two months after Edward Hopper's sketch of *Night Shadows* had been sold at Sotheby's, on New Bond Street.

Ernst Grip walked from Marylebone, one subway stop away. The building he entered had a nice stone facade and a doorman. He phoned, and then Grip was allowed to take the elevator up.

Ayanna opened the door and looked at him for a second. They hadn't seen each other since they'd said good-bye at the airport gate in Nairobi.

"Come in!" She was barefoot and obviously felt at home in the apartment.

"Wow," said Grip, walking from the hallway into the living room.

"I can afford it," she replied with a shrug, "given what I brought with me."

"Not for long, at this rate."

"It is not mine. I am renting."

"Even a grand piano."

"I give piano lessons now."

"Is that the plan?" Grip asked, looking up at an oil painting. He couldn't decide whether it was an original or a copy.

"Now you are being stupid."

"I'm sorry, I didn't mean it to sound that way, but I think you're underestimating yourself. Is that what you're going to use the money for, renting an expensive apartment to give piano lessons?"

"And you overestimate what is possible, for someone like me."

"Not for you, never for you. So tell me, what's really going on? Not

, you sat playing in a bar in Djibouti, and now you're sitting
and piano in London's most exclusive neighborhood."
s a pianist at a bar in Djibouti, I met one sort of person, and as a
no teacher for children here, I meet quite another."

"You mean, the fathers have an excuse to come over?"

"Something like that."

"Is that painting an original Repin?"

"Given the person I am renting from, certainly. There is a Maksi-
mov hanging over there. But it is not only Russians who come here.
For piano lessons, I mean."

"And in the long run, then?"

"Meeting someone who is divorced, or ready to divorce."

"Financial types?"

"Those are the only ones who can afford my lessons for their
daughters."

"And now you get to play Gershwin, and even entire pieces by
Chopin again?"

"Mostly, I listen to badly played Bach and Prokofiev, to be honest,
but this is far better than the bars." She came close and gently put her
hands on his chest.

"What are you wearing under there?"

"A protective vest. I have a one-hour break."

"We could have had lunch."

"We could have."

She lowered her hands.

"I know," she said in a low voice, "you came for something practical. Not for this."

He swallowed, and she looked away for a moment. "Something
that barely existed cannot be lost, and I am not talking about money.
But," she said then, clearing her throat, "let's get down to business . . .
Timur did everything he promised, and then took his third. There
are instructions on how to obtain the rest of your money, in the envelope there."

"And the other thing I asked you to do?"

"I did as you said, put in the bids, it was not difficult. An⸍ delivered it here."

"How is it packaged?"

"It was framed. I have not seen it. It is still wrapped up." Grip looked around. "Not in here," she continued, "you will get it when you go." There was silence; something had been left hanging.

"Do not be disappointed," she said. He looked bewildered. "Disappointed in me," she tried to explain, putting her hands on his shoulders so that she could actually feel him.

"I need this, want this," she said. "I want to have you again. You are in London sometimes?"

"It happens."

"Come here then. You want it too. It is just that I also need to think a little further ahead, while you want to burn and disappear. Come whenever you are running away from something else. But when I finally find my husband here in the banking district, then I will no longer answer your calls."

"Do you want children?"

"Exactly the kind of life you do not have in you. And I do want that, a home and a family. But you, who knows what you really need." She paused a moment and then smiled. "I will miss your shoulders. The kind of banker that I will end up with will not have those."

"I'll probably be back in town in a month or so."

"Well then."

She disappeared but came right back. There was the rustle of wrapping paper, when Grip put the package under his arm.

"What will you say to your colleagues when you show up with a package?"

"That I bought a framed poster at lunch."

"And what will you do with the rest?"

"You mean with the money?"

"Naturally, I am talking about the money."

"Next time I'll invite you to dinner."

"It should cover much more than that."

aybe I'll tell you then."

don't need an excuse to see you."

"No, but maybe I need one."

He leaned forward. She smiled but guarded herself against what would have been a kiss on the cheek.

"You do not need to play polite. I just want to know if we will meet again."

"About that, I'm all but certain."

60

The rule of thirds had worked: Ayanna and the Russian at the casino had received their shares, and Grip himself would get the balance. They probably felt they'd earned their third, unlike him. Still, he'd allowed himself to buy that drawing. What remained was a staggering sum that weighed heavily on him.

In the Stockholm offices of Scandinavian Capital, by Stureplan Square, the lights had been dimmed for the night. Yet a silver mist seemed to hang in the air, from the bright white Christmas lights that had been lit a few days before, in the streets outside. It was so late that even the most ambitious new hires had left their desks and headed home.

A lone cleaning woman pulled her cart across the dark wood floor. Once again, the rule of thirds came into play. For two-thirds of the day, the office was used for managing investments, and for the last third, someone earned only enough for bare essentials. It was called the evening shift; at best she finished at three o'clock in the morning. The desks and chairs had all been dusted, and the toilets cleaned, so only the vacuuming and mopping remained. She knew the rounds; it was simply routine. Five nights a week, and on Sundays she cleaned it all in broad daylight. If she was lucky, for that shift she'd have a coworker keeping her company.

She heard steps behind her.

"Sorry," she said, turning around. At work, all her sentences began that way. It happened now and again that someone would appear to deal with an emergency in the middle of the night. Swiftclean's white

...ne on her shirt in the silver mist, and she smiled at the man, ...y you do when sharing a night shift. She stood up for a mo-
..., to see which part of the office he belonged to.

No, I don't work here," he said.

"You have gotten lost," she said, with her accent. "I can show you the way out."

"In a moment. I wanted to see this office and exchange a few words with you."

She looked at him cautiously but wasn't afraid. They stood next to a coffee machine. Beside it was a bowl of fruit and a counter-top fridge with glass doors, filled with perfectly straight rows of expensive water, beer, wine, and, at the bottom, even a few bottles of champagne.

"Ideally, I'd like to make you a cup," he said, "but the coffee isn't mine, and I get the idea that you'd feel uncomfortable touching any of this." She said nothing. "And you might be uncomfortable enough, as it is."

"Who are you?"

"I'll let that go unsaid, but you work for your brother who owns this cleaning company, and your husband is Cismaan Delmar."

"He is not my husband anymore. We are divorced now."

"So, night work gives you a little more to live on?"

She shrugged and said irritably, "If this is about Cismaan's debts, take that to him. I live my own life now, and he lives his."

"I'm sorry, I don't care about anyone's debts. I'm here for an entirely different reason. Until recently, you were regularly receiving envelopes containing money."

"They were from my son."

"Exactly."

"He just wants to help out with the rent and other things."

"You have deserved that money in every way. Could you please sit down for a minute?"

Her eyes darkened as she reluctantly shifted from cleaning lady to mother. "Are you from the police? Has something happened to him?"

"Here you are." He rolled over a desk chair for her and sat d
on an identical one.

"Tell me now!" A wounded demand, laid bare before a comple
stranger.

He opened his hand and showed her the bracelet with its wooden
beads.

She trembled as her fear turned to certainty and grief, wrapped up
in the same emotion.

"I didn't know him, but this belonged to him."

She had already taken the bracelet and was rolling the balls in the
palm of her hand.

"Where?"

"Not far from Barawe," he replied. "I don't know the name of the
place, but he has a grave."

"Who did it?"

"I don't know."

"I do not believe you."

Grip looked down at the floor and said instead, "The money you've
been getting, he left that behind."

"His brother died trying to flee," she replied. "And now, I come
here at night, while both of my children lie in graves down there.
Why, can you tell me? What does God mean by this?"

He sat quietly, making a feeble gesture of apology.

Tears rose up, but he couldn't hear that in her voice. Then: "Do you
understand what it feels like when nothing has meaning? Nothing."

"Maybe not." He stood up. "This may not mean very much . . . but
here is the key to a storage locker downtown. It has all you will ever
need."

"Do you want me to be grateful?"

"That is the last thing I want, but I want you to know where the
money comes from."

"I have no idea what to use that money for."

"You can stop working the night shift."

"I could stop working altogether, but what would I do? Hands

. have something to do." And only then did her voice break, and turned away with her hand over her eyes.

Grip looked at his watch. "In a quarter hour, a taxi will be waiting outside. Just go home, or to your brother's. Your car is already paid for. In any case, Scandinavian Capital can start one day without a shiny floor."

He started walking.

On his way out, he stopped next to a magazine rack, where someone had left a copy of *Yachting World* on the table. It had a huge white sailboat on the cover, surrounded by unnaturally turquoise water. The image must have been taken from a helicopter flying over, photographing it bow to stern. At the helm was a woman standing alone, her feet wide apart and in full control, her white clothes matching the sail. And in front of her, with her back to the camera and the wind in her hair, also dressed in white, sat a confident-looking girl on the deck.

He stopped for a moment to look at the cover, then stuffed his hands in his pockets and kept walking.